About the Author

Paul Anderson lives in Adelaide, South Australia. He is a surgeon who specialises in upper gastrointestinal and hepatobiliary surgery. Born in Rotorua, New Zealand, his tertiary education began at Waikato University before he went on to further studies in Scotland, California, and South Africa where he completed both a Ph.D. and a medical degree before becoming a surgeon. The passion for writing has latently manifested, thanks to the encouragement and direction of many friends.

Paul G. Anderson

OLD LOVERS DON'T DIE

AUSTIN MACAULEY
PUBLISHERS LTD.

A CIP catalogue record for this title is available from the British Library.

ISBN 978 1 78455 705 8 (Paperback)
ISBN 978 1 78455 707 2 (Hardback)

www.austinmacauley.com

First Published (2015)
Austin Macauley Publishers Ltd.
25 Canada Square
Canary Wharf
London
E14 5LB

Printed and bound in Great Britain

Does It Hurt To Die, Medical Mystery Thriller by Paul
Anderson, 2nd Edition available online
www.doesithurttodie.com.au

If you see the stable-door setting open wide;
If you see a tired horse lying down inside;
If your mother mends a coat cut about and tore;
If the lining's wet and warm -- don't you ask no more!

Foreword

With any writing, there are many contributions. They are all extremely valuable, each in a unique way adding to the vibrancy of the story and hopefully the pleasure of reading. Pre-eminent on the ladder of gratefulness, is the family that supports you. They are biased, but there are days when you need and love their bias. Their belief in your writing and its value to others as entertainment is an invaluable spur when the creative well has only a few lonely drops in the bottom.

Gabrielle, a more wonderful sister you could not have, and my favourite son, Jordan. Independently both are of inestimable value. Gabrielle's unswerving and consistent enthusiasm astounds me. Jordan has read so many books that it embarrasses his father; but in having done so, he provides invaluable analysis and critique. Peter, your reaction to the first novel, *Does It Hurt to Die,* was the greatest encouragement, which provided momentum for this sequel. Richard, for the ongoing reminder two of the important things in life are, fishing, and green tea. Moreover, that you ignore them at your peril. Vanessa, thank you for your analysis and encouragement of this manuscript as it surfed the rough waves of its beginning.

There are many others, far too many to name, who in a world enamoured with critique, run contrary to the herd and encourage. If I named them all I might run the risk of offending some, who might inevitably leave out.

Prologue

A terrorist attack on a church in Cape Town in 1989 kills twenty people. Jannie de Villiers, a well-known liver transplant surgeon, narrowly avoids death, but is seriously wounded. The uproar over the killings by a radical black group hides the more sinister involvement of the apartheid government. Two weeks later, while recovering at home, Jannie de Villiers is murdered. With too many inexplicable circumstances surrounding her husband's death, Renata takes her four year old son Christian to live in Australia.

As Christian grows up, he becomes more and more interested in what his father might have been involved, in South Africa. He repeatedly researches the death of his father on the Internet, trying to find the reasons he might have been killed. There is little to satiate his curiosity until one day he discovers a blog site set up by an old anti-apartheid activist. The blog site claims that his father worked for the Bureau of State Security in the old apartheid government, which was implicated in atrocities against black and coloured population groups. Initially, Christian is devastated by the discovery, as the little that he had been able to read up to that point had all been positive about his father. He then becomes convinced that there is a mistake, and wants to return to South Africa to find out more about his father's work.

His mother, Renata, is initially opposed to Christian returning to South Africa, fearing that some of those who might have been involved in her husband's death may threaten her son. Christian pleads with his mother and returns to Cape Town shortly after his eighteenth birthday. Unbeknown to him, his return to South Africa is monitored by the National Intelligence Agency and a white underground Afrikaner supremacist organisation. They both have knowledge of Christian's father's genetic research on

11

racial profiling and believe that he also had a folder containing highly sensitive material on chemical and germ warfare. Both organisations consider that Christian may have information which will help them find his father's folder with its racial research and highly embarrassing links to international governments.

Christian, when he arrives back in Cape Town, finds changes under the new post-Mandela South Africa; however, vestiges of the past are everywhere. While legal separation is no longer constitutionally enshrined, years of separation and brutality live on in attitudes, undermining trust and harmonious living. Friends of his father help Christian build a picture of what it was like for his father growing up in apartheid Africa. As he meets more and more people associated with his father, he begins to understand his father's involvement with the previous government, and he realises that he is being watched by someone or by some unknown organisation.

Christian's search for the truth about his father is then further complicated when he meets Isabella, the beautiful daughter of his father's theatre scrub nurse. He falls in love with Isabella but is shattered when she turns out to be his half-sister. After much anguish and soul-searching, they determine to complete the journey of discovery together. Christian discovers his father's research in an old folder buried in the garden of their house in Wynberg, after one of his father's old friends delivers a cryptic note. Included in the folder is evidence of the apartheid South African government's involvement in germ and chemical warfare programmes and the development of nuclear arms. Christian shares the contents of the folder with Isabella and it becomes increasingly apparent to them both that their father was heavily involved in and a trusted member of the apartheid government's President's Council. A council so secret, they discover that it was answerable only to the Minister of Defence and the Prime Minister. The primary aim of the Council was to be able to use any means possible to preserve the white government in perpetuity.

Within the folder are also details of the apartheid government's involvement in the development of nuclear weapons with Israel, and germ and chemical warfare programs with nations who were openly opposed to apartheid. They soon realise that the information has never been released, and understand that

12

it has the potential to embarrass many governments who covertly supported the apartheid government. In a section which has his father's name at the top of it, Christian and Isabella find encrypted genetic research on racial groups, which his father had discovered during his research into the rejection of liver transplants. Christian recognises that the encryption has a code not dissimilar to code that he noticed on the back of a photograph of his mother and himself in Adelaide. He suggests to Isabella that if he can get his mother to find that code and send it to him, they may be able to decipher his father's research.

Once it is known that the folder has been discovered, the National Intelligence Agency and a secret white Afrikaner supremacist group pursue Christian and Isabella openly. Christian and Isabella are taken hostage by the white supremacist group who demand the key to the genetic research, which they now know that Christian's mother Renata has. Held in an underground mine, Christian and Isabella have to persuade Renata to send the code to unlock their father's research, knowing that it may be used by the white supremacists to eliminate thousands in the black population in the pursuit of a new white homeland. Once the code is supplied may mean their deaths.

Saved from the white supremacists, Christian and Isabella find their relationship frustrated by the distance between them. They, with great reluctance and heartbreak, return to their respective countries Australia and South Africa.

Chapter 1

"De Villiers!"

Bolt shouted across the sanitised white Emergency Room at the Royal Adelaide hospital. Christian felt his name reverberate off the walls as interns and nurses turned to look at the source of the minatory guttural sound. The voice belonged to Dr. Adrian Bolt, the senior surgical registrar who had become the scourge of the trauma unit at the Royal Adelaide Hospital.

Adrian Bolt liked to give the impression the trauma unit was his own medical fiefdom. Within the confines of his personally constructed kingdom, judgement and commands were to be acted upon instantly. His word, he considered, was fundamental law and as with many short men, he had inherited the gene for belittling taller male individuals with acid sarcasm.

"De Villiers, stop trying to bloody chat up that nurse and get your stupid slack arse over here! We may have a gunshot trauma coming through that door; there is no time to be organising when you next get laid. I need you to be thinking resuscitation - not sex, and to be able to react instantly."

Christian stopped talking and returned Bolt's stare. Bolt was daring him to respond; the insecurity of his size desperate to manifest in a more belittling comment. Christian considered a cutting reply; this was his last week in the trauma unit before he went overseas for a year. It would almost be worth the vitriolic holocaust that would ensue to repay Bolt's abuse in kind.

Adrian Bolt had passed his fellowship in surgery six months previously and was hoping to become a full consultant. That he had not yet been appointed clearly irked him. For most every other senior registrar, it was an automatic acclamation after graduation. The delay suggested to everyone that Bolt was either not good enough or not well enough liked. Christian had seen that he was a good surgeon. The only reason he could imagine that he had had not been appointed was that he had seriously pissed off the authorities in the Department of Surgery.

In contrast to his meticulous medical knowledge, Bolt cared little about his appearance. His black hair was receding on both sides; a few small tufts remained above each ear accompanied by unruly irregular strands crawling down his neck. Bolt allowed the hair uncontrolled growth for months. Periodically, he would sweep it out of the way with a carefully manicured hand, unconcernedly showering dandruff in every direction. This created a mini snowstorm, from which the medical students took sudden and evasive action. On a bad day, he had no shame and would take some of the lubricating jelly from the trolley on the ward and plaster his hair into place.

Medical students on ward rounds over the years had listed Bolt's hair plastering as one of the 'official' causes of nausea. Ranked fifth on the list, it was a favourite answer at the annual quiz night, the answer which students had learned over the years and would shout out 'Bolt' at the appropriate time with great alacrity and laughter. Christian personally thought that the great tufts of unruly black primal hair emanating from his ears should have been added to the list. However, that was overruled when he had suggested it to the student committee; it was not considered truly nauseating, as they were difficult to see consistently if you were below average height. For someone who was so unconcerned about his personal appearance, Bolt's approach to general and personal hygiene was also somewhat unusual. He insisted that on the ward all students and nurses fastidiously use the alcohol wash bottles.

"Do not bloody infect patients; wash your hands," was one of his favourite invectives.

Yet his personal hygiene appeared to lack the same consistent rigor. His hands were clean from the constant use of the alcohol antiseptic bottles, but his body odour suggested that the rest of him needed a good bath. Stale sweat impregnated his blue surgical overalls; mixed with old blood and fast food, it created an olid reaction under the hot fluorescent lights of the Emergency Department. Another inexplicable peculiarity of Bolt's was that he did not change his surgical overalls regularly; he seemed oblivious to the pungent smell which had started days before he decided to change them

The blue surgical overalls, which Bolt favoured in the emergency department, were a curiosity in themselves. All overalls for use in the department were delivered from the central sterile supply room neatly folded. Bolt's overalls appeared on the ward with ironed creases. The strange thing was no one seemed to care about whether his or her overalls were ironed except Bolt. That created another favourite question on student quiz night for which no one knew the correct answer. He did not have a girlfriend and none of the nurses liked him, which ruled both out as surreptitious ironing women. There was a rumour that he sent them to his mother who lived in the small town of Whyalla. Small packages wrapped in brown paper, with a Whyalla postmark, turned up at the Emergency Department every two to three weeks addressed to Dr. Adrian Bolt. That however was just medical student speculation, for no one really knew, and no one dared ask.

The other strange thing about Bolt's surgical overalls was that they always seemed a size too small. The cuffs squatted a good five cm above his surgical clogs, suggesting they were two sizes too small. On closer inspection, this was due to the fact the overalls rode up under his crotch. Bolt took the trousers and rolled the top down before tying them tightly below his waist. As a result, the trousers pulled up into his crotch, displaying various parts of his anatomy not normally visible. Christian thought that not only did it look uncomfortable but also it must have made standing up to pee almost impossible. The medical student's analysis was that in pulling his pants into his crotch, it made him feel taller than he was. Christian thought that was too simplistic an explanation and wondered whether there was something a bit more perverse, knowing Bolt the way that he did. In that strange mind of his, it was more likely Bolt was trying to demonstrate that not all of his anatomy derived from the same gene that had dictated his height.

Adrian Bolt's only redeeming feature that Christian could see was that he was damn good at surgery. The unshakeable belief in his own knowledge ensured that he had a good base from which to teach. Coupled with the desire never to display weakness or fear meant that if you could tolerate the sarcasm, excellent medical and surgical learning was almost compulsory. Not that Christian was enthusiastic when the time came at the thought of doing another rotation with Bolt. He could easily recall with the embarrassment the first time when Bolt had picked on him as a medical student. The medical students and Bolt had been rehearsing positions for a potential trauma. Marked out on the floor in the trauma unit were positions for each of the assisting staff as well as the senior registrar or consultant. Footprints in different colours permanently glued to the floor indicating where everyone was to stand. This was to ensure rapid and effective deployment of medical staff. Christian could remember that in his haste to get to the yellow footprints as the third assistant, he had ended up standing at the first nurse's station. Bolt at that time had taken great delight in pointing out his stupidity and making him kneel in his position as they went through the rehearsal.

"While you're down there, pray that you are not as stupid again. We are here to save lives, not to have you lose them."

Christian could distinctly remember the look of disgust from Bolt at committing so basic an error, but also the pleasure he got from belittling him in front of the other students. Christian enjoyed neither. Opting to do six months as a surgical trainee meant possibly more of the same abuse. He had thought long and hard about whether he wanted to endure that again and then rationalised that despite Bolt being arrogance personified, he was the best teacher. Christian also knew he had learnt a lot from this first rotation despite the regular humiliations. He knew that to be a surgeon, he needed the exposure to significant trauma, which provided an excellent background to dealing with other surgical emergencies. Enduring six months of Bolt would, in the overall scheme of his training, be worth it.

"Can't you move any faster than that, de Villiers?"

Bolt's voice sliced through the silence that had now descended upon the Emergency Room as Christian moved to take up his position where a potential trauma victim might be waiting.

"And don't just stand there like some lanky beanpole without a brain, make sure you have some large bore intravenous catheters and the peritoneal lavage set in your hands ready to go."

Christian was again tempted to say something confronting. He fought the urge and reminded himself there would be learning in this exercise and he would shortly be going overseas. He thought about asking a question and then remembered that even asking a question was to invite a comment on one's stupidity. Bolt expected everyone to learn by watching what he did; seeking verbal clarification indicated that you were not concentrating sufficiently. There was some small consolation. Bolt dispensed his arrogance without favour to all who ranked below him: doctors, medical students, nurses, and orderlies. The only real exception was if you were significantly taller than Bolt, then you had to expect a greater dose of sarcasm.

At 195 cm, Christian had always been a prime target .He was also easily spotted and therefore frequently picked on. There was nowhere to hide on the big wide wards, even if he attempted to try to crouch behind some of the taller students. Bolt took great delight in finding him. There were days in this latest rotation, where Bolt's comments had become so frequent, that Christian had longed to ignore the lessons of the past and respond in kind. Either that or one good punch to his short fat nose. He had managed to control that urge, knowing that any kind of response would see him shifted off the trauma unit; such was Bolt's influence. He picked up the peritoneal lavage catheter and took his place.

"Good work de Villiers. It may have taken six years but I can see that at least you can recognise a peritoneal lavage catheter. The next question is do you know where to put it."

Christian did not look up but just briefly imagined plunging it into Bolt's abdominal cavity. The catheter with a sharpened spike he had used to assess whether there was any ongoing bleeding inside the abdomen. A small incision was made in the abdomen, which allowed the catheter to be inserted. If blood came back up the catheter, that indicated bleeding inside the abdomen and mandatory surgery. Given speculation that Bolt only had ice in his veins, stabbing him with a catheter may have little value. They stood waiting for the next ascerbicism when the nurse manager pushed her way past Christian to stand next to Bolt.

Maureen Maxwell had spent fifteen years in the Emergency and Trauma Department; she owned it and was the one person of lesser rank that Bolt appeared to defer to. Maureen's hair cut was extremely short in the style of a United States Marine; the efficiency of hairstyle complimented by her triathlete's body suggested she was not a person to be messed with. Every finely sculpted inch of her body projected authority; you argued at your peril. Bolt and Maxwell together made a strange but hugely efficient team, with medical students often speculating as to what kind of children they would have in the unlikely event that Bolt was the only male left on the planet.

"There's been a bikie brawl in Hindley Street, four suspected gunshot victims, and two stabbings; they will be here in fifteen minutes."

Maureen Maxwell spoke in a matter-of-fact way that belied not only the unfolding drama, but also her experience in dealing with emergencies. Nothing ruffled her, not even the eminent arrival of four gunshot victims.

Bolt turned and faced Christian.

"De Villiers, come with me. The rest of you stay the way you are and be ready. Sister Maxwell, alert the other teams that they will be needed stat and it will need all the theatres open and the anaesthetists on-call notified."

Christian followed Bolt through into the front of the emergency department. Lines of trolleys were neatly parked next to each other, thirty in total he had once counted, anticipating a major catastrophe. Orderlies, in their grey overalls, gathered in one corner to help with the transfer of patients from arriving ambulances. Through the bulletproof glass, which lined the front of the emergency unit, Christian could see the flashing lights of the first ambulance approaching.

"So de Villiers, time to find out whether you have learnt anything. You are going to assess the first patient. Tell me what you do first. If you don't get this right, I'm sending you to drink coffee with the bloody nurses."

"Check airway patency, check breathing, and check circulation. Stop any obvious haemorrhaging."

Christian repeated the mantra that Bolt had taught them ad nauseam.

"Establish venous access; prioritise resuscitation of the patient. Identify injuries at a rapid first assessment; determine need for surgery before second assessment." He continued before Bolt could say anything.

"Not bad for a lanky beanpole.' conceded Bolt. 'Let's see whether you are any good at putting that theory into action."

Christian watched as the paramedics rushed the first bikie up the ramp and into the emergency assessment area. He took up position at the head of the trolley. The paramedics had already established venous access and that the bikie was breathing, but his eyes were closed and Christian was uncertain whether he was conscious. He made a mental note that a Glasgow coma score was automatically six, indicating possible major brain damage.

As Christian looked down at the bikie, he was confronted by a dishevelled beard matted in blood; there was no movement other than shallow breathing. Another mental note: he may be paralysed. Not therefore to be moved, without the placement of a spinal board. The first superficial examination quickly completed, Christian could see blood now soaking through the badly torn faded denim shirt. Fortunately, there was no obvious gushing of blood, which would indicate a major arterial puncture; a pulse rate of 120 bpm indicated that there had obviously been considerable blood loss somewhere.

The paramedics, in their rush to get the victims to hospital, had not cut any of the victim's clothes off. Christian reached for the scissors on the emergency trolley as well as the surgical gloves. He was about to cut through the shirt when Sister Maxwell walked past and, with a look of feigned horror, handed him the protective glasses from the trolley.

He attempted to quickly cut through the blood-soaked shirt, but the scissors were old and blunt, and kept catching and locking on the matted blood and denim. Christian discarded them and ripped the blood-soaked shirt so that he could see most of the upper body.

Underneath the shirt was black hair that any primate would have been proud of. It covered most of the torso, making any identification of a potential wound difficult. The lower abdomen by contrast was covered in a myriad of tattoos. Swastikas, tridents, tattooed words venerating the Hells Angels, death, and the devil. Some words were indiscriminately tattooed where there was available skin: Touch Me I Will Kill You/Death To All Spades and one tattoo which was centred on his belly button, Fuck All Pigs. As Christian scanned for a possible bleeding site, he remembered what Bolt had always said about tattoos. The number of tattoos on any body was inversely proportional to the intelligence of the tattooed. The more tattoos that you had, the less intelligent you were. Bolt would often quote many a sports star known to be covered in tattoos, as hard evidence that this was a not theory but scientific fact. He also constantly reminded medical students that one in five of any tattoos that they saw would possibly be hepatitis C positive; such was the lack of sterile control in tattoo parlours. Christian looked at the bikie and his tattoos, thinking the first part of Bolt's theory would remain unproven unless the bikie regained consciousness.

Checking to see whether he could see a small stab wound beneath one of the ribs, he glanced up to see a growing pool of blood gathering beneath the beard.

"Sister, we going to need to remove that beard. Can you give me the electric shaver?"

"We may need a scrub cutter to deal with that piece of undergrowth."

"No Sister," said Christian looking up and smiling. "I'm sure the battery-operated razor will be fine."

Christian positioned himself so that he could remove a significant part of the beard from the right neck and jaw. As he applied the battery razor to the beard, it was no match for the congealed blood and quickly seized. Christian tugged at it trying to dislodge both hair and clotted blood. Clumps of blood and hair came away with the razor as he pulled, which caused two immediate reactions.

A gush of bright red arterial blood, powerful enough to reach his eyes, splashed on his protective glasses. Thank you, Sister Maxwell, he quietly said to himself. He quickly put his gloved finger onto the spurting vessel, which stopped the flow. Then he looked round for an intern to continue the pressure while he finished the examination. Whether it was the pressure that he applied to stop the bleeding or tearing of the blood-soaked beard, the bikie suddenly opened his eyes. Coal black, chillingly dispassionate eyes turned and fixated on Christian. Without warning, his massive hand reached up with the speed of a giant cobra and grabbed Christian roughly around the throat.

"You cut off my beard and I will fucking kill you. I know your fucking name now, dipshit, shave that off and you will die."

Christian was startled but immediately pulled back breaking the grip and looked at the bikie, feeling evil and hatred emanating in a continuous deathly stare. It was like confronting some alien life form. How someone be that close to death, weakened by significant blood loss and yet could retain such physical power, defied basic physiology. Such power seemed to have some kind of evil supernatural component. Christian briefly wondered whether this was what he had trained eight years for, and whether the world would be a better place if he released his finger from the carotid artery. Despite the attractiveness of the thought, his training was to preserve life, irrespective of whom the life belonged to and no matter how evil they seemed.

"Let's go with another litre of Haemacell, Sister. Cross match blood and notify theatre that we need to do an exploration of his neck."

As Christian looked up, he noticed Bolt standing behind him. He had obviously heard the threats from the bikie.

"Have you done your second examination yet?" Bolt asked. "And he won't remember your name. Hypnovel, which he will get in theatre, takes away the memory. He won't remember your name if he wakes up."

Bolt's comment took Christian by surprise; it was the first time that he had said anything to Christian that was not belittling.

"No, I have not done a second examination yet, so he may have another gunshot or stab wound; I was about to do that now."

"Let's get to theatre. You can do the second examination in there while I'm scrubbing up. Sister Maxwell, make sure security knows, in case some of the other gang come looking to try to finish off what they started. Now where is that bloody intern when you need her? She can apply pressure to the neck."

Bolt looked around, annoyed that that the intern was now helping another registrar with the third bikie to be wheeled in. Walking over to her, he tapped her on the shoulder, turned and pointed at Christian and said,

"That's where you need to be. And don't take your finger off that bloody neck until we get him into theatre."

Christian signalled to the orderlies. Rupert, the older orderly with grey hair and a limp, quickly took control of the trolley and propelled the bikie towards the first emergency theatre. Christian walked ahead, guiding the head of the trolley and as they neared theatre, he pushed in the access code to open the double doors. Inside through the glass window, he could see Bolt scrubbing and beyond, Peter Jones the anaesthetist drawing up drugs.

"He has a small stab wound to his abdomen." Christian said to Bolt as he walked into theatre

"I will do the neck first." Said Bolt from the scrub bay. "Then you can open the abdomen, de Villiers."

"Shit, he's losing pressure," was the shout from Peter Jones as he struggled to get an arterial line positioned.

"I think you're going to have to do the abdomen first."

"De Villiers, get scrubbed. I am going to open the abdomen and you can fix whatever is inside. What's the intern's name— Donna?"

"Yes," replied Christian

Christian, from the scrub bay, could see the scrub sister rapidly applying a mix of alcohol and iodine skin preparation as an antiseptic to the abdomen. As it dried, it created a surreal yellow backdrop for the mosaic of tattoos, which now appeared two-dimensional. By the time drapes were flung into position, he was standing opposite Bolt.

"You guys better hurry. His pulse rate is up to 160 and his blood pressure is down to 80/40. He must be bleeding inside his abdomen."

"Sister, give de Villiers the scalpel."

Christian looked at the abdomen; it was now significantly distended and rapidly filling with blood. He had made incisions on the abdomen for trauma so he knew that once they entered the abdominal cavity, the bleeding would no longer be contained. Blood would flow all over the operating table and they would need to be able to quickly contain the bleeding. He would need to place a large number of abdominal packs inside the abdomen and very quickly stem the flow. As he looked down to see how far below the umbilicus he would make his incision, he saw the words tattooed just above the belly button. Fuck All Pigs, in old English script.

"How quaint is that." Bolt said sarcastically looking at the Fuck All Pigs tattoo. "See whether you can curve your incision to go through the F."

Christian made the incision starting high up on the abdomen and curving slightly through the F as requested by Bolt. It meant deviating from the midline, which was unusual, but he was not about to question Bolt at this point. On entering the abdominal cavity, fresh blood rushed up to greet them as predicted.

"Suction, Sister," said Bolt as Christian placed one large abdominal pack after another into both sides of the abdomen. The bleeding finally slowed after the placement of seven large white abdominal packs. Bolt applied the suction and Christian could see there was a tear in one of the larger veins.

"You repair that and I'll retract for you." Bolt said taking the metal retractor, which allowed Christian to see the bleeding vein.

Christian repaired the vein with fine sutures and then checked to see if whether there were any other bleeding sites. The stab wound had been quite lateral but there was no other bleeding from the entry wound.

23

"Well, that was an easy fix. We will have a quick look around, then we can close up his abdomen and fix his neck."

Christian sutured up the first layer of the abdomen with a heavy nylon suture and was surprised when Bolt said he would do the skin layer. That was usually the junior surgeon's job. He was also surprised when Bolt moved to his side of the operating table and rejected the skin stapler and insisted on a continuous suture. A continuous suture would take much longer than just stapling the skin together. Bolt, who was not renowned for his patience, made using the suture even more of an unusual request. Christian watched and assisted as Bolt slowly sutured the top half of the wound, then paused at the point of the tattoo where Christian had partly incised the F of the tattoo Fuck All Pigs. With a few small deft sutures, Bolt turned the F into an S. Then he completed the lower half of the wound, neatly tucking the suture in after tying his surgical knot. Looking over his surgical mask at Christian, he laughed and said.

"That should make for more interesting reading in the future."

The next morning Christian took the lift up to the eighth floor where all post-operative patients were sent. The previous night they had not finished surgery until 2:30 am. Christian did not mind the tiredness this morning; it was his last ward round before he had a year off. He had successfully negotiated with the College of Surgeons to have a year off before starting formal training. He felt deep inside he needed to see some of the world to expand his medical and surgical horizons beyond Adelaide. There was also the other factor, which was the uncertainty in his love life. He had never been able to match the chemistry he had found with Isabella. Over the years, he had wondered whether it was impossible to recreate the chemistry with her. There had been a few other girlfriends but the intensity had not matched what he had had with Isabella. He needed to resolve that crisis with time away or possibly finding her again

As he walked out of the lift and down the corridor to S Ward, he was grateful that the bikie, whom he now knew as Anton Kauffman, had only a puncture wound to a vein, not an artery in his neck. That had been a relatively easy suture repair as well. Unfortunately, the other bikie had died on the operating table, a 9 mm bullet shredding his aorta and spinal cord. There was no way they could repair the aorta, despite the intervention of one of the best vascular surgeons in Adelaide, Rupert McKnee.

Christian punched in the code 911E for the last time and opened the door to the ward. Sally, whom he thought was the most attractive nurse on the ward, looked up and smiled at him from the nurses' station as he walked in. Sally was a second-year nurse with an infectious amount of enthusiasm and a blonde ponytail, which she loved to twirl as she talked to you. He had been tempted to ask her out several times. Nevertheless, despite her obvious interest in him and her attractiveness, there was something missing which he could not quite define. He knew he needed to work out the Isabella legacy in his life; otherwise, he might never find someone to share his life with.

"Late night I hear," Sally said, twirling her ponytail as Christian approached.

"Yes, it was and all a bit dramatic in the end."

"We have moved Mr Kauffman into a private room. I have to warn you that there are four of his gang in there refusing to leave."

"Probably ensuring that one of the rival Bandito's gang doesn't come back to finish off. How come we have no police up here?"

"No one is saying anything; you know what it's like with gangs, if no one says anything, then charges can't be laid."

Christian pulled the small table out from the side of the ward and retrieved Kauffman's notes from the pigeonhole above. He read quickly through Sally's notes; there had been no change in Kauffman's condition overnight, which was gratifying to see. He could report to Bolt that everything was stable and that would be his last action on the ward.

"Do you want me to change his dressings?" Sally interrupted his thoughts.

"No, you can leave that for forty-eight hours," said Christian remembering Bolt's handiwork and that any gratitude that might be coming, should be Bolt's alone. As he closed the folder his mind turned to the discussion he had had with his mother about where he was going to spend the next year.

Chapter 2

"So Dr. de Villiers, now that you have done two years as a trainee surgeon, you are going to leave Adelaide and explore the world. Four more weeks to go, have you finalised all the possible destinations yet?" Renata enquired, standing in the doorway of Christian's study.

Christian turned from the computer screen to see his mother standing in the doorway smiling. She had her hair pulled back into a tight bun with a nine-carat gold hair clip holding it tightly in place, her fine Flemish features freshly burnished with a cream that he remembered cost almost as much as his monthly iPhone plan. Most of his friends could not believe that she was forty-six years of age, as she looked so much younger. Perhaps there was something special about the Retinoic acid in the cream she used, a fact she would often refer to with no little hubris, whenever he teased her about the cost of the moisturising cream.

Christian looked at his mother, a beautiful picture framed by the doorway and wondered how much different her life could have been, had his father survived and not been murdered. There was a persistent sadness surrounding his mother, which he could not explain other than in some way it related to his father's death. Her sadness detracted from a natural beauty; her almond-shaped blue grey eyes were never really smiling. He wished on many occasion he could find the key to alleviate her personal darkness.

Once all the details of his father's involvement with the Bureau of State Security in South Africa had been revealed, he thought she might find greater peace. Christian knew that he was relieved to discover that his father's involvement with the apartheid government had not been entirely corrupt. His father had been more a victim of his own pride and ego, than an active supporter of the regime that brutally enforced racial segregation.

In the end his father had seen the immorality of the government and tried to rectify some of his mistakes. For Christian, that made his actions a little easier to accept. Strangely, the discovery seemed to have the opposite effect on his mother and she now refused to talk about his father at all. That was difficult to understand; there had to be something else that he did not understand about his father.

"You know you don't have to decide on which specialty you want to follow straight away. In actual fact it would be quite a good idea just to gain experience in some other specialties before you make up your mind."

"That's what I was thinking about doing when I first decided to go overseas, and it would also give me a different perspective on medicine before I finally committed to surgical training."

"Well, I know that's certainly what many young doctors are doing now, although I think, like your father, you are suited towards a surgical specialty. So where are you going to spend all this time; let me guess... South Africa?"

Christian looked at his mother and smiled, thinking that she knew him so well, loving the way that her intuition on occasions manifested. Moreover, she had refrained from mentioning Isabella, which she nearly always did whenever South Africa came up in the conversation.

"In actual fact you are in this instance right but only about the continent not the country."

Christian deliberately shortened the sentence so that it did not give the full amount of information, knowing that it would cause his mother, in that very familiar way of hers, to scrobiculate her brow. It was her distinctive way of indicating that she wanted more information but did not know whether it was polite to ask. They stood for a few minutes looking at each other smiling; understanding each other so well. Christian knew she wanted more information, and Renata knew that if she waited long enough, Christian would tell her what she wanted to know. They had played this game among themselves on many occasions over the years.

"Okay, I give in this time," said Renata. "So where is it that my adventurer son is intending to go?"

"Rwanda."

Christian looked at his mother, trying to anticipate her reaction. He had been uncertain as to whether she would approve and knew that he would have to give her more details as to his decision. Nevertheless, it was always the initial reaction from his mother which was an indication of approval or otherwise.

"Having two parents who are doctors and who have a need to both achieve and help people often means that the children of those parents may inherit some of those characteristics. Not always, and in many instances, children with achieving parents feel that they are not a priority. Those children end up with a determination within their own lives to be more family centric. You clearly are the former, and it would be impossible I think for anyone to distract someone as focused as you on what they want to achieve. I am delighted that you are now an independent achieving young man. I was incredibly impressed with the way that you dealt with the discoveries about your father in South Africa. I know that any decision you now make will have much thought behind it, great sensitivity, and maturity as well as having a remarkable chance of being both successful and enriching."

Christian got up out of his chair and walked towards his mother. Renata hardly ever used long sentences; her inclination was to be short and to the point. He had heard her lecture during his pathology course in third year. Always succinct, almost surgical in the way that she ensured the information was presented, amongst the forest of histology, she made sure everyone could see clearly the pathological trees. That is how she had always been as a mother, direct and to the point.

"You know you are a pretty cool mum," he said as he stood in front of her and took in a bear hug. "You have never said anything like that to me before. That really means a lot to me."

Christian rested on his chin on the top of her head: he was now a full head and shoulders taller than his mother and her head fitted perfectly on his shoulder. Although when he hugged her it now, with their height differences, it felt a little awkward, as he looked straight down on the changing colour of her hair. He momentarily thought about playfully lifting her off the floor when he felt a dampness seeping through the top of his shirt.

"Are you okay, mum?" he said as he disentangled himself and held her at arm's length.

Renata wiped her eyes before turning and heading towards the kitchen.

"Yes, I'm fine; sometimes I forget how grown-up you have become and how capable you are of dealing with life."

Christian followed her into the kitchen. Cook books, mostly Jamie Oliver and Nigella Lawson, lay open at various pages at the far end of the bench. Next to them were multi-coloured chopping boards, green for vegetables, red for meat, yellow for chicken, and white for fish. The colour coding was part of his mother's belief that cooking needed science; colour separation was a memory aid, which she argued reduced cross contamination of the bacteria in foods. His mother loved cooking and Christian had been the recipient of many of her wonderful cooking experiments throughout his life. Garlic was an ever-present smell in the house, and there were few dishes that garlic did not find its way into. Christian, however, was not certain from the large amount of garlic that his mother used, whether it was added to each dish purely for flavour, or because she believed that it had certain medicinal properties. Garlic was one of those strange quirks, which was his mother. Her training was in evidence-based medicine, which she normally insisted on if he was to convince her of his argument. Moreover, being the Gradgrind that she mostly was, it fascinated him that she would put her faith in the medicinal properties of things like Echinacea and garlic for which he could find no evidence. When he had started studying medicine, he had done Medline searches to try to convince her. Quoting the research to her in this instance had made little difference. After a while, he no longer puzzled as to how that exception worked and just accepted that is how it was with his mostly scientific mother, and no one was perfect.

Renata simmered the chopped garlic and onion for a few minutes in the frying pan. As she added the pasta sauce and basil leaves, the aroma again changed. The new smell distracted Christian from the discussion and reminded him of when he came home late from university. Opening the backdoor, the various aromas would envelop him stimulating his hunger. He watched as his mother fiddled with the arms of the pasta maker, sensing her uncertainty about how to proceed after his question. Throughout his life, she had never been comfortable with emotional statements. Any small emotional discussion that they had had over the years was usually followed by an uncomfortable silence. It was like a compensatory pause after an irregular heartbeat, a pause required to overcome the natural disinclination to talk about things emotional. He felt that tonight, would be no different; she would busy herself with the pasta and then with her composure regained, would initiate the conversation around another topic. On this occasion, he decided that he had more to talk to her about and venturing into the refractory period would be acceptable. Before he had a chance to speak, his mother surprised him and broke with tradition. Without turning to look at him, she said,

"I think I know why you want to go to Rwanda," she said. "You found out that your father once went there."

Christian had realised for some time following his intern year that he had a decision to make. It was now nine years since he had been back to South Africa looking for information on his father. He had mostly closed the book on that in his own mind, although he did still wonder what had happened with his father being in Rwanda.

"That's partly true, mum, which is something that I wanted to ask you about. It wasn't clear when we came back from South Africa. I know looking through dad's papers that he visited Rwanda and went down to a small town on the border of the Congo called Garanyi. I just thought it would be interesting to go back to a place where he had been which has not been tainted by all the issues of apartheid and corruption that we discovered in South Africa. And when I looked it up on the Internet, the hospital there has 300 beds and serves a catchment area of one million people on both sides of the border which would give me heaps of experience in medicine and surgery."

Renata listened, not turning to face Christian, part of her not really wanting to hear what he was saying, hoping that the chapter, which was Africa, had truly gone from their lives forever. In her heart of hearts, she understood that Christian was truly his father's son, and that part of his father which she had loved, the desire to help the less fortunate, was present in Christian. That desire needed to be fulfilled. She put down the sheet of pasta and turned to face him.

"I can understand your desire to go somewhere where your father has been. However, there are certain things that you should consider in making that decision. Your father was only there two weeks, I seem to recall, and it was on some kind of government business, therefore it might not have been medically related. He was never specific about why he was there, only suggesting that it had to do with his genetic research. Nevertheless, at the time, and with the information that we now have, it might have been related

30

to trying to obtain some of the rare minerals from the eastern Congo, for the nuclear development programme in apartheid South Africa. Even if he did work at the hospital, which I cannot recall him talking about, I doubt that they would remember him. Going there with your limited experience in medicine and surgery may not be regarded as a useful experience with regards to a future specialty."

"I realise that my experience is not great, but I do have two years surgical experience now and my time in the Trauma unit, which will be helpful, and certainly I will learn a lot. Also it would just complete things in so far as I'm concerned, being in a place where my dad was, in trying to imagine that he was there helping people."

Christian looked at his mother and could see that she was not entirely convinced.

"Christian, you can probably sense that I am not happy. There has been genocide there and there are still countless reports of rebels in that region. I think you would be better going to South Africa. However, I know that being the person that you are, trying to stop you would be counter-productive. My underlying concern as a mother will always be for your safety. There has been ongoing conflict on the border between Congo and Rwanda and I don't want you caught up in anything."

"I do understand that, mum, and I have already been in contact with the Department of Foreign Affairs in Canberra. There are no travel advisory notices for that area; it is regarded as a safe region to travel to. Besides which, you know me after the South African adventures, I now have an intuition that hopefully allows me to avoid dangerous situations."

Christian finished the last sentence with a smile and winked at his mother hoping that his humour would break the impasse, as it normally did. Renata looked back at him understanding his strategy and holding his gaze to let him know that she understood he was using his youthful charm to try to win her over.

They looked at each other for what seemed to Christian like an age. It was on occasions like this that he wished his father were still alive. His mother had tried to bridge the gap; but at times, he just longed for a true male perspective. In some strange way, he felt the last nine years of medicine in Adelaide was something that his father would have approved of. On more than one occasion, he had wondered whether his father was out there watching somewhere with a sense of pride. He would have loved to discuss many things with his father and particularly to try to have understood how he felt about the new South Africa. He wondered whether his father would have adapted to a country where legal separation no longer existed. However, from what he had observed, it was a long way from the rainbow nation that everyone now claimed it was. From what he had seen, there were still only three primary colours: black, brown and white, a long way from a multi-coloured carefully integrated rainbow.

The living conditions for the majority of the black population had also not significantly changed since the era of the white government. Building programmes had been undertaken, but it was nowhere near what was needed. The social needs of the black population were not being met and there was growing discontent amongst the youth who were advocating nationalisation of industry as a way of redistribution of wealth. Would his father, he wondered, have said integration is such an unnatural thing that it produces systematic chaos, or would he have been of the opinion that integration requires generations to overcome racial bias in order to succeed.

"Have you thought about catching up with Isabella if you go?" Renata again interrupted his thoughts.

Christian again looked at his mother. He had never really discussed with her what had happened to the relationship that he had with Isabella. However, he knew that she sensed that they had had an intense albeit short affair. The chemistry was something that he had not experienced since and not something that he thought he could discuss with his mother. He was also uncertain as to whether it was unique to Isabella, or whether such intensity was because it was the first time for the both of them. Strangely, he had not been able to replicate that intensity with other girlfriends. Inside, part of him longed for the intensity again where colours were brighter and desire became an all-consuming fire. He knew if he was to have any peace and success in future relationships, he needed to find out if the chemistry he had with Isabella was just a first relationship phenomenon. If it was, he needed to accept such intensity could not be replicated and move on.

That the relationship had not survived due to the distance he could understand. However, that the flame for Isabella still flickered after all these years intrigued him. Looking back, there were so many things that they had in common, so much so that initially he had even thought about trying to study medicine in South Africa, so he and Isabella could be together. When they had enquired about whether he could, they discovered the difficulties of being admitted into medicine in South Africa for someone who was white and Australian. Finally, he had been persuaded by Renata to return to Australia and leave Isabella behind. To Christian at the time, it all seemed so desperately unfair; two people who had a wonderful attraction for each other could not be together.

They had tried to maintain the relationship when he returned to Australia. Certainly, for the first few months the combination of e-mails and Skyping maintained their intensity and hope. Christian even planned to return in his first holiday break to Cape Town; however, as the full immersion into university life in Adelaide progressed, the intensity of their relationship seemed to diminish. They could both sense it and in the end, they agreed that given the distance between them, it was better just to try to remain friends.

"Well mum, we have maintained a friendship but Isabella has moved on and has another boyfriend now."

"Is that so? I had an e-mail from her mother Nadine the other day who suggested that Isabella still asked after you, suggesting I would have thought that she is still interested."

Renata looked at Christian with the small smile she reserved for occasions when she wanted him to know that, despite not having had a relationship since his father, she still understood them.

"Mum, it is probably too difficult for people such as Isabella and me, from very different cultural backgrounds to have a successful long-term relationship."

"That sounds like a well-thought-out response, or a reason not to try again, but thoughts don't always effectively deal with emotions. I think you should see her and make sure the flame is not flickering." Renata said with another knowing smile.

Christian was a little taken aback; he was not used to his mother venturing into his emotional space. She had been a brilliant mother in terms of providing support and organisation, but he had always found it difficult to discuss the emotional side of his life with her. It was not that she lacked emotional intuition; he knew that she did from several things that she had said during his various relationships. However, that is all they were, comments with no real emotional depth or understanding. Fortunately, the mother of one of his friends from primary school had an uncanny ability to both bridge the age gap and understand emotional conflict. Gabriella had become his confidant, and in many ways she was like a big sister to him, providing him with the inside into relationships as he grew up. It was Gabriella, whom he talked most to about Isabella.

Christian looked at his mother, wondering whether to respond in the way that he had with Gabriella. Past experience suggested it wouldn't be a discussion but more an analysis and recommendation. Then he thought about how Gabriella had taught him to always be prepared to take a chance. Her favourite 'The heart that's afraid of breaking, will never learn to dance.' He decided to take a chance.

"Mum, Isabella was my first love. She was the first girl I had sex with. The intensity of that whole experience invaded my whole being. I felt like I had been taken over by a greater force, which was propelling me in a direction that I could not and did not want to control. Part of me found it difficult to deal with that lack of control, but part of me loved the feeling. You know that I have had relationships since then without the feeling that Isabella generated. I can now see that that intensity was possibly all part of the first experience, and that what we had was probably surreal and not survivable. The girls that I've since been out with, that intensity or chemistry has been lacking, even though they were each in their own way a wonderful experience." Christian rushed through the last few sentences wondering whether his mother was embarrassed by what he was telling her.

"Now it's my turn, my favourite son. I have never heard you talk like that about something that was obviously important to you. That is such a privilege that you wanted to share that with me, you cannot know how many times I wished you had in the past. I know that Gabriella has been a fantastic emotional resource for you, but there were times when I was so envious that she could discuss things like this with you. I realise also that is not one of my abilities, but that never stopped me wanting to share the special emotional side of things with you. Just remember, and this is my humble contribution accepting I'm outside my area of organisational expertise, but the reason that I never had a relationship with anyone after your father, is that there is no one who lit my fire like he did. There are many of my friends who have successful relationships, but from what I have observed, many are also business partnerships. I would much rather be single than have to get the warmth in a relationship by sitting at the fireplace."

Christian stood looking at his mother for quite some time, neither of them speaking. He after all these years now at least partly understood why there had been no man in her life. She had not been prepared to compromise on love just to have a relationship and sex. Perhaps therefore it was not just an intensity associated with a first relationship with Isabella; it had been something so special that he had not been able to find anything similar since.

"Okay young man, I can see that you're deep in thought so let's get back to the facts of what you want to do. You want to go and spend time in Rwanda. Have you any idea how you going to get there and where you are going to stay?"

"I've made contact with the superintendent at Garanyi hospital, and he has a house close to the hospital where I could stay."

"And how are you going to get there?"

"I'll go to London and then fly into Kigali. Or I could go via South Africa?" he completed the sentence with a slow deliberation, winking at his mother and enjoying her responsive smile.

"I know that you are teasing me but in my humble emotional opinion, you need to see Isabella and sort out your feelings. Something to think about in the next few weeks as you finish up your duties at the Adelaide hospital."

Chapter 3

Christian was not looking forward to visiting the travel doctors. Travelling to Rwanda, he knew, meant eight vaccinations. He could either have them all at once, as one of his friends William had suggested, although he seemed to remember that Will had felt quite strange afterwards to the point of vomiting. The alternative was to have them as two separate series of injections a week apart. As he walked up King William Street in the large cool shadow that stretched across the western side of the street, he still had not made up his mind which option to take. Getting closer to Hindmarsh Square and the travel doctors, he made up his mind. He would take the chance of feeling unwell for twenty-four hours and have the eight injections; getting it all over with at one consultation was the right decision.

The travel doctors had a bright yellow banner advertising their presence on the front window, as well as a small mobile sign in the street. With no wind blowing, the sign hung lifelessly, its large arrow pointing enervatedly at the front door. As Christian approached, the door automatically opened and he walked into a small reception area with a large map of Africa painted on one of the walls behind the receptionist. In the middle of the map he could see, straddling the East African Rift Valley, the small nation of Rwanda. He stood in front of it for a minute absorbing the vastness of Africa and the remoteness of the country he was intending to visit. Rwanda, he had read, was the most densely populated African country with eleven million people, although shortly after the genocide a census had indicated there were only ten million people, one million people having been killed in the genocide. For such a small country, it seemed inconceivable that it should have such a violent history. From what he had read, it fascinated him that it was still described as a Garden of Eden.

The resolution of the genocide fascinated him as much as its history. Two major tribal groups, Hutus and Tutsi, were apparently now in peaceful coexistence despite the hatred which had driven them to kill each other. What would he find in such a remote part of the world, he was wondering, when the woman behind the appointment counter spoke to him.

"Good morning, Dr. de Villiers, you have an appointment with Dr. Jaeger I think."

"Yes, I am having vaccinations done as I am travelling to Rwanda."

"He's running about ten minutes late so if you don't mind waiting, I will let him know that you're here."

Christian took a seat opposite the large map on the wall. The chairs were wooden, with small, dark green cushions tied to the top. The backs were made from bare wood with African woman ornately carved into each panel. The legs had African animals, mostly monkeys, carved into them. The arms, except for a small wooden shelf to rest your hand, were inlaid with white shell. He had not seen anything quite like the chairs before and wondered which country they had come from. He made a mental note to ask Dr. Jaeger.

"Dr. de Villiers." The lady who had greeted him when he arrived moved from behind the desk and sat down next to him.

"We need some details from you, past medical history and allergies, but I guess being a doctor you understand the need for all that information. I'll leave that there with you; if you have any questions just ask."

Christian looked at her and smiled. He realised, despite being qualified for three years, he had still not really fully adjusted at times to being called Dr. de Villiers. That in itself was strange, as he had looked forward to the honour for such a long time. There was a time, he remembered, just after starting medical school, when he was flying to Melbourne with his mother and he looked at his mother's boarding pass with Dr. de Villiers printed on it. He wondered at the time what it would feel like and how proud he would be to achieve the title of doctor. Now that he had been qualified for three years, he had mostly adjusted to the title, but knew deep down that each time he was called doctor, there was still a degree of pride in what he had achieved. What he had not adjusted to was the different ways people reacted when they knew you were a doctor. From many, there was a recognition that you had achieved something substantial which allowed you the privilege of being able to save lives and treat people.

For others the reaction was different. It was that being doctor was glamorous and sexy. He remembered all the discussions with his friends about how people reacted once they knew you were a doctor. The consensus he recalled, was that there had been so many television programmes promoting glamorous doctors that this is how doctors were generally now seen. He had worked enough late nights in Accident and Emergency and been sleep deprived and seen enough stabbings to realise medicine was far from glamorous and sexy. However, when he thought about it and was brutally honest with himself, he had to admit he did not mind someone thinking he was sexy because he was a doctor. The eye contact from the receptionist he thought fitted into that category. Recognising such a reaction he was capable of, but knowing how to deal with it he had found difficult. He remembered what his good friend Sophia had tried to tell him during one of their many relationship research sessions at their favourite student pub, The Elephant and Castle.

"Be cool, Christian; do not immediately return eye contact until you're certain that you want more. Then if your peripheral scan is positive, remember shyness, or apparent shyness, is very appealing. It gives the appearance that you are unused to this kind of attention and do not quite know how to deal with it. Very attractive from a woman's point of view, it even suggests that you might be relatively untouched from a relationship point of view."

Christian looked at the floor, or more correctly at his feet on the floor, as he reflected on Sophia's advice. He had always felt awkward making eye contact; he did not have to feign shyness. He picked up one of the travel magazines and began flicking through the pages in what he hoped was a nonchalant manner. He looked at the photographs replaying in his mind Sophia's advice when he heard the reception phone ring. He looked up and the woman behind the reception desk said,

"Vanessa speaking, how can I help you?"

Vanessa's hair was cut short, coal black hair cropped neatly into her neck. On her right side, she had hooked it behind her ear. The curl of the hair drew attention to her high cheekbone and eloquent neck. A light blue T-shirt, with Travel Doctor embroidered across the front in large dark blue letters, matched her blue eyes and stretched itself over her pert breasts.

"Dr. Jaeger is quite busy but I will certainly bring that to his attention, and I'm sure he'll get back to you as soon as he can."

Christian quickly switched his gaze back to his travelling magazine. However, not quickly enough. Vanessa had noticed his covert appraisal. Christian felt uneasy; it was as though he had been caught doing something that he should not have been doing which brought with it a strange sense of guilt. Why that happened, he was never quite certain. Vanessa was very attractive and it was a natural instinct to admire beauty. Nevertheless, he had never been able to fully transition from 'it's rude to stare', which he had heard as a child, to a guiltless appreciative appraisal. When he had discussed his problem with Sophia at yet another of their pub research sessions, her advice had been unhelpful. Get over it, she had said, everyone stares, just learn to do it with style. She had not elaborated on how he could achieve that which had quietly annoyed him. Instead, she had said in the forthright manner, which was particular to her,

"Part of your problem is that you think you need to project the confident doctor, accepting all attention as adoration of you and your medical degree. That you do not is more attractive. Stick with the appearance of shyness, but for God's sake learn to look at a woman when she looks at you—not the floor!"

As Christian thought about the advice, he realised that he really hated his shyness. Medical school with all its requirements for grand rounds and presentations had eliminated his tendency to shyness on a public level but not on a personal one. He was confident in presenting to other doctors and even talking in public; he had done that many a time in his training and quite enjoyed it. It was just that somewhere deep inside, there remained a part of him that he did not want to or that he could not expose easily. He had been unable to figure out where that came from, a trait he thought he could not have inherited from either parent given their confidence. Although when he thought about it, he didn't really know that much about his father. Perhaps the beatings his father had endured from his grandfather on the family farm in South Africa were because his father was not confident enough to stand up to him. Another question about his father that he knew may never be answered.

Deep in that thought, he barely noticed that Vanessa had moved out from behind her desk to come and sit in the other ornately carved seat next to him. As she sat down clutching an information sheet attached to a blue clipboard, she said

"While you're waiting, if you could give me some of your details that would speed up the process."

Christian moved into recovery mode noting that everything seemed to be colour-coordinated, from the clipboard to the paper. He wondered whether that was also Vanessa's influence.

"And don't forget to put your phone number in there."

As she got up from the chair next to him, she left him with the clipboard and a knowing smile which annoyingly caused his shyness to resurface. Despite Sophia's advice that shyness was attractive, he wished that on occasions such as this he had the ability to overwhelm it.

Filling out the form, he was conscious in his peripheral vision of Vanessa now glancing over at him. He briefly wondered if there was something funny that he could say that make her laugh - one of Sophia's more helpful suggestions he remembered.

"Always remember," she had said, "making a woman laugh means you have touched her soul, and touching her soul inevitably means that she might trust you with touching other parts."

How Sophia had ended up having so much personal wisdom when it came to relationships intrigued him. It was not that she had had many boyfriends. He seemed to recall there had only been three or four, one more serious than the others. Perhaps it was more related to the fact that her mother was a psychiatrist and as a family, she had witnessed lots of discussion about life and personal issues and how best to deal with that.

Christian decided that if he had to think about what would make Vanessa laugh that it probably would not. He stood up to give the clipboard back when the side door opened slightly. A racing bicycle appeared. Christian placed the clipboard on Vanessa's desk as she turned to see who was coming through the door. The bicycle was followed shortly by someone whom Christian assumed was Dr. Jaeger. He looked every inch a serious cyclist, dressed in a white and black hooped Lycra top and shorts.

"Good afternoon, sorry I'm late, dam P platers slowing down the traffic again."

Christian watched as he disappeared with the bicycle into his office. A few minutes later, Christian could hear the shower start followed by less than tuneful singing.

"Well, she's all you'd ever want, She's the kind I like to flaunt and take to dinner, But she always knows her place, She's got style, she's got grace, she's a winner."

Christian smiled to himself. The singing itself was not that good, although Dr. Jaeger had a deep voice which should have been melodious. Christian was not quite sure either of the words of the song or who had sung the original version. What he did remember was that it was a song that his mother played often. There was one month particularly in the year when she always played it. The week before Easter, if he remembered correctly, although now that she had an iPod he had not heard it as often as he used to. He resolved to try and remember to ask her what the song was and who sang it. Dr. Jaeger's singing continued and he noticed that Vanessa was smiling. She was obviously enjoying the singing without the slightest embarrassment that Dr. Jaeger's voice was filling the waiting room.

A few minutes later Christian heard the shower stop with the singing becoming a low humming and shortly after the surgery door opened.

"Dr. Villiers, I presume. I'm Dr. Mark Jaeger, please call me Mark."

Christian took his outstretched hand and decided instantly that he liked Dr. Mark Jaeger. There was a kindness in his eyes, which Christian had always taken as a sign of inner goodness in people. Not that he had any science to back his observation it up. Conversely, he had learnt to be wary when there was no warmth or kindness. In countless patients high on methamphetamines, there was blackness as if their soul or the soul connection had gone into hiding.

"Vanessa tells me that you are going to Rwanda." Dr. Jaeger interrupted his thoughts.

"Yes, I'm planning to go to a small hospital down the Congolese border at a place called Garanyi."

"That's adventurous, no tripping off to a safe comfortable place like New Zealand or Asia to further your medical experience!"

"I wanted to go to some place which would be medically challenging and where my medicine and surgery would be useful."

"Well, Rwanda will certainly do that for you. It may interest you to know that my wife and I visited a hospital in a place called

Goma about six years ago, which is just across the border from Garanyi in the Congo. It was a hospital, which had a strong Australian link as it used to be visited each year by an Australian surgeon, who did a fantastic amount of surgery. If I recall, there was another German surgeon who used to come down and help from a mission hospital that he ran in the mountains of Rwanda.

"That is an amazing coincidence." Christian said. "My mother is worried about the safety and whether it will help or hinder my medical career. It all seems quite calm now, although I am aware that there are number of gangs active across the border in the Congo. Did you get concerned for your safety when you were there?"

"We were never really concerned, but you need to be careful and aware that from time to time violence can erupt. There are number of vested interests that are championed by various militias and political factions, centred on primarily the exotic minerals in the Eastern Congo. You need to have awareness about what's going on and always have at the back of your mind a plan for a quick exit."

"Not something I suspect my mother would like to hear."

"Christian, I think walking across the road is a danger in itself, but that danger can be minimised by an awareness of what may happen to you. The potential to learn in a situation, such as you want to go into, is significant even at your stage of medicine. Not only did that experience contribute significantly to my medical knowledge, it impacted the rest of my life. I subsequently have done a Master's degree in tropical medicine and I'm looking at joining Specialists without Borders, who teach doctors in developing countries."

"Thanks," said Christian. "I have also heard about that organisation, and it sounds like it's a fantastic way to be able to give back."

"Yes, it is an amazing concept, analogous to teaching people how to fish so that they may therefore supply their own needs, rather than just going in for a short period and doing everything medically for them. I had thought about *Medicines Sans Frontiere*; however, they generally need you for longer periods than I could afford. Now Doctor, have you decided you want all the vaccinations in one injection or do you want to come and see me again?"

"It has been amazing to chat with you and thank you for your encouragement and much as I would like to hear more from you, I think I'd rather get them all over and done with at once."

"Very brave. Do you realise having eight vaccinations at once you may not feel well in the next twenty-four to thirty-six hours?"

"Yes, one of my friends had all the vaccinations together and felt totally washed out for three days. But I figure that it's better to get that over with rather than the possibility of having two lots of three days feeling terrible."

"Okay, take your shirt off and let's get started."

Chapter 4

Christian knelt at the side of toilet. It was three o'clock in the morning and he had been throwing up for an hour.

"Are you okay, Christian?"

Renata's voice appeared from somewhere behind him as Tia the golden retriever pushed her nose into the bathroom, concerned about the unusual noise.

He was just about to answer Renata when he vomited again. As he pushed back from the toilet bowl, he felt his mother reach forward and wipe his mouth clean.

"I have some Stemetil in the medicine cabinet. Let me give you an injection and that should stop vomiting."

Christian kneeling, half turned to see his mother standing in the bathroom doorway. Renata had switched on the kitchen light so he could see her outline: dressing gown pulled tight round her waist, sleeves rolled up, and a towel in one hand. In her inimitable doctor way, she had taken control of the situation. On many occasions, he had had to fight to be able to determine his own direction; in this instance he was pleased he could trust her to take over and make him feel better.

"Just stay as you are. Christian, keep your head over the toilet bowl in case you want to vomit again."

Christian watched as she swabbed his shoulder with an alcohol swab and then he felt the sharp jab of the needle. The anti-emetic she injected quickly; he was tempted to try to smile a thank you but did not trust himself to turn away completely from the toilet bowl to look at her.

"That will take about five minutes and the nausea and vomiting should settle."

Christian nodded his agreement, knowing that it would take that long for the Stemetil to be absorbed but hoping that it would be shorter. Tia, as if sensing it was safe left Renata's side, pushed her head in beside him, tail wagging. Within three minutes, he was feeling better and able to stand up although not without threatening to fall over. Renata held onto him for a moment to steady him.

"I know mum, don't say anything – I know I should have done the vaccinations in two sessions but I honestly thought I would be fine."

"Now, would I say anything like that to someone who wasn't feeling well?"

Smiling, Renata guided him towards his bedroom.

"That would be taking advantage of you when you weren't feeling well; you know I wouldn't do that, much better to save that for the morning when you're feeling better." She said as she helped him into bed.

"Thanks mum."

"That's what mums are for. I hope you sleep okay now, but here's the towel and a plastic bag in case the Stemetil wears off. Although it has a six hour half-life so you should be fine, and I will make an exception for Tia on this occasion she can sleep in your room to keep an eye on you."

Christian slowly opened his eyes; he could hear his mother was in the kitchen moving pots and pans around. He had slept soundly and not vomited again; hopefully though, his mother was not preparing bacon and eggs as she normally did on a Saturday morning. The nausea had settled but he did not want it challenged by anything that was fried. As he pulled on his dressing gown and walked into the kitchen, Renata turned to look at him.

"Not quite the son I know, but certainly a better variation of the one that I saw last night."

"Thanks mum – and good to see it's not the normal bacon and eggs this morning. I don't know whether I would be quite up for that, given last night's experience."

"How about coffee, then? You will need some fluid replacement. Do you think you can manage coffee?"

"Coffee sounds fine, mum. Thank you."

"So what happened at the travel doctor yesterday, other than obviously having all the vaccinations at once?"

"Well I met and had a great chat with the doctor there, Dr. Mark Jaeger and as it turned out, there was a very interesting coincidence; he and his wife had been and worked at a hospital not far from Garanyi on the Congolese side of the border."

"That is an interesting coincidence. When was that that he worked there?"

"From what he was saying, I think it was about seven years after the genocide, so that must have been around about the year 2000."

"Did he think it was now safe?"

"Yes mum, but he said as an every situation in life, you need to have an awareness of potential difficulties and a plan to deal with them."

"So have you finalised your travel arrangements yet?"

"Yes, I'm going to go directly to London."

"So you are not flying via South Africa and in particular Cape Town. You know there is a direct flight from Cape Town to London."

"I know what you're hinting at mum, but I thought Isabella was going to be in Mauritius with her mother."

"My information, which may be more up-to-date than yours, is that she's going to London to do a tropical medicine course. Moreover, being the interested mother that I am, I checked with Nadine, and unfortunately your arrival does not coincide with her course. Now on another topic: should we plan a farewell dinner similar to what we did last time, after your last day on call at the hospital?"

"If it's okay, I'd rather not this time. Last time it coincided with my birthday, so perhaps we can just make it a dinner here on a Sunday night with Sophia and a few friends?"

"That's fine with me, and the money that we save from the restaurant, I'll contribute to your trip."

"Thanks mum, that would be great as I was going to take some medical equipment with me which I could use that money to buy. Dr. Sudani, the medical superintendent of Garanyi, had said that they needed intercostal drains."

"You let me get those. I have contacts and we might even be able to get them donated, so keep the money that I'm going to give you as a contingency fund, agreed?"

Christian looked at his mother and knew from experience that while it sounded like a question, it was actually a statement that just needed his confirmation. They had done this many times, so he looked at mum straight in the eye, smiled and said,

"Sounds good to me, mum."

Renata laughed. She really was going to miss him, he knew her so well, and the way that he responded to her assertion was never confrontational.

"Oh, there was something that I wanted to ask you. When I was in the travel doctors today, Dr. Jaeger was singing a song that I've heard you play but I wasn't quite certain what it was and forgot to ask him."

"Can you tell me the words or sing it for me?"

"I could play the first few bars for you on the saxophone and then I'm sure you would recognise it."

"Okay, let's hear it."

Christian walked through the open door into his bedroom. His saxophone sat alone in the corner, stabilised by a pair of old running shoes. It was ages since he had played it: studying medicine left little spare time to practise. As he picked it up and wiped the mouthpiece, he felt a slight misgiving about playing the song that Dr. Jaeger was singing. That misgiving he knew was related to the fact that when his mother played it, there was often a tear in her eye. The song obviously had an emotional association with something in her past. Maybe it was the memories of his father. Not wanting to stir up any of those emotions, he put the saxophone back in the closet and walked back into the kitchen.

"I don't think I can remember the notes well enough to play it, mum."

Renata turned to look at him.

"I've known you now for twenty-seven years. I know your ear for music. I know once you have heard a tune, you do not forget it. If you do not want to play it, say so. But now you have me extremely curious, so if you don't mind, I would really like to hear it."

Christian walked back into the bedroom annoyed with himself that he had tried to bluff his mother. In addition, he was doubly annoyed that he had not been smart enough to realise the potential emotional association with his father. The only thing to do, as he picked up the saxophone out of the closet, was to hope that it was just the words in the song that affected his mother emotionally. Hopefully, the saxophone by itself would not have the same effect. Sitting on the wicker chair in the kitchen with the saxophone he thought he would try one last time.

"Mum, I remembered when I heard you listening to the song that it seemed to upset you. I'm sorry I don't want to play it if it brings back some painful memory for you."

"Thank you for your consideration, my sensitive son, but just for your information, there are quite a few songs that can do that to me just because of the way they are sung. So stop fiddling with that saxophone and get on and play it."

Christian fiddled with the keys a little more and then blew into the mouthpiece a couple of times before playing the song as best as he could remember. As he finished, he looked at his mother who was now staring quite intently at him, and she did have a tear in the corner of her eye.

"You see mum, I didn't want to do that."

"It's okay. I asked you to and while it still affects me, it is a song which is really special and it gives me a chance to share that specialness with you now."

"It's related to dad in some way, isn't it?"

Renata looked at him for a few seconds before responding.

"Yes it is. That is an old Tom Jones song called 'She's a Lady'. Your dad used to sing it to me. He used to love Tom Jones. I can still remember the last time he sang it to me. It was our fifth wedding anniversary not long before he was killed. He did not have a very good singing voice, unlike you, and perhaps for that reason I can remember most of the words."

Renata picked up the soup ladle and pretending that it was a microphone softly sang,

"Well, she's all you'd ever want
She's the kind I like to flaunt and take to dinner
But she always knows her place
She's got style, she's got grace--she's a winner
She's a lady
Oh, whoa, whoa, she's a lady
Talkin' about that little lady
And the lady is mine '

Christian looked at her as she finished the last line. The tear in her eye had disappeared. She was smiling at him in a way that he had not seen previously and with a shyness that he was not used to. Maybe that is where his shyness gene derived. Looking at his mother and noticing that she seemed relaxed with the memory, he wondered whether it was the fact that she now had shared it with him, which made the memory less painful.

"Well there you go, now you know that your dad was a big Tom Jones fan," Renata said interrupting his thoughts

"Not quite my cup of tea mum but, great words, but just out of interest now that you're talking about it, I can't imagine you relating to that third line: *'But she always knows her place'*."

Renata laughed.

"Yes, we used to laugh about that quite often. Initially I thought that was one of the reasons, with your dad's South African background, that he liked the song. We certainly talked about it often and I think your dad deep down did like it that it was in there but just because it got my attention, and in the end it was really our special song for our anniversary. That's why you used to hear me play it, for it reminded me of all the good things about your dad."

"Well there you go, mum. Now there's something else positive I know about my dad."

"Okay young man, enough talking about the past. Tell me a little bit more about where you're going to go."

"I will, mum, but firstly one last duty at the hospital."

Chapter 5

"That was such an action packed last night at the hospital, let's just go through and check some of the things and make sure you've got everything. Now you have passport, yellow fever and vaccination certificates?"

"Yes mum – you went through all that last night and nothing has changed since then – provided the golden retriever didn't steal them in the night."

"Now, do not be cheeky," said Renata smiling at him a way that was the opposite of admonition.

Christian looked at her and smiled. He would also miss having someone to tease, and with his mum there was usually a guaranteed response, which made it even greater fun. They walked together to where he had placed his two suitcases next to the front door. Sitting in the doorway next to them was Tia. Her head was on her paws and she looked at him disconsolately. Strangely, she always seemed to know when he was going away and parked herself next to the suitcases at the front door. Her big brown golden retriever eyes down cast but staring intently at Christian, willing him to take her with him and a perfectly still tail waiting to spring into action should she be invited along. Christian knelt down and scratched her behind the ears. She did not respond as she normally did by sitting up, tail wagging uncontrollably. Instead she just stared back at him, unmoving, knowing that he was leaving and would not be back for some time.

Tia had arrived in the house as a puppy when he was sixteen years old. His mother had told him she was the only puppy in the litter. Subsequently without any competition at her mother's milk bar, Tia had rolled into their house looking more like a polar bear cub. Her subsequent antics and playfulness soon captured their hearts and she became part of the family. While his mother had undertaken her training, she had firmly become his dog.

"Don't look at me that way with those big brown eyes," Christian said holding both her ears, imagining she understood his every word, before giving her one final stroking and standing up. Tia did not move, her head remained on her paws and her eyes just followed him seemingly begging him not to leave.

"I'll be back before you know it."

Christian reached and took hold of both the suitcases, determined not to look back but feeling she was still intently looking at him. As he took both the suitcases out to the car, out of the corner of his eye he could see that she had moved to the front window, her eyes still watching him intently.

As he half ran up the front steps not wanting to make eye contact with her, he recognized part of him did not want to leave her either.

"Okay, I'm already to go. Have you said goodbye to Tia?" Renata called out from her bedroom.

"Yes mum, I have."

The drive to the airport was well-known to each of them. They had both done it a number of times together and usually chatted all the way. This time they hardly said more than a few words to each other. Christian could understand and feel his mother's anxiety over this trip to Africa. She had not been concerned about his last trip to South Africa, until he had been kidnapped and held to ransom by a white supremacist organization. She in the end had been the key to their freedom, supplying the encrypted key to the genetic research that had eventually led to their release. Those memories obviously were still fresh in her mind.

"You sure you don't want me to come in while you check-in."

"No, I'll be fine if you just drop me at the Qantas departure point, and that way we'll both avoid any tears."

Renata pulled up between two taxis and flipped the boot open. Then getting out of the car, she walked around to the boot. They then both lifted the suitcases out in silence. Stacking them on the sidewalk, Christian looked around for a trolley. As he did so, his mother tugged at his shirtsleeve.

"I want you to take this, honey. It's US$500 that I've had and it might come in handy somewhere. I also joined you up to the frequent-flier lounge. Now give me a hug and I'm going to get back in the car and leave you because I don't want you having your last image of your mum with tears in her eyes."

"Thanks mum – you're fantastic and I will e-mail and Skype you when I can."

Renata turned and quickly closed the boot of the car and with one final wave, Christian watched her disappear down the exit ramp and into the traffic again.

Christian checked his bags in at the Qantas desk. His first stop was Singapore; he had decided just a stop rather than a stopover, even though he knew that would make it an extremely long flight. He was delighted therefore when the lady behind the Qantas check in counter looked him up and down and said,

"Dr. de Villiers, with your height I think we need to find you extra legroom in an emergency exit seat. Let me have a look and see what's available."

As she checked on the computer, Christian thought it would be a great start to the adventure to have at least a comfortable seat.

"I'm assuming as a doctor that you are happy to act in the event of an emergency."

"Yes, of course," Christian said trying to contain his smile.

"Well that's done then and all the way through to London – so enjoy your trip. Is it business or pleasure?"

"A bit of both, I'm hoping," said Christian.

As Christian walked into the frequent-flier lounge, it reminded him how different this was to travelling as a student. There was a bank of computers for businessmen, multiple coffee machines, tables with newspapers and magazines on them—more comfort than he had been used to in his backpacking days. At a quick glance, all the tables looked like they were occupied. Then he spotted one table, with a newspaper and half a cup of unfinished coffee on it; either someone had just left or if they had not, he hoped they wouldn't mind him joining the table.

He put down his overnight bag next to the table and checked his iPhone. Three messages were blinking. Obviously one from his mother, and one from his good friend Greg, the other from Sophia. He knew his mum's message would be: '*I'll miss you, travel safely*' so he started with Sophia's. '*Be confident. You never know who you will meet and have fun*', *i*t read. He smiled thinking how much she had to know him and how much fun it was having a friend who had that much insight into you. He had thought on many an occasion, that it was a pity there was no chemistry between them as they had such a great friendship. However, they had talked about that many times trying to work out what it was that was missing. They both agreed that they ticked so many boxes for a relationship, but that whatever was missing was something that fell into that category of a *je ne sais quoi*. They had even talked about having a physical relationship to see whether that took the friendship to a new level, but decided that there was too much of a chance that it would ruin the friendship. In addition, he loved having her as a good friend too much with all the advice that she was able to provide. He was about to check Greg's message when he heard someone approach from behind him.

"So you'd like to join me."

Christian heard the voice behind him and turned to see that it belonged to a tall attractive woman in a business suit. You knew it was one of those suits which was expensive from its fashionable and tailored cut. Light grey fine wool with very thin pink stripes, shoulders slightly padded, a waist trimly tapered. Christian looked up and smiled.

"I hope you don't mind me joining you; it appeared to be the only table that was half free."

"Not at all. My name is Petrea Williams and you are...?" She held her hand out.

"Christian de Villiers."

"Haven't you left out something?" she said, looking down at his overnight bag and smiling.

Christian looked back at her somewhat puzzled.

"Isn't it Dr. Christian de Villiers?"

"Yes it is." Christian said smiling. "Sometimes I forget."

Thinking that reply sounded very unworldly or falsely humble, Christian quickly added,

"I hope you don't have an allergy to doctors." He partly mumbled trying to remember Sophia's advice about the need to be confident when it came to the meeting people, strange women in particular.

"No, no allergies, especially not to good-looking young doctors."

Christian could feel Petrea looking at him as she finished her sentence to see what kind of response she received.

"A bit shy I see, Doctor de Villiers; I like that in a man."
Petrea continued, "I really am teasing you a little, and that's
unfair having only just met you, but it's a technique that I learned
which helps establish really quickly whether there is more behind
flashing blue eyes that might be much more interesting. I do
suspect in your case, from my quick analysis, that there is."

"Well, if you don't mind me asking, why is it that you need
that technique at all?"

"Fair comment, there must be some surgical inclination in
you, Doctor de Villiers, if you cut to the chase that quickly, and if
you will forgive the pun. It is partly related to what I do and
having to assess people very quickly to decide whether you can
trust them or not. I work for the International Criminal Court and
most of the people that we deal with through the prosecutor's
office cannot lie straight in bed at night, let alone tell the truth.
Not being able to discern the truth can mean for very long days. I
have just been back to visit my parents in New Zealand and I am
on my way back to The Hague via London."

"I have read about the International Criminal Court. It was set
to prosecute individuals for crimes against humanity, war crimes,
and genocide."

"That's correct. It was partly in response to the genocide in
Rwanda and Serbia. Although we cannot go back and prosecute
beyond the date that we were established, which was July 1,
2002. And then we can only get involved with those states or
individuals who commit crimes against humanity and war crimes
progression if the countries signed the original treaty which is
known as the Rome Statute of the International Court."

"Have many signed up to the original treaty?" said Christian,
fascinated not only by such an attractive stranger's flirty
complements, but also by a stranger with an interesting
occupation and history.

"One hundred twenty states which include nearly all of
Europe and half of the countries in Africa. Most of South
America, but not all, have ratified the treaty and therefore
accepted our jurisdiction. In actual fact, countries like China and
India have been very critical of the court."

"And that's just because they feel that their authority might be
usurped?"

"That and they don't want international publicity which they
have no control over."

Christian looked again at Petrea. When she talked, it was with both her eyes and hands. Her hands she used to round out the scenes that she was describing. There was no indiscriminate waving; her hand actions were directed and purposeful. Her hands were such a part of her articulation that it did not surprise him that they were beautifully manicured with nails that matched the pink stripes in her suit. At the end of some sentences, when her hands momentarily hesitated, her eyes would hold his for a second to ensure he understood what she was saying. Everything about her suggested an efficient prosecutor. Her blonde hair was cut short, not too short that it was masculine, but short enough to imply consideration had been given to practicality. High cheekbones suggested some kind of Scandinavian gene and a small straight nose added to the authority that she projected. Christian imagined she must be in her early thirties, ten years older than him.

"How did you end up then with the ICC?"

"Well, I finished my law degree in Auckland, and my dad, who owns a big shipping company, wanted me to do a business degree and work for him. Fortunately, I was offered a place in Cambridge reading international law."

"And that smile means that you did not get on with your dad?"

"Let's just say that my father is driven; he was an only child and an orphan. He immigrated to New Zealand with little in the world and no family. So that when I arrived on the scene, I was his first real biological link. He doted on me, which was only partly because I was very cute, and mostly because for the first time in his life, there was DNA to relate to other than his own. Therefore, letting go for him was extremely difficult. Knowing his history as I did, I didn't want to hurt him so being offered a place at Cambridge allowed him to feel really proud of me and provided a genuine reason for me to be able to develop as my own person."

"The ICC followed on from doing really well at Cambridge?"

"I did quite well, not a first but an upper second. However, during my time in Cambridge I went to The Hague and just hung out with the prosecutors. I got to know many people and decided that it was an area of law where outcomes were achievable. What impressed me was that the ICC was not just being seen to be a conscience, but a conscience in action. There was a real sense that people would be held accountable for their inhumane actions. I must have impressed someone as that is where I was offered a job."

"And being attractive and good-looking would not have been a minus." Christian said looking at her unblinkingly, surprised at his growing confidence.

"Well listen to you. And I picked you more for the shy and retiring type. But don't get me wrong—courage and confidence is an intriguing mix."

Christian wondered where the courage and confidence had come from. It was almost as though part of Sophia was with him prompting replies. Although he rationalised that while she might have planted the suggestion of confidence, it was more likely his subconscious decision in the presence of someone who exuded confidence. He found Petrea an intriguing mix of beauty and intelligence, someone who also had control over her destiny.

"So I've talked about me, now here's the reciprocity. You need to tell me where you are going and why you are going there in ten minutes because that is all you have before they call my flight. Christian looked at Petrea, fascinated that she would want to know more about him, but also concerned that he did not have a resume as interesting as hers to talk about. He had already decided that he liked her and wondered whether she was just going to be gone in ten minutes. One of those chance meetings beyond serendipity, but which never fulfilled a hidden potential. He decided to give her the abbreviated version of his resume.

"I'm going to London and then on to Kigali in Rwanda. I'm going to work at a small hospital down on the Congolese border for three months at a place called Garanyi which is where my father once worked as a surgeon."

"Wow, impressively concise. So much information in two sentences. Let me see how I decoded it. You are going on the same flight as me, your father was a surgeon, and you are imbued with an adventurous nature and quite possibly possess a philanthropic gene."

"Well to be honest, I didn't really know how to start and you said there was only ten minutes"

"Well, you have got my interest, and I want to know more and now there's only five minutes."

"Perhaps the detail wouldn't be as interesting."

"No, I'm a fairly good judge if you'll pardon the expression; I think the detail would only be interesting. How good a judge of character are you? Do you trust me after knowing me for fifteen minutes?"

Christian looked at Petrea while she held his gaze waiting for him to answer. Everything about her seemed to personify integrity. Even after knowing her for such a short time, he not only liked what he saw but also trusted her and wanted to know more about what she did and stood for.

"I trust you." He said with a large querulous smile.

"Okay, give me your ticket and your boarding pass."

Christian looked at her, then reached down into his bag, took out his ticket and boarding pass, and handed them to Petrea.

"Good," she said as she stood up.

"I'll be back in two minutes. If I'm not, you'll know that I've met someone else and we are both flying to London together."

As Petrea walked off towards the frequent flyer service desk, she turned and winked at him without breaking stride.

Christian sat looking at his passport, suddenly the victim of a wave of post-cognitive dissonance. Was he that insecure that, after being flattered by an attractive woman for fifteen minutes, he had given away his ticket and boarding pass? He could imagine trying to explain it to his mother. He had just made up his mind to go and find Petrea and ask for them back when he saw her stride around the corner holding his ticket and boarding pass in front of her.

"There you are, and for trusting me, you can sit next to me on the plane to London and fill me in on the details."

Christian reached out and took both the boarding pass and airline ticket and was about to put them both back into his bag when he noticed on the top corner of his boarding pass there was a small sticker which said business class. He looked up as Petrea was bending over to pick up her bag. She stood up, looked at him, smiled, and said,

"That's what happens when you trust people. Good instincts Christian. You will go a long way following those instincts, so let's go and board and I can find out more about what drives you, which I'm sure will be interesting. Certainly it will be more interesting than sitting next to Gloria Monkhouse, the mining magnate."

Chapter 6

Christian reached up and placed his overnight bag and laptop into the overseat compartment. It was a tight fit; he needed to move Petrea's laptop further inside the compartment so that it would close. As he moved the laptop, out of the corner of his eye he saw the Qantas hostess looking at him, a little strangely he thought, as she poured the first glass of champagne. He stopped adjusting the laptop and looked back at her, wondering whether he was doing something incorrectly with the overhead locker; she just smiled at him when he caught her eye. It was a more knowing smile than the welcome aboard type. Perhaps she could sense that he was not a normal business class traveller but a young male upgraded by an attractive woman with all the implications that possibly had for the mile high club.

"Making new friends already?"

Petrea gave him a wink as she put her hands on his waist and slid past him to the inside seat.

Christian laughed and, for the first time despite their age difference, felt a little more at ease with Petrea. He realised he enjoyed the way that she had put her hands on his waist as she brushed past him. The momentary touch felt like an approval of sorts. Given his penchant for over-interpreting, he looked at Petrea again as she sat down.

That small fraction of doubt which had hovered, was removed by the look that she gave him; holding his gaze for a few seconds, it was an approving look. He relaxed a little. His normal confused state when it came to understanding women was not interfering for once, although Petrea's look was difficult to misinterpret. The only thing that puzzled him slightly from the little that he had already learnt about Petrea was that an approving glance was not what she would utilise. He imagined that someone with Petrea's experience and worldliness would tell you they liked you, removing any doubt from looks and glances. But then again, she had been talking about signs and how men should interpret them. Perhaps that was his first test and he had passed.

"So are you wondering about me or the Hostess? Remember I made friends with you first."

Christian laughed again.

"Yes, I do remember that you made friends with me first. That was fully fifteen minutes ago. And yes, I was thinking about you and the nice feeling that being with you engenders."

"So now I'm surprised. It looks like I have someone who is going to be seated next to me who is not afraid to talk about their feelings and emotions. That should make for an even more interesting trip to London."

Christian closed the overhead compartment, thinking about Petrea's comment while adjusting his laptop to sit neatly on top of hers, wondering whether that was a metaphor of any kind.

"A glass of French champagne for you both?" asked the hostess.

"Yes," said Petrea, looking at Christian who nodded his agreement. As the glasses were put on the tray between them, Petrea took her glass and touched Christian's.

"Here's to our friendship."

"To our friendship," Christian replied.

"So do you want to tell me a little bit more about why you're going to Rwanda and what motivated you, or do you want to tell me about your last girlfriend and why she isn't here with you?"

"Are you always that direct?"

"Part of being a prosecutor, I'm sorry. Does it make you feel uncomfortable?"

"No, not uncomfortable. It just takes a little bit of adjusting to. My background is white South African mixed in with lots of Aussie; both are quite direct cultures, but I don't think I managed to receive that 'out there' gene which seems to be so typically Australian."

As he finished talking, he briefly thought about which option he would be most comfortable talking to Petrea. To tell her about his father would take him at least half an hour, even for the abridged version. His father, the liver transplant surgeon in apartheid South Africa, who was brutally murdered. He sensed that with her background in the ICC, she would be interested in the corruption and intrigue, in which his father had been involved. However, part of him also sensed that Petrea had a worldly experience and to have her input into his love life, or lack of, would be a potentially valuable discussion. He looked up from his champagne; Petrea was studying him.

"There looks to be more in there than I suspected," she said, eyes smiling. "A few girlfriends and you are processing which one to discuss?"

Christian smiled back.

"Not as many as you may think. I was wondering whether to tell you about my father, particularly as there is no current girlfriend. Girlfriends and relationships I don't seem to have been particularly successful with, so I'm always fascinated to have any kind of female input into relationships and how they work."

"Well, let's start with the easy things," Petrea said laughing. "Fathers are straightforward and mine is no exception. So we can swap father stories and then after a few glasses of champagne and somewhere over Cairns, will be ready to really deal with the deep and intriguing aspects of what makes the world go round: relationships."

"Just so we have an understanding: is this where I share my experiences and you share yours. Or is this more about your experience guiding my inexperience?"

"What would you like it to be?"

"I'm not sure," Christian said. "Part of me wants it to be on an equal footing, but I know that I probably don't have your experience when it comes to relationships to really be able to offer sage advice in return. Then there is the other part of me that is attracted to you which doesn't really want to know about your past experience."

"Don't complicate it just yet. I like you too and what you represent, but now the *sine qua non* is not that I am thinking about making love to you in the business class toilet. It is far too small for someone your size. Seriously, you may not have the experience that I have, but I suspect that you have a sharp mind. That in itself is very attractive and what usually goes with it is the ability to provide insight into whatever I might tell you. That generally means the possibility of presenting me with a number interesting dimensions that I might not have thought of. So I do see you as having potentially an equal footing, just not in the very boyish way that you may be thinking."

"Perhaps we should talk about our fathers first," Christian said, feeling a little uncomfortable with such directness from someone he had just met.

"We can, but I think we both are establishing boundaries for a much more interesting conversation. I am sorry if my statement sounded prosecutorial; sometimes my work interferes with my private life. There, we have already established that there is something that you could give me advice on."

Christian decided to buy a little more time before he replied and took a sip of his champagne.

"You're going to tell me about your father, aren't you?" she said before he could reply

"Very intuitive. I take it that comes from scrutinizing many witnesses in trying to determine the truth before it emerges, or I suspect more often determining whether it's a substitute for the truth."

"Partly true, and it's partly what women do. We have radar that is more finely attuned to the emotional parts of human beings. Evolutionary psychology is the more scientific term. I studied that as a free subject at Cambridge along with epigenetics."

"You mean evolution had a significant psychological component worthy of study?"

"Spoken like a true sceptical scientist. Psychology was an important part of survival in the hunter-gatherer period especially for women. In the days when it was all about strength, a woman's advantage was to be able to know intuitively how man was going to react. Women understanding any situation, particularly involving men, often determined not only her survival but also mateship and preservation of the species. Men were good at hunting and gathering, women were good at risk assessment. Then as we evolved, those genes became more sophisticated evolving into the radar that we use today. Something which is called epigenetics, the evolutionary modification of our genes."

"So that's where women's finely tuned intuition comes from, evolution and epigenetics. Women learning over the years and being able to influence their genetic code so they end up emotionally smarter than men in the way that they react," Christian said, unable to contain a wry smile.

Petrea laughed. "You are right, although I see your scepticism is alive and well. Intuition is built on thousands of years of assessing males genetically, working out what works, and discarding that which doesn't."

"And you seriously studied that."

"Yes. And seriously back at you, I thought it would help me in my job as a prosecutor, understanding not only plaintiff's body language but also my own counsel. However, it became fascinating as a subject in its own right. One of the things women do, I learnt, was a subconscious visual scan similar to you and me in the Qantas lounge. That scan determines interest or otherwise, based on a number of well-defined evolutionary anatomical points. Over the years we have evolved to a secondary peripheral scan with more sophisticated elements."

"Okay, you have my interest. Tell me about this visual scan."

"For a female in the early days, it was all about a continuation of the species. Therefore, the scan centred on body shape. Shapes were subconsciously identified with protection and successful healthy procreation."

"So males who were big and strong would be what a female was scanning for. That does not sound too different to the modern-day situation, considering the emphasis on six-packs in the magazines."

"It's not, but what we do now, or have evolved to, is scanning for someone who is attractive to us not just as a protector/provider. There will be elements of the past embedded in our genes, but it's no longer completely about procreation. Attractiveness and projected personality/intelligence has been added to our visual scanner, both male and female."

"So what you're saying is if I see a woman in the street, some part of my primitive brain is processing her shape and that determines future action."

"Correct. Think about situations where you have been walking down the street or in the gym and something just registers with you that suggests there is a pleasant shape in your peripheral vision that you want to examine more closely. Ever had that experience?"

"I have. I can remember being in the gym one day, and a woman walked past and without looking at her directly, I can remember feeling she seemed really nice."

"That's evolutionary psychology in action. Your brain processed her shape, referred it to your genetic centre of evolutionary assessment, and sent a pleasant feeling to your

62

temporal lobe. And then you did a more sophisticated secondary scan, am I right?"

Christian laughed. "Yes you are right, although I don't know that you would describe it as more sophisticated. Her shape caught my attention, I liked her hair, the way she walked, the way she smiled and I then looked at her as she walked along and thought she was really nice and in many ways my type."

"But you did not follow her and ask her out?"

"No, I did not because that's the frustrating thing, how do you tell whether there is real bilateral interest?"

"That's what you boys don't do well; you don't have confidence in the signs that you reading and you have this hugely disproportionate fear of being rejected. In the past, man never had to deal with rejection. The need for procreation overrode everything else. That is partly why it is such a problem for men now, this huge lack of evolutionary development. You are now being forced to evaluate and make choices based on limited experience and retarded evolutionary history."

"I do remember reading somewhere that over 60% of males have no idea how you progress from that point after they see someone who is attractive to them."

"That research could, despite sounding like it comes from one of those authoritative woman's magazines, quite possibly be possibly true. Most males end up being so worried about being rejected that they do not do anything. On the other hand, if they manage to get close enough to a work colleague that they fancy, they make very weak enquiries about what she may be doing or where she is going at the weekend, hoping that that will initiate a relationship. From an evolutionary point of view, you can understand that kind of unsophisticated approach. Unfortunately, they have no evolutionary experience on which to build greater sophistication, as mostly it was the females who initiated preselection. There were exceptions, such as a few dominant Neanderthal males just selected a female and dragged her back to the cave by the hair. Either way, rejection was not something that males had to face back then which is why they have a crisis with that now."

"From the rejection point of view, I think I'd prefer to go back to days of the cavemen, much simpler than trying to sort out the complexities of attraction nowadays and whether you are wanted and for what reason. It appears broad shoulders, strong arms, plus a large club might have made things a lot easier."

"Back then procreation was the driving force so that approach was fine but now what the female wants is a relationship. Men haven't evolved fast enough to deal with the current reality of relationships."

"Isn't that vaguely sexist?"

"No. Well yes, but it is the science of evolution talking. Men have to get better at reading the signs. Men, young and old, are hopeless when it comes to reading the signs we give, a woman almost needs to come up and say, "You're the most attractive thing I have seen on this planet," before you ask them out. And then, we still have man mistranslating that into we want to have instant sex with them."

"Okay, I admit my difficulties in that area of reading signs that you give us; perhaps that's why there has been such an explosion of Internet dating. Men can take their time, look at lots of people whom they think they will fancy without the rejection. Women have cooperated, understanding means inadequacies in this area. However, while the Internet allows you to do the equivalent of a preliminary scan, you still have to do your secondary scan when you finally meet them. I guess, though, it eliminates a lot of potential rejection. Nonetheless, to my way of thinking, it is just delaying and complicating the process and in addition, you cannot find out about potential chemistry looking at a photo where you don't know how authentic it is."

"So now we know you have tried Internet dating, Christian?"

"Not really. I had a look at it, and probably like every other male, was intrigued by the fact there were so many people who believed it was the answer to the relationship problem. It is still an interesting phenomenon to me, but it depersonalises the whole aspect of relationships. From the point of view of initial attractiveness and getting to know someone, it appeals to the voyeur in us and deceives us into believing there are many potential great relationships out there. In so far as I can see, all the Internet has done is give a wider range of people the opportunity to look at carefully constructed profiles and photos. You still need to go through getting to know someone in person to determine whether there can be a great relationship and more importantly, great chemistry. That is the essence of a great relationship and you cannot tell that from the Internet. Even with new innovations like Tinder, which allows you to scroll through dozens of photos from Facebook pages closed to you, it doesn't determine personal interaction, only attraction at a superficial level."

"Have you ever tried it?"

"No, but like you, I have looked at it and found it fascinating partly because so many of my friends use it, but the real answer would be no, for all the reasons you have just mentioned. In addition, and this will sound arrogant, I have never had an issue finding men, although finding the right one has been difficult. So I have been tempted to revert back to the Internet but then dissuaded by my friends who tell me that over 50% of the people they meet are completely different to those represented in their profile. In addition to which, many falsely represent their status as being single, when actually they are married. They turn out to be not interested in a relationship, but in sex. As you imply, a hot photo does not guarantee chemistry. I tend therefore to stick to picking up interesting men in airport lounges."

Christian laughed. "Well, we are agreed on the Internet but for different reasons. So you had better up-skill me with this sign reading and evolutionary relationship development."

"Let's start with that girl you saw in the gym. What happened after your preliminary scan? Did she at any stage walk back past you and glance at you?"

"Yes she did, about ten minutes later. She looked at me as she walked back past, just a quick glance and then looked away."

"Now that glance, in pure evolutionary psychology terms, meant she approved your shape and was interested. If she had not been interested, she would have walked past you looking at the floor. Did you smile back at her, give her a small wave, or get up and looked like you wanted to talk to her?"

"No, I did not. I thought she may have had a partner or that she was just being nice. I know that probably confirms the evolutionary rejection theory. Nevertheless, getting beyond that preliminary encounter has always been one of my issues. I'm so busy processing the secondary scan in thinking how nice it would be to be with her but the opportunity disappears or perhaps I allow it to disappear."

"Christian, you just need to get to learn the signs better and decide that they are real signs and women, through those signs, are giving you permission to get to know them."

"So now, you're going to teach me next about evolution of body language and how to interpret that?"

"Well, since you appear so interested. There is now clearly much more to attraction and successful relationships than just a primary and secondary scan even if they are more sophisticated. As we have evolved and developed an instinct for what we like in a partner, there is not just recognition of someone who will protect us and possibly be a good sperm donor, but who will also satisfy this growing list of sophisticated emotional needs."

"That could be simplistic things like colour of hair, length of hair, haircut, long or short neck, long or muscular legs which have evolved as part of our individual relationship requirements and are built into our secondary scan."

"Mostly correct but the second scan is not at the subconscious level. It is no longer about recording data points based on primitive genetic selection. It's now about consciously evaluating a profile that is involved in us and that we have constructed of someone we would like to get to know better. That may include some of the things that you recognise you like, but for some people, it will be just a good feeling that is generated by saying something which has evolutionary roots they can't really define."

"And that applies to women as well as men?" said Christian.

"Of course with women it's a little bit more refined as you would expect." Petrea's mischievous smile had returned. "Despite what the common magazines say, we are looking for signs after a basic scan of attractiveness that tell us a man is intelligent with an innate sense of goodness, projects authority and appears to have the potential to be a successful provider."

"I get all that, and there are many shapes of women that I find attractive, but for me, it's still it's how to read the signs and does any of that give me an indication whether my scan is reciprocated. Clearly, you can have attraction between two people who identify with each other's profile. The only problem is that men are, as you said, useless at recognising it, which makes it difficult to get to the next step of establishing chemistry—the secret of all good relationships."

"Ah, chemistry. I wondered whether we would get to that; some would say without chemistry in a relationship, you only have a friendship. Many in fact do not ever find chemistry and argue that it is an illusion; in many ways that may be easier and potentially be the safer option. Having a nice managed relationship without any chemistry can clearly be very successful."

"But having found great chemistry once, I don't want to settle for something less, Petrea."

"Tell me what you define as great chemistry."

"With Isabella, there was obviously mutual attraction. From the time we first met, there was this overwhelming feeling of attraction/desire. That in turn ignited this incredible passion. I loved her body and mind and everything about her; even our orgasms were in sync from the first night. It just seemed like 100% match on all levels."

"Well I can understand you wanting that again. That does sound like great chemistry. Not the type of chemistry that the modern media tries to get us hooked on. They have created this fantasy of chemistry around these illusions of big boobs and six-packs. Yours is the real chemistry which I personally think you can have with more than one person, even though you haven't yet found it with anyone else other than Isabella. So tell me about me more about Isabella. I might learn something."

"Did you ever see the movie, *Mad Dog and Glory* with Robert De Niro and Uma Thurman?"

"I think everyone has seen that. It's a classic, why?"

"Do you remember the intensity of the passion when they made love?"

"I seem to remember they devoured each other."

"It was that kind of intensity when I met Isabella. The lovemaking was almost uncontrollable. As though every part of us, all our senses of smell, sight, hearing, suddenly were much more alive and just wanted to interact with the each other at a frantic pace."

"Okay, so I can see you skipped the evolutionary scanning bit and just went straight to the chemistry, thereby arguing I take it, that chemistry overrides evolution," Petrea said smiling.

"The primary and the secondary scan happened but just very quickly. It was the next step which was so different; there was no confusion with signs, just this laser lock of attraction; when we met each time, it was like a virtual neon sign of desire was turned on, if you will, by how she looked, how she moved, how she smelt, and how she smiled."

"Why isn't she here with you now?"

"Circumstances. She had to complete medical school and so did I and the relationship just drifted, irrespective of how hard we tried to maintain it. We both remain friends and she has had other relationships and so have I. But as I said, nothing with kind of chemistry which I had with Isabella."

"So one of the things you wonder, was that chemistry unique to Isabella, and therefore it's impossible to have that level with anyone else?"

"Well, I haven't got close with anyone else when it comes to that kind of chemistry. I have considered it from many angles. Was it just because it was the first time, and our hormones were unleashed upon each other raw and uncontrolled? That it was like climbing Everest for the first time, so that whatever you did after that could never have the same intensity."

"Firstly, there is an intensity which is hard to replicate with a first love if it's a good experience. That is the same as anything for the first time that is new, wild, and uncontrolled. Secondly, it is possible to have the same kind of intensity and chemistry with someone else. Believe me, I have had with more than one man an amazing chemistry between us."

"So if I could return the question, why are none of them sitting here with you now?"

"Most of the men that I have known suffered under the illusion that if they were attractive physically, chemistry was guaranteed. What detracted from all of that was unfortunately, most were self-focused and self-absorbed, which possibly guarantees good sex, but good sex is not great chemistry. It is a bit like driving a Volkswagen when you could be in a Ferrari."

"I like that analogy, but surely in your profession with all the intelligence and attractiveness, there must have been some Ferraris you could have parked in your garage."

"Very cute, Christian. The men I meet mostly have all the necessary ingredients that meet my requirements: tall, athletic, attractive, intelligent, and successful. The prominence of the 'how great I am gene' locks them emotionally into the 1800s, an era when chemistry was unheard of, other than the claims that it resided in abundance in red light districts. Let me quickly add that, despite your inability to read signs, from what I have gleaned through talking to you, I think your emotional side is more evolved than many men I have met."

Christian smiled at Petrea, delighted that, firstly, he did not blush, and secondly that she choose to flatter him. Perhaps he was evolving, he thought.

"I take it that's one of those prosecutorial things that you do to maintain the interest of the defence or distract their thinking?"

"I can see that you're onto me."

"Chemistry is both an old and new phenomenon. Women in days gone by limited their passions partly because sex was a primarily procreational exercise and wild passion was associated with weird forms of sex. If they ended up having great sex, that was a supernatural bonus. Now we know what it takes to make sex outstanding. It's not just passion or attraction."

"You're suggesting, if I'm following, that freedom to express passion is just one of the components of chemistry?"

"Passion translates sex into something more than a physical act. Sex for many can be just shag with little if any passion, which means physical compatibility gets confused as chemistry. Some of my friends quite happily settle for that. For them it works and companionship is more important."

"I have friends like that too; that's not what I want to settle for either although many of them seem very happy."

"I would much rather be dead or celibate than just exist in a functional business arrangement. A relationship without chemistry for me is worse than cheap wine. My choice is not to taste or drink something which does not enhance at least one of my senses. I agree, for many it seems to work until they by chance meet someone who ignites all those feelings and then they realise what they have missed for so long."

"That is my problem is a nutshell," Christian said. "Once you've had relationship with chemistry, it's difficult to settle for anything less."

"Okay, we have established, in the short time that we've been talking, that you are a romantic and passionate. I do not need any more details about your chemistry with Isabella, although a little kinkiness at 39,000 feet could be good for both of us. I think the only way you are going to sort out your problem is to meet up with her again."

Christian reflected on how easy it had become to talk to Petrea. He was somewhat flattered that she appeared to find him attractive. As he was about to reply, the Qantas hostess interrupted and topped up their champagne glasses. While he watched the bubbles, he thought with all the talk about the chemistry with Isabella, he had not noticed how seriously immersed he had become with Petrea and how much he was liking her company.

"You were wondering about what?" Petrea said as she watched Christian staring into his champagne.

"I was thinking about how easy you are to talk to and how you have this ability to easily talk about relationships and how easy it was to tell you about Isabella."

"That's a relief! I thought I might have been too forward for you and had thought about apologising. I think I also got caught up in your description of chemistry. I think I was slightly envious"

"I like your honesty. It's refreshing. You don't need to apologise for that. I was thinking that if I was going to trust anyone with that kind of information, it would be you"

"Now that we know each other well, there was something I did want to ask. That look that you gave me when we were in the lounge?"

"I liked your shape and I wanted you to know that so that I would get to know you more. Did you read that sign correctly?"

"To be honest, only in retrospect." Christian smiled.

"Don't worry. A primary and secondary scan does not tell me your inner thoughts and it's not completely foolproof, and I have been known to be wide of the mark on occasions, especially when it comes to chemistry."

"Just to reassure you, I'm not worried. If truth be known, a little flattered that after such a short time you could determine that I was interesting enough to sit next to."

"That look you gave me was similar to what Isabella used to give me."

"And you want to know whether I am as interested as Isabella was in you or just that we have the same way of looking at you?"

"I was thinking the former, but now that you mention it?"

"I see, Christian, that you are getting the hang of interpreting signs, or at least mine. In addition, if we weren't at 39,000 feet, things may happen. I can see, though, if we continue this line of thought, we both may become very frustrated and you need to sort out Isabella first. Let me tell you about some of the things that you need to know going into the Congo. "

"That would be good."

"Always remember that in the Congo, humanity tends to be at its worst not its best. Human life has no protector; animals have a greater chance of survival in some areas. You need to be extremely careful. I am going to give you a list of four names before we get off the plane. You will need to promise me two things. Firstly, if you come across them, avoid them at all cost. They will kill you just to satiate a bloodlust. Secondly, I'm going to give you my personal number so you can let me know if you do hear where they are."

"Hopefully, I don't see any of them. Am I allowed to use your personal number for anything else?"

"There is something I need to tell you first before I give you carte blanche to use my personal number."

"What is that?"

"On the personal level, I think you need to find Isabella and either become convinced in your mind that she is unique for you and make her an offer she cannot refuse. If that doesn't work out, then call me."

"It would be great to remain in touch informally."

"Of course we can. It has been great fun talking to you and I would enjoy doing that anytime. And you never know, once you sort out the Isabella thing, you might also discover some of your chemistry answers lie elsewhere."

"Thanks, Petrea, it has been great talking to you. Now we should try and get some sleep."

The Qantas hostess tapping him on the shoulder woke him up before reminding him that it was twenty minutes before the descent into Heathrow. Christian was surprised that he slept so long. He looked across and Petrea still had a blanket pulled up around her neck, asleep. He leaned over and whispered.

"Time to wake up."

Petrea opened her eyes, looked at Christian and smiled.

"I dreamt about you."

"I hope it was a good dream."

"You were very good." Petrea laughed. "And that's all the detail you are getting. Let me go to the bathroom and then I need to give you that list of rogues and killers in the Congo and also how to get hold of me if you need to."

Christian thought he would not worry about shaving; he knew there would be a shower and shaving facilities in the lounge at

Heathrow. He brushed his hair roughly into place. Petrea squeezed out past him.

"Going for the rough and unkempt look this morning, I see."

Before he had a chance to reply, she quickly walked up the aisle to the bathroom. Even the way that she walked attracted his interest. Deliberate long strides, with just a small sway of the hips. He was wondering whether they would meet up again when she paused, before opening the curtain in front of the bathroom, and looked at him and smiled. An answer, he wondered? Would it ever be more than what it was now? A few moments later as she walked back towards him and squeezed past him to the inside seat, she deliberately touched him on the thigh; it was a simple but personal communication of approval.

"Reading the messages?" she said as she sat down.

Christian laughed. "Correct me if I'm wrong but was that so I did not misinterpret that you would like to see me again?"

"Ten out of ten. You have come a long way on this flight."

"Great teacher!"

"Flattery will get you everywhere, but this is the list of people whom you need to be extremely cautious of if you know they are around. Kariba Offengowhe. Bosco Demungu, aka Bosco the Brutal. They are both notorious evil warlords. There are, in addition, two buyers of mineral resources, who are equally unscrupulous: one, a Jewish Frenchman, called François Segal, and the other a Syrian, Raoul Assad. We would prosecute both of them for crimes against humanity and corruption as well as arraigning them for child and sex and slavery charges."

"Hopefully, I will not come into contact with any of them and just can get on with learning more medicine and surgery."

Christian looked down at the envelope and on the back was Petrea's mobile number.

"One big hug before we go is the deal."

"I like a forceful man. Consider that a deal and remember the list of people to avoid that I gave you; if things work out when I see you again, I want the whole 195 cm of you intact, please."

Chapter 7

Raoul Assad knew he was a fat bastard. However, since he had become rich and powerful, the only person who could say that to him and remain alive was Kariba. Kariba Offengowe controlled all the Casserite ore, gold, silver, and diamonds in the Northern Congo. Raoul bought everything that Kariba could force out of the ground with his army of emaciated enslaved children. The recent discovery of tantalum, and its use in microchips for phones and computers had made the metal the new platinum. The Congo, and therefore Kariba, owned 30% of the world's supply. Selling refined tantallum to the electronics companies was a licence for Raoul to print money. Raoul loved money almost as much as he loved the young African girls, which Kariba supplied.

Raoul initially supplied arms as well as money to Kariba in exchange for exclusive access to the resources. Fortunately, there had been a ready supply through his friend, General Alaki. The donations to the general's retirement fund had become more demanding but they ensured the regular delivery of arms, which had maintained the balance of power in Kariba's favour. In the ten years that he had known Kariba, they had formed a successful team. For the first five or six years, Kariba was unchallenged, other than small individual gangs of subsistence workers who attacked his mining gangs. Kariba would hunt them down, ruthlessly, execute them, and hang their bodies in the trees as a deterrent for others. For some time that deterred further attacks. However, as others saw his growing riches, opposing gangs started to become more organised. Kariba saw the need to develop an army to protect his personal kingdom.

Then in the last two years, two more serious threats to their wealth emerged. On the one side was the Congolese army, whose political masters coveted the massive profits Kariba made. They made repeated attempts at a takeover of Kariba's mines, but their organisation and firepower was so pathetic that Kariba's well-armed men easily repelled them. On the Rwandan side was a far more serious threat. A gang lead by Bosco the Butcher was better trained and a greater threat. Bosco used the same type of violent intimidation that Kariba used, competing perversely for the title of most depraved inhumane atrocity. Raoul had heard that Bosco's growing influence was that he was supported by Rwandans and Chinese desperate to gain access and control all of the North Congo's resources, especially tantallum. Plans were already underway to develop a microchip processing factory and mobile phone industry in Rwanda's capital Kigali. Kariba had suddenly decided the answer to both problems was chemical weapons. He knew that Raoul, with his Syrian contacts, could access them for him.

Raoul told Kariba that he was fucking mad no one had chemical agents in Africa, and that's the way it should stay in order not to attract world attention. If word got out, it would lead to an outrage, which would completely stuff up their business. Kariba had looked at him for a few seconds before saying,

"No one gives a fuck what happens in the Congo as long as they can use their fucking mobile phones and computers. Either get me the fucking gas or Segal will take over."

Kariba smashed his hand on the desk and stood up. Raoul knew that Segal would not hesitate to find chemical weapons for Kariba. Anyone could find them if they had the money and Kariba would ensure that Segal had lots of money. He finally agreed and told Kariba he would check with his contacts in Syria and have a reply for their next meeting. The next meeting would be in June, he had replied, and that is when he would expect Raoul to deliver the weapons

With an alternative supplier in the unscrupulous Segal, it was now Kariba who was able to dictate terms to Raoul, a situation Raoul detested immensely. All his life Raoul had been in charge. He also hated that he could do little about it. Kariba was now so drunk on not only money and power, but also the drugs that Segal supplied that Raoul's influence had diminished. Segal was an unprincipled whore, even by Congo standards, and now had 40% of Raoul's ore supply from Kariba. In previous years, Raoul would simply have had Alexey or Pierre bury Segal in a convenient, fast-setting concrete foundation. He wondered momentarily if he was getting too old adjusting to a 60% share of the resources; moreover, he should also have Segal killed as a warning to anyone else trying to muscle in on his business. However, he knew if Segal suddenly disappeared, Kariba would suspect that Raoul had killed him, and that might interrupt the supply of young African girls.

Raoul arranged an appointment in Damascus. Initially his friend General Alaki had refused; Raoul's final offer of a US $5 million dollar donation to Alaki's retirement fund finally changed the General's mind. Despite having persuaded Alaki to supply Tabun nerve gas, Raoul considered not going through with the deal several times. Kariba was becoming too unpredictable, even by his own wild standards. He was certain that this change in his behaviour was linked to Segal supplying Kariba with mind-altering drugs. Kariba had jived his way into their last meeting complete with sunglasses, earphones, and with his whole entourage talking to each other in some kind of strange finger sign language. This had all magically stopped, when Kariba held up his hand, and then spoke to him in some kind of black American jive language.

"Shit man, you need to chill out. Ice yourself down. You are tighter than a fat broad's underwear."

That had been a signal for Kariba's entourage to laugh outrageously and start clicking their fingers and jiving again. What annoyed Raoul more than the fat insult, which he was used to, was the constant clicking of fingers and the rhythmic nodding of heads. Then one of the entourage had twirled to his left, jinked and pointed his weapon indiscriminately at whomever he felt like. Raoul thought that either Alexey or Sharif might protectively shoot one of them. That was not the way that Raoul liked doing business. The only consolation, despite all the clicking noises and sunglasses, was that deliveries were on time and the money continued to flow. In addition, he needed to keep the whore Segal from gaining any more advantage.

A nerve gas such as Tabun would be dropped or exploded above Bosco's men. Alaki had agreed to supply the latest Syrian quad copters, which would enable Kariba to release the gas from treetop height, killing hundreds of Bosco's men on the ground. Each of the quad copters was a million dollars - it was another $4 million donation into the general's retirement fund. Even with such a delivery system, Raoul did wonder, with Kariba's men high on drugs, that there was the potential for them to gas themselves. Outside of the irony of that happening, the more significant issue was that if they did learn to fly the quad copters, then there was no guarantee as to who else Kariba would not use it on. He had to go ahead with the supply of the Tabun and the meeting in June in the Congo; his addiction demanded it.

Raoul's private car met him at Goma airport and quickly whisked him past all the shanties and begging children to the Ihusi Hotel. He walked slowly up the loose stone pathway of the Ihusi Hotel. He had to walk slowly; stone pathways in the Congo were treacherous when you were as obese as he was. On either side of the path were small, neatly cropped trees shaped to resemble African animals and birds. Mostly they were carefully trimmed small elephants, lions, and hippos, but the last two trees were shaped like large green vultures hovering above prey. Raoul always paused in front of them for a few minutes and offered a silent prayer to an unknown God. The tree vultures had their talons outstretched like small knives and neatly sharpened beaks; they were a reminder to him that unless he was careful in Africa, he could also be a carcass picked over by the increasingly deranged human vulture he had come to meet, Kariba Offengowe.

The Ihusi Hotel was normally one of his favourite places to stay, washed on both sides by the calming waters of Lake Kivu. The one exception was the month of June, the month that Kariba had demanded a meeting. June was the prelude to the rainy season in the Congo and the humidity was disgusting. Five minutes after leaving his air-conditioned car, Raoul knew his obese body would be overheating and unable to cope with 96% humidity. Perspiration would be soaking his shirt, making it stick to him like some giant rubbery spider's web. His wet shirt would wrap around between his rolls of fat, emphasising his huge stomach, which would bounce repulsively as he walked. He hated such a conscious reminder of his physical unattractiveness. The reminder of how fat he was threatened to destroy the remaining vestige of vanity to which he tenaciously clung. He constantly tried to reassure himself that being a large size in Africa was a sign of prosperity. Despite his ratiocination, he always tried to disguise his fat stomach by wearing his shirt loose. That did not work in June in the Congo, for the humidity made it like a wet T-shirt contest for repulsive satyrs.

"Fuck Kariba," he said loudly to himself.

Walking from the pathway up the steps to the reception area, he caught a reflection of himself in the large picture window. He tried to ignore it, knowing it would probably confirm his worst fears. His vanity instantly overrode his inhibition. He glanced quickly at the reflection and physically recoiled in horror from what he saw. Perspiration enthused by the smug humidity was gathering on his head; small pools coalesced around his temples before running down in rivulets through the grey-black stubble beard that he grew to hide his double chin. The remaining hair on his head was plastered to his bald scalp, greasy strands falling on either side in front of his ears. The image repulsed him.

"Fuck Kariba to hell!" he shouted to himself again.

His reflection in the window had also made him instantly depressed, the opposite of the mood required to effectively deal with the maniacal vulture Kariba. Another reason to have all his faculties fully alert was that he had noticed Kariba, since he had been on drugs, was developing an unbridled evilness. No longer just killing to protect his ore mines, he was now killing and brutalising for pleasure. Women were raped then sexually brutalised, Kariba's men leaving them in a state where they could no longer function as women. That disgusted even a paedophile like Raoul.

Walking up the stairs which ran up the side of the hotel, he could feel the coolness of the air but it did little to change his mood. He stopped in front of reception out of breath, dripping with perspiration, and angry. Michael, the African receptionist, dressed in a freshly starched perspiration-free white shirt, greeted him from behind the counter with a cheeriness which irritated him.

"Welcome back, Monsieur Benefactor."

Raoul looked at Michael without his normal welcoming recognition, ignored his greeting, and put his hand out for the keys to his room. A shower and clean clothes would make him feel less repulsive. Michael, he knew from previous experience, would be upset at the lack of warmth and recognition in his greeting; he would sulk for a few days but recover when Raoul left his normal tip.

Providing a generous tip was always part of what Raoul did to ease his conscience. He was uncertain why he had the need to do that, given that he had screwed so many people in his life without a second thought. To make the millions in this world, it helped to have no conscience. To be able to screw people on a whim was a necessity, which ensured success in his line of business. Life, he believed on some level, demanded balance, the bad set-off against the good to maintain stability. Yin and Yang applied to the business world. Without some kind of balance, the poison of life would seep unashamedly into all parts and stuff up the workings of the whole world. The reality was also that the judicious spread of largesse in the form of money provided information and warnings. An investment of a few dollars could pay off with a warning needed for his survival.

The hundred thousand dollars that he contributed to the local hospital each year had nothing to do with the yin and yang of business, or even guilt as Kariba had once suggested. Neither was it motivated by aberrant altruistic need, as his ugly first wife had suggested. It was a self-preservation investment; if he became unwell on one of his trips to the Congo, there would be somewhere medically half-decent to treat him until he could be evacuated to a Western medical facility. There was also another selfish reason, despite local officials being convinced his donation was related to his generous nature. Raoul was desperate to prevent situations happening, like the one where one of the eleven-year-olds that Kariba had bought him in the beginning had turned out to be HIV positive. Eventually he had persuaded another Syrian family to take her on, but the condition was that he paid the family a monthly allowance to keep her and he had to supply retro viral medication. Now with his donation to the local hospital, there was no longer that risk; any girls Kariba gave him were examined and blood tested before they flew out with him. However, his last contribution nearly caused a situation that he was desperate to avoid. Médecins Sans Frontières heard about the donation and the local director insisted that he appear in their monthly magazine. Raoul refused to participate, as he did when they nominated him for local citizen of the year. That kind of media attention could bring scrutiny of his part in the rape of the Congo resources.

Room fifty-four was the luxury suite which they always reserved for Raoul. The only issue was that it was located on the second floor of the hotel. This location was something he had complained to the management about on multiple occasions. He

78

even offered to pay to build a luxury suite on the first floor so he did not have to climb the stairs. The old French owners had refused to consider the plans that he had drawn up, or the alternative suggestion he had of installing a lift to the second floor. It would not be in keeping with the overall 1950s appearance of the hotel, they had finally advised him in a sharply worded letter.

Sweating even more profusely after having walked up the stairs, he cursed the French owners and Kariba again. He walked along the walkway at the top of the stairs until he recognised the small black Baobab tree, etched around the security eyepiece on the door of room fifty-four. He looked at the familiar black flat-topped tree and unlocked the door. Once inside, he headed straight for the air-conditioning switch on the far wall. He turned it down to 19 degrees, immediately feeling its cool breeze. Basking in the coolness for a minute, he looked up, taking in the view through the large sliding windows. In the distance, he could see a few anglers in small wooden boats, the waves from their bobbing prows and nets disturbing the calmness of the Lake Kivu, the small ripples running slowly to the distant shores of Burundi.

He locked the door and placed a wedge underneath before pulling the chain across, his survival instinct not impaired by his disgruntled demeanour. He knew that meant he would have to get up and unlock the door in a few minutes, when his luggage arrived. However, since everyone seemed to have a key to every lock in Africa, he had learnt to take precautions to prevent any unwanted surprises. He would wait for the bags to arrive before he had a shower.

He fell back with a wet soggy squelch into the large leather lounge chair feeling the relief of the cool air. As the cool air blew over him, he started to feel cold and hoped the bags would soon arrive so that he could have a warm shower. Looking around the room, he saw the bottle of his favourite Monkey Shoulder whiskey, which had been left on the table as a welcoming gift. If he closed his eyes, he could almost feel the smoothness in his throat. He licked his lips and was tempted to get up and have a quick shot when the knock at the door distracted him.

Pushing himself out of the chair, Raoul walked to the door so that he could peer through the eyepiece. It was Robert the concierge with his bags. Raoul opened the door and greeted Robert in French.

"Mettre ces sacs la-bas," Raoul said pointing towards the bedroom.

The door wedge he eased only slightly, his survival habit manifesting instinctively. Looking along the walkway outside his door, he could see Alexey and Sharif, his two bodyguards, entering the room next door. Their arrival always made him feel more comfortable especially since they were closely connected to his room by an internal door. Under normal circumstances he would have only needed Sharif, whose Syrian background was similar to his own. Kariba however had become so unpredictable in terms of his demands and actions, he had had to bring Alexey as well this time. Two bodyguards meant more potential firepower.

Sharif he had purchased from the military intelligence directorate in Damascus on the recommendation of his great friend, General Alaki. The general believed in looking after his good friends, although such help did not come without a considerable price. Jokingly, the large sums were referred to as a contribution to the general's retirement fund. Once a year, the general's close friends were invited to view the top 10 recruits in military intelligence. The recruits had to display their abilities in hand-to-hand combat fighting, handling of small arms, and the use of explosive devices. If you liked what you saw there, you entered a bid in an unsophisticated auction. Sharif was only five foot ten inches, but in hand-to-hand combat his size did not matter for he was unrivalled; that he also placed third in the explosive section made him a good acquisition for Raoul. The $500,000 successful bid had been a small price to pay to ensure his personal safety. Sharif on two occasions had repaid that amount in full when he had killed those who had intended to kill Raoul.

Alexey, his second bodyguard, was by contrast a huge brute of a man. He stood five inches over six feet with hands the size of feet, knuckles thickened from the repeated smashing of bricks, which he did in his spare time to dissipate his anger. Raoul never really understood why Alexey was so angry, but then growing up in Russia, he thought, would make most people angry. Alexey was trained by the Russian federal security service and after several years of service had been gifted as a personal bodyguard to the Russian oligarch Oscar Benveninski. Oscar who lived in London was a close friend of Raoul's and laundered most of Raoul's profit through the major banks. When Oscar had died of a heart attack, Raoul contacted his friends in the FSB and sought permission to take over Alexey. That required the intervention of the Russian prime minister; permission was granted on condition that he still passed information to his Russian handlers. Raoul had agreed and Alexey became the club to Sharif's rapier, a counterbalance of talents which worked well in ensuring his survival. He thought he would need them both given Kariba's recent escalating demands and increasingly erratic behaviour

Raoul knocked three times on the interconnecting door. He listened as the bolt slid across, the door opened, and Sharif walked in followed by Alexey.

"Is the nervous package from Aleppo on schedule?"

"The Antonov will land tomorrow morning with the package on board. General Alaki has men on board protecting the package and they will only sign it off to me."

"Good. You will both stay here initially with me for the negotiations. If Kariba is juiced up and becomes irrational, anything could happen. Alexey, remind me to take my Glock pistol and silencer; see whether the hotel has a smaller room than that bloody big dining room. A small room limits the number of idiots that Kariba brings with him and gives us a bit more protection if things get out of hand."

"I have already found a room that suits our purposes. It'll take a maximum of six, three of us and three of them," said Alexey.

"Good. If everything goes well we should be out of here by tomorrow night, and even if everything doesn't go well, we should be out of here by tomorrow night. The Lear jet is locked in the hangar at Goma airport?"

"Yes, it is, and we have changed all the external locks and have set a motion sensor inside the hangar which is connected to Alexey's phone. It has been refuelled and the pilots are one floor down."

"Keep an eye on them tonight and make sure they don't try and sample any of the wildlife."

Sharif and Alexey nodded at each other before leaving through the interconnecting door.

Raoul sank back into the lounge chair and thought about the growing unpredictability of negotiations with Kariba. He took another swig of the Monkey Shoulder; at least whiskey was predictable in its effect. He felt its warmth go down his throat and pool in his stomach. Then on cue a few minutes later, he felt the knock-on effect from the previous swig, not yet the alcoholic dysphoria he liked but still enough to relax him slightly. He leaned back in the chair enjoying the effect when the smell of his own perspiration reminded him that he still had not showered. He thought about it and then looked back at the bottle of whiskey. He would shower later.

"Good morning, Major." Sharif said, demurring to Raoul's ex-military rank, as he joined him at the breakfast table.

"Sleep well?" Raoul replied, not looking at either Sharif or Alexey.

"We did a patrol at 2 AM and 4 AM. Everything was quiet, both pilots were sleeping."

"That's good; I don't want to have to get rid of another pilot because he developed AIDS after a visit to the local whorehouse."

"Michael says that Kariba is expected at 10 AM," said Alexey.

"And his whole fucking drugged up circus," Raoul said. "Sharif, get a message to the pilot. I have this feeling that Kariba is so high and unstable that anything is possible. His men at the airport are there to load the ore on the Antonov for the return flight, but if they're on whatever Kariba is on, they may think about holding the plane for ransom or worse, destroy it."

"Will do." Sharif said, getting up from the table.

As the clock in the main hall struck ten, Kariba flowed into the reception area at the hotel, accompanied by his band of rapsters. Large gold chains hung from their necks, chinking discordantly to the rap music blaring from small portable players. On this occasion, the entourage wore matching robes in bright greens and reds, interlaced with embroidered pictures of African animals. Each of the edges of the gowns was threaded with gold, silver, and diamonds. All had black, shoulder length hair in ringlets dyed with streaks of pink. All they needed was a lion tamer to be a circus act.

Raoul watched from the distance of the dining room. The music and the constant jiving movement already made him nauseated. He looked across at Alexey who had noticed the guns visible beneath the flowing robes. Alexey passed the Glock pistol under the table to Raoul.

"Bonjour," Raoul said in Kariba's direction, as he walked through the interconnecting glass doors from the breakfast room, robes flowing behind him.

"What's with that French shit? We are so not into that. You need to loosen up, Raoul. Free that Syrian brain of yours. Get with it, man. Make your life interesting. Loosen up. Chill out."

Raoul had almost decided after the delivery of the Tabun, this was going to be their last meeting when he caught a glimpse of the two young African girls that Kariba had brought with them. They were tall and clearly Sudanese. He had never had beautiful young Sudanese girls before.

"You're right, I need to loosen up a little, but then I don't have that African gene for rhythm that you have."

"Those who have the rhythm never need to lie, and those who have the rhythm, their hearts never die, and those who have the rhythm have souls which learn to fly."

Raoul looked at Kariba and wondered whether he had taken one tablet too many. He wondered which philosophical giant had supplied the words. He did not intend to ask but he did not have long to wait to find out.

"Black Dog. The coolest rapster on the planet," Kariba said as though that was sufficient explanation.

"Shall we get down to business?"

"Chill out. Your black pussy will wait. My boys need to check out the room."

Raoul could feel the imprint of the Glock, which Alexey had given him in the back of his pants. Kariba now irritated him so much, part of him wished he did not need him and could just shoot him.

"There is only room for three of yours and three of mine in that room."

Raoul watched as Kariba wandered off, his long flowing gown nearly catching the edge of one of the chairs. Two of his entourage high-fived each other before falling behind and walking almost sideways to what he assumed was music from the famous Black Dog.

Alexey was already in the room when Raoul arrived. He had positioned himself on the far side of the table, his back against the wall, a view out over the lake and more importantly through the doorway. Alexey, from his position, controlled the room, a fact reinforced by the Uzi which rested comfortably on his knees. Kariba sat at the table, two from his entourage standing behind him. There was no jiving now, but the earpieces and the sunglasses remained. Sharif and Alexey would be happy to see that; sunglasses might look cool in a slightly darkened room, but it decreased visual acuity. That could be the difference between staying alive and being shot. Raoul pulled the two briefcases out from under Alexey's chair.

"Twenty million American dollars in cash. Fifteen million has been deducted for the Tabun. This is the receipt for a deposit into your Swiss bank account, twenty million from the last shipment as agreed."

"I'm more interested in the package that you have for us."

"That arrives tomorrow morning once we have completed our agreement today."

"We have enough ore to fill the Antonov. I have enough diamonds to keep Antwerp cutting and polishing for a year. The success of your package determines whether there is a next time."

"It's a variation on Sarin nerve gas called Tabun. It's less volatile and comes as a dispersible liquid which is more easily handled and less likely to kill you than Sarin."

"I knew you could deliver," Kariba said glancing quickly at his two protectors. They both nodded without any understanding.

"You may not need to use it. I hear Bosco has handed himself in to authorities and wants to be prosecuted for his crimes in The Hague."

"Yeah, that's because he's got lung cancer and he's going die a horrible death if he stays in the Congo. Fucking serves him right for trying to take over my kingdom. He knows he is going to die in nine months and giving himself up to authorities means that he gets the best medical treatment overseas. Man, that Bosco is smarter than I gave him credit for. The time is right while there is no new leader in sight to smash the remains of the M 23 gang so no one else gets any ideas and the Chinese go home."

"You will have to learn how to deliver it for the maximum effect. I have supplied two large drones, but someone will have to learn how to fly them to be able to deliver the liquid."

"You don't think Africans are fucking smart enough to do that, do you, Raoul?"

"I did not say that."

"When you've got rhythm, you just know things. You white motherfuckers always under estimated us, but now we have the brains and the power."

"Two of the men arriving with the package will stay behind and teach your man how to fly a quad copter and how to deliver the gas. We will meet at the plane at midday tomorrow."

"You want to talk about the other part of our arrangement."

Raoul nodded and looked at Sharif and Alexey, indicating with his head to leave the room. Alexey was the last to leave, closing the door behind him. Raoul sat in silence looking at Kariba and feeling his scrutiny.

"Is it the black pussy or just that it's difficult to get them this young anywhere else, when you are so fat and old?"

Raoul did not blink, nor did he reply to Kariba's question. It was the same question every time and they both knew the answer; he was fat and old and addicted to child sex. The only reason that Kariba repeatedly asked was that it was a rare chance to claim some kind of warped moral superiority. It was the same every time the exchange of girls took place; Kariba would sit and stare at him, and Raoul would stare back at him. Raoul knew there was no moral high ground for either of them to claim; Kariba's depraved treatment of woman and abuse of children ensured that. Raoul endured the stare, accepting that it was part of the price he paid for the young girls that Kariba supplied. However, he had determined not to look away once Kariba started staring at him; he could never accept that his deviancy was worse than Kariba's depravity. Looking away would have suggested that to Kariba. He would never give him that satisfaction. Besides he was convinced that most of the men in the world were deviant in some way. Some admitted it but most did not and claimed piety. He knew that 50% of the world's men did pornography while the other hypocritical 50% did not admit it. Moreover, Raoul looked after the girls Kariba gave to him and did not mutilate them the way Kariba did with those he raped. Once the girls reached twenty years of age, he usually gave them to his good friends as house cleaners. To his way of thinking, if there was anyone, it was Kariba who was on the fast track to hell, not him. He retained his basic decency, which had long disappeared from Kariba's activities. A light knock at the door interrupted his thoughts and broke the staring deadlock as it usually did.

"Entre," he called.

The door opened and two young, tall, black African women glided into the room. Dressed in long flowing white gowns, they looked virginal. Kariba spoke to them in Swahili for a few minutes after which they smiled at Raoul. They were perfect, Raoul thought, young and elegant and in twenty-four hours, he would have them both in Damascus. The youngest first, he thought. Putting up with Kariba's increasingly erratic and wild behaviour suddenly seemed of little consequence; they were both beautiful.

"They will be at the plane tomorrow when the package arrives, but until then, look and touch but nothing else," Kariba said pushing back from the table.

Chapter 8

The flight to Kigali had had taken about seven hours; it was nowhere near as interesting or as comfortable as the flight in business class with Petrea. Christian had caught up with his downloaded emails, although Petrea kept intruding on his thoughts.

"Au revoir; don't forget to call me," she had said as they waved goodbye at Heathrow.

Given their respective circumstances, Christian thought realistically that it was unlikely they would meet again - unless fate intervened. However, he had never really believed in outcomes controlled by some strange force or God. Fate, like gambling, had no predictability when it came to outcomes, which is not what he preferred. Medicine taught that if you had enough knowledge, you could predict disease outcomes with reasonable certainty. He felt much more comfortable with predictability; it made the world easier to relate to, although it did not explain all phenomena in the universe.

He had often thought about the concept of a supreme being while studying medicine. Evolution by itself did not seem to provide a complete answer. The probability of a finely tuned machine such as the human body evolving with all its intricate systems, mathematically at least was improbable. He remembered specifically marvelling at the permeability in the kidney, the amazing ability that it has to secrete and reabsorb micro molecules. Other than the mathematical improbability, such were the fine tolerances at which it operated. It appeared far too sophisticated to have evolved from a primal soup. Evolution suggested chance but science argued against both chance and fate when it came to the human body.

The only problem with the alternative to evolution, the concept of a God with infinite wisdom, is that he had not been able to be convinced that there was any scientific proof of that as an alternative. The thought of a supreme being in charge of a celestial supercomputer somewhere in space was intriguing, but with no proof it was an unconvincing theory. Not that considerable effort had gone into trying to convince him that there was evidence. Eleanor, a happy clappy Christian friend in his fifth year medical group and Shamash, a Muslim friend in the same group, had both tried at various times. Eleanor had suggested the way to know God was for Christian to disconnect his brain and think with his heart. She had suggested he sit quietly alone with the Bible open, and ask God to come unto his life and show Christian that he was real. Then, according to Eleanor at least, he would develop faith, the other ingredient necessary to understanding how God worked. Despite her impassioned plea, he could not get his mind around the concept of disconnecting his brain and thinking with his heart.

He remembered a quote from Dr. Christian Barnard, who did the world's first heart transplant, "the heart is only a pump"; he did not mention, he could recall, anything about it being a brain as well. Moreover, if anyone should have known, Christian would have thought it would have been Dr. Barnard. Shamash, in his quiet understated way, had been a little bit more convincing when he suggested that the laws of science, logic, and common sense suggested that life did not spring from non-life. That was more Christian's line of argument in that at least it involved the word science. Shamash followed that point with the point that if the universe exploded into existence, who had caused the explosion? Since science could not explain it as a scientific phenomenon. That vaguely interested Christian for a short time, partly because the question had no answer.

He had not closed his mind entirely to the prospect of a God; however, when he had taken Eleanor's advice, nothing really had happened. Sitting alone with her Bible open in front of him, all that had happened was that he had imagined some fanciful romantic mischievous god orchestrating interesting meetings to overcome heavenly boredom. The imagery of that taking place on some cloud amused him for a few seconds but there was no blinding revelation. When he had told Eleanor the following day, she had just shrugged her shoulders disbelievingly and taken her

Bible back. It was, he thought, going to be intriguing with his level of disbelief, to be going to a country like Rwanda where 95% of the population, not only admitted to a Christian belief, but enthusiastically practised it.

Christian finished his emails and to stop the recurring thoughts of Petrea, read again the National Geographic article on the Rwandan genocide. He knew that much had been written about the French involvement in the genocide and the lack of support from the United Nations. Nearly everything he had previously read suggested that the world, and in particular the United Nations, had failed Rwanda in its hour of need. President Clinton had stated that one of the great stains on his administration was the inertia concerning Rwanda, a statement that underscored the fact that the genocide with the right leadership may never have happened.

The origins of the conflict went back to 1000 BC when there was an influx of Bantu-speaking Sudanic and Cushitic peoples into Rwanda. Approximately 1500 years later, these groups had merged into a single society, and within that single society were two major groups, the Tutsis and the Hutus. The Tutsis with their Sudanic origins were tall and with more aquiline features. Hutus were physically shorter with broader features. In the late 1800s, the Germans colonized Rwanda, but then following the First World War and the Treaty of Versailles, Rwanda was traded to the Belgians. The Belgians gave the taller Tutsi favoured status, creating an artificial ruling class, with which they would exclusively deal. However, that created deep divisions and enmity, which finally erupted in 1993 into genocide with nearly 1,000,000 killed in a bloodletting, which shocked the world.

"We will be landing in twenty minutes. Please ensure your seats are upright and all electronic equipment is switched off," the hostess said in English, before repeating her request in French.

Christian switched off his computer and put his seat back in the upright position. The six and a half hours had gone quickly and caused him to momentarily wonder whether he was really prepared for what lay ahead in the most densely populated country in Africa. Once the plane landed, he would be in a place, often referred to as deepest, darkest Africa. His exact presence would be largely unknown. No friends to call and ask for advice in an emergency, he would find out how good his medical training had been. He finished putting away his laptop and his friends, Australia, and his golden retriever suddenly felt as though they were a lifetime away. Those thoughts were unexpectedly replaced by thoughts of his father arriving in Kigali so many years ago. Would there be any trace of his father to find, he wondered, as he clipped the buckle of the seatbelt.

He could feel the plane started to descend and he looked left out through his window. In the distance, he could see Kigali airport appearing as though perched on the top of a hill. At either end of the runway, there was a downward slope, which slowed you down either when you landed, or allowed you to gather speed as the plane took off. At both ends, there were thousands of earthen shacks. As the plane further descended, it was possible to see a little more detail, roofs, and chimneys, of each of the mud brick houses. Layers of wood smoke, which appeared to wander languidly and unconcernedly between the dwellings, denied him a better view. The pervasive smoke gave the false impression of a huge soft mattress, which you could safely land on. On most days, he could imagine the smoke haze could also be a landing hazard, which would be good reason for the airport to be on a hill in a relative smoke-free zone; someone clearly understood the energy needs of Africa when it had been created.

The smoke haze reminded him of the first time he flew into Johannesburg airport. Smoke, morphean in its insouciance hanging indulgently above poor shantytowns, seemed unaware of its endemic health hazard; its fire was used for warmth, cooking, and light. Carbon emissions were not a tradeable item, but a signature of survival in Africa. Most were unaware that it poisoned the atmosphere and the lungs of those who inhaled it. Wood fires provided not only a link to the past but way of surviving in the present without the regular supply of electricity. There was little alternative in Africa, and Christian knew that there was some electricity in Rwanda, but from all accounts it was not reliable.

"Thank you for flying with Brussels Air and please remember to take all your belongings off the plane," the hostess said once the plane had come to complete stop outside the terminal building.

Christian watched through his window as the stairs were rushed across the tarmac and adjusted next to the plane's front door. Three African men in dark blue uniforms secured the steps against the side of the plane. After a tap at the window, the hostess struggled a little with the lever but finally opened the door. With the door fully open, the woody smell of Africa drifted in to the plane. Warm, unfiltered air with rough lashings of wood smoke surrounded Christian and instantly brought back more memories of South Africa ten years ago.

"Watch your head," said the hostess.

Christian ducked beneath the front door of the plane. Momentarily pausing at the top of the stairs, he watched the sun starting to set and in the distance, the lights of Kigali beginning to twinkle. As the number of lights increased, Christian noticed a darkness creeping up on the mountains surrounding the city. Without the bright ambient light of most major cities, there was a greater blackness to the arriving Kigali night. The darkness pushing its way stentorially up the surrounding mountains, nonchalantly covering the verdant green forest with a black blanket as it advanced. As he watched, the darkness reached all but the peaks of the four highest mountains until summits only remained, silhouetted by the setting sun. Four large black shining bald heads protruding in the evening sky, the wood smoke encircling each like the wispy grey hair of an old man.

Walking slowly across the tarmac, Christian inhaled the woody smell and enjoyed the warm African night. Midges and mosquitoes, visible in the light from the terminal building, circled him as he walked, a reminder that malaria was always stalking. As he stood in line and waited for his visa to be processed, strangely he could sense no lingering genocide animosity. In a country which had known so much killing and death, everyone seemed to be genuinely happy.

"Welcome to Rwanda," the customs officer said, handing Christian his passport and visa.

He took his passport, putting it in his neck pouch before walking down the stairs from immigration, wondering where he would get a taxi to take him to the Gorilla Lodge Hotel. At the bottom of the stairs, he spotted a large semicircle made out of orange coloured rope. Beyond the rope barrier, young Rwandan men waved various signs for the different hotels in Kigali. The scrum of people exiting the customs hall made it difficult to approach them. Christian noticed a sign with Dr. Chris in big letters as he headed towards the exit. He ignored it initially, not thinking it was his name as it had no surname. Without fully understanding why as he walked through the exit, he glanced back at the person holding the sign, and saw he had a Gorilla Lodge Hotel T-shirt on. He decided to go back and ask directions.

"Excuse me. You wouldn't happen to be able to take me to the Gorilla Lodge Hotel, would you?" Christian said to the smiling Rwandan face holding the sign.

"Are you Dr. Chris?"

"Well I am a doctor, Dr. Christian de Villiers."

"Well, welcome to Rwanda, Dr Chris. I am Willy Twiragu. When the superintendent from Garanyi hospital asked us to meet you, we weren't sure how to spell your name."

The large perfect smile returned, but Christian could also detect a genuine kindness of spirit. There was warmth to Willy's greeting which he had not noticed in South Africa. He wondered briefly whether that was peculiar to Willy or whether he would find it more widely reflected in Rwandans. Willy was quite tall with aquiline features and Christian thought that he must therefore be a Tutsi.

The trip from the airport to the Gorilla Lodge Hotel, Willy said, would only take about fifteen minutes. He quickly picked up one of Christian's bags and indicated that he follow him. They walked out through the airport front entrance, Willy glancing around intermittently, to make sure that Christian was following.

At the bottom of several flights of steps was an old cream and red Ford panel van. On one side of the van was painted a giant silverback gorilla, arms extending over most of the van and down onto the bonnet. The gorilla's huge white teeth gleamed in the reflection of the airport light. Unfortunately, nothing else, other than the painted gorilla, had been updated on the van. Pieces of wire precariously held the exterior mirrors on the mudguards in place. The usefulness of the side mirrors on the door was questionable as they pointed to the road. The mudguard also had a large piece missing on the top where the aerial had been attached. Through the rusty hole, the size of a fist, the tyre was clearly visible. Christian noted from what he could see that it was smooth - without any tread. The gorilla, on closer examination, had been recently repainted, the edges of the painted-over gorilla still visible, which created a new gorilla that up close appeared two-dimensional and slightly out of focus.

"That's how big they really are," said Willy as he watched Christian examine the gorilla on the side of the van.

"Up to 260 kg, I hear."

"You must go and see them, Dr. Chris, while you are here."

Christian wondered whether he would have time once he was working full time at the hospital, but knew that it was something he also would love to do. Willy put his bags into the back of the van and then he slid open the side door for Christian to get in. Willy told him to be careful where he sat. Looking down, Christian could see why; there were holes in the floor of the van through which he could see the road. As he made a decision to step only on the firm runner, he wondered where it was safe to put his feet down at all. He glanced up to see Willy looking at him examining the floor.

"Rwanda air-conditioning," Willy laughed as he climbed in the driver's seat, lashing the door closed with a piece of green rope.

Christian smiled, wondering whether the floor was a specific deterioration or whether it applied to the whole vehicle. He guessed he would soon find out. Sitting on part of the seat which did not have springs protruding, he wondered whether they would make it to the hotel. Perhaps it would have been better to take one of the motorcycle taxis, which might have, in many ways, been safer. Since Willy had now closed the sliding door, he would have to take his chances. Willy turned the key and started the motor; immediately exhaust fumes suffused fimicolously up through the holes in the floor. Christian started to have serious second thoughts about survival in Willy's van. He was on the verge of telling Willy to stop - that he would get out, when they started moving and the fresh night air rushed in through the many holes, diluting the exhaust fumes.

Leaving the airport, the van was surrounded immediately on all sides by small bright lights. The lights were in constant motion; motorcycles, each with a paying passenger, were weaving and constantly tooting while gesticulating to everyone to move aside. Motorcycles of all shapes, sizes, and colours swarmed around them, clearly the choice of transport for most who lived in Kigali. Experience and intuition appeared to be the only prerequisite for survival.

Willy tooted back and weaved unconcernedly. Christian watched as one motorcyclist waved wildly and then cut in front of them. Strangely, no one seemed to get upset. The tooting and waving always seemed to be accompanied by a smile. Rwandan road rage did not appear to exist, at least on the main road from the airport. Even allowing for that, he could not help but think the emergency department fracture unit in the local hospital could be very busy on any given day.

Willy accelerated towards the first judder bar, a raised concrete mound placed across the road to slow down traffic. This caused the van to leap in the air and bounce several times in an unstable manner when it landed on the other side. Not only did it not slow the van, but it also appeared to be part of the enjoyment Willy got from driving. After the fourth and last bounce, his grin was again lighting up the van when a motorcycle and its pillion passenger passed on the outside with much tooting and waving. Willy was mortified to be overtaken by a motorbike; it was a personal affront. He accelerated in pursuit, changing the bouncing into a nauseating side-to-side movement.

The swaying in the van caused Christian to reach for the inside door handle for support; as he grabbed at it, the van swayed to the right and the door handle promptly fell at his feet. He sat back, resigned to the skill or otherwise of Willy's driving. Peering out through the side window into the darkness, he wondered whether all those years ago this was how his father had made his way into Kigali. His thoughts of where his father might have stayed were interrupted as he looked up and saw they were approaching another judder bar. He quickly moved so that he could use his legs to brace himself against the driver's seat. This time to Willy's great delight, the van leapt at least two feet into the air, returning to the road with an enormous screech as the chassis ground into the asphalt. That caused part of the floor next to Christian's feet to disintegrate with the exhaust pipe then visible, discharging its fumes directly into the van.

"Open all the windows, Dr. Chris," said Willy over his shoulder after quickly glancing at the hole in the floor. He turned his attention back on the road ahead, and the challenge of the disappearing red light of the last motorcycle.

Christian changed position so that he straddled the exhaust pipe and opened all the windows.

"Put your head out the window," Willy said, as he started to cough, the fumes beginning to irritate his lungs.

Christian moved to the window and looked around the van. Even with all the windows open, the carbon monoxide could still be toxic to them both. The other danger that became obvious was that in leaning too far out the window, stray motorcyclists trying to pass, may hit him. As he thought that there was nothing he could place over the hole in the floor to stop the influx of fumes, Willy quickly looked around and lifted up the floor mat from under his feet. He then handed it to Christian in such a nonplussed manner that Christian could not help but think that exhaust pipes appearing in the back of Willy's van were a regular occurrence. Christian quickly draped the mat over the exhaust, reducing the amount of fumes somewhat; he hoped it was not too far from the hotel or otherwise they might well have to contend with the smell of melting rubber as well as the carbon monoxide.

The first stop sign appeared out of the night like a glowing red ember invoking another unusual driving practice. Firstly, Willy put his foot on the brake, which caused a sound, not unlike fingernails on a blackboard, but which did little to slow the van. The sound, Christian understood, meant that the brake pads were now non-functional and just a figment of the van's history. Not that that seemed to perturb Willy too much as the second part of the routine for slowing down appeared to be a well-practised art. He rapidly changed gears using the engine to slow the van down before bumping into the curbing at regular intervals to bring the van to a stop just in front of the red light. Christian thought it was such a skilful performance, it really needed an ovation; therefore, to Willy's great delight, he clapped his hands as the van sat quietly at the red light. After looking both left and right, Willy coaxed the van, with several hops, onto the main road into Kigali. Christian with his head out the window relaxed enough to smile at the numerous motorcyclists alongside.

"Here we are, Dr. Chris," Willy said turning off the main road.

The bright lights of the Gorilla Lodge Hotel felt like the end of a survivor episode. And he knew he could not be certain until the van came to a complete halt. There was still the car park in front of the hotel to negotiate. Willy started his routine of changing down gears but this time appeared to be moving too quickly. Willy showed no concern for clearly he had something up his sleeve. Then right on cue, he turned left and headed for the small grassy bank next to the car park to bring the van to a complete and well-rehearsed halt. Willy then quickly jumped out of the cab and put a stone under the front wheel.

As the swaying movement in the van finally came to a halt, Christian went to slide back the door before remembering he had pulled off the handle. He sat back relieved that he had arrived safely and waited until Willy opened the door from the outside.

"I will take your bags, Dr. Chris."

"Thank you, Willy."

Christian walked up three small concrete steps to a small wooden veranda that led to the reception area. Inside was a small wooden desk and the person sitting behind it was someone who could have been Willy's brother. His T-shirt, with the ever-present large silverback gorilla, slightly cleaner. His smile also almost as perfectly formed as Willy's was. It had to be the Rwandan diet Christian thought, as he knew there were only eight dentists for eleven million people.

"Good evening, Dr. Chris," he said. "I hope you had a good trip."

"Yes, it was an excellent flight, and Willy's superb driving got us from the airport very quickly."

"We have you in a small room upstairs, which has a toilet and a mosquito net. There is a shower that all the guests use down the hallway."

"That sounds good to me. I'm in need of some sleep."

"I will come back in the morning," Willy said, "to take you down to the genocide memorial."

"Thank you, Willy. Are you sure the van will make it?"

"Oh yes, Dr. Chris. I know the way to go where there are no judder bars."

Small mercies, Christian thought. He would deal with that issue once he had had some sleep.

"Breakfast starts at 7 AM. If you are not down, we will come and knock on your door," said Willy's lookalike from behind the wooden desk.

"Thank you, Willy. I guess I will see you tomorrow."

Chapter 9

The smell of freshly brewed coffee percolated through the door and the mosquito net. Christian stirred and opened his eyes. He felt refreshed. and was delighted to have slept so soundly. He could not remember sleeping so soundly after flying previously, and briefly wondered whether there had been any contribution to his sleep from the carbon monoxide in Willy's van. The rich smell of the coffee wafted in the door again, stimulating his cerebral caffeine centre and he decided he would shower and shave later; he needed to investigate and organise his caffeine fix for the day.

Walking down the stairs, he could hear enthusiastic voices coming from the dining room. Accented voices, American perhaps, although he could not be certain of their origin, partly due to the fact they were loud and very enthusiastic. At the bottom of the stairs, a doorway led left into the dining room. At the far side, he could see two women sitting at a small round wooden table talking very animatedly and laughing. He stopped for a moment and listened. It was their voices, which he had heard, and they were American. From where he stood, they looked like they were sisters; each had blonde hair pulled back tightly into two short ponytails, fine features, and both with gold hoop earrings. He made for the spare table next to them, under a large indoor palm tree, when they both turned towards him, waved and called out.

"Come and join us."

Christian smiled and pulled the spare wooden chair out from the table. As he sat down, he introduced himself if somewhat formally as Dr. Christian de Villiers.

"I'm Cindy." The first blonde ponytail on Christian's left said smiling without considering a surname was necessary.

"And I am Donna, but we are not sisters which is what everyone thinks."

"Where are you both from?"

"Well, you probably already established the United States. I am from the Bronx in New York and in Rwanda as part of an aid program associated with my church. Donna is from Houston and is training to be a teacher."

"And you, Christian, here to work in a hospital?"

"Yes, at a hospital close the Congolese border in the little town of Garanyi."

"Good morning, Dr. Chris. Would you like some nice Rwandan coffee?"

"Albert, if you're getting some coffee for Dr. Chris, could I have a refill please?" Donna chimed in.

"Can you do a long black, Albert?" asked Christian, as Donna finished.

"I will get that for you both and don't forget there is fresh fruit over there that you can help yourself to."

Christian looked in the direction Albert had pointed. All kinds of fruit from pineapple to pawpaw were neatly cut up on square white plates. It looked very enticing.

"Albert makes the best coffee, just you wait and see," said Cindy.

"Mais oui, and now we know that you're a doctor, we also know where to get our drugs." Donna added with a small laugh.

"You speak French?"

"I teach French and was hoping to improve it in Rwanda. That's their first language, although most speak English."

"Yes, I'd heard that was the case and was hoping their English was better than my French."

"From what we have experienced, almost 80% would understand English, but it may be a little bit different when you get to your hospital, as that is close to the Congo." said Donna

Christian was pleased to hear the statistic; he had learnt French at high school, but doubted that was going to be adequate to work effectively in the hospital. There had been a decree in Rwanda recently that the official language that would be taught in schools in the future was going to change to English. It was partly because the French had never fully apologized for their role in facilitating the genocide by supplying arms to the rebels. He wondered also whether it had anything to do with the fact that

Rwanda was the democratic darling of Africa, with most of the aid supplied from the English-speaking United Kingdom and United States of America. Having English spoken as the first language undoubtedly would facilitate business with English-speaking countries.

"We are all going to the genocide memorial tomorrow if you would you like to join us, Christian."

"Well, I was hoping to do that. Willy who brought me here last night is returning with his van this morning, but I would do anything to avoid travelling in that van again so that would be good."

"He drove too fast," said Cindy.

"The answer to that is probably yes, given that the absence of shock absorbers, brakes, tyres, and floorboards should have mandated a top speed of five km/h for any safety."

Cindy laughed. "I think you have to get used to that here. That sounds very similar to one of the taxis we had."

"Any other plans for today, Christian?"

"Drinking more of this coffee, I think. This Rwandan coffee is the best I have ever tasted."

"Albert has a little hand grinder so it's always fresh. We are having a meeting at lunchtime with our local supervisors. Why don't we meet back here for dinner? There is one more in our group you haven't yet met; Rafael is a German engineering student who is going to help out with a hydroelectric project in Shyra."

"Sounds good to me," Christian said. "Shall we say about 4:30 PM back here?"

At 4:30 PM, after another sleep to deal with his jet lag, Christian went down to the reception desk. Neither Cindy nor Donna had arrived and as he looked round, he felt a tap on his left shoulder.

"If you are Dr. Chris, then I'm Rafael," said the heavily accented German voice as Christian turned round. Rafael's rotundity suggested he had a good student allowance in Germany. Covering his ample frame was a large green T-shirt, in the centre a bright yellow light bulb. Underneath was written in italics *light to the entire world"* with the sponsoring German company, whose name Christian could not read. At a touch over six feet, Rafael had an exuberance about him that projected well into

Christian's space, and reminded him of the character from the Jolly Green Giant cartoon.

"Would you like to try the local beer, Mutzig? It's very good," said Rafael.

"Love one," said Christian.

"Count me in," said Cindy who had just walked in the front door.

As Christian looked up, he saw Donna also walking in, and she just shook her head.

"I'm a Pepsi girl," she added quickly.

The beer arrived accompanied by the smiling Albert; it was chilled to the point where it could have been an Australian beer. That was an excellent starting point when it came to beers. Christian was then not too surprised that it tasted so good, and was very similar in taste to Carlton draft, an icon Australian beer. At the equivalent of three Australian dollars a bottle, it could also be a cheap evening he thought.

"The water in the beer comes from Lake Kivu which is where your hospital is situated. That could be a good sign," said Rafael, laughing loudly.

The evening turned out to be one of great fun with Donna finally capitulating and switching from coffee to Mutzig. After a few Mutzig beers, they all ended up laughing and telling stories from their student days; all seemed to have done remarkably similar pranks despite their different origins. Rafael had told the story about rewiring the common room in the girl's dormitory at his university. Every time the lights in the common room were switched on, the fire alarm came on; this caused all the girls to run out of their rooms in various modes of undress. While Rafael laughed at the memory and Christian thought it was quite clever, Cindy just raised her eyebrows at Donna. However, a few beers later, Donna appeared to be the one most relaxed, perhaps because she was not used to drinking beer. By the time the third beer arrived, despite reassuring Christian that his lack of French would not be an issue, she was offering to be his French interpreter if needed. This brought a playful reproach from Cindy.

"And what particular phrase were you thinking of helping him with, soixante neuf?"

They all laughed which Christian noticed caused Donna to blush slightly. When Albert closed the bar at 11 PM, Christian felt like they had all become good friends. As they said good night, they agreed to meet for breakfast at 8 AM, and then go on to the genocide memorial.

Christian slept until about 7 AM when the coffee smell again caused him to stir. He was surprised that the mosquitoes had not bothered him with their buzzing in the night. Cindy and Donna had complained the buzzing kept them awake most nights. Christian, despite feeling very relaxed after drinking quite a few beers, had thoroughly checked the mosquito net before he went to bed, finding two little holes which he had managed to close with two paperclips. He reminded himself to tell Cindy and Donna to check their nets for small holes.

He showered and shaved, remembering to keep his mouth closed in the shower and not use the tap water to wash his teeth. Keeping his mouth closed in the shower was a tip given to him by Rafael; it was a way to avoid getting gastroenteritis from the local water. Towelling himself dry, he briefly wondered what Petrea was doing. She had probably completely forgotten about him. He quickly glanced at his phone to check and there were no messages. He unpacked a change of clothes, inhaled the coffee aroma drifting up the stairs, and headed down to breakfast.

"Good morning, Christian. Did you sleep well?" Cindy said, watching him come down the last few stairs.

"Wonderfully well, thank you."

"It's that Mutzig beer; it should be marketed as an antidote for insomnia," Rafael said smiling.

"We have a taxi organized for 9 AM to go to the genocide memorial."

"How expensive is the taxi?" asked Christian.

"Nothing seems to be expensive here, with the exception of course of certain American French interpreters."

Christian laughed remembering the banter from the night before. There was no reproachful look from Cindy this time, just a smile to suggest that she had also enjoyed the previous night's interaction.

"I hear the genocide memorial is a very emotional journey which takes about an hour and a half."

"I think, from what I've heard, the fact that it has interactive screens and videos of victims describing the horror of seeing family members hacked to death, leaves you feeling emotionally drained."

"It sounds like we will definitely need some Mutzig therapy afterwards then," Rafael added, the practicality of an engineering student relating any kind of emotional issue to an alcohol solution.

The taxi that turned up to take them to the memorial was a Mazda circa 1970s. Its original colour had been a bright red, but over the years had faded to a colour somewhere between burnt orange and rusty pink. At a cursory glance, Christian could see no parts missing, as distinct from what parts were left on Willy's van. While it appeared a huge positive, it did not necessarily suggest that it was going to be any safer. An elderly Rwandan driver emerged who appeared to be from the vintage before cars themselves. His neck bent from arthritis, he could only look at the ground as he walked slowly to meet them, taking the stairs one at a time to reach the small landing at the top. Christian also noted as he walked through the door at the top of the steps, he had cataracts in both eyes and a small tremor.

"Good morning. I am George, your driver," he said as he reached the top of the stairs, puffing slightly, a toothless grin accompanying the greeting.

"Twenty dollars American for everyone to go to the genocide memorial."

"Ten dollars," said Rafael. George looked at him for a minute and then nodded, his toothless grin endorsing the price.

"Always halve whatever gets quoted to you," Rafael whispered in Christian's ear. "It's expected."

They walked down the concrete steps in front of the hotel and with a degree of trepidation climbed in the Mazda. Christian was delighted to see no holes in the floor and that each door had a door handle which appeared to work. The back seats had been repaired with duct tape but there were no springs visible. They all climbed in, having voted for Rafael to sit in the front, arguing humorously that he had the most cushioning should they bump into anyone. Christian, Cindy, and Donna squeezed into the back seat, the duct tape in places sticking to them. The driver's window contained no glass at all which Christian thought was reassuring should the exhaust pipe decide to follow the example of Willy's van.

Passing through the centre of Kigali, Christian was amazed at the lack of traffic. The roundabout in the centre of the city had almost been in gridlock the previous night, with the number of cars and motorcycles trying to make their way through. There was no waiting this time, just the odd motorcycle and passenger and George did not have to try to push across in front of other motorcycles or vans.

"Where is all the traffic?" Christian asked Cindy.

"It's Sunday and 90% of the population will be at church. Rwanda, as you know, is a deeply religious country and practices its faith vigorously."

"This would be the time to invade them if you were a foreign nation," said Rafael from the front seat, his practical nature forcing its way to the surface.

The taxi ride turned out to be as equally eventful as the van ride with Willy the night before, albeit for slightly different reasons. George firstly drove very slowly peering intently over the steering wheel. His intense concentration was clearly driven by his diminished ability to see very far ahead. The thought that they might hit something due to his poor vision was reassuringly tempered by the fact that there could be little damage, given the speed he drove at. The slowness of the travel had another positive: it minimised some of similarities with Willy's van. The Mazda had, like Willy's van, little by way of effective shock absorbers and tended to bounce and sway at the slightest unevenness in the road. However, at the slow speed, the bouncing was not as vigorous or as nauseating as it had been in Willy's van.

The genocide memorial they found up a dusty winding road on the side of the hill. Lining the road on either side were small earthen huts. The majority were made from orange sun-dried mud bricks, rendered as a plaster finish by another layer of brownish mud. Roof tiles of hardened dried mud had become a faded pale orange, thanks to the hot African sun. On either side of the central door facing the road were two small windows. The design reminded Christian of the drawings of some of the very young patients in the paediatric wards. To their drawings, they had consistently added smoke from a chimney, now also coming from most of the Rwandan houses. Smiling faces, which children also consistently drew, were the only things missing from the windows.

George drove the Mazda slowly into the car park and parked in one corner. Along one side of the car park was a dark grey granite wall onto which thousands of names were etched, a stark commemoration to those who had violently died in the genocide. Each name was a memory of someone who had been hacked to death. Climbing out of the taxi, they all stretched and stood for a moment just looking at the wall and feeling the enormous sense of tragedy that it projected. It was such an overwhelming feeling that no one felt able to speak. The thousands upon thousands of names, all senselessly dead, many buried beneath their feet. They walked in silence towards the main entrance as George pointed out open graves to their left. Bodies were being laid in neat rows, more victims who had been recently discovered.

Inside the memorial building, the genocide had been recreated in vivid detail. Large poster-style pictures of decapitation immediately attacked all senses and produced a feeling of revulsion. Holograms and other gruesome pictures drove home the horror of wanton killing. Nearly 1,000,000 people were senselessly hacked to death, many of them young children, while the world stood idly by. The scale of the killing and its graphic nature was nauseating. However, it was the videos in which children talked about watching their parents being hacked to death, which were the most heart wrenching and emotionally draining. No wonder the sheer scale and depravity of the slaughter had produced universal guilt, and then an attempt to assuage some of that guilt with overwhelming aid.

After an hour and a half, they slowly and quietly made their way back to the entrance. They were emotionally drained, sitting in silence for quite some time, each trying to comprehend the extent of man's inhumanity to man, woman, and children. Christian, as he sat, wondered if the memorial was made compulsory viewing for every human being, would it decrease the chance of it ever recurring anywhere else in the world. Given man's capacity to inflict grotesque mayhem on his fellow man and the history of Germany and Bosnia, it was a wishful thought. Primal bloodletting once unleashed ignores basic, let alone sophisticated, emotional restraints.

The trip back to the hotel failed to stir them out of their sombre mood. George managing to avoid all the major potholes was one small consolation. His driving, however, was not flawless for he did manage to find at least two judder bars, which caused them to brace themselves for the inevitable hard landing and chassis scraping on the other side. They experienced a momentary distraction from the emotional sadness that they were all feeling.

Arriving back at the hotel, Rafael suggested a cold beer almost as soon as they climbed out of George's taxi. However, no one seemed enthusiastic about taking up his offer and no one seemed to want to talk about the experience of the memorial. As they walked into the hotel, Cindy hooked her arm through Donna's as her act of emotional solidarity. Christian was about to head to his room when he noticed Willy standing next to the reception desk. The contrast to their mood could not have been greater. Willy was not just smiling as he usually did; he was beaming his smile that penetrating their collective sea of darkness.

"I thought you might like to talk about the memorial," he said. "People usually come back from that visit very depressed."

"I'm not sure that we are ready to do that just yet," Christian said, looking at the others to see whether there was any dissent. "I think we just need to take in what we saw, the enormity of the genocide. Perhaps we can talk about that tomorrow."

"I would like to pray for you, so that you are not contaminated by the spirit of death from the genocide memorial. That can contaminate your spirits and give you weird dreams."

Christian looked at Willy; clearly, he was on a mission. Spiritual exuberance he could see radiated from every pore. He was as charged up as a twelve-volt battery. Then Christian remembered it was Sunday. Willy, being the fervent worshipper that he was, would have had four hours of charismatic Christianity channelling. He would be so infused with God's love he would believe that everything could be and should be dealt with prayer.

"I would like you to do that," Cindy said without looking at any of the others.

Willy's smile took on lighthouse proportions. No shadow in the room was safe.

Christian looked at both Donna and Rafael. Neither of them appeared convinced that this was the antidote. Christian was equivocal but curious. Having Willy pray for him, he could not imagine it would do any harm and it would give him insight into the Rwandan people, or at least Willy.

"You can pray for me, Willy," Christian said as Donna and Rafael shook their heads and headed off upstairs to their rooms.

Willy directed them to a small table in the dining room. Although it was close to dinner time, there were no others in the room. Willy seemed to have organized exclusive access through Albert, his spiritual partner in crime. Christian held the chair for Cindy as the beaming Willy stood and waited for them both to be seated. For a moment, nothing happened. Willy stood in front of them, eyes closed murmuring to himself. Cindy looked at Christian and raised her eyebrows indicating that she thought it was going to be more than just a silent prayer. Christian shrugged his shoulders just as Willy opened his eyes and said to them.

"Do you believe in Jesus?"

Cindy nodded quickly while Christian did not respond. He had been through the religious challenge many times and not come to any scientific conclusions. There was no such doubt in Willy. He believed he had the answer and he could see in Willy's eyes that he was desperate for some affirmation. Christian shortly wondered with his lack of spiritual belief, whether he should make a declaration and possibly exclude himself. He had almost made up his mind to get up and leave Cindy to whatever was about to happen, when Willy looked at him with such kindness and expectation, he could not abjure. He nodded to Willy.

Christian lost count in the next fifteen minutes of how many times he heard the name Jesus. Giving Willy permission to pray he imagined was going to be the easy part. Stopping him before midnight would be the greater challenge. As he sat there, he learnt about Jesus the Saviour, Jesus the Redeemer, Jesus the Shepherd, but mostly Jesus who died on the cross, and spilled his blood for all humankind. Certainly more cheeses than he had ever heard in his life before. Willy then moved on, prayerfully washing them with the blood of Jesus, cleansing them, he said, of the spirit of death that might have clung to them from the memorial. After invoking the Holy Spirit to be with them, he walked around the small table placing his hand firstly on Cindy's head and then on Christian's.

"Father God, by the power that you have invested in me, I release them from any spirits that may have rested on them. By the blood of Jesus, I command you to protect them."

Silence followed for what must have been at least a minute but seemed like five. Willy sat down on the spare chair at the table, seemingly exhausted from all the exhortation. Christian wondered whether he was waiting for God to respond and give further instructions and whether this was an opportune time to take his leave. Christian looked across at Cindy, he could see her eyes were tightly closed, and there were tears streaming down her face. Clearly, Willy had had some effect on her.

"Are you okay?" Christian whispered across the table. Cindy nodded without opening her eyes.

Willy then started to pray again before Christian could get up.

"Father, forgive them for what they have done. They know not what they do. Forgive my neighbour who killed my brother and sister. Forgive the nuns who sheltered my family in a church and betrayed them to the Hutus. Forgive the Hutus at Ruhengeri who slaughtered my cousins in their church. Forgive those who killed 5000 children at Butare."

Willy then took a deep breath and paused before saying, "And thank you, Jesus, that you have brought Cindy and Christian here to help my people."

Christian watched as Willy then closed his eyes again making the sign of the cross before telling them the spirit of death had been lifted. Willy's prayer did not have the same effect on Christian that it had on Cindy, whose hand Willy was now holding, while he murmured to himself. Although the prayer had not had an impact Christian realised he was starting to understand a little more of the people in the country he had come to work in. Contriteness and forgiveness excessively expressed as compensation for blatant disregard of the cornerstone Christian belief of that shalt not kill.

Ongoing enmity and unforgivingness had the potential to destroy Rwanda as a nation. Mandela had healed wounds in South Africa using a similar principle through the truth and reconciliation commission. The creation in Rwanda of centres for forgiveness and rehabilitation was an admirable concept; however, it would only work if the majority believed strongly in forgiveness. It was clearly a way forward for Rwanda and a great example of developing harmony through abject despair. Christian did wonder if the rivers of blood returned whether the principle of forgiveness would survive. If Willy represented the greater majority the possibility at least existed. While, he was not certain that the spirit of death that ever been part of their company, Willy's prayer in many ways had contributed to an understanding of Rwanda beyond the memorial.

"Thank you, Willy," Cindy said as she got up wiping her eyes and kissing him gently on the cheek.

"Thank you, Willy," said Christian, not knowing what else to add, feeling that any other words would not enhance what he had just experienced.

"God can do amazing things, Dr. Chris," Willy said standing up. "I will see you in the morning. The bus for Garanyi and the hospital leaves at 12:30 PM and I will take you down there. I am sure you will have no nightmares tonight."

Chapter 10

As he walked down the steps to reception, Christian wondered how Willy would get their entire luggage into his van without the floor collapsing. From the top of the steps, he could see Cindy, Donna, and Rafael's luggage; there was no way they could even get it all into the van, irrespective of the state of the floor. Willy, however, was leaning on the reception desk, chatting amiably to Albert and looking completely non-plussed about the pending problem.

"Good morning, Dr. Chris. You look very relaxed. It must have been that cleansing prayer from last night," beamed Willy.

"Thank you, Willy. Yes, I did sleep well and I will let you take some of the credit as I did not dream about any of those horrific killings."

"Neither did I." Rafael chipped in. "But I think my good sleep was down to the spirit of Mutzig, not the Holy Spirit that Willy dispenses."

Willy for a moment looked crestfallen before realising that Rafael was teasing him, and after a few seconds smiled broadly again.

"I do not think we're going to get all our bags in your van, Willy. Even if we can, your exhaust pipe is too dangerous. I think we should get two taxis."

"Don't worry, Dr. Chris. I have fixed the holes in the floor and my friend has fixed the exhaust."

Christian looked at Cindy and Donna, hoping that they might insist on a taxi. They just looked at him and then shrugged their shoulders, as if to say it was fine with them to go with Willy; that was the only sign to Willy and Albert. They quickly walked down the steps and started to put all the bags besides the van. Christian followed them down the steps, carrying his own bags. He turned and waited at the bottom for Cindy and Donna, watching as Albert started handing bags to Willy inside the van. As the bags started to disappear into the van, Christian put his rucksack down and knelt down on the ground. He gazed underneath the van, and amazingly, there were no bags visible through the floor; Willy had repaired the floor with planks of wood. Christian looked inside the van and saw that Willy had also placed folded blankets over the springs in the seats.

"That looks great, Willy! Where did you get the planks from?"

"God provided," Willy said beaming.

"So they just appeared out of the night and ended up on the floor of your van all neatly cut?" Rafael said, struggling to hide his scepticism.

"I was talking to the pastor of my church and he said that they had a number of old pews that I could use. Therefore, that's still God providing," he said, concerned that Rafael did not fully appreciate what he considered a small miracle.

"That's fantastic, Willy," Cindy said which encouraged Willy's widest smile of the morning.

Christian looked in the back of the van and had to admit that Willy and Albert had done a great job of getting the entire luggage in, although they had used part of the backseat. Christian sat with his rucksack resting on his knee in the middle seat while Cindy and Donna took the backseat alongside the luggage. Rafael quite unconcernedly climbed in the front seat. Considering previous experiences of driving with Willy, Christian would have been tempted to have called it the suicide seat. Once they were all in, Willy slid the van door closed. There were shouts of goodbye to Albert through Willy's open window as they drove off. Willy started more slowly with his large load and took a route which avoided the busy city centre roundabout. Fortunately, on the route that Willy had chosen, there were no judder bars and few motorcycles. Willy, once he had the van up to speed, informed them that the driver of the bus they were taking was a friend of his called John, and he had reserved special seats for them.

Fifteen minutes later, as they descended out of the main section of Kigali, Christian spotted several buses at the bottom of the hill. Thousands of people surrounded the buses for the bus stop was at the local market. Willy pointed to a bus at the far end of the stalls. Christian looked in the direction that Willy had pointed and saw a faded yellow mud-splattered old bus with certain similarities to Willy's van. The advertising on the side of the bus appeared to be its most modern and best-kept feature. There was a picture of the president of Rwanda with gleaming white teeth painted along the side of the bus. The only other section free of mud had a large safe sex banner complete with outsized condom. The images were sufficiently graphic so that the medical advice in Kinyarwanda alongside needed no translation to understand its message.

The queue waiting was twice as long as the bus itself. Christian could not imagine how the people, let alone their luggage, were going to fit in. The queue was mostly Rwandan woman and their children, returning from a day's shopping in Kigali. Many had large bags of rice balanced delicately on their heads; others had old suitcases stuffed with shopping alongside. It was a scene of great colour. Rwandan women, whatever their financial circumstances, had an instinct for fashionably bright, beautiful African colours: vibrant ecstatic colours, bright yellows, dark reds, light greens, set mostly against a black background. A spectacular ocean of colour was offset with Elysian jewellery. Earring hoops the size of softballs, golden neck chains with large religious crosses, and golden bracelets from wrist to elbow were some of the most favoured. And despite the practical issues of walking, long dresses predominated. It was a unique alfresco fashion display, the likes of which he had never seen anywhere in Africa before.

The second thing, which caught Christian's interest, was that each of those queuing had numerous additional earthly attachments. Mostly it was luggage; old faded brown fabric suitcases dominated, many of which were struggling to constrain their contents. Several were under such duress that rope had been tied around them to prevent their contents discharging onto the road. For some of the suitcases, that was still not enough; socks, scarves, T-shirts, food packages, and even the occasional bra poked through the gaps between the ropes. Children ran uninhibited in the gaps between parents, live chickens, and the occasional goat. The children in their enthusiasm were treating the line of would-be passengers as an adventure playground; seemingly unconcerned, they frequently knocked over the cans of water or upset the chickens and the melancholy goat.

Willy pulled his van over in the normal fashion using the curb to slow the van down; although this time, he miscalculated slightly, bumping the goat in the queue as he came to a stop. Fortunately the goat seemed to take little notice. Willy then jumped out of the van, remembering to put the rock under the front wheel, before he waved vigorously in the direction of the yellow bus and John the driver. He made his way over to the bus. Christian could see that they were good friends; there were lots of hugs and enthusiastic handshakes. After a few minutes, having exhausted their greetings, Willy returned to the van holding the bus driver's hand. Willy introduced John, explaining that he attended the same church as Willy and wanted to be a pastor. The last part was obvious given John had on the same *Jesus Saves* T-shirt that Willy had been wearing the previous night. After shaking all their hands and blessing them, John returned to his bus queue where he walked up and down the queue checking small pieces of paper. Looking at the tickets, John then rearranged some people in the queue; Willy explained they were the ones who would have a seat. They had paid a little bit more for their tickets; the others would have to stand for the entire three-hour journey to Rhuengeri, their first stop. Christian was pleased to see that when John got to the end of the queue, there was no change in the goat's position.

John finished organising tickets for those to be seated and then turned his attention to the goods and the luggage. With the number of passengers, it was obvious that most of the luggage and goods would have to go on the roof of the bus. The top of the bus had a rusty red rack designed originally to run the entire length of the bus. This allowed luggage to be stacked securely and lashed with rope to the roof rack to prevent it from falling off. The rack, however, had seen better days. Rust cancer had completely eaten through the rack every meter or so leaving large gaps; it would be a miracle if any of the luggage or livestock managed to remain secure for even a small part of the journey.

John made his way down the queue for a second time, selecting the biggest bags and crates. After surveying them for a few minutes, he whistled in no particular direction. A young man sprang out of the waiting throng and stood expectantly in front of John, who pointed to the roof of the bus. The young boy then climbed up onto the spare wheel attached to the back of the bus, before adroitly pulling himself up onto the roof. John placed a table next to the bus onto which the passengers put their larger bags. The young boy on the roof dangled a hook on a rope, which John connected to the luggage before it was hoisted up to be positioned on the rack. Quickly stacking the larger bags in the corners, the young boy then turned soccer goalkeeper, catching the smaller bags thrown by up by those still standing in the queue. He wedged the smaller cases inside the larger bags. Christian could start to see the logic. The large bags spanned the areas where the rust had removed sections of the bus rack. The smaller cases wedged everything in tightly, and hopefully none of the luggage would then move or fall off.

The exchange of large and small bags proceeded with very little communication but great efficiency, a little bit like a silent movie. Once all the large and small suitcases were lashed down, live chickens in crates were passed up. A cacophonic protest of squawking accompanied each of the crates of six chickens. Baskets of vegetables were the last to be loaded. The vegetables jammed between the large suitcases and small suitcases, and then the young boy lashed everything into place.

John walked around the bus and inspected the roof-loading process, nodded approval to the young boy, and then started boarding the rearranged queue. Those to be seated were the first to get on the bus. Like an aircraft captain, who needed to balance the weight of the airplane, John selected the largest passengers to come to the head of the queue. John then seated them in the middle of the bus. All the other passengers were then seated around them at the front and rear of the bus. Having seated all the Rwandans, John smiled and nodded at Willy.

"Time for you to get on board, Dr. Chris," Willy said. "I hope you have a safe trip. God bless you, and maybe I will see you in Garanyi, God willing."

"Thank you, Willy. It has been wonderful meeting you. I hope we see you down in Garanyi as well."

Christian, Cindy, and Donna climbed up the steps of the old bus through the front door, which the young boy from the roof had temporarily tied open. He then showed Donna, Cindy, and Christian to the back seat of the bus, which was the only seat now unoccupied. Walking down the aisle of the bus, Christian noted another disconcerting similarity with Willy's van before he repaired the floor. The floor of the bus had similar air-conditioning vents, large holes in the floorboards, through which the road was clearly visible. Christian silently hoped that the bus did not have a similar exhaust problem to Willy's van, although the strong smell of diesel inside the bus suggested that, unfortunately, it might.

Cindy and Donna took off their backpacks and sat down on the back seat. Christian put his backpack on the floor next to them, as he looked past them to the back side window. On either side of the back, windows were completely missing. At least he thought that would mean that they could get a flow of fresh air in the worst-case scenario where the diesel fumes were overwhelming. Moreover, with Donna not feeling well, having fresh air blowing through the open window would possibly help reduce her nausea.

Finally, with everyone seated, John started boarding the standing passengers and the eight remaining livestock and goods. Baskets of dead chickens he and the young boy placed in the racks above people's heads. Extra vegetables, water bottles, and small collections of firewood were packed in alongside. The rope netting, which held all of the goods in place above passengers' heads, started to bulge threateningly. Christian's concern was growing that a large pothole in the road would probably cause it to release its constraints on everyone underneath.

"I'm glad we're sitting down in the back and there is no overhead rack above us," said Cindy as she watched another load of firewood placed above a young boy's head.

"You might be required to do some emergency treatment before we get to Rhuengeri if that rope netting gives away," Donna said looking at Christian in amazement as more objects were placed in the racks above the passengers.

Eventually with the racks full to bulging, crates of live chickens were stacked three high in the aisle. Sitting at the back of the bus, it was difficult for Christian and Donna to see the front. Once the aisle was fully stacked, the goat was led on board by the young man. Christian thought it was either a nanny goat kept for its milk, or a frequent traveller, as it was so relaxed, trotting up the stairs and lazily making its way down the aisle. Confronted by live chickens, it did a few disdainful sniffs and turned to face the front of the bus.

Four extinct volcanoes surround Kigali; they varied in height up to 4000 metres and had to be climbed to get to Rhuengeri and beyond. Serpiginous arms of smooth black asphalt were deceiving as to the mountaineering task which lay ahead for the bus. Each section of road cut into the mountain at an angle of about 40 degrees. John started the bus, which began to shake in time with the revolutions of its motor, perhaps fearful of the climbing task ahead. Once John was certain that the engine was well-warmed up, he engaged first gear which then caused the bus to start to sway gently. Very quickly, everyone and everything in the bus started metronomically swaying left to right. The gentle swaying of everyone on the bus reminded Christian of a Southern American Baptist church choir. All that was required to complete the imagery was for everyone to lift their hands in the air and sing a halleluiah chorus. Given his experience to date with Willy, he would not have been surprised if that happened.

John eased the bus onto the road and it began to heave and sway its way up the hill, diesel, as predicted, percolating up through the air-conditioning holes in the floor. As the bus laboured, John changed gear and extra clouds of brown diesel flowed up through the floor irritating the chickens, producing a rap cacophony of squawking. Unfortunately, the increased agitation caused spurts of chicken poo, which splattered the crates and aisles around the crates. The smell of diesel and chicken excrement was an overwhelming combination.

Christian cast a glance along the seat at Donna to see how she was managing. She had changed places with Cindy so that she could be next to the window. She had her face resting on her hand with the top part of her head out the window. Christian could see she had her eyes closed so it was difficult to tell how she was feeling; her general greyness indicated that the smell of the chicken excrement and diesel was having a deleterious effect. He had seen that look many times before in accident and emergency, and he knew it was a prelude to vomiting. As if on cue, Donna vomited loudly and prodigiously out of the back window. He motioned to Cindy to change places so he could sit next to Donna. As they were in the process of changing places, Donna vomited again. He sat down next to her and quickly felt for her radial artery. Her heart rate was regular and about 80 bpm. Clinically while she looked unwell, she was not at the stage of decompensating due to dehydration; however, he knew that unless she stopped vomiting, dehydration would quickly occur and with it possibly renal failure. He wondered, given the filthy conditions in the bus, whether he could give her an intramuscular injection of Stemetil, an antiemetic he carried in his bag. One more vomit, he thought and he would take the chance.

The blaring of horns temporarily distracted him from Donna's vomiting. He tried to peer around the chicken crates but could only see the backs of those standing in the forward part of the aisle. He looked out the side window past Donna and could see that they were still steadily climbing but were now on the opposite side of the road. They were attempting to pass a small truck that had stopped in their upward lane. Donna then vomited again as the bus lurched back rapidly onto the right side of the road, narrowly, or expertly missing a bus which had come around the corner just prior to the apex of the climb. The water that Donna had tried to take in between the vomits immediately was lost out through the window in a continuous stream. Christian unzipped his bag and found the container which held the Stemetil. He had six needles that were blunt-tipped for drawing up medications, the six others for injecting. He quickly told Donna what he was planning on doing and she weakly nodded her consent. As he drew the Stemetil into the syringe, people all around him started to look at what he was doing. Three young children, who had been sitting on their mother's lap in front of the back seat, peered over their mother's shoulders, wide-eyed and with great curiosity. By the time he had taken the needle out of its sterile container, more faces were appearing around the chicken crates, and most of those in the back of the bus had stood up to see what he was going to do next. Smiling at all of the faces, he rolled up the short sleeve on Donna's arm, wiped it with an alcohol swab, and plunged in the needle before injecting the Stemetil. He heard some of the children gasp. Then, as he pulled out the needle and checked the syringe to make sure the full five mg had been delivered, all those who were watching burst into spontaneous applause. Donna mouthed a thank you to him and put her head back out the window.

Half an hour later having crested the top of the hill, the speed had increased significantly. More importantly, flows of fresh air flushed out the diesel and reduced the impact of the smell of the chicken poo. Importantly, Donna had not vomited again. Christian turned to Cindy.

"Would you like to sit next to Donna again now that she is feeling a little better?"

"No." She smiled. "I've always believed you should share a good doctor."

"Very cute. I'm relieved that she is feeling a little better. It would have been awful leaving you at Rhuengeri if she hadn't been."

"Well, at least we can try and concentrate on what there is to see around us now that she's feeling a little better."

Christian could see the flat road that they were now on was really just a connection between volcanic ridges. Looking up at the surrounding peaks, every possible inch was cultivated. Horizontal furrows were constructed all around the distant mountains to the very top. Rich volcanic soil provided a life-giving underbelly to everything from potatoes to bananas. Every 1500 m up the mountain, he could see there were small one-room huts. They had four walls, approximately a metre and a half wide, each with a small door, a chimney but no windows. Some had smoke gently drifting out of their chimneys, suggesting occupation. People who cultivated the soil obviously lived in the huts so that they did not have to climb the whole mountain each day.

It was like nothing he had ever seen before, a reminder of one of the human endeavours in Africa required to survive. In another life, he wondered whether he could have existed in a similar small hut. As he thought about the daily grind that would entail, he noticed the 50 km to Rhuengeri sign on the side of the road. For the last few kilometres on either side of the road, there were increasing numbers of people walking with various forms of produce. Some rode or pushed bicycles, which had large water bottles for filling, or branches of trees cut for sale as firewood. Some of the bicycles were so overladen with firewood that there was no room to ride them; the rider was walking alongside the bike while trying to maintain balance.

Rhuengeri quickly came to meet them with its markets and throngs of people. As a town, it was not dissimilar to Kigali, although unlike Kigali it was entirely flat.

"I guess this is where we say goodbye," Cindy said, looking dispiritedly at Christian.

"Perhaps not goodbye then, just au revoir. I feel like we are destined to meet again."

"And hopefully not just for your medical expertise, wonderful though it was," Donna added, her vomiting greyness replaced by a healthier pink colour.

"That injection that you gave me has made the world of difference. Thank you so much. I'm sure you'll make a huge difference to the patients at Garanyi Hospital where you're going."

Christian felt both sadness and excitement. Sadness that he was losing his travelling companions whom he had, over a short period, grown to know and like, yet excited about the challenge which lay ahead.

"Well, you can always come and visit me, as friends of course, not as patients." He laughed. "I hear it's beautiful on the shores of Lake Kivu where Garanyi Hospital is situated."

Christian looked across to his left and out the window. John was expertly bringing the bus to a halt next to another long queue. Remarkably, nothing had fallen from the roof. As the bus's motor was switched off, Christian felt the sensation of the rocking motion of the bus continuing for a few minutes. John then reached through one of the missing door panels, untied the front door and the disembarkation proceeded in the reverse order to boarding. The chicken crates in front of them however remained in position and Cindy and Donna had to manoeuvre around them by climbing over the seats. Christian held onto their backpacks and once they were outside, passed them out of the window. Realizing that they would have to remove some of the luggage from the roof, Christian also decided to exit via the missing back window.

"Time for one last goodbye," he said as he landed on the ground next to the backpacks.

He stretched out his arms and Donna walked quickly towards him producing a prolonged grateful hug. Turning towards a broadly smiling and open-armed Cindy, he breathed deeply and enjoyed the temporary escape from the diesel and chicken pooh.

"Now don't forget, the orphanage is only about an hour from Garanyi Hospital. If you get a free day, come and visit."

"I had been meaning to ask who runs the orphanage that you're going to teach at."

"The Chinese. It's one of their new humanitarian outreaches."

"Well, that could be very interesting from a cultural point of view at least; I would definitely be interested in coming and visiting you and the orphanage."

"Be careful, Christian. There are reports of lots of Congolese militia and armed groups not far from where you are."

"I will take care," Christian said, climbing back in through the bus window, trying to imagine what was behind the Chinese humanitarian aid. The Chinese had always put their business interests first, especially when it came to Africa. The sceptical part of him wondered whether the proximity to some of the world's most wanted mineral resources was behind the sudden desire to help the poor.

Chapter 11

Christian looked back out through the side window as the bus eased its way through the throngs of people gathered at the Rhuengeri market. Donna and Cindy stood like two life buoys in an ocean of colourful humanity, waving energetically as they pulled away. The bus, after a few minutes, turned onto the main road to Garanyi and he finally lost sight of their waving arms.

The two-hour ride to Garanyi was more of the dark rich Rwandan soil cultivated to its last life-giving centimetre. Greenness, in its darkest Sherwood Forest shade abounded, undoubtedly due to the multiple trace elements bequeathed by volcanic activity over the millennia. As Christian looked from the small-cultivated patches at the side of the road to the mountains in the distance, he thought if ever there was a place on earth where life had begun, Rwanda and its pristine beauty would have to lead the list. The overwhelming lushness is what he imagined would be a pre-requisite for any Garden of Eden.

The bus had been traveling for about an hour when Christian noted the lines of people walking on either side of the road expanding to three deep and more uniformed military personnel with automatic weapons. The Congolese border was getting closer. As the bus rounded a long slow corner, an area of rare uncultivated flatland appeared. A ten foot high fence topped with barbed wire surrounded hundreds of large blue United Nations tents. It was the refugee camp for those fleeing atrocities in the Congo, which he had read about in the news. At the front of the camp, a double gate protected the entrance. Four armed guards on the inside of the gate were checking people in and out. Inside he could see hundreds of people, mostly women and children, wandering around or sitting next to small fires. He imagined that many would be seen at the hospital that he was going to, before they made it to the camp.

From the time of his first setting foot in Rwanda a few days ago, its beauty had dominated his senses, irrespective of the surrounding poverty. Such beauty should have prepared him for Garanyi, but it did not. After an hour's driving beyond the refugee camp, John announced they were approaching Garanyi. The bus again laboured up the side of a hill and then entered a canopy of trees on the road leading down to the town of Garanyi. Half way down the slowly winding hill, the trees suddenly retracted their protective canopy; the effect was like a curtain in a cinema being flung open for the major film. Racing to take centre stage, was a lake of expansive dark green beauty—Lake Kivu, with its attendant smoke, haze, and small wooden fishing boats. The lake, stretched miles into the distance, towards the nations of Congo and Burundi. Trees abounded, squatting in clumps around the lake, some trekking down to the shore, branches gently moving at the water's edge as the lake breeze stirred.

The hospital was situated at the bottom of the hill, and the road then ran on to the border. As the bus slowed for the hospital, Christian could see a dusty dirt road leading off from the hospital entrance to the town centre. Interestingly, situated two thirds of the way down the main street was the spire of a mosque. This was the only mosque he had seen in Rwanda of the Muslim religion. He wondered how the religion even had a toehold, given that Rwanda was 95% Christian. The spire was a nugacious protest in the overwhelming sea of counter belief.

Christian was surprised when the bus stopped outside the hospital, expecting the main stop to be in the town itself. A smiling John soon appeared next to his open window.

"You can get off here, Dr. Chris."

He could feel the eyes of some of the passengers on his back as he climbed out the window after passing his backpack to John.

"Thank you, John, and have a safe trip back."

"I hope we didn't put you off chicken."

"No, not at all." Christian said laughing and looking back in through the open window at the crates of now docile feathers.

After picking up his backpack, the first thing that he noticed about the hospital, other than it desperately needed painting, were the stone ovens dotted around the grounds, each surrounded by family groups. The ovens were made of grey volcanic stones, each the size of a square rugby ball, placed one on top of the other. Formed to have a meter wide square base, they allowed cooking from four sides all by four separate families. Above the large stones was a corrugated roof, which offered some protection against rain. Smaller stones he could see had been placed on top of the roof to hold it in place.

At a quick count there were half a dozen ovens, with families chatting and preparing food to be cooked. Large faded yellow water containers lay on the ground next to small containers of rice and dead chickens. A nanny goat tethered to the fence watched over proceedings, its morphean chewing a contrast to activity surrounding the ovens. A metre from the oven base, colourful blankets spread irregularly over the rocky ground and acted as tablecloths and places to sit. Those who were not involved in cooking sat and watched, some plucking the feathers from the dead chickens. Smoke from the ovens hovered and then drifted indolently when fanned by gentle lake breezes.

A little further down the hill, beyond the stone ovens, there were three old shipping containers. Rusty brown, the P and O insignia of the shipping line was still recognizable. The containers had had windows cut in their sides and a door added to serve as accommodation for patients and nurses. A third container had 'X-Ray Department' painted expertly on the side. X-rays were stacked alongside the container, the sunlight drying them and generating the needed exposure.

Dr. Emmanuel Sudani was the superintendent of the hospital with whom Christian had been in email contact. He had been very enthusiastic about Christian coming to help for three months and suggested his surgical experience would come in handy. From what Christian had read online, Doctor Sudani had trained in Uganda as a haematologist. He had been superintendent at Garanyi for fourteen years, first working at Rhuengeri hospital. Christian had worked out with his mother that it was probably fifteen years since his father had visited the hospital. It was unlikely therefore, that Dr. Sudani would remember him even if he were the superintendent at the time. Christian in correspondence had been tempted to ask about his father, but in the end, had decided not to in case Dr. Sudani thought that that was his primary purpose in coming.

From where he was, standing outside the hospital, Christian could see the entrance to Dr. Sudani's office. The word

'Superintendent' painted in capital letters above the door was unmistakable. Christian reached down to get his phone from his backpack, thinking that he would record his first impressions before heading to the office. As he unzipped the small side pocket, a small, brightly-coloured gecko scampered away from underneath his backpack. It was unlike anything that Christian had seen before. It was large by gecko standards - ten or eleven cm in length. What separated this from any other geckos that he had seen were the striking colours. All the colours of the rainbow represented in a sparkling iridescence. It looked as if it had been painted with shiny strips of metallic paint. He watched, fascinated, as it scurried away, a bluish purple iridescent stripe catching the afternoon sun. Another argument for the Garden of Eden theory.

The waiting room outside Dr. Sudani's office had three wooden chairs. Each of the chairs was carved in a fashion that reminded him of the waiting room at the Travel Doctor in Adelaide. An overhead fan, sitting above the chairs, was motionless; wires protruded from the roof suggesting that even on a hot day, it would be still be motionless. A slightly yellow light bulb protruded from a broken socket in the ceiling, suggesting that it contributed little, other than appearance of a working electrical supply. Christian put his backpack down and was about to sit down when Doctor Sudani strode out of his office and stood a metre in front of him smiling.

"You must be Doctor Chris. You are exactly like your photo although slightly taller than what I expected."

"Doctor Sudani. It is very nice to meet you and nice to be in Garanyi finally."

"Well we can certainly do with your help. Over one million patients have access to our hospital from either side of the Rwandan/Congolese border. Now with all the rebel activity in the Congo we have to treat even more patients. You will have seen the constant stream of people passing in front of the hospital as you came in."

"Yes I did notice that. There seemed to be a steady stream heading towards the Congolese border."

"There is plenty of work there in the mines and such is the desperation of many people they suffer the enormous brutality from the militias and rebels if it means being able to feed their families. We then unfortunately get to deal with the aftermath.

However, enough politics. You will learn about that quickly enough. I am under strict instructions from my wife to bring you back to our home and not put you to work straight away. I hope you like vegetarian curry; meat is in very short supply as we tend to keep our goats for the milk."

"Curries are a big favourite of mine."

"Great, get your bag and come with me. Chantal, my wife is waiting to meet you. It's just a short drive, ten minutes from the hospital towards the border but a five-minute walk from the lake's edge. And please call me Emmanuel."

The Toyota utility parked at the side of the hospital was an unwashed camouflage green suggesting its military use in another life. The word Ambulance had been roughly hand painted in French on the bonnet, and there was a partially shattered windscreen on the non-driver's-side. Christian smiled to himself thinking how he was adapting; viewing Rwanda out of open windows now second nature to him. The back tray of the Toyota had been removed to allow easy access for two stretchers, each bolted to the floor, preventing the stretchers from being stolen.

Emmanuel turned the ignition key several times until the diesel engine finally coughed into life. They then drove slowly out through the front gate, waiting for a break in the throng of people, before making their way down the hill towards the lake.

"There's not anyone swimming," Christian said, looking out the side window towards the lake.

"Schistosomiasis exists in the lake - what you probably know as Bilharzia. Worms from freshwater snails. We have had an education program going for some time now. It's even in the churches and mosques along with posters so the people are slowly understanding."

"It is the eggs in the adult worms that get into bladders and the small intestine of those who go wading or swimming, which then creates an inflammatory response. If it's not correctly treated, patients get blood in the uterine and stool as well as very large livers."

"Excellent response, Doctor Chris. You are indeed well prepared; I knew you were a good choice."

After a further 100 metres, Dr. Sudani slowed to a stop and waited until those walking had passed the front of the Toyota, before he drove up a short driveway. The driveway was lined with grey chips of finely compacted volcanic rock. On the left side, majestic apollonian palms protected the house from the late afternoon lake breezes. The fronds of the palms draped themselves across the driveway, creating an arch with a two metre high hedge. The driveway forked to the front and to the side of the house. Two stories high, it was quite different than other Rwandan houses and reminded Christian of some of the houses he had seen in South Africa. At the front, it had a very similar veranda or stoep to Cape Dutch houses he had seen in South Africa. The windows were shuttered and had security bars, which was remarkably similar to what he had seen in Cape Town. Emmanuel turned left and stopped front of the veranda.

"I can see what you're thinking," he said turning to face Christian. "Not your traditional Rwandan house. Many years ago, we thought that we were going to get the services of a Dutch surgeon. This house was built on his instructions, the land belonging to the hospital. When he did not arrive, the house became the superintendent's."

Emmanuel walked up onto the veranda and rang the front door bell. It opened on the third chime.

"Welcome to Garanyi, Doctor Chris. I am Chantal; Emmanuel's wife and we are delighted to have you here with us. Please come in."

Christian followed Emmanuel and Chantal down a short hallway. The floor he could not help noticing was a dark rich teak wood, similar to Jarrah floors common in South Australia. As if reading his mind, Emmanuel without looking behind said.

"All imported materials, Christian, but finished by local craftsmen. Quite different to what you will see anywhere else in Garanyi. Although with increasing numbers of people and wealth in Kigali, there are several similar designs."

Chantal turned left through a door half way down the hallway. Judging by the wonderful curry smells wafting through the door, it was the kitchen.

"I'll show you where you can put your bag and where you will be sleeping and then we can come back and sample Chantal's wonderful cooking."

Christian's room was to the back of the house. The room held a single wooden bed and a small open wooden closet for his clothes. There was also the obligatory mosquito net hanging from the ceiling tied into a neat bundle, which was released for sleeping under.

"The door opposite is a toilet and shower. All of our children have left home so it is just two servants, Chantal, and me. We have a security code and deadlocks, which we will explain to you. Being on the main thoroughfare to the Congolese border we have to be more vigilant than otherwise would be the case."

"This used to be a back lounge but when our two children were growing up, we divided it to give each their own room. When you're ready come through into the kitchen, I know that supper won't be too far away."

Chantal's kitchen was a testament to her love of cooking. Approximately ten to twelve cookbooks sat in a neat rack at the end of the bench. Most had French titles, although the one that was open on the central island was in English. Garlic hung in bunches from the wall and small herbs grew in pots along the windowsill.

Chantal's figure was still slim suggesting that she controlled the desire of all good chefs to sample what they created. Her long black hair was gathered up, and held on top of her head, a small thin wooden clip straining against the thick hair. It exposed a long thin neck, fine cheekbones, and aquiline nose that Christian had come to associate with the Tutsis. At nearly six foot tall, Chantal also had elegance about the way that she moved. Christian sat on one of the stools and watched as vegetables were quickly chopped and disappeared into the curry base.

"It will be ready in half an hour," she said, looking up and smiling at Christian.

"It smells delicious, Mrs. Sudani."

"That's very polite. But if you call me Chantal, I will stop calling you Doctor Christian!"

"That sounds like a very good deal," said Christian laughing.

Emmanuel walked back into the kitchen and motioned to Christian to follow him. The lounge which he led Christian to had a green leather three seater sofa and two reclining comfortable chairs, all facing the front window. Despite the fine curtain, Christian could still see the constant pedestrian traffic heading towards the border and the shores of the lake in the background.

"The lake looks inviting, doesn't it? You would not know just looking at it that it could be the source of so many medical problems for us in the hospital."

"Looks like some children are getting ready to go for a swim."

"Unfortunately we cannot educate them all. Let me just quickly tell you a little about the hospital and then we can settle back and enjoy Chantal's cooking. We usually do ward rounds at 8 AM. That is for both surgery and medicine. Patients accepted into our emergency department remain there until we see them. Some of those may not have been seen if we have been deluged by emergencies from the border and will need to be triaged. Given your surgical experience, we thought we would put you in with the surgical team. Currently we have no full-time surgeon, just one of our graduates who has done a bit of surgery. In many things, you might well be more experienced than he is, but our doctors here have to do everything from gynaecology through to urology and orthopaedics. You said in your letter that you had done some rotations in gynaecology and orthopaedics?"

"Yes that is right. I did a rotation in gynaecology in outback Australia. I have done about thirty caesarean sections and then a rotation at Alice Springs in orthopaedics. So I should be able to help with most things other than the really complicated orthopaedics."

"That's good. I will introduce you to Doctor Theodore Nikita. He will show you around the theatres and explain to you how everything works as well as outpatients. We do not have any real anaesthetists as you know them, just anaesthetic technicians. Anaesthesia in Garanyi is basically monitoring the patient and supplying oxygen, and a sedative drug of choice. I usually walk up to the hospital. That takes about twenty minutes and it's quite safe although one of the staff will come back with you if it's late at night."

"Come on you two, food is ready and you can continue the discussion over supper." Chantal's voice drifted down the hallway and into the lounge where they were sitting.

Chapter 12

The Accident and Emergency ward was attached to the side of the old hospital. It had been added on, jutting out from the main medical and surgical wards, like an inadequate afterthought. The hospital itself had an H shape accommodating 300 beds. Each side of the H had 150 beds. Medical and surgical wards were on one side of the H, Gynaecology and Paediatrics wards on the other side. The Accident and Emergency mutated from the middle of the H bringing it conveniently closer to the dirt roadway, which ran round the outside of the hospital. That meant the ambulance then could stop outside the entrance and quickly transfer patients.

The front door leading from the roadway consisted of two halves, which opened internally to allow stretchers and wheelchairs through. When Christian arrived with Emmanuel the following morning, both doors were tied back. Patients who could not be accommodated inside were sitting in the dirt at the front door, wounds crudely bandaged. One patient, Christian noticed, had a stick tied roughly with string, acting as a stabilizer of the obvious fracture. Another elderly man next to him seemed to be asleep, but Christian could detect no respiratory effort and he wondered whether he was dead.

Emmanuel carefully stepped over the patients sitting on the ground before stopping at the old man. He bent down and felt for a carotid pulse. After a few seconds he stood up, looked at Christian and shook his head; the old man was dead. Inside the front doors were six beds. Corrugated iron beds were painted white to hide their age, each with thick, dark, red blood-stained plastic mattresses. There were no sheets on any of the beds which were surrounded by grey floor tiles. Dried blood created Dali like art on the floor tiles.

There were two patients on each bed; if there were two males, they were head to toe. One bed strained under the impact of two woman and two children. Under four of the six beds, Christian could see patients with intravenous lines, the bags of saline which ran through them attached to the window catch. Others patients sat on the floor in between the beds apparently uninjured and were therefore most probably family.

At the end of the ward was a small wooden table, at which a young man in a white, neatly pressed shirt sat writing vigorously. Four patients were crowded onto the bench next to him waiting to have their details recorded. Standing behind him in a white coat, with a stethoscope around his neck, was Dr. Theodore Nikita. Broad shouldered with shiny black leather shoes, he did not look up as they entered, continuing to scrutinize patient notes, while intermittently asking questions of the young man at the desk.

"Dr. Nikita." Emmanuel said, stopping next to him.

"Good morning, Doctor Sudani. As you can see, another busy night. Most of these came from across the border in the Congo after militia burnt down another village. Well, I should correct that - some of the ones who survived came here."

"I see there is one outside the front door who didn't survive."

"Yes, we couldn't deal with anymore at about 2 AM and I had to close the front doors. I found him this morning and he had no pulse. We are going to get him taken to the morgue."

Emmanuel nodded. "This is Doctor Christopher de Villiers. He has come to work with us for three months from Australia. You might remember me telling you about him and that he had some surgical experience that we could do with."

Christian stepped from behind Emmanuel to shake Doctor Nikita's hand. Before he could do so, Nikita turned from both of them reached up and took a white coat from a peg on the wall. Then he turned and thrust it in Christian's direction, avoiding a handshake.

"Let's see what you know and how useful it's going to be. They don't have malaria in Australia, do they?"

"Thank you," said Christian taking the white coat and slipping his stethoscope into the pocket. "We do have cases of malaria in Australia, but those are usually patients who have been to Southeast Asia. So there's a great awareness about its presentation in medical schools."

The greeting, or lack of greeting, Christian could understand. Doctor Nikita had been up most of the night, still had many patients to see, and did not need a medical tourist. He had always assumed that he would have to earn his stripes.

"I'll leave you two to it. Christian, you can find me in the office. Theodore will explain how surgery and the theatre work. I will see you later."

Theodore Nikita put down the folder that he had been reading and picked up a new folder from the desk. Without saying anything to Christian, he headed towards the patients on the right of the wooden desk. One woman got off the bed as he approached. The other woman who remained on the bed was partly covered by a bloodstained blanket. Her long black hair was matted with blood, her face partly hidden by the blanket, contorted in pain. In her right arm was an intravenous line, the bag of saline to which it was connected almost empty. Nikita bent over her and felt for her pulse before pushing the blanket down to listen to her chest with his stethoscope. He touched her abdomen and she winced and cried out several times.

"She needs to be first on the theatre list," he said, straightening up and talking to a sister in a tight ill-fitting uniform.

Christian was surprised that he had not removed the blanket from the lower half of the woman. The gentle touch on the abdomen, which caused a painful reaction, indicated peritoneal irritation to the extent that she required urgent surgery. Something was seriously wrong inside her abdomen.

"What do you know about recto-vaginal fistulae?" Nikita said without turning to face him.

"In the western world, they are usually the result of obstetric difficulties. Poorly applied forceps at the time of delivering the child can cause a tear in the uterus and the rectum resulting in a communication between the vagina and rectum resulting in faecal discharge out the vagina."

"How do you repair them?" Nikita continued, still not looking at Christian.

"If the bowel contents have discharged into the abdominal cavity, we would at the time of surgery repair the hole in the vagina and the bowel and leave the patient with a colostomy."

"Have you done any?"

"Not recto vagina fistulae repair, but obviously laparotomies and colostomies."

"You can assist me this morning then," Nikita said finally turning to look at Christian. The scrutinization from Nikita, Christian assumed, was a well-practiced look, designed not only to assess but to inform.

"This was not the result of obstetric accident. Congolese militia raped this young girl, repeatedly. Not content with that, they then brutalized. It would not be fair to say that she is lucky that she is alive but in the extreme inhumanity, which you encounter here, she is. If you're going to work here and make a contribution, you will need to be familiar with this kind of injury and how to deal with it."

Nikita pulled back the blanket far enough that Christian could see a large broken stick protruding from the young woman's vagina. Nikita watched while Christian tried to take in the gross brutality. The image repulsed him; it assailed every decent sense he had built up over twenty-seven years. Waves of disgust rushed at him. He could not imagine how any one human being could brutalize another in such a fashion. He could not control the shock that appeared on his face. He knew Nikita had wanted to shock him, to see whether he was capable of dealing with the brutality that he was going to encounter. Christian looked at the young woman whom he estimated to be almost the same age as he was, crying and grimacing with pain. She had no family beside her, no support group, no one to turn to. Christian reached down and pulled the blanket up before walking to the far side of the bed opposite Nikita. He sat down on the bed, took the young woman's hand, and as he did so, her eyes opened, fear and the pain openly transmitted. Christian bent over and, struggling to remember his high school French, said:

"Nous allons prendre soin de vous et de vous faire une meilleure," which he hoped translated into a reassurance that indicated she would be well looked after and recover. The girl squeezed his hand, and closed her eyes. "Tres bien, a good start, you may turn out to be better than the other five medical voyeurs that we've had here," Nikita said dismissively before he turned towards a middle-aged plumpish woman in a white coat, who had just walked through the front door.

131

"Matron Malasu, this patient needs an urgent laparotomy. Take her to theatre and arrange some large overalls for this tall Muzungu doctor."

Christian smiled in the direction of Matron Malasu. She looked over the top of her glasses, perched precariously at the end of her nose, and said,

"Come and see me, tall Muzungu Doctor, when you are finished with Dr Nikita."

Christian followed Doctor Nikita to the next bed. Lying on it with a distended belly was a twelve-year-old girl with long hair, a clump of which she was holding in her hand. Standing next to her, holding her other hand, was a woman in what Christian had come to recognize as traditional female dress: a blue-green floor-length skirt with a red sash draped over one shoulder hiding a T-shirt with a picture of Nelson Mandela. Her hair she had pushed up in a bun, decorated with beads and two pink ribbons. Christian assumed it was the mother of the young girl. Sitting under the bed were a young boy and girl playing with a wooden comb.

"She is a repeat offender," Nikita said standing at the foot of the bed and looking down at the young girl. "She swallows things which block the bowel. She has had two major operations already and now looks like she needs a third. Examine her and tell me that I am right. We will operate on her after the previous patient."

Christian looked at the young girl; to him she did not look dehydrated or distressed which was a good sign. He asked her to put out her tongue and noted that it was well hydrated, something that did not fit with a bowel obstruction. Surgery may not be as urgent as Doctor Nikita was thinking.

"Vous vomissez?"

"No, she hasn't been vomiting," the woman said who was standing next to her. "You can speak to her in English; she understands English well."

Christian smiled at the woman, and explained that he was going to examine the young girl's abdomen. He tapped her abdomen gently and noted that she did not react or wince in pain. That was another very good sign; it meant that the abdominal contents were not providing irritation. Taking his stethoscope, he placed it on her abdomen. There were low-pitched bowel sounds present, another good sign indicating that things were working relatively normally inside her abdomen. If there were no obstructions, she would not need surgery. He could feel Doctor

Nikita watching him intently, willing him to confirm the diagnosis of obstructed bowel and the need for surgery. As he moved his stethoscope to the lower abdomen, he noticed a large clump of hair the young girl was clasping in her hand.

"Does she eat her hair?" Christian asked the mother.

"For as long as we have known her, she has done that. We adopted her when she was five. Both her parents were killed in the Congo by Kariba's militia. "

Christian examined the young girl's head and found many clumps of hair missing. Those clumps could be matted together in her stomach causing the distension of her stomach. It would be, he thought, a better explanation of the symptoms. However if he suggested matted lumps of hair as a diagnosis, it would conflict with Doctor Nikita's management. Moreover, to contradict Nikita's diagnosis would possibly compromise the rest of his stay in Garanyi. If he was right, the condition possibly could be treated without surgery from what he had recently read.

"So you agree with my diagnosis?"

Christian looked up from his examination. He did not reply immediately but put his ear on the young girl's abdomen above the stomach. He then gently shook her side to side with Nikita watching.

"She has a succussion splash suggesting the outlet to her stomach is obstructed."

"Well she still needs surgery."

Christian stood up and looked around the ward. The article that he had read, just before coming to Africa, had been on exactly this girl's condition—gastric bezoars or balls of hair in the stomach. The study had found that the obstruction could be overcome by getting the patient to drink Coca-Cola. The very acid nature of the drink dissolved clumps of hair and overcame the obstruction in many cases. In the far corner of the ward was a half-empty bottle of Coca-Cola. If he could persuade Nikita, it may well save the young girl from a further operation. Christian looked at Nikita who was now standing at the foot of the bed, arms folded, his body language suggesting Christian not challenge him. Christian briefly wrestled with the thought of not replying, however something within him would not allow him to deny his findings. If it meant damning his visit on the first day, so be it.

"I think we might be able to get away without surgery," he said, straightening up from the side of the bed so that he could look Nikita straight in the eye.

"So you're disagreeing with my diagnosis."

"Yes. I think she's got a gastric bezoar and from what I recently read, that half-finished bottle of Coca-Cola over there may relieve her obstruction."

Nikita looked at Christian for thirty seconds before replying.

"If you're not right, don't come back tomorrow. Sister, give her that bottle of Coca-Cola and we will see her after surgery this evening."

The rest of the ward round became a bit of a blur for Christian. Out of the corner of his eye, he could see the young girl sipping away at the Coca-Cola. He felt certain his diagnosis was the correct one, but would that be enough Coca-Cola to dissolve the hair?

They saw another young boy who had water on his brain, and then a prisoner from the jail across the road who had been badly beaten by other prisoners, but whom Nikita didn't think needed surgery. A young man was the final patient they reviewed. He had fallen off his motorbike and badly lacerated his head. Nikita told Christian that his job would be to suture the laceration after the major surgery was finished. They would review the prisoner later in the day.

Christian followed Nikita out through a side door. A smooth concrete pathway led twenty metres to a faded pale green wooden door, which had 'Theatre' in large red letters painted on it. Several trolleys for transporting patients were parked on either side of the pathway. In their original state, they were white. Now they had faded to a dirty cream with parts of the enamel chipped off exposing bare metal, which was mostly stained by splashes of blood. There were no mattresses on any of the trolleys. Just literally, they had the bare essentials on which to transport the patients from accident and emergency down the hill to theatre.

Nikita knocked on the door and waited. Christian stopped behind him thinking about the young girl with the gastric bezoar. If he was right and it resolved the obstruction, he was not sure still how Nikita would feel. Would he view it as a challenge to his authority rather than a good clinical outcome for the patient?

"Good morning, Dr. Nikita", said the voice behind the door. "Come in. The anaesthetist is not yet here."

Christian followed Nikita into a tired, grey-tiled reception area. A small wooden desk in one corner had patient notes scattered over it. Huddled in the other corner was a large used oxygen cylinder waiting to be refilled. Next to the cylinder, was a small portable sterilizer, the door of which was open revealing several broken shelves and the charred remains of internal wiring. Two opaque windows of the type frequently seen in public toilets provided some filtered light.

"That is the changing room," Nikita said, pointing to the door which led off from the left-hand side of the room. "And the other door over there goes through into the theatre."

Christian looked in the direction of the changing room. There was no door to the changing room and it was no bigger than a large broom cupboard with half a dozen large hooks on the wall for clothes. He could see a collection of male and female clothes. As if reading his mind, Dr. Nikita looked at him and smiled before saying,

"Not quite what you're used to Australia, everyone in together?"

"No, we have separate changing rooms. To suggest that we all change together would produce a fierce outcry from the female staff. Although I do recall when I was working in South Africa, we had a very glamorous German medical student who insisted on changing in the male changing room. All the surgeons started their lists on time for the duration that she was there."

It was the first time that Christian had seen Nikita smile. Not a full smile, just the hint of one which adumbrated, he hoped, greater acceptance.

"To preserve dignity here, we have an agreement that the female staff get changed first, twenty minutes before an operation, and then the male staff, ten minutes before surgery."

In the corner of the changing room was a pile of neatly stacked blue surgical overalls. Christian found the large pair that Theresa had left for him, and put them on. Over shoes, he found next to the doorway. They were only one size and he struggled to get his size 12 shoes into them. The one on his left foot tore a little exposing his shoe and the dustiness of the outside world. He was searching for another to cover the torn defect when Nikita walked in.

"There are masks and hats in theatre," he said without looking up. "What do you think we use for anaesthesia here?"

"Ketamine intravenous as a 75 mg standard dose."

"You have done your reading. What do you need to look out for postoperatively?"

"Hallucinations. It's one of the most distressing things for the patients, I believe. Otherwise it would be the perfect anaesthetic drug for developing countries, particularly as it doesn't have a marked effect on respiration."

"Well, at least that's a better answer than the last German doctor we had here. He could only tell me that it was a date rape drug."

Nikita pulled on blue surgical overalls followed by surgical gumboots. Originally white, the boots had faded with constant washing to a yellow cream colour. There were pink outlines where blood had etched itself into the waterproofing, resistant to constant washing. In places, the stains coalesced to give the appearance of an unmarked map of Africa. On the heel of the boots, Nikita's name was written with ballpoint pen. Nikita pulled on his boots and stamped his feet into place before calling over his shoulder, in Christian's direction, as he walked through the door,

"Come with me. I'll introduce you to Sister Teresa. She has been the scrub nurse here for twelve years. She does minor surgery and likes to think that she could do major surgery. Despite that, she is invaluable and she will also be your assistant when you start your own surgical list."

Sister Teresa looked formidable, dressed in similar blue surgical overalls. Christian had always wondered about the original selection of surgical overalls for surgery; they always seem to be badly fitted and more suited to those who needed to crawl underneath cars. Sister Theresa's were no different. They were tight around her bottom and in front battling to constrain large breasts, which threatened to open all the buttons with any sudden movement. A mask hid most of her face, and a mass of tightly woven hair was held in place with a cloth cap with a Red Cross insignia emblazoned on the front. Her boots were similar to Nikita's, although much less bloodstained; they had two red hearts drawn in ballpoint pen over the toes of each boot which he could never imagine on Nikita's boots. Green surgical gloves completed the impression of an overweight sensitive plumber intent on clearing a drain rather than an experienced scrub nurse.

"Sister Teresa, this is Dr. Christian de Villiers from Australia who will be joining us for three months."

Sister Teresa looked up from the surgical instruments that she was arranging, briefly looked at Christian, and said,

"Make sure you wash your hands for two minutes."

Christian looked down in the direction where she had been looking, and saw a large red plastic bowl to wash his hands in and a single piece of soap; there was a well-used grey hand towel folded neatly alongside. The theatre itself was the size of a small bedroom. All of the walls were lined with grey enamelled tiles. From a central pivot in the ceiling was a large surgical light. On the operating table directly underneath lay the patient, the piece of wood protruding offensively from her vagina.

The abdomen and pelvic region had been liberally coated with the antiseptic betadine. Christian noted as he walked into theatre, that there was no ventilator, just a large oxygen bottle, similar to the one he had seen in the waiting room, connected via a mask to the patient. The operation would utilise only oxygen and ketamine. Christian knew from his reading that that would mean not only that there was not muscular paralysis, but the patient would be disconcertingly moving around on the table as they operated in a semi-conscious state, although unaware of pain.

"Would you take it out first or leave it in?" Nikita said as he washed his hands in the red plastic bowl.

"Leave it in until we have opened the abdomen so it's possible to trace any damage to uterus/ bladder and bowel."

Nikita dried his hands before walking through the open door into theatre. Christian noticed the anaesthetic person strapping the arms down as the patient started to move under the effects of ketamine. Nikita stood on the right side of the operating table. On the left-hand side were the instrument tray and the considerable size of Sister Teresa. There was little space for Christian. As he pulled his surgical gloves on, he wondered how he was going to be able to see into the abdomen to assist Dr. Nikita efficiently. He stood alongside Sister Teresa who provided him with no extra space. As Christian placed his hands on the part of the abdomen covered by the surgical drapes, he felt the patient move and heard the disconcerting moan that was part of the hallucinatory effect of the ketamine. Sister Teresa began talking very quickly in her national Kinyarwanda dialect as she handed Nikita the scalpel.

Nikita looked up at Sister Teresa, before he made a cut in the abdomen with the scalpel, and said in English,

"No, you are not the assistant. This one is different than the last medical tourist. He has clinical knowledge. Move down and let him in."

Christian moved opposite Nikita as Sister Teresa reluctantly made room for him. Nikita then made a lower midline incision as Christian placed his hands on the pelvis of the patient as she started to move on the table. Out of the corner of his eye, he glanced in the direction of the woman administering the oxygen and the ketamine. She had her head buried deep beneath the drapes listening to the woman's breathing and checking her pulse.

"Penetration of the uterus and the bladder, but no bowel. That was lucky."

Christian looked inside the abdomen. Considerable force had been used to drive the broom through both the uterus and the bladder, the roundness of the tip the only thing that had saved the more mobile bowel from being ripped apart. After placing sutures to mark the penetration through the uterus and bladder, Nikita pushed the broom out through the pelvis.

"No colostomy will be needed." Christian said as both a question and as personal relief for the patient.

"Despite western research suggesting that a colostomy is the surgical approach which works best, we clean the bowel and join it back together; no colostomy. In Africa colostomy bags fall off, and patients return with faeces discharging directly onto their abdomens. Close the abdomen with a nylon suture after I finish the washout."

Nikita finished the washout within the abdomen, slid his hand between the woman's thighs and removed totally the broken broom. Christian moved around to the patient's right-hand side and took the Rutherford forceps Teresa had handed to him. He placed them on the edge of the fascia and handed them to Teresa to hold. He could feel her eyes watching him, judging, unbelieving of his competence.

"Could I have the one nylon suture please, Teresa?"

Teresa took the suture from its packet, straightened the nylon out, and gave it to him on a needle holder.

"Thank you, Teresa," he said as he began suturing the layers of the abdomen while she retracted the skin. The abdominal wall closed neatly and he could sense Teresa's appreciation of his skill. It wasn't anything that she said, just a diminution in the hostility of her look. Christian decided to chance his arm, as there was something that he had wanted to know about the brutality of this particular woman.

"Teresa," he said as he placed the final suture in the abdominal fascia and looked over his mask, engaging her eyes.

"Yes, Doctor de Villiers."

"Why do you think these women get brutalized in this way?"

Teresa held his gaze during a long pause. He had the feeling that she was trying to make up her mind whether replying would concede acceptance of him on that side of the table as the surgeon.

"Raping a woman is not about sex. Whether it is in the western world or here, it is about power and degradation. It is a return to the animal kingdom where the male dominates, and the strongest male dominates in any way that he enjoys. Only here, there is not just the urge to dominate but to physically destroy and mutilate any who do not comply with their commands. It is unbridled evilness, in which one group tries to outdo the other. It is like the primeval blood thirst that drove the genocide. They are worse than animals and they know no one cares and no one will stop them as long as the world gets its share of resources."

Christian looked at Teresa over his mask. There were several things which had surprised him about her reply. Firstly, that she had replied, or considered him worthy of her reply. Secondly that it was not just a passionate disgust that she was evoking, although that was implicit in her explanation: it was more the identification and understanding of the root cause of such mephitic depravity.

"Why do these militia groups continue to exist? I thought the United Nations had a peacekeeping force to control them."

"Most foreigners think that. In addition, they think that this is still an ethnic conflict, which should therefore be left to the locals to sort out. That Kariba's militia are exiled Hutus and the group named M 23 are Tutsi from Rwanda who want to keep the exiled Hutu in the Congolese Bush."

"And clearly that's not the case," Christian said as he surveyed the table Teresa was using for his surgical instruments and sutures, looking for a suture he could close the skin with. The patient for the first time had stopped moving as he was suturing and Christian wondered for a minute whether she was still alive. He glanced towards the anaesthetic technician who was showing no alarm. Perhaps without the significant stimulation of protecting the abdomen and cutting through the tissue, the ketamine was in a dominant phase.

"Could I have that 30 nylon, Teresa?"

Teresa handed him the nylon on a needle holder after first straightening the memory of the nylon before continuing her explanation of the brutalities.

"Expecting that moronic bunch of United Nations peacekeepers to control this conflict is like using a fly swatter against elephant. The Congolese army is pathetic. In some instances they are almost as bad as the militia groups, except the militia groups are the better armed. This conflict does not have its roots in ethnic cleansing. It is about the rape of the Congo's resources and the corruption that goes with it. The militia exist in the Bush to facilitate the extraction and transport of rare minerals. They kill each other to preserve their supply lines to their minatory political masters. They kidnap and press-gang children to be killers, they rape and brutalize woman just so the political and commercial needs of the world are met."

Teresa looked away as she handed Christian the 30 nylon to close the skin. He wondered whether she felt that she had said too much.

"Thank you, Teresa. I can understand how deeply this affects you. Thank you for sharing that. I clearly have a long way to go to understand what is going on in this region."

Christian finished the final suture, picking up the individual sutures with the blunt end of the artery forceps to ensure that the continuous suture had even tension. As Teresa dabbed the incision with Betadine, she looked at him again over the top of the mask holding his gaze for a second. He felt it was a glance of approval and was about to say when could they talk again when he was aware of movement behind him. As Teresa placed a dressing on the incision, he looked over his shoulder to see Nikita standing in the doorway. For the first time that Christian could remember, he had a smile on his face.

"Your young girl in accident and emergency drank Coca-Cola and overcame her gastric obstruction. She has completely recovered and I have sent her home. I guess that means you are doing your own surgical list tomorrow morning. Teresa, you will be assisting me. We can get Sister Margarita for Christian."

Chapter 13

Leaving theatre, Christian discovered the changing room had no lights, or - no lights which worked. Faded, broken, yellow light shades hung from the ceiling, without any light bulbs. In the light, which filtered through the doorway from theatre, he could see his clothes hanging where he had left them on a hook in the corner. Walking into the changing room, he placed his dirty theatre clothes in a bin, and took his shirt off the hook. As he put his shirt on, he noticed that his trousers had their pockets turned inside out. There was nothing of value in his pockets, as Emanuel had reminded him before he had left that morning, to leave all things of value in his rucksack in the house. However, even the tissues that he carried had been taken from his pockets. The disappearance of the tissues, he thought, could be something of a metaphor for Africa: stark poverty providing a value for anything. He tried briefly to imagine their new owner, a child perhaps with a runny nose. As he disposed of his overshoes, the room suddenly became a bit darker. He looked up to see Teresa still in her theatre overalls standing in the doorway.

"The only place that has an active connection to the Internet at this time of night is the pharmacy. Theatre has one key. You might like to contact your family or girlfriend and you can then give the key to the matron of the medical ward, Elizabeth, who is a friend of mine," Teresa said, holding out the key.

Christian looked up and smiled. "That is very kind, Teresa. Thank you. It's about a week since I heard from anyone and I haven't purchased a local SIM card for my phone yet."

"It's the doorway just before you go into the hospital. There is a light inside the front door which works with the password *medicine*. And if you are purchasing a local SIM card, make sure you get MTN. They have the best coverage."

Christian closed the door to theatre, leaving Teresa to lock up. He looked up the pathway to Accident and Emergency and thought about going back to see how the young girl was doing. The African night had not yet descended but a few cicadas had begun their distinctive chirping and he could feel the gentle breeze blowing up from the lake. Wood smoke drifting across pathway reminded him that the patient's families were preparing supper in the ovens around the hospital. He decided to go to the pharmacy and quickly log on and reassure his mother. The door to the pharmacy was like an old wooden farm gate. Nevertheless the key turned easily in the lock, and the light worked when he flicked the switch just inside the door. Locking himself in as Teresa had suggested, he could see wooden shelves along each wall. Mostly they were empty, and a few were stacked with medications. There were no windows and towards the back, large cardboard cartons were piled on top of each other. It clearly doubled as a storeroom as well as a pharmacy.

The computer terminal was on a small table next to where the drugs were dispensed. He sat down and switched the computer on, searching for the Big Pond website and Australia. As his webmail came up, he could see there were three emails from Renata, the last of which he saw first, expressing concern that she had not heard from him in over a week. He hurriedly sent a reply telling her not to worry; he was safe and enjoying himself. There were others from friends in Adelaide, which he quickly scanned, and then one from Isabella. She was, she said, in London finishing a tropical medicine course and wondered whether she could join him on her way back to South Africa for a few weeks. He hesitated about replying, uncertain about how he really felt about seeing her in the current circumstances. It was now nearly ten years since they had seen each other. He knew that he needed to see her to resolve some of the issues, but he had doubts that they could do that in the midst of the Congo. Then the excitement of his first real sexual encounter and the chemistry that went with it flooded into his consciousness. He needed to know whether it was unique to Isabella or whether it was just a first love and he should move on. As he tried to deal with all those feelings, he read on and saw that as she had finished a six months tropical medicine course in London, she also therefore would be hugely useful in Africa. He quickly replied that he would need to ask Dr. Sudani, the superintendent of the hospital, and promised to get back to her as soon as possible. He quickly scanned to see whether there were any other emails that he should reply to before heading to the Sudani's for supper. There was one from Petrea with a warning; they were close to bringing a case against Kariba Offengowe, the leader of one of the notorious militia groups. The International Criminal Court were about to announce that they would offer a five million dollar reward and seek to extradite him for crimes against humanity. The publicity coming from the ICC seeking to prosecute and extradite him could result in Offengowe committing even more atrocities to demonstrate his complete disregard for their authority.

Christian switched off the computer, checking to make sure there had not been any immediate reply from Renata before locking up and heading back out into the African night. Outside the pharmacy door, the African night was rapidly approaching. The cicadas now in full song, no longer a hesitant susurrus .The wood smoke was now dominated by the smell of various foods cooking around the hospital. He was not certain from the smell what was being cooked, although assumed, given the number of live and dead chickens he had seen, chicken would be a good guess. Whatever it was, it made him realize that he was hungry. He dropped the key off with Margarita as instructed.

He walked quickly back up the concrete walkway and around Accident and Emergency unit to the dirt path, which led down to the main tar-sealed section. The flow of people heading towards the Congolese border had slowed to a trickle, one or two people every thirty or forty metres. In the still night air as he walked, he could hear them talking and could not help but wonder what they would be discussing.

Turning left into the street, which led down to the lake, he was quickly at the Sudani driveway. The light on the front porch had been left on for him; however he walked around to the back door as Chantal had warned him that she often didn't hear a knock at the front door. As he walked on the pumice stones pathway to the back door, Chantal must have heard his footsteps as she looked up from the kitchen bench, waved and then went to unlock the back door for him.

"Welcome back, Dr. Chris. I hear you had a very interesting and challenging first day, and managed to impress Dr. Nikita, which let me tell you is no small feat. So, well done; you must be hungry. I hope you're ready for a vegetarian curry."

143

"Sounds wonderful, Chantal. I am really hungry."

Christian followed Chantal into the kitchen where Emmanuel stood stirring one of the pots on the gas stove.

"Good evening, Christian," he called over her shoulder as he stirred the contents of the pot with a large wooden spoon. "I was telling Chantal that you managed to get a good pass mark from Dr. Nikita, which is not an easy thing to do on the first day. Well done. I'm sure you are going to impress everyone even more in the months ahead."

Christian sat at the small wooden table. Chantal had set out three place settings, each with a white placemat with the black outline of an African hut, the roofs of the huts made of fine grasses tightly arranged and glued for authenticity. People had been drawn standing around the huts cooking meals and drawing water. He wondered whether it was something that Chantel had made, as he had seen nothing quite like that previously in Rwanda. He picked up the placemat to see whether there was any inscription on the back.

"Made in Garanyi by Chantal Sudani," Chantal said, smiling as she saw Christian turning over the placemat. "If you like them, I'm sure we can organize for you to take some back when it's time for you to go."

"Now don't get him thinking about leaving. He has got lots of work to do in the next few months," said Emmanuel before Christian could reply.

"I had an email today from a friend who has just finished a six month course in tropical medicine in London. She wondered whether there would be anything that she could contribute for a month if she came to Garanyi on her way back to Cape Town."

"Those with African experience we always welcome. They know what to expect, and they have experience in the diseases that we need to treat. Tell her to send me her CV and we can then make a decision quite quickly."

The vegetarian curry was delicious. It reminded him greatly of the curries that he had liked so much when staying at Mike and Sian's in Cape Town. He wouldn't have guessed that it was possible to create something so flavoursome in the middle of Africa, given the different spices and ingredients that were required to normally achieve such a taste. For Christian, it was yet another interesting experience of life's contrasts in Central

Africa, such as omnipresent abject poverty, with small insinuations of a more luxurious western life.

"You have to get Emmanuel to show you the flourishing market in town. Just off the main street, just past the entrance to the mosque. You can get anything there from food and spices to instant repair of any clothing," Chantal said interrupting his thoughts and answering his own silent question on spices.

"I'm pretty certain he's going to be busy for the rest of the week once we get him started with surgical lists. I'm sure with Dr. Nikita's approval, we will soon have you also doing caesarean sections as well."

"I imagine we start each day in Accident and Emergency at 7:30 AM? I have also been meaning to ask if there is a big Muslim community here in Garanyi. That is the first mosque that I have seen in Rwanda."

"We have one very vocal Imam; unfortunately he has built up a considerable following, particularly after he became the town mayor. He is not the type who wants Sharia Law; in fact, he seems to be more moderate, but he has tried to gain influence over the hospital. And he always comes to the hospital meetings to suggest that there should also be a chapel in the hospital for Muslims to worship in. We have resisted up to this point, because it would cater only for very small minority, and we do not have the funds. Recently he has suggested that he has received a sizable grant from Saudi Arabia to construct a chapel. I think there are greater priorities than a chapel in our hospital, that that money could be used for. Starting with the theatre that you were in today having an anaesthetic ventilator and proper monitoring would be a much better use of those funds. And yes the day does start at 7:30 AM in Accident and Emergency."

Christian went to gather up the plates but was stopped by Chantal. She suggested that they all have coffee in the front room, leaving the dishes to Anna their house cleaner. Christian hadn't seen any sign of a house cleaner up until that point, but took his cue from Emmanuel who had pushed his chair back, and was headed for the front room.

"Come and have a look at this," he said as Christian sat next to him.

Christian looked at the magazine open on the table. It was the July edition of *Newsweek*. A quarter page photograph of the notorious Kariba Offengowe headlined a story: "Atrocities in the

Congo." There were further colour photographs of child soldiers and burnt villages.

"This is something that you should read if you're going to understand this part of the world. Most of the information in this article is correct, although they do not fully understand that he continues to exist because of the support of western and eastern governments, and corporations interested in the profits that can be made from this part of the world. But if you read it, we can talk some more and I can answer any questions that you may then have."

Christian picked up the magazine and noticed that it was complete with maps detailing mineral extraction and points of conflict. Chantal placed the coffee plunger and three cups on the table as he placed the magazine next to him. The aroma from the Rwandan coffee briefly took him back again to Mike and Sian's house in Cape Town. It was where he had first experienced the strong aroma and the smooth taste of Rwandan coffee. Emmanuel poured the coffee and Christian learnt that Chantal was a teacher at the local primary school. One of her passions was in developing African art, the placemats she told him being one of her classes' projects. The major problem was the lack of materials and often she would have to take the children outside for their art lesson and they would draw with a stick in the dirt. Then they would use the same stick to draw characters and scenes, leaving them to be admired by the other children at playtime.

Chapter 14

Christian and Emmanuel walked out through the front gate, going up the short alleyway to the main road. Despite the fact that it was 7:15 AM in the morning, there was already a constant stream of people, two to three deep in places, heading to and from the Congolese border. It was a reminder that Rwanda, with twelve million people, is the most densely populated country in Africa. The major export crops of coffee and tea provided work for some; however for the vast majority, there was no work. The Congo with its numerous mines and employment provided the potential to stave off starvation irrespective of the atavistic violence they had to endure.

"Here's hoping we don't get too many of those people back tonight in our emergency room or operating theatre." Emmanuel said as they walked on the opposite side of the road to the mainstream of people heading towards the Congolese border town of Goma.

"I found Sister Teresa an interesting person yesterday. But she's not going to be assisting me today?"

"She gave you the thumbs up as well, which is important since she runs theatre. She usually assists Dr. Nikita but they're both going to do an outpatient clinic at the orphanage that you passed on the way down here."

"I met an American girl who was due to work there for three months. She travelled on the bus with me from Kigali."

"We visit there every two weeks and I'm sure that we can arrange for you to go and do a clinic with Sister Teresa. I am sure Dr. Nikita would be delighted not have to travel up there. We do have some concerns as the orphanage is run by a Chinese foundation. While they provide buildings for the children, we are concerned about links to the Chinese government and corporate interests in the Congo. They have a manager Kim Yao, who gives the impression of caring deeply for the children. However, there have been some irregularities with some of the older boys disappearing from the orphanage. There are also unconfirmed reports of her having been seen near the Chinese mine at Bisie across the border."

"So theatre this morning without Dr. Nikita or Teresa, that will be a challenge I assume."

"Sister Margarita is very different to Teresa. She is much more outspoken for she has been with us for twenty-two years. Watch out or she will close the wound for you!"

"Thank you for the warning."

Christian found a similar crowd outside Accident and Emergency as the previous day. Fortunately, there did not appear to be anyone who needed to bypass Accident and Emergency and go directly to the morgue. As he walked in with Emanuel, the greeting was in contrast with the previous day. The three nurses all looked up from their patients and smiled, the young man filling in the paperwork behind the wooden desk greeted him with a 'good morning, Dr. Chris'. Emmanuel looked at him and winked.

"Word travels fast here if you cut the mustard," he said.

Christian knew from the previous day that theatre would start at 8 AM and he had half an hour to sort out who else needed to be operated on. There was one young man who had a badly lacerated scalp from a machete attack. The bandage that had been applied to his head was soaked in blood, which was now trickling down and into his left eye. He would need suturing earlier rather than later. Another young man had fallen off the back of a motorbike and had an open fracture of his forearm. A two-year-old boy whose mother had brought him in with an infected spider bite on his lower leg needed cleaning and debriding. Hopefully it wasn't a Buruli ulcer, which could consume the whole leg and need a skin graft. He told Sister Masuli he would start with the badly lacerated head and then reduce the fracture.

Sister Margarita was in the changing room when he arrived. He had forgotten that the protocol was to allow twenty minutes for the female staff to change. He should have arrived at 8:10 AM. Margarita had only the top half of her surgical overalls on. They were fortunately sufficiently large that they reached down to her mid-thigh. She was unconcerned by Christian's appearance, standing and looking at him before calmly reaching for the surgical trousers and pulling them on in front of him. Christian turned his back to provide some privacy and heard Margarita from behind him say.

"Good morning, Dr. Chris. I am obviously Sister Margarita. You can come in and get changed and don't feel embarrassed. I have brought up four boys, and I'm sure you're not worried about how an older granny like me looks half dressed!"

Christian smiled to himself. He still did not turn around, waiting until he heard Margarita walk through from the changing room into the theatre.

"You can turn around now," she said laughingly as she disappeared through the second door into theatre.

Christian took about five minutes to change. By the time that he had done his compulsory three-minute wash-up in the red bowl, the patient with the lacerated scalp was on the table, with an intravenous line running. They had the same anaesthetic woman from the day before. Teresa had quietly informed him that her name was Satilde.

"Good morning, Satilde," he said as he pulled on the surgical gloves, watching as she applied pressure to the dressing which was oozing considerable blood underneath her gloved hand.

"Teresa, let's have all the sutures ready before we take the bandage down. And I may need you to apply pressure to control the bleeding while I suture."

Christian quickly cleaned the area around the bandage with betadine and then with Teresa standing opposite, removed the bandage. Blood quickly spurted, staining his surgical top. Remember to bring glasses tomorrow, he reminded himself. While his tallness was a barrier to direct HIV contamination via the eye, it was not completely foolproof. As Teresa applied pressure, he reached across to her operating tray for a large suture. He ran it under the bleeding artery. The haemorrhage was controlled when he tied the knot in the suture. Teresa could remove her hand from the control point and he assessed the rest of the wound. It was 10 to 12 cm in length running just from above the right eye down to the left ear. He could see the protective covering of the bone. That did not appear to be breached. Christian cleaned the wound out with betadine before asking Margarita for a finer suture to close the wound. As he was just preparing to tie the final knot and wondering about the chance of infection, they heard a loud commotion coming from the small reception area. Margarita looked through the doorway to see if she could see who they belonged to as Christian started to take his gloves off. As he started to remove his surgical gown, John, the clerk from Accident and Emergency appeared in the doorway. Initially he stood there looking at Christian as if dumbstruck.

"What is it, John?" Christian said.

"Dr. Chris! Dr. Chris, you need to come quickly. A truck has driven through the front fence of the hospital and there are people trapped underneath." He tugged at Christian's surgical top trying to hurry him up.

"Margarita, finish bandaging the patient and I may need you and Satilde at the front of the hospital."

Christian did not worry about taking off his overshoes and he followed John up the concrete pathway. As they approached the rear of the hospital, he could already hear the crying and children screaming. At the front of the hospital, a large section of the fence was missing. Hundreds of people had already gathered around a large truck which had crashed through the fence and ended on its side inside the hospital grounds. Its brakes having failed coming down the hill, the driver had swerved to avoid the stream of people and had hit one of the large potholes. This had flipped the truck onto its side, trapping those walking past the hospital underneath.

There were a few plaintive cries coming from those who were still alive but trapped underneath. Christian knew if they were going to survive, it meant getting the truck off them as soon as possible. At the rear of the truck, he could see one young boy trapped; people were digging feverishly to try and free his leg. They were making little progress against the jagged volcanic rock.

"John, can we get as many men as possible on the side of the truck closest to the hospital?"

Christian thought it might be impossible, given the amount of screaming coming from those caught underneath the truck and their families. John, however, anticipated the problem and let out a loud and high-pitched whistle. There was a momentary pause in the wailing cacophony. Everyone for a second turned and looked at John.

"Nous aurons besoin de tous les hommes sur le côté du camion," John shouted.

The response was swift; fifteen or so of the men quickly assembled next to Christian and John.

"John, what we need to do is get them all along the side of the truck and we will try and lift it at once."

John quickly got the men into position and once everyone surrounding saw what Christian was trying to achieve, rapidly joined the men on the hospital side of the truck. With over thirty people in position, Christian shouted to John.

"On the count of three, John."

"Une Deux Trois." John shouted slowly and deliberately.

Slowly the truck started to rise. At twenty cm off the ground, it teetered and threatened to collapse again on all those underneath. As all thirty strained to hold the truck, Christian could see out of the corner of his eye a woman reached in and pulled out the young boy at the end of the truck. For what seemed like an age, the truck hovered above those underneath. Then more hands and shoulders rushed to help. John shouted again and with one extraordinary effort, the truck was righted.

Christian quickly surveyed the human carnage. In the back of his head he could hear Bolt's voice.

"Prioritize, Prioritize, Prioritize. Decide who is dead and who you can save quickly, otherwise those whom you might save will be your worst statistic," he used to shout incessantly at the medical students in the trauma unit.

Christian quickly worked his way amongst the bodies. He looked for fixed dilated pupils and checked for pulses. He heard a young boy crying and knew that he needed immediate evaluation in case he was bleeding. He looked up and saw Satilde standing next to John. He pointed her in the direction of the young boy and shouted that he would need intravenous fluids. Quickly he triaged the others who had been trapped. There were no other survivors, including the last woman and her newly born child; he counted six as dead. Despite the death and destruction, the stream of people going past the hospital had quickly re-established itself. Not many he noticed stopped to look at the dead bodies. Perhaps death was too common in Africa; it was never very far away, almost bromidic. Christian waved John over to where he was arranging the bodies.

"John, can you organize for them to be taken to the morgue?" He deliberately avoided using the term bodies as most still looked like they were sleeping; rigor mortis was hours away.

"Yes, Dr. Chris, and I think that young boy up there needs your help. He is in a lot of pain and his leg is broken."

Christian joined Satilde as Teresa arrived with intravenous fluids. Satilde quickly inserted an intravenous line and started the saline running. She had also brought a hypodermic syringe and a vial of morphine.

Christian, looking at the young boy, thought he was about twelve years of age. He was dressed in a long flowing white gown. The lower part of the gown was soaked in blood, but he could still detect the boy's right leg at an angle that indicated it was broken. He lifted the lower part of the boy's robe; it was a closed fracture—there were no bones breaking the skin edge. Repairing it wouldn't be difficult however, he needed to know whether there was any further injury. He tore the upper part of the boy's gown so that he could examine his chest and abdomen. The abdomen was distended, so possibly two broken ribs on the left-hand side were indicating his spleen was bleeding. He was going to need to go to theatre urgently.

"Satilde, Teresa, this young boy is going to need a laparotomy. I think he's bleeding internally."

"He's the son of the local Imam," said Satilde. "Someone will need to tell him."

"He will be up at the mosque preparing for afternoon prayers, which is probably where his son Yusuf was heading," Teresa said. "Mark, over there helping John, knows the Imam quite well. I'll get him to go and get him urgently."

"Satilde, if you take off your white coat, we can use that as a stretcher and get him to theatre."

Satilde quickly took off the white coat and laid it on the ground next to Yusuf. Christian instructed several people as to what he wanted as Satilde translated into French. He could see the growing pain on Yusuf's face as his abdomen was became increasingly distended. They would need to move him carefully so as not to cause greater pain with his fractured leg. They all then picked up a corner of the white coat as the crowd parted around them to let them through. Yusuf's eyes by this time were closed, and Christian noticed that his heart rate had increased. They did not have much time if they were going to save his life.

Teresa rejoined them after instructing Mark and proceeded ahead to clear a path through Accident and Emergency and down to the operating theatre.

Fortunately, the operating table was cleaned from the previous operation and the next surgical pack was ready to be opened. Time was of the essence getting into Yusuf's abdomen and normal sterility procedures had to take second place. Christian ripped open the surgical gown as he watched Teresa do the same. They did not wash their hands, quickly putting on surgical gloves as Satilde administered fentanyl and ketamine. At least for a short while Yusuf would have no pain.

Christian was about to make the incision in the abdomen with the scalpel when the theatre door loudly crashed open followed by raised voices in the reception room. Then he heard John's voice instructing the intruder that he could not go into theatre. As he looked over his left shoulder, he saw the ashen face of the local Imam, Yusuf's father.

"If I don't operate on him, he's going to die," Christian said over his shoulder.

"Let me pray for you both first."

"It will need to be a quick prayer."

"To Allah the Almighty God we belong, if it please Allah let his angel Izareel call his humble servant home and let the sun of the world continue to shine through Yusuf. May the wisdom of the prophet Mohammed guide the hands which care for him."

"And may the one true God look after us," whispered Teresa.

"Thank you," Christian said smiling inwardly at the thought that, despite the crisis, it was still necessary for each to assert their religious belief. Turning back to make the incision, he said, "We will need many large packs, Teresa."

Christian made the incision in the skin down to Yusuf's navel. As he did so, Satilde commented that Yusuf's blood pressure was going down. That meant the bleeding inside the abdomen was getting critical. He could see Satilde squeezing the saline bag to encourage extra fluids into Yusuf. It was critical that he stop the bleeding. As he opened the fascia over the abdomen, blood gushed out over the surgical drapes and down onto the floor. Teresa quickly placed a retractor into the abdomen and handed him five large surgical packs. That would get rid of some of the blood, but he needed to isolate the splenic artery to stop the flow of blood. Reaching inside Yusuf's abdomen, he could feel the lacerated spleen. Blindly he clamped the artery. The blood stopped welling up and, relieved, he put more packs in to dry up the blood. Satilde was busy putting up another litre of saline as he introduced another clamp, divided the archery, and removed the badly lacerated spleen.

"Don't dispose of that until we have checked with the Imam."

"I think that's only with death that the body parts have to be returned but you can ask them when we're finished."

Christian washed out the abdomen with the saline before closing the abdomen with a nylon suture. He still had the leg fracture to set but at least now, he could take his time. As Therese placed the dressing over the incision, he looked at Yusuf's right leg. There was no x-ray to be able to check the alignment, so it would have to be his best clinical judgment.

"Teresa, do we have any plaster of Paris to make a cast?"

"Yes, we do, but someone will have to get it from the pharmacy. I will see whether John is still out there."

Christian looked at the lower leg; the deviation was lateral approximately half way between the knee and the ankle. He put one hand on the inner side just around the knee and the other opposite to that just above the ankle. One short sharp push with his lower hand pulling down realigned the leg. Now all he needed was the plaster of Paris to keep it in position. He peeled off his gloves and gown and peered through the theatre door to the reception area where he could see the Imam. He was sitting on the ground in the corner looking anxiously towards the theatre door. Christian smiled reassuringly as he walked through and sat down next to him.

"It's going to be a difficult few days, but I think he will make it."

"Praise Allah. I am most grateful that he guided your hands."

"I had to remove his spleen, and although we can live without spleens in this environment, we going to need to see whether we can get him vaccinated. Do you know whether he has been vaccinated against TB or measles?"

"Yes, we run an education program through the mosque about vaccinations, and he has also had the smallpox vaccination."

"That's good because without his spleen he will have impaired immunity and would be very susceptible to certain infections. I have his spleen inside if you require it; I was not sure what the Islamic teaching was for body parts. Please call me Christian."

"Thank you. I am Mohammed Sharaf. It is only with death that we like to have all body parts together. However, it is not a critical teaching. I am so grateful that you have saved my son. I would insist that you come and visit us when he's better."

"That might be a week or two, but I'm sure that we will be seeing each other regularly as he recovers. We will take him up to the surgical ward in a few minutes. One thing that fascinates me is the fact that there is a mosque in this part of the world. I would not have thought that is possible given the fact that 95% of Rwanda is Christian."

"Christianity is the predominant religion, as you say, and you probably know central to its teaching is peace on earth and goodwill to men. In the genocide, that principle teaching was abandoned. Many people, in addition, were disillusioned with the God who did not protect them from such atrocities. Some of those former Christians now worship at the mosque."

"Does not the Quran say to cast terror into the hearts of the unbelievers? And doesn't it also exhort all true believers to fight and kill those who believe the Messiah was the son of Allah?"

"I see you've read the Quran. Not all Muslims are jihadists as not all Christians are extreme fundamentalists. Those who undertake jihad in Africa often blaspheme in the name of Allah. They are more interested in power and control than people's souls. Unfortunately because of those extremists in Somalia and Mali, sight is lost by many of the common ground that could be shared by Christian and Muslim, to make the world a better place."

"I'm not sure that you will convince me of that Mohammed, but we are all one on this planet together and so let's get your son well and I'm sure we will talk more. Now if you'll excuse me, I must go and check on your son and then need to go and identify those who have died and been taken to the morgue."

"Bless you, my son, and if there is anything that I can do in any way, please let me know. Could I give you my mobile number in case there is any problem with Yusuf?"

"Of course we will let you know. But I haven't had a chance to get a new SIM card for my mobile phone; however you would be more than welcome to have my number once I do."

155

"I will organize an MTM SIM card for you tomorrow; one of our brothers sells them in the market."

Chapter 15

"I hear you've made a friend of the local Imam," Emmanuel said as they sat down for Chantal's supper of spicy fried chicken.

"I'm not sure that I've made a friend. He was obviously very concerned that he was going to lose his son and therefore very grateful that we have managed to save him so far."

"Margarita and Satilde were very impressed at the way that you operated on Yusuf."

"He may need a blood transfusion. Is there any way that we could obtain four units of blood, Emmanuel?"

"It would take three days to organize from Rhuengeri."

"Fingers crossed then that there is no more bleeding."

Christian watched as Chantal used a pair of aluminium tongs to lift the fried chicken out of a large battered black iron pot. She would shake each piece to remove any excess oil, before putting it on a plate. Next to the pot was a new black flat frying pan, which Christian had not previously seen, gently simmering what appeared to be bananas. He thought it would be an interesting side dish with spicy fried chicken. He was a bit worried about the brownish colour until Chantal explained that what she was cooking was Plantain, a vegetable that looked like a banana. When they turned brownish black, they were sweeter and ready to eat. To the sizzling Plantain, Chantal then added a little vegetable oil, cayenne, and a pinch of ginger. The smell accelerated his hunger and reminded him that he had not eaten since breakfast that morning.

The combined plate of spicy chicken and plantain, when placed in front of him, almost overwhelmed his salivary glands; it was a shame that he was so hungry that it did not linger longer on his palate. With his last mouthful, Emmanuel interrupted his gustatory joy.

"There was an email from your friend Isabella today. Her curriculum vita is very impressive and we would be delighted to have her. We could certainly use her on the medical ward and medical outpatients, particularly in helping with the children who have malaria."

"When does she think she would be arriving?" Christian said, reluctantly wiping the last piece of chicken from his lips with the paper serviette.

"She said she would be flying into Kigali at the weekend and then come down the following week."

"Is there anywhere that you could suggest that she could stay?"

"I have already talked to Chantal and she is welcome to stay with us. I had thought we would send you up to do an outpatient clinic at the orphanage next week. There are three hundred children ranging in age from one to sixteen, so having two of you there would be very helpful. We usually send the ambulance with you in case there are any children who need to come back."

"That will be interesting; I should see whether I can contact Cindy the American friend that I met who is working there. I could possibly phone her if you have a number for the orphanage as the Imam is only getting me a SIM card tomorrow."

"Is he indeed? Hopefully not one which has Sharia style restrictions on it," Emmanuel said with a wry smile.

"Emmanuel, we need to try and work with everyone for the greater good of our people," Chantal quickly admonished.

"It's all very well saying we ought to all work together but there's a great difference between belief and practice with that religion. I can appreciate there is a commonality of belief, but the practice of their belief involves superimposing that belief system on everyone whether they are Muslims or not. Not only that, it often involves severe punishment, if there is not compliance. That is not freedom to worship; that is a loss of freedom if you do not worship in the prescribed way. In addition, trying to appeal to the community down here on the basis that Christianity had failed and allowed the genocide is disingenuous and shameful. "

"Lots of grounds for interaction there then," Chantal said challengingly, while standing up, collecting the dishes, and looking at Christian with her eyebrows raised.

Christian was about to reply when the phone rang in the front room and Emmanuel got up to answer it. He could hear

Emmanuel's voice from down the corridor, saying yes he is here, before he shortly reappeared standing in the doorway leading into the kitchen. He stood there for a second, smiling at Christian, before saying.

"It's for you, Christian, the young American woman that you are talking about from the orphanage. She would like to come down and visit next week, I think just before Isabella arrives, if you are lucky!"

Christian smiled at the gentle teasing and walked into the front room to pick up the old green phone. Cindy sounded genuinely excited to hear his voice. She quickly explained that she had been assigned a class of boys to teach, aged between seven and ten. That was all going well and there were seven other volunteers from different countries also helping. However, her voice changed somewhat after telling him that and she almost whispered into the phone. There was something that she was concerned about that she needed to discuss with him. Could she come down to visit and get his advice, as she did not want to discuss it on the phone? Christian suggested Sunday, as he was less likely to be operating or working in the hospital. He added that she could stay with Emmanuel and Chantal. Cindy then told him she would be coming by bus and would see him on Sunday before quickly putting the phone down.

He walked back into the kitchen wondering what it was that was troubling Cindy so much that she couldn't tell him on the phone. Emmanuel and Chantal were embracing each other as he walked in.

"It's not only the young who can do love." Emmanuel winked at Christian as he kissed Chantal on the cheek and put the ground coffee into the coffee pot. Christian laughed, delighting in the fact that they felt comfortable enough in his company to demonstrate their feelings. It also momentarily distracted him, from the concern that he had detected in Cindy's voice.

"Cindy would arrive tomorrow night if that's okay. She seems to be concerned about something that's happening at the orphanage."

"We will prepare the spare room," Chantal said.

"I will be interested also to hear what Cindy has to say as there have been some concerns about what goes on at that orphanage."

After Chantal's meal and the long day operating, Christian slept soundly. The next morning when he did his ward round, he found Mohammed sitting next to Yusuf's bed quietly praying for him. Besides looking a little bit pale, Yusuf's observations were all normal. Christian waited until Mohammed had finished praying and then informed him that he was happy with Yusuf's progress. He had decided to heed Emmanuel's advice about becoming too familiar with Mohammed, although he could sense that Mohammed found his new detachment difficult to understand. On Sunday morning, he asked Yusuf whether he had passed any wind out his bottom. When he nodded and smiled, Christian put his stethoscope on his abdomen. There were early bowel sounds; Mohammed would be delighted as they could start getting Yusuf something to drink. As Christian stood up and smiled, Mohammed sensed the good news.

"Praise Allah, my prayers have been answered," he said with a broad smile without waiting for Christian to speak.

"They may well have been, but this is a normal part of bowel recovery after an operation," Christian said, not wanting to ascribe to the supernatural something that was natural.

"Would you come and have a meal with us and allow my family to pray for you?"

"Thank you, but buying me a SIM card with so much credit on it is more than enough."

"Does prayer frighten you, or is it just that you don't like Muslim prayer?"

"Neither actually," Christian said, a little annoyed at the implication of bias in both directions. "I have my own beliefs and would prefer to keep them personal."

"I'm sorry. I hope I didn't offend you. That was not my intention at all. I would like you to meet my family and my wives. They are all extremely grateful for your skill; both my wives are very good cooks. Perhaps you could also come to our malnutrition clinic and then stay for lunch afterwards."

In the two weeks that he had been at Garanyi, he had not heard about any malnutrition clinic outside of the hospital. There was obviously a great need given the number of children that he had seen with pot bellies and a reddish tinge to their hair suggesting severe protein deficiency; malnutrition was endemic. He wondered why Emmanuel had not mentioned the clinic, and where the medical and dietary advice was coming from in the clinic that Mohammed had established.

"If it's not on a day that I'm operating next week, I will come."

"I will check with Teresa. Her brother now shares our beliefs, and he can coordinate a time with you."

Christian could feel that he was irritated; he was not certain he had not been manipulated into the decision. His response was a half-smile, which he hoped conveyed to Mohammed that he would visit out of professional interest. That was the truth, but there was part of him that was still curious about a religion, opposed openly by so many, which not only existed but also was apparently thriving.

Having finished his ward round, he went and found the key to the pharmacy on the medical ward. Checking through his emails, he found one from Isabella confirming that she was arriving and saying that she was very excited and looking forward to catching up with him again. She had been in touch with his mother, Renata, who had asked her to buy a telephoto lens for his camera, as Renata's birthday present to him. It was to be a surprise, but Isabella felt that she needed to be certain about what lens would fit his Canon camera, given how expensive it was. Christian quickly replied that he was also looking forward to seeing her and the telephoto lens suggested by his mother was the correct one.

The next email from Petrea caught his attention. She said she missed him and then went on to precisely explain the five million dollar bounty that had been placed on the head of Kariba Offengowhe. It was payable if he was captured or if he was shot. DNA evidence was required if he was shot. No one knew who was providing the bounty but it was suspected that a corporate conglomerate associated with the Chinese government was responsible. The removal of Kariba would allow access for groups, such as the Chinese, who were currently frozen out of the region. Information from the CIA indicated that the Chinese government was actively supporting Bosco the Butcher with arms in an attempt to control a major portion of the world's supplies of tin, tungsten, and tantalum. 'Be very careful' she ended her e-mail. The removal of Kariba would not only change the dynamics of supply and possibly freeze out the West, but may also provide a power vacuum in which the smaller militias may seek to take over, causing an increase in the number of atrocities. Since the

Congo was one of the few places which supplied tantalum, used in all mobile phones, the world spot price would go through the roof. The PS at the end of her e-mail said that she thought he should leave, and to please destroy the email after reading it. He should not reply to her until he was out of Africa. Text messages to her personal number should be his avenue of communication.

Christian sat and looked at the email. He knew that Petrea was taking a huge risk by sending it to him. She had possibly breached protocol at the ICC by revealing such sensitive information. Ignoring such advice would be at his own peril. He would text her on the personal number that she had given him, to say that he had received the message, and thank her for the warning. He looked at his phone and realised his stored addresses had not been transferred with the new MTN SIM card. He needed another phone similar to his bluetooth to add the addresses to his new SIM card. He hoped Cindy had a similar phone.

The least he could do in the interim, he thought, would be to stop Isabella coming next week. He quickly dashed off an email to Isabella suggesting that he had received information that it was becoming more dangerous to be in Garanyi and he suggested that she not come. Her reply was instantaneous. If you are there, I am coming. I am a big girl now and capable of looking after myself. Look forward to seeing you next week with your birthday present!

He switched off the computer, locked up the pharmacy, and returned the key to Elizabeth. He had subsequently learned that Elizabeth did not speak much French or English. However, the wide welcoming smile that she gave him each time he went to the ward did not need translation. As he walked out the front of the medical ward, he could see right along the front of the hospital and down to shores of the lake. He joined the constant stream of people heading to the Congolese border before peeling off, and walking the short distance to the Sudani's. Chantal had left a note explaining that they were out at a community meeting and that he was to help himself to the left-over ratatouille.

As the mouth-watering smells from heated ratatouille started to wander through the kitchen, he wondered briefly whether he should bring forward his departure. Petrea would not have sent such a warning unless she was seriously concerned. He then remembered that Emmanuel had mentioned a Chinese manager at the orphanage where Cindy was working. He would ask Cindy what she knew when she arrived, which may help him make a decision.

The next morning, he slipped out quietly while Emmanuel and Chantal slept. He wanted to briefly check on Yusuf before he met the bus and Cindy. When he walked into the ward, Yusuf was sitting up, smiling, and drinking soup that his family had brought in for him. Two women sat next to him, both wearing full veils so that he could not see their eyes. They both stared at the ground as he checked Yusuf's chart. Christian assumed they must be Mohammed's wives. Women venerated as mothers he could understand, but restricted in areas where their talents may well have contributed to improving the world, made it more difficult visualising the common ground, about which Mohammed had previously spoken.

The bus overloaded with people and animals was strangely on time. Bags of belongings hanging precariously from the roof along with cane baskets with live chickens squawking incessantly reminded him that in life some things never changed. Word obviously had gotten around about the disaster from the week before as he heard the bus engage lower gear and begin to brake from close to the top of the hill. The braking sound was not very reassuring. It was the metal on metal sound he had come to associate with absent brake pads. The slow speed of the bus was reassuring and after avoiding several potholes, it stopped in front of the hospital. He quickly scanned the bus and could see that Cindy had positioned herself at the back. She waved out the open window he had exited a few weeks previously. John, he could see, was not the driver; perhaps John had been promoted to assistant pastor. As he walked to the back window, Cindy passed out her backpack and then quickly followed.

"Hello, hello, how nice to see you, Christian," she said, giving him a big hug as she landed on the ground next to her backpack.

"It's great to see you too. I didn't realize it would be this soon."

"So this is the hospital that you've been doing all the great work at," Cindy said as she stood surveying the hospital.

"I'm not sure about great work. We have been very busy what with refugees from the Congo and a recent tanker disaster."

"Yes, we had heard about the tanker rolling over in front of the hospital, and the new tall Muzungu doctor saving the local Imam's son. Good news travels fast in these areas."

"It has been a fascinating few weeks and I can't wait to talk to you and find out what's been going on at your end. Follow me," Christian said picking up her rucksack. "The Sudani's is about a fifteen minute walk from here."

"Only if you promise to show me the hospital later."

"I will show you the hospital, but I'm interested to hear about the orphanage as well."

Cindy put her arm through his and on the walk down the hill, told him how well the orphanage was run. Three hundred children not only had schooling but three meals a day. Everything was regularly cleaned and the children beautifully dressed. The orphanage was even looking at supplying some of the older children with laptops that they could wind up, after a significant donation from Zhanghou, the large computer and mobile phone manufacturer in China. The Chinese woman that managed it, Kim Yao, was so efficient, that at times Cindy felt she would not have been out of place in the military.

Christian thought about the last remark, in the context of Petrea's email, and was about to ask Cindy about her concerns with the orphanage, when they arrived at the Sudani's house.

"What an amazing house. It's quite unlike anything that I have seen so far in Rwanda," Cindy said.

"Yes. It was apparently designed by a German or Dutch surgeon who was due to live and work here, and then for some reason did not arrive after the house was built."

"You will find that there is a real shower down the hallway with hot water. I'll put some of the best coffee on that you have ever tasted and you can tell me more about the orphanage and your concerns."

"Sounds good to me. I'll have a quick shower."

Christian made his way back to the kitchen thinking how infectious her enthusiasm was and how naturally she just put her arm through his as they walked along. The hand grinder for coffee beans, bolted to the sink, had a wooden funnel for the coffee beans and a matching wooden base, on which was a small hand-carved picture of Lake Kivu. As he ground the beans, he remembered it was not the caffeine in coffee that produced the stimulatory effect; it was rather the smell of the freshly ground coffee beans. He inhaled the aroma of the coffee beans before he put them into the coffee pot; their smell was delightful, although he could detect little stimulation. Within a few minutes, the coffee pot was percolating its dark rich aroma throughout the kitchen. As it started to whistle, Cindy appeared in the doorway, a towel wrapped around her wet hair.

"Perfect timing," he said turning towards her. "Black, white, sugar or no sugar?"

"Black with no sugar would be great, thank you."

By the second cup of coffee, Christian realised that they had found out an enormous amount about each other. Cindy had grown up in Wisconsin on a small farm with two older brothers and one younger sister. She described it as a tightly-knit family, and she had been expected to do her fair share of the chores. There was no distinction made just because she was a girl. As Cindy talked, he could not help but feel a small degree of envy for her family life—such a distinct contrast to his own as the only child of a single parent. It was so easy chatting to Cindy that he had almost forgotten that he wanted to ask her about any strange happenings at the orphanage. When he finally did ask her, she looked at him rather quizzically and said,

"It's more of a feeling that something is not quite right there. There are many meetings at the orphanage but the vehicles that bring people to them have darkened windscreens. You would not know who was inside. Kim Yao, the manager, tells us they are Chinese benefactors wanting to see how their Yuan or dollar is spent. There are special quarters for them, which are separate and completely secure from the orphanage. However, after one of these meetings, four or five of the older boys disappeared overnight from the orphanage. When I asked one of the staff about it, she had said there were entrepreneurs at the meeting who had offered the boys good jobs and free lodging so that they had gone with them when they left. That all seems to be a bit strange as one of the boys, Michelangelo, I knew quite well. He was very proficient in English and French, exceptionally gifted in mathematics and I know he wanted to go to University. I can't imagine him accepting a job without a future."

"Do you think the boys are being traded or sold as cheap labour?"

"I don't know, just that I don't have a good feeling about whatever is going on. Then the same staff member came to me a few hours later and said I should stop asking questions, that I was there to teach and they were there to make the orphanage the success that it was."

"Are you allowed to go anywhere near the quarters where these guests stay?"

"No. As I said, there is a separate locked compound, and when guests arrive, they drive through the locked gates and park at a separate entrance to the quarters, which you can't see from the orphanage."

"Well, perhaps when we come up the week after next, we should have a look around."

"I'm not sure that you would be allowed to."

"I wasn't thinking particularly about asking for permission," Christian said with a wry smile.

"And here I was thinking that you were a very straight-laced doctor whom I could rely upon for an ethical approach to the problem! Although I do like the fact that there is a little bit of rebellion mixed in with all the straight-laced doctoring stuff."

While Christian wondered how to respond to the coquettish look that accompanied Cindy's last statement, the front door opened and Emmanuel and Chantal called hello down the hallway.

"Would you be happy discussing your concerns with Emmanuel and Chantal?"

"I think let's leave it until you've been up to visit so we know that it's not all in my imagination."

Chapter 16

The phone rang in Kim's Yao's office, the green light indicating it was Lee Kaiping from the embassy in Kigali. The meeting at the orphanage had gone well, Kim thought; Lee would be ringing with further instructions. There were never any congratulations; lack of condemnation was the highest form of Chinese political praise. Kim picked up the phone, listening as she heard the embassy secretary quietly say,

"Kim Yao is on the phone sir."

"You have failed in your responsibilities." Lee Kaiping screamed down the phone.

"The party doesn't tolerate incompetence or failure. There is an iPad missing from the secure briefcase. I told Beijing not to send me another stupid woman. You have one hour to find it and call the embassy or you get sent home."

"One of the Rwandan businessmen at the meeting might have mistakenly taken it," Kim interjected.

"Don't insult my intelligence. Our security people scan all guests before they get back in their cars. Either it is in the room and you have missed it or someone else has taken it. You now have fifty-five minutes to find it."

Kim listened as the line went dead. The information on that iPad in the wrong hands could lead to an international incident. It would embarrass both the Rwandan and Chinese governments. In addition, she would be sent home in disgrace.

Kim hated the thought that she might have failed. Her whole life in China had been shaped by the fact that she had born a woman. Being a female in China made being a success almost impossible, unless subservience was regarded as the highest achievement. Her father had been desperate for a boy to help him work in their fields around Laoshan. He had never attempted to hide his disappointment that she was, he said, an inferior girl.

When she was five years of age, she tried to help him in the fields; however, he had just looked her up and down disparagingly and told her to go home. At six years of age, her cousin had informed her that her father had tried to give her up for adoption, but no one had wanted her because she was such a puny girl. Kim remembered that she cried herself to sleep for over a year and then resolved that she had to prove that she was better than any male. After school, she went for walks through the village. Initially she would walk to the hills and then take her sandals in one hand and tuck her dress into her underwear so that she could run up the hills. In a glade, close to the top of one of the hills, surrounded by chinaberry and tallow trees, she would do sit-ups and push-ups until she started shaking from near exhaustion. Some days she would just lie on the ground wishing that she had been born a boy, oblivious of the beauty of the red and gold tallow trees and the chinaberry dropping its yellow seeds around her.

Exercising as hard as she did meant that she was always hungry. However, there was never any spare food at home. If there were any leftovers, they went to her brothers because they were working in the fields with her father. When she started falling asleep at school, she was told that part of her punishment was that she had to clean the kitchen after school. As she cleaned, she ate the leftovers that were destined for the local piggery. After about six months, she felt strong enough to compete with the boys. Initially, most boys laughed at her and waved her away. However she waited, biding her time, and one day when the boys lined up for a running race after school, she quickly joined them and beat them all. After that, none of the boys talked to her and she was banned from being anywhere near them or competing against them.

In gymnastics, she found she could use her newly developed strength, representing Shazikou prefecture in floor exercises, but it produced no recognition from her father. It seemed the more she tried to prove that she was better than any male, the more she distanced herself not only from her father, but also from her mother. No one seemed to want a girl who was better than the boys in their village.

Yang Tao was the only family male who took an interest in her. He was his father's brother by about ten years and offered her a job packing shoes in his factory. Kim initially was filling in for a sick worker during her school holidays. She had to pack shoes into boxes as they came off the production line, but after a week she saw a more efficient way of packaging. When she told her uncle, he was impressed, and promoted her to work in his office after school and at weekends. She had started to feel valued for the first time in her life, then one night when everyone had gone home, he forced her to lie on his desk, tore her underwear off and raped her. A half empty jar of ginseng facial cream was the only sop to losing her virginity at fifteen years of age.

Yang, once he had finished grunting and thrusting, pushed her off the table and said not to tell anyone; otherwise he would have her sent to a labour camp for spreading false rumours. Kim knew about the labour camps. The police could lock people up in a labour camp for four years without trial. Her auntie's daughter was raped when she was ten. Auntie Tang Won tried to prosecute the man, and was locked up for a whole year for malicious gossip. The rapist was a friend of the town prosecutor and a prominent member of the local Communist Party. She also knew that one woman in the village, who complained to the Communist Party officials in Shazikou about the local mayor demanding sexual favours, had acid thrown in her face and was blinded. Her uncle was the chairman of the local Communist Party.

She left Yang's office, hating that she had something of him in her. She walked to her glade in the hills and stayed until it was dark. Looking up through the branches of the tallow trees at the stars in the sky, she felt so alone. The stars were twinkling as though there was something to celebrate; they did not understand her pain and the disgust she felt. The universe did not care. She did not want to cry: the anger was too deep for tears, the insult too brutal. Then the tears flowed and slowly soaked the grass between her feet.

After many hours, she finally walked slowly home thinking that ending her life was an option, but concerned there could be dozens of Uncle Yangs waiting on the other side. She knew too little of the afterlife, and only knew she would never dream of being a boy again. Never would she lie in her little glade in the woods wishing she could change. Boys and men were disgusting creatures, lower on the evolutionary scale than rats with the plague. The only solution for a woman in China was to be stronger and more powerful and then determine her own destiny.

It was after midnight when she unlocked the back door and judging by the quietness, everyone was asleep. She was desperate for a shower to try to wash away Uncle Yang's stains; however, she knew her father would shout at her for waking everyone up. She crawled into her bed and pulled the blanket over her head trying to ignore the stench of Yang. She could not sleep, for every time she closed her eyes, Uncle Yang was in front of her, grunting and thrusting. In the morning she tried to tell her father as he brought the wood in for the fire in the desperate hope that he might show that he cared. He didn't say a word, looking at her and shrugging his shoulders as if to say what could he do.

The arrival in Laoshan of recruiters, a month later, from the Ministry of Defence and the People's Liberation Army, offering scholarships to Shanghai University, was a way out of her personal hell. The entrance exam she passed with flying colours and was told she would study information technology, not mathematics, which she always thought was her best subject. She would have studied anything to get away from her family, her uncle, and the depravity of the village. That she was told that she would have to spy on fellow students mattered little; it was a chance for freedom.

Shanghai University was a revelation and a refuge. The university buildings were surrounded on all sides by large green poplar trees which provided a foliage umbrella, where she would often retreat and sit under. Some days she would just watch people walking past, noting how different they were to those in her village, neatly dressed and mostly they looked happy. She was amazed at the number of bicycles and that often she would see a man on a bicycle with children in a little basket seat behind him. In the village, men never cared for the child—that was a woman's job.

She had her own small room in an apartment half a kilometre from the main campus on Shangda road. The apartment was like all the other student apartments, a bedroom with a small kitchen and no bathroom. Twenty students shared a communal bathroom at the end of the building. There was no door to the kitchen and all the rooms were painted a grey white. A small collapsible wooden table next to her bed sat under a small window and had a wooden chair. When she studied, she could look out of towards her favourite poplar trees and see other students walking below. The smallness of her apartment did not really concern her. It was the first place that she had lived in where she could lock the door. She felt safe for the first time since Yang raped her. She became friends with some of the other students who lived in the other apartments on her floor. Their parents were mostly Communist Party workers in Shanghai and worked in the shipyards. To them, though, it did not matter that she was from a small village; they included her in most of the things that they did.

Kim knew that she was being observed; she would often look out of her second-floor window and see someone in a PLA uniform sitting under one of many poplar trees. He would occasionally glance up at her window. That same person she would often see sitting in the furthest corner of a sushi restaurant, where she went with her new friends. None of her friends seemed to notice, or if they did, no one talked about it. In a strange way, Kim thought it was quite nice to have someone who was interested in what she was doing and approved of her. She felt someone was at last looking out for her.

Her contact in the People's Liberation Army, Ruan Diu, initially visited her every two weeks. He encouraged her to go to any meetings on campus, a minimum of four a month, and report anything contrary to what the party expected. What the party expected, Ruan initially explained, was loyalty without criticism. He gave her a dossier on party policy and said that she was to read it and be familiar with it. He also gave her a list of students and their photographs to try to befriend. The first case he wanted her to report on was a German student. Kim was to film secretly all those attending. She was be given glasses to wear to the meeting which contained tiny cameras, and which broadcasted to a PLA truck which would be parked outside the meeting.

Kim had heard about the German student; her parents were diplomats and she was trying to improve her Mandarin. She had invited people to her parents' home for an evening of German music. The PLA knew she was doing research on the one child debate and suspected she wanted to interview students.

A small quartet playing German music greeted Kim as she was ushered into a large room at the back of the German Embassy. Approximately twenty students were already there listening to the music and enjoying European food. Heidi walked over as Kim entered and introduced herself in very good

Mandarin. She told Kim that she was interested in getting to know more about China, as she wanted to come and work in Shanghai. Kim listened as Heidi also chatted about Germany and its freedoms, wondering to herself why a woman with so much potential freedom would want to come and live in a country which was so limited for a woman. As she listened to Heidi talk, she wondered whether the PLA, might have been misinformed about her intentions. Then the quartet stop playing and Heidi took over the microphone. She explained that she was doing research and that she would really appreciate everyone's assistance. They were to put up their hand if they believed they should be allowed to have more than one child in China. Kim looked around as the room went silent. No one put up his or her hand. Heidi asked the question again and still the same response, no hands were raised, and now was an embarrassing silence. Kim realised that the students knew someone would be watching and listening. Kim looked around the group, and there were at least three who had glasses similar to hers. The quartet started to play which broke the silence, but by that time, most of the students had started to make their way out through the back door

Kim's first assignment pleased Ruan. The pictures were clear; they could hear the conversations and Kim had moved around to allow them to identify all the students at the meeting. The German student would not have her visa renewed at the end of term, he told her. Kim was assigned to another room in the apartment, two levels up, which had a built-in shower.

In her second year, Kim was top of her class in computer science and was invited to attend the People's Liberation Army unit on the outskirts of Shanghai on Saturday mornings. The Ministry of Defence building was a large grey twelve story building. The fourth floor contained one of the biggest and fastest computers in the world. Ruan wanted her to be part of the team writing encrypted programmes. Her office was a desk with six others, each with the latest computer. She was given unfettered Internet access that allowed her go to websites, otherwise routinely blocked by the Communist Party. She knew that any site that she visited would be monitored. Nevertheless, it was privilege almost unheard of except for the senior Communist party members. She felt trusted and valued.

On most Saturday mornings there were six students. She was the only female, supervised by one of the professors of computer forensics at the University, Jin Sanwong or Professor Jin as he insisted everyone called him. Interestingly, he did not dress in a PLA uniform, which meant he had a very high standing in the party. Kim wondered whether he modelled himself on the Macintosh founder Steve Jobs, as he only ever seemed to wear black leather shoes, a black shirt, and black trousers. The only contrasting colour was his silver hair and rimless spectacles.

"Good morning," Jin said on their first Saturday morning. "I would like to welcome you all here and let you know what a privilege it is for you to have been selected. You have one of the highest security clearances and the chance to further all of your careers within the party. We will start with small tasks to challenge you as a group."

Kim noticed another anomaly; Jin did not use party language for everything he spoke about.

"Analyse, analyse, analyse. Don't use words when you can use an equation, equations cannot be misinterpreted in any language."

Initially Jin considered Kim the token girl in the group and of limited value. He ignored her and concentrated on the five boys. When she spoke to Ruan about her exclusion, Ruan had told her not to worry. He did that with everyone until they proved themselves, and it had nothing to do with her being a woman. Kim was not convinced, even though there seemed to be more acceptance of woman in Shanghai. Jin seemed to be more like those men from her village. She did not feel comfortable next to him.

To begin with, the tasks were small, learning how to hack into websites of not-for-profit organisations around the world. Kim learned quickly as she ran variations of people's names, birthdates, and high schools as simple algorithms. It really was not much of a challenge. To impress Jin, she accessed the bank account of one of the biggest not-for-profit groups, Give to the World. When she showed Jin, he said disdainfully,

"China has enough money. With information you are far wealthier."

Kim quickly realised that the rest of the students were the best in their disciplines and small tasks like hacking into websites proved little challenge to any of them either. One Saturday morning while waiting for Jin, they were talking about their new found skills and that there had to be a greater goal. Their speculation stopped when Jin arrived and gathered them together saying he wanted to introduce them to someone important.

"Good morning," he began in his nasally voice. "You have done well in the tasks that we set you. Then, we knew you would because not only were you the brightest in your class, but you all are competitive. You have the instincts and the loyalty to the party that we need for your next task. We also wanted to make certain that you could work together as a group. That is going to be important in your next assignment. I am going to introduce you to someone who is going to challenge you."

Kim looked around the room, but there was no one else present for Jin to introduce.

"Come with me," Jin said while walking out through the door and heading back up the corridor. Kim hurried to catch up and saw in the distance three PLA security members standing in front of a red door. Kim had not seen anyone pass through that door previously. Jin stopped in front of the three PLA security officers and showed his pass. Jin then turned and the security officers opened one of the two red doors and Jin led them inside. They filed in and in the middle of the room was the largest computer that Kim had ever seen. As they stood looking at banks of computer terminals and screens, Jin did not speak, allowing them to take in its impressive size and computing power. After they had taken in impressive array of computer hardware, he turned to them and said,

"This is Hei Long. You will not discuss Hei Long or Black Dragon with anyone. You will not be allowed to tell anyone that you have seen Black Dragon and if there is a suspicion that you have, you will spend five years in a labour camp."

Jin then went on to explain that Black Dragon was the latest in artificial intelligence, and they were to use it as part of China's intelligence gathering from foreign universities and countries. Around the central module were individual computer screens, each with a seat.

"Select a screen," Jin said. "You will see a task on the screen. You will not leave her until your task has been completed. There is a toilet at the far end, and food will be brought at regular intervals."

The first task on Kim's screen was to access the physics database at the University of Berkeley in California. The university supplied information to the National Aeronautical and

Space Programme, calculating solid and liquid fuel ignition times, information useful in China's space programme. Within four hours, Kim had found the password by running an algorithm based on the University's history. She was the first to complete her task and knew that Jin would be impressed. She put her hand up and Jin came over and stood behind her screen. He said little as he stood behind her screen. They waited half an hour and then accessed the database through the personal computer of the university's physics professor. That way Jin explained, they would leave no electronic footprint. Kim was disappointed that Jin had one of the others hack into the professor's computer. She knew she could have done it faster. However, Jin offered faint praise when he used Kim's algorithm and was able to access the National Aeronautical and Space Programme database. He quickly extracted the firing sequence for the Saturn rockets.

"Our North Korean friends should be interested in that. Now let us all go and celebrate at Ma Dongs Sushi kitchen," Professor Jin shouted.

Jin had sat next to Kim, and ordered the first course, ginger chicken and coconut soup. As that arrived in small dark blue bowls, he reached over and touched on her lightly on the thigh, indicating he wanted to say something to her and she should move closer.

"The senior party officials are very impressed with your group's ability and organisation. They have a very important task for your group, which they have called the Sheng Long, the Living Dragon. I will explain that to everyone tomorrow, but if you are successful, which I know you will be, you will be given the highest security clearance. Zhang Liu, who is the senior adviser to the president of the China Institute of Contemporary International Relations, on my recommendation would like to interview you."

"Forgive my ignorance, but what is the function of the CICIR?"

"They are an advisory group on international affairs and strategies to our security services."

"And why do you think they would be interested in me specifically?"

"They need intelligent gifted people for overseas missions. Women attract less attention and are less threatening."

"And I'm to meet Zhang after the next assignment if it is successful. What is the next assignment, Prof Jin?"

"Please call me Jin. The party would like some of the anti-Chinese press disrupted. They want you to break into the international news feed at the New York Times and corrupt their computer system. You are to leave no trace. That is to demonstrate that we have the ability to strike where we would like."

"You know that that's not much of a challenge for us."

"I realise that," Jin said, touching her thigh again. "However, it's part of a two-step strategy, and the senior party officials need convincing of our capabilities."

Kim looked down at the hand which now remained on her thigh. For all the time that she had now spent in Shanghai, she had never had to deal with that revulsion which followed her uncle's attack on her. She looked at Jin's hand, commanding it to leave as her nausea returned, but it did not.

"The second part of the strategy," Jin said, sliding his hand further up her thigh, "And I'm telling you with this first, is to manipulate the international money markets."

"I thought you said it was information which gave the wealth, not money," Kim said feeling his grip tighten on her thigh.

"It's not the money that we are seeking with this assignment," Jin said leaning closer.

"The Federal Reserve Bank in America is symbolic to most Americans. Outside of Fort Knox, it is considered one of the financial cornerstones of their society. We want you to penetrate their database and insert corrupt data that they will use as the basis of their next economic forecast. That information will suggest that unemployment in America is decreasing, and that the Reserve Bank is about to decrease quantitative easing. That will have an immediate effect on the stock exchange and cause the American dollar to plummet. Such a disruption should cause the stock market to fall by one or two per cent. Then senior Communist Party officials will buy stocks at lower prices in great volumes. When the Reserve Bank discovers the corrupt data, the stocks will recover and we will sell our purchases. The proceeds, of course, will go to the Communist Party, not to the members or officials. The other part of your assignment is to leave traces enabling authorities in America to trace this attack to North Korea."

Kim did not reply, but looked frantically around the Sushi Bar for her other students. They had left her alone with Jin.

"We will need to take over the North Korean government's education computer. Once we give them the rocket sequence starter, they might even provide free access," Jin said with a smirk, oblivious to Kim's silence and growing discomfort.

"I have great faith in your abilities, Kim, now that I've got to know you and understand you better. And if you know the right people in the Party, who I can introduce you to, means that you could go far." Jin winked.

"Now let us enjoy the honey-glazed quail, and then I can walk you home," Jin said giving her thigh an extra squeeze. Kim felt the nausea start to build up in the pit of her stomach. She wished she was the quail on the plate in front of her. Being dead was preferable to having sex with Jin.

She could not eat; knowing that if she refused Jin, not only would she no longer be part of the group, but also that he had the power to revoke her place at university. Jin pushed the quail into his mouth and then looked at her, licking his fingers suggestively.

The walk back to the apartment took ten minutes from the restaurant. Jin constantly touched her backside as they walked, rubbing it in a suggestive manner. She suppressed the urge to scream; perhaps it would be over with quickly and he would not bother her again. Going back to her village, she could not manage. Jin talked nonchalantly as they walked, telling her that she was going to do so well in the party when he put in his recommendation. When they reached her room, he followed her in and hung his coat behind the door. The small talk stopped.

"Take off your clothes," he said as he went back to the door and removed a syringe from his coat pocket.

"You have an excellent body. It must be all the martial arts training," Jin said as he filled the syringe from a small vial in his left hand, staring at her nakedness.

"Lean over the table. I like doing it from behind."

Kim hoped that he had nothing sexual that she would catch; she imagined she was not the only female student subjected to coercive sex. As she turned to face the table, out of the corner of her eye she saw him inject the syringe at the base of his penis. Then she felt the lubricant being rubbed between her legs. At least she thought she would not have the horrible lasting images that she had from Uncle Yang grunting on top of her.

Nevertheless, the anger at the impending violation rose rapidly. She lay on her arms across the table, willing herself not to put a thumb in both of his eyes as she felt his body behind her. He placed his hands around her waist and pulled her roughly towards him. There was no penetration; she could feel he was not hard enough. The injection hadn't worked, and his hardened arteries were unable to dilate to create an erection. Several times he tried, including what she imagined was trying to masturbate his penis to hardness. Then suddenly he stopped and quickly put on his trousers, taking his coat from behind the door.

"Don't say anything to anyone about what happened," Jin said as he walked out the door and closed it behind him.

Kim wiped the lubricant with a towel from the bathroom and got dressed. She made a cup of green tea and sat at the table thinking about what had happened. Then she smiled briefly to herself thinking that even in situations of subjection, there can be natural justice. She half smiled to herself before coming back to the thought that all men in China were disgusting and depraved. The only solution she could see was to get out of China. After several minutes of wondering how she could achieve that, she got up and walked to the wardrobe, wrenched her martial arts uniform out, and decided to take her anger out on the punching bag at the gym.

In the special group meetings after that encounter, Jin never looked directly at Kim. The group successfully hacked into the New York Times, Lehman Brothers, and the Bank of America in addition to the Reserve Bank. Insinuating their data had caused a predicted two per cent drop in stocks and shares. North Korea had been successfully blamed for the attack and a senior official from Beijing turned up one Saturday morning to congratulate them in person. He also said 5000 yuan would be deposited in their scholarship accounts.

Several days later Kim was summonsed to meet a Zhang Liu in a small office on the campus. She had received an e-mail telling her to be there at 9:30 AM sharp. Jin, despite his disastrous attempt at sex, had obviously kept his word. At precisely 9:30 AM, she knocked on the door. Interestingly for an organisation which made recommendations to China's major security agencies, there was no security check.

"Come in."

Opening the door, she could see the office was large by university standards. Four big red lounge chairs faced an ornately carved green wooden table. On top of the table were a blue vase and a red lacquer box. Both she recognised were from the Qing Dynasty. Zhang Liu did not get up from behind his desk as she entered, merely pointing at one of the large red lounge chairs. Kim took the one closest to the window.

"You come highly recommended."

"Thank you. I enjoy my work," Kim said, grateful that Zhang Liu had not added 'for a woman' to the end of his sentence.

"We have something more challenging that we think you might be suited to."

"Prof Jin had mentioned something."

"And that you managed to survive his overtures without laying a complaint to the party has also been noted."

"Thank you."

"China's Institute of Contemporary International Relations was formed to further Chinese ambitions internationally. You may be aware that China has never really been known for its humanitarian aid. We have come to realise that in developing countries, where there are resources, offering some kind of humanitarian aid would allow us greater control of those resources. We are therefore looking for ways to expand our influence while not attracting international criticism for hegemonic activity. Rwanda provides a stable environment. We have set up an orphanage which we support and which you will manage. The objective is to take control of the resources in the northern Congo. Chinese industry desperately needs the ore/copper/tin and especially their tantalum, which is essential in all microchips. Sanwan, our largest electronics company, is creating a factory there. We will also take over a South African managed smelter by making it unmanageable. We have managed, in conjunction with our Rwandan friends, to interrupt its electricity to the point where it no longer works. You will help reinstitute that and be fully supported by our embassy in Kigali. You will be given background lessons of history and culture in the next week and then be fully briefed on whom you deal with by Lee Kaiping, your controller at the embassy in Kigali."

"Do you have any questions?"

"What kind of technological assistance will I have?"

"You will have access to secure communications at the embassy. You will report to me by live link once a month. I cannot emphasise enough to you that need to secure the resources by any means possible, without coming to international attention or by creating an international incident. We expect you to use ruthless determination to succeed."

"When do I leave?"

"We will create a profile for you, and delete all reference to you being associated with the People's Liberation Army, then you will fly out in six weeks and be met by Lee Kaiping. He will complete your briefing. You may go now."

Lee Kaiping did not meet her at Kigali airport, rather just a driver from the embassy who carried her name on a sign. He did not speak to her, picking up her bags and expecting her to follow him. The first thing that she noticed was the quality of the roads. She remembered reading in her briefing notes that China had supplied large amounts of equipment to Rwanda, to ensure an efficient connection between the resources of the Congo and the ports in Tanzania. A preparation ultimately for, the briefing papers stated, China's exclusive control of the Congo's vital industrial resources.

The driver circumnavigated the central roundabout, weaving between the sea of motorcycles, before driving up the Boulevard de la Revolution. The Chinese embassy had walls twelve feet high covered by razor wire with multiple video cameras. Opposite the embassy was a nine hundred bedroom luxury hotel. She knew it was being built by a Chinese construction company, in anticipation of future business. The driver parked in front of a giant reinforced steel doorway, in front of the embassy. A small camera on a retractable arm descended and peered in through both windows, which the driver had lowered. A green light appeared on the camera indicating that they had both been positively identified. The doors then slowly opened, steel spikes in the ground retracted, and they were able to drive into a large cobbled courtyard.

Kim's driver got out and opened her door before leading her up the steps to a reception area. Twenty feet high portraits of Mao adorned two of the courtyard walls, alongside and lower down the wall were smaller paintings of Premier Xi. The remaining wall had a giant portrait of a golden peacock, elaborately painted. The head of the peacock was almost as high as Mao's portrait and had been crafted with gold filaments. Rubies and emeralds had been implanted into the painting, creating a spectacular and colourful plumage. The peacock in China, Kim knew, was revered for many of its characteristics: a clear voice, a careful walk, appropriate behaviour, moderation in eating and drinking, knowing how to be content, existing together, not being obscene, and always returning. In addition, she remembered, the larger the portrait, the greater the implication of authority. Admiring the portrait, she heard footsteps descending stairs behind.

"Good morning." The greeting was in Mandarin.

Turning around she saw a man dressed all in black. Slightly taller than her, he had dyed black hair neatly parted on the left-hand side. A small scar under his right eye distorted his lower eyelid.

"I am Lee Kaiping," he said. "Welcome to Rwanda and may you be as successful as we expect. Maising, the driver who brought you here, will show you to your room. You will stay here for three days for briefings and then we will take you to the orphanage. You will report every week here in the embassy. I expect all those reports to be positive. Here are your briefing papers and the secure briefcase. The code is 78931." Lee then turned and made his way back up the steps.

Kim watched as he walked up the stairs. He was typical ex Chinese army. Well-trained, well prepared, ruthless when needed, and expecting the same standards from anyone who worked with him. Failure, clearly, was not tolerated. She looked at the briefcase that she had been handed; it was all metal with no distinguishing Chinese insignia. From experience, she knew it was designed to destroy all documents if the wrong code was entered in attempting to open it. In addition, it would be bullet and bombproof. The understanding was that the code was never written down, it was always spoken, and if you didn't remember it, you were reassigned. The code that Lee had given to her she repeated, 78931, silently to herself.

The orphanage was, Maising had told her, a three-hour drive from Kigali. He loaded her bags into the black SUV and handed her sandwiches from the kitchen. Once they were out of the city, she opened the briefcase and went over her briefing papers.

The instructions were simple; she was to set up a meeting with Rwandan and Chinese executives within six weeks. That meeting would be chaired by Lee Kaiping and would require

Bosco Bunarama, or Brutal Bosco, the leader of M 23 - the armed gang which they supported, to attend. Bosco needed more arms which China would facilitate the delivery to Kigali, and the Rwandans would coordinate the transport of the arms to Bosco's base on the Congolese border. In addition, a warehouse in Kigali would be supplied by the Rwandan executives, with Chinese finance, and they would repackage all arms disguising their Chinese origin. In the interim, she was also to come up with a strategy to deal with the warlord Kariba.

The orphanage was spread over six grassy acres, manicured to impress all who visited. Gardens beds were bright with colourful flowers, a few concrete Chinese dragons discreetly sculpted, juxtaposed alongside elephants and giraffes. Granite stones, chiselled into small squares, surrounded all the grass beds forming neat borders. Slides and swings confirmed the appearance of a well-funded humanitarian project. The driveway of grey granite chips weaved eight hundred metres through the gardens to the main entrance. As Maising pulled up, a Rwandan woman approached the car and opened the door.

"Welcome," she said with a large friendly smile. "I am Ruby and I will show you to your room."

Kim's quarters were separated from the main dormitory by an enclosed walkway. At each end were solid security doors made out of steel, imposing and secure. Ruby waited at the second door and knocked three times. Within minutes, the door opened to reveal a Chinese woman in a dark blue tracksuit, who introduced herself as Cusang. She explained that she would be Kim's assistant. Kim liked the look of her; her short boyish haircut and athletic build suggesting she would be a veritable challenge to any man, African or Chinese.

In the first few weeks, Cusang introduced Kim to the routine at the orphanage. Breakfast for the boys was at 7 AM sharp and finished on time at 8 AM, at which stage they could either shower or do schoolwork. School was between 9 AM and 3 PM, with a lunch break from 12 PM to 1 PM. Dinner in the evening was from 5:30 PM to 6:30 PM. Depending on the number of volunteers available, there was supervised homework and lights out at 8:30 PM.

The orphanage had ten volunteer teachers, six from China, and four from America and Australia. Cusang explained that it was policy to always have more Chinese volunteers than other nationalities. Six weeks passed quickly and Kim felt that she was rapidly adapting to life in Africa. The weekly meetings with Lee Kaiping had been professional and respectful. She had detailed the discussions that she had had with Bosco, and presented his list of armament requests, including more Chinese RPGs to deal with Kariba. The week before the meeting at the orphanage to coordinate a strategy to take over the resources in North Kivu, Kim had made a special trip to the embassy to assure Lee Kaiping that security was in order and to get agreement on the agenda. Lee had told her the Secretary for Commerce was arriving, the military attaché, the vice president of the electronic company Sanwong, as well as Zhang Liu. There would be six Rwandan politicians and executives. Lee indicated that the embassy would supply six extra staff for security. They would arrive early in the afternoon and thoroughly inspect the site; one would then remain at either doorway with four inside the meeting room. Details of China's offer would be on an iPad in Chinese, French, Kinyarwanda, and English to avoid any misinterpretation. The iPads would be collected at the end of the meeting by security, supervised by Kim.

On the day of the meeting, Bosco Bundarungu arrived in a large grey four-wheel-drive with black tinted windows. Stopping in front of administration, the front doors of the SUV opened; two large bodyguards got out. Both were well over six feet tall and very muscular, which Kim thought would make them Tutsis like Bundarungu. After a few seconds the back door opened, a small cloud of cigar smoke wafted out followed a few seconds later by Bundarungu. Dressed in army fatigues with a Marine style cap, he stood in the sunlight looking around the grounds like a general surveying his battleground. Kim stood back, the Chinese custom being to wait for him to approach her. He ignored her for another few minutes puffing on the cigar, creating another small smoke cloud which temporarily lingered on his right shoulder. Kim motioned to Cusang to take his briefcase; however, that was quickly waved away. Bosco, she then realised, was not standing and enjoying the view, or the sunshine; as someone military trained, he was scrutinising each section for any potential threat. With that kind of approach, he would be good to work with, thought Kim.

Lee Kaiping led the meeting with the efficiency she had come to expect from him. There was no joviality, but a discussion simply on what the Chinese could supply in terms of light arms/mortars and explosive devices. Kim had been instructed to watch carefully for Bosco's reaction. Lee wanted Bosco to feel indebted but did not want him to be the controlling force. Bundarungu, during the entire discussion, kept a poker face making it difficult for him to ascertain whether he was pleased with the Chinese offer or not. During the discussion, he also kept smoking his cigar, until one of the Rwandans got up and opened a window, looking disapprovingly at Bundarungu. Control of the meeting clearly resided with Bundarungu. When Lee stopped speaking, Bundarungu put the cigar on the table edge and stood up.

"There are no handheld surface-to-air missiles that we requested. We need handheld surface-to-air missiles if we are going to put Kariba out of business. If he can no longer bring the Antonovs in, he cannot get his ore out and that will dry up his money source. That is the head of the snake that we need to cut off. We also need boy soldiers from the orphanage; Kariba killed ten of ours last week and we have abducted all eligible boys within a 30 km radius of our camp. If we are going to attack him at the Goma airport next week, they need to be delivered to our Rumangabo training camp in the next few days. The fuel tanker that we ordered to resupply our trucks will need to be at Goma airport."

Lee looked at him for a few minutes before replying, clearly irritated at the commanding tone of his request. Kim knew it would be highly embarrassing for Lee to be spoken to in that manner in front of his Chinese visitors.

"Your request was considered by the Ministry. There is too much chance of an international incident if you shoot down an aircraft as large as the Antonov. We will provide more rocket-propelled grenades to destroy the planes on the ground. The fuel tanker that you requested will be there at the border in three days. Miss Yao will organise six boys to be delivered within twenty-four hours."

Bosco picked up a cigar and took a long drag, then again blew smoke in the direction of the businessman who had opened the window.

"The rocket propelled grenades are difficult for boy soldiers to carry. Unless we can interrupt Kariba's air supply, the snake will continue to survive. We have also heard rumours that he is also attempting to get chemical weapons through one of his suppliers, Raoul Assad. Do you have any information on that?"

Kim watched as Lee conferred with two of his assistants.

"Our information is that Assad will not supply chemical weapons. We will give the additional information to the Ministry about surface-to-air missiles and communicate their response to you shortly."

"I will look forward to your reply," Bundarungu said, sitting down and blowing more smoke in the direction of the Rwandan businessman.

Lee then declared the meeting closed and four boys brought hot food from the kitchen for all the guests. The boys, Kim ensured, were checked as they entered the room, and again as they left. There was little discussion, and Kim could see that Bosco wasn't happy with the outcome. As soon as he finished eating, he nodded to his bodyguards and they left without saying anything to Kim or Lee. Lee, she could see, was seething at the way Bosco had treated the delegation. He stormed out saying nothing to Kim as he left. It was a few hours later that she received a phone call from him.

"Did you check that all six iPads were placed back in the secure briefcase?" Lee screamed at her again.

Kim's heart raced; she had left that to Cusang.

"No," she replied, "that was Cusang's responsibility, but I will now go and check to see if there is one remaining."

"You stupid woman. Need I remind you the party does not tolerate mistakes, nor do I. There had better be one remaining in the meeting room. Otherwise you will go back to China tomorrow in disgrace."

Kim went back to the meeting room, but the door was locked. She walked around the outside and then saw the open window. Below the open window were a series of small footprints. She went back and unlocked the door, and looked inside the room. There was no iPad to be seen, just a small slip of torn paper which suggested that not all the handwritten notes had been shredded. She had trusted Cusang to clean up and secure all the iPads. Perhaps Cusang had found the extra iPad, however the footprints outside the open window concerned her. She shouted for Cusang who came running from the main office.

"Did you find an extra iPad?" she asked barely containing her fury. Cusang shook her head. Kim turned and headed to the dormitory where the two boys who were trusted to serve would be getting ready to go to bed.

"Stand outside, everyone," she shouted as she walked into the boy's dormitory door, eyes blazing.

"Search the room," she said over her shoulder to Cusang who had caught up with her. Together they turned the beds over and looked in all the drawers but found nothing.

"Go and tell them they will all stand outside in the cold until they tell us where the iPad is."

For the next hour, the six boys stood outside on the stones, not saying a word. Kim watched from the office, increasingly annoyed by their resistance. Aware that Lee would soon be phoning, she marched out and picked up the youngest of the boys by the collar dragging him into the office. Once Inside the office, she closed the door and beat the young boy with her hands and fists until he cowered crying in the corner.

"Where is the iPad?" she screamed at him.

The knock at the door distracted her from continuing her beating.

"Who is it?" she shouted angrily.

"Cusang."

Kim opened the door and as she did, the young boy ran crying from the room. She was about to grab him when Cusang held up the iPad.

"Which one had it?"

"I found it in one of the other dormitories in the bed of a friend of one of the boys outside, a boy called Michelangelo. When I took it from him, he was using it to play minesweeper with that new American volunteer, Cindy, who has befriended him."

"The information on the iPad tells about the supply of arms by China to Bosco Bundarungu. If she read or understood any of that information, it could expose our operation and embarrass the Chinese/Rwandan governments. Not to mention what Lee would do to us."

"Those six boys standing outside and Michelangelo can go to Bosco's training camp tonight, in case they have learnt anything."

"They might, with any luck, be killed in the fighting at the airport next week," added Cusang with a wry smile

"From our perspective, that would be the best outcome. Any potential evidence would then be buried."

"Cusang, what about that do gooder American teacher? If she saw anything on that iPad, that could be real trouble. Have her come to the office in the morning and I will interrogate her."

"She has left this evening to visit a friend at the hospital at Garanyi near the border. She will be away, she said, for three days."

"I will talk to her when she gets back and when Lee Kaiping calls in a few minutes, I am going to tell him that the iPad was found safe in the secure room. Do you understand that, Cusang?"

"I understand that," Cusang said as she bowed and walked out of the office.

Chapter 17

Christian was looking forward to the weekend and then the following week driving up to the orphanage to meet up with Cindy again. It had been a busy week. In his last case, he had had to drill a hole in the skull of a young woman who had fallen off the back of a motorbike. With no crash helmet, he had suspected that she might have fractured her skull. However, they had run out of chemicals in the X-Ray Department, so he could not be certain. When her coma scale started to decrease and she became less and less responsive, he knew intervention was the only way to save her. Fortunately, the drill hole had been right over her brain hematoma and he was able to release the pressure. He was sure she was going to recover. As he bandaged the wound, he started thinking about Isabella who was due to arrive on Sunday. Her phone call from Kigali the previous day had surprised him. Her voice was different from when he had first met her in Cape Town nine years ago. There was a sense of control and maturity in the way that she now talked. In many ways, he guessed she would now be like a stranger, despite their previous intimacy.

"Christian."

He looked over his shoulder in the direction of the doorway, which led into theatre. Doctor Nikita stood in his civilian clothes with a concerned look on his face, peering across the top of his rimless glasses towards Christian.

"There has been a major trauma across the border at Goma airport. Bosco and Kariba's gangs shooting at each other. A diesel fuel tanker has caught fire and exploded. There are approximately eighty dead and unknown number injured. Medicines sans Frontiers are flying in a team via Goma, and they have asked whether we can do the initial triage until they get there. We will send you now to help triage and see whether there are any patients we could possibly treat here."

"Do you have intravenous fluids, analgesia, and bandages that I can take in a kit, and is Satilde available to come with me? If there are burn patients, we will need to do some surgical debridement and having someone to look after the anaesthetic would be helpful."

"That's already taken care of; Jean Miguel is going to be your driver. We have resurrected the old ambulance that can transport four patients if necessary. An emergency kit, which we have, has all of the requirements for trauma triage. The hospital will provide emergency documents to cross the border."

"If it's okay, I will also take some surgical scrubs from theatre. I'll also pick up a few things from the Sudani's on the way."

"Good, Jean Miguel will have everything ready in thirty minutes."

The resurrected ambulance looked like something straight out of a M.A.S.H. movie. The green camouflage cab had had a small, red cross painted on each door. The windscreen was completely missing. The rear of the ambulance, with its old green canvas covering torn in so many places, that ultraviolet radiation was a significant risk to any patient being transported. None of the tires appeared to have any tread, but it had been cleaned, and was ready to transport patients. Christian just hoped that it had avoided the terminal brake disease that most vehicles in Rwanda seem to be infected with. The consolation and contrast was Jean Miguel. Fit and athletic, sporting a broad smile, he was in his early twenties and literally bounced out of the truck when he saw Christian emerge from the front of the hospital.

"Dr. Chris, Dr. Chris, over this way." He waved one hand, holding the cab door open.

Christian walked to the passenger door, Satilde, he noticed, was already there, and she moved across on the bench seat to make room for him. He could see through the torn canvas that there were two permanent stretchers and two collapsible stretchers loaded as well a very large wooden box, which he assumed was the emergency kit. As he climbed into the cab next to Satilde, he said,

"Thank you for coming. Have you checked everything in the back?"

"Yes, Dr. Chris. Dr. Nikita and I went through everything twice and Jean Miguel has all the papers."

The border crossing was in two parts. For those on foot there was a separate queue, which on both sides of the border stretched for half a kilometre and was three persons wide. He could only imagine the uncontrolled chaos in 1994 when 10,000 to 14,000 tried to squeeze through following the eruption of the Nyirangongo volcano in the Congo. For those traveling by road, there was a queue of five vehicles waiting to be processed and passed through the checkpoint. Five military personnel with automatic weapons supervised the process on either side of the border. Jean Miguel handed the official papers out the window, said a few words, and they were quickly waved through. Jean Miguel explained that the hospital was about fifteen minutes from the border. Hawker's stands dotted the roadside, selling everything from fruit to souvenirs, and clothing.

The hospital entrance was a large wrought iron gate that had been tied open. On either side, a white plastic fence extended for twenty metres. A small wire fence continued from the plastic fence around the perimeter interrupted every four or five metres by missing segments. Driving through the gates, Christian could see the sealed road stretched and curved eight hundred metres up a slight hill to the hospital entrance. Six large white marble-like pillars dominated the front of the hospital. Set back from the pillars was main section of the hospital. Unlike Garanyi hospital, it was constructed out of rendered plaster, and had been painted white. Difficult he imagined to keep clean but true to its historical 1950s development.

On the flat lawn in the front of the hospital, tents were being rapidly erected. Blue plastic sheets had been thrown on the ground as a makeshift floor. Jean Miguel drove past the tents and stopped on the roadway in front of the pillars. As Christian opened the cab door, he was greeted by multiple voices, speaking rapidly in French. Satilde slid along the seat and quickly joined him next to the truck. She addressed one of the men in a white coat who was closest to Christian and appeared to be in charge. After a few minutes, she explained to Christian that they wanted to take the ambulance out to the airport to retrieve more patients. They would unload the emergency kit and take it down to where the tents were being assembled. The wards were already overloaded and they would need to triage the new patients down in the tents.

Christian looked back down the hill and in the distance could see the first ambulance approaching. They would hardly have time to get the emergency kit unpacked. Under Jean Miguel's direction, the hospital workers lifted the emergency kit off the back of the ambulance and Christian followed it down the hill to the first of the tents, which had now been fully erected. The side of the tent, closest to the main entrance, had been rolled up and the space within would allow thirty patients to be laid on the floor. Christian shouted to Jean Miguel to have the emergency box placed close to the entrance. He could hear the sound of the ambulance and knew that they must only be six or seven minutes away. Burn patients needed to have the intravenous fluids and pain relief ready as they arrived.

Five minutes later the first ambulance stopped in front of the tent. Six patients were brought in and placed on the clear plastic. Christian was shocked to see that they were all young boys ranging in age he thought from ten to sixteen years of age. Some were grimacing, others were crying out unable to bear the pain of the burns. He quickly scanned the young boys, looking for ongoing bleeding. Beneath two of them, he could see a red pool of blood starting to enlarge on the blue plastic floor.

"Satilde, these two are going to need IV lines and fluids."

Christian moved to the first of the two young boys. His pulse was rapid, suggesting significant blood loss. The pair of scissors that he had taken from the emergency kit he used to cut off his bloodstained shorts and T-shirt. He had a bullet wound through the thigh, and the exit wound had destroyed a substantial amount of it, suggesting a high velocity bullet. Fortunately it was on the outer aspect of the thigh, and therefore away from the major artery. It would respond to a pressure dressing. He called Jean Miguel, demonstrating with his hands what he needed. The next boy had a gunshot to the upper arm, which was a flesh wound. That also would respond to dressing. He quickly moved to another young man with a pool of blood developing beneath him. As he approached the young boy, his breathing became rapid. Christian frantically looked for a bleeding site and then with a small sigh, the young boy stopped breathing and died in his arms. Christian closed his eyes and moved on.

By 9 PM he counted, they had twenty-three young men side-by-side in the tent. They had run out of intravenous fluid after the arrival of the twentieth patient. Satilde had called Dr. Nikita for more supplies; however, he could not supply them as the ambulance was already out on another emergency call. Christian realized that some of the boys would die, whom they could save, if they had intravenous fluids. He took his mobile phone out of the zip pocket on his pants. He dialled Mohammed; desperate times needed desperate actions. He quickly explained the situation to Mohammed. Four young men on motorcycles would be there within the hour Mohammed assured him, with as much as they could carry. Would Christian please alert Doctor Nikita? Christian said he would, hoping that Emmanuel would also understand.

Within the hour four motorcyclists arrived, baskets in the front and back bulging with bandages, intravenous fluids, and medications. Satilde and Jean Miguel, whom Christian had quickly taught to insert an intravenous line, moved amongst the remaining boys to give them fluids. Christian estimated that more than forty per cent of the boys whom he triaged had burns covering more than half of their bodies. The ones with the severe third-degree burns were ironically the lucky ones at this stage. Deep third-degree burns melted the two layers of the skin and destroyed the pain receptors. Their pain would come later with skin contraction. The others who had first and second degree burns needed pain relief. Christian decided to call a brief meeting and prioritise treatment. He indicated to everyone the boys who had first and second degree burns. They were to be administered ketamine and were to be regularly examined, to make sure that they were not overloaded with intravenous fluids.

"You need to sleep," Satilde said as he finished his briefing. "We have done everything we can and we are going to need to do surgical debridement on some of these boys tomorrow."

Christian could feel the adrenaline ebbing and with the creeping tiredness, he knew from experience, would come a blunting of his surgical sharpness.

"Where do we sleep?"

"The small tent, just behind this one. We are all sleeping there."

There were still cries of pain as he did one final visual check. Four nurses had arrived from the main hospital and Satilde had given them instructions on dressings and looking after the intravenous fluids. He waited for her to finish giving instructions, and heard her say in French, as she joined him, where they would be if they were needed by any of the patients. The tent was the size of a small room, similar to the one his mother had once taken him camping in the Flinders ranges outside of Adelaide. In the moonlight, he could see four mattresses, each with a sheet and a pillow as well as the outline of a small primus stove with coffee and cups balanced on top. Next to the stove were four fresh bottles of water. He quickly handed one to Satilde before consuming three quarters of one of the other bottles. The constant activity and heat had left him dehydrated. He was also hungry but knew that there would be no food until later that day.

Satilde crawled under her sheet without removing her surgical scrubs. She turned on her side pulling the sheet up over her head and said good night. The sheet pulled up over her head, Christian realized, was going to be her mosquito net. He climbed under his sheet without taking off his surgical scrubs until he realized he was too hot to sleep. Peeling off his surgical top and trousers, he tucked them under his pillow before pulling the sheet over his head fractionally ahead of the first mosquito. Intent on a blood meal it settled on the sheet over his ear, amplifying the annoying buzzing sound. He could not stand it, and swatted at it with his right hand uncertain as to whether he had exterminated it. There was no tell-tale smudge of blood on the sheets and five minutes later, the dreaded sound returned. He wondered whether it was the same mosquito seeking revenge for the attempted assassination, but there was more than one buzzing sound and he knew it had probably passed its bloodsucking message to family and friends.

The next noise to wake him was the pan on the primus stove. He opened his eyes and noticed it was early morning. Exhaustion had overwhelmed the annoying sound of the mosquitoes, so that he had slept. In the corner of the tent was someone he did not recognize cooking tomatoes and eggs. He looked at Christian as he heard him stir and smiled.

"We have brought new supplies," he said in perfect English. "Mohammed also thought that you would need something to eat which was fresh."

Christian rubbed his eyes and noticed small red welts on his arm. In the night, his arms had come out from underneath the sheet and the mosquitos had had their revenge. Not everyone, he told himself, got malaria from being bitten; he had to hope that he was one of those. Just in case, he would ask one of Mohammed's motorcycle couriers to pick up his doxycycline on the next trip back to Garanyi.

"Thank you and tell Mohammed we are extremely grateful."

Christian pulled his surgical scrubs on and noticed that both Jean Miguel and Satilde had left the tent. As he looked out through the rolled-up front flap, he could see them in the distance already checking intravenous lines and patients. He hurried through the scrambled eggs and tomatoes, understanding the need to have some energy source for the difficult day which lay ahead. A half cup of unfinished coffee that sat next to the primus stove completed his breakfast.

"Thank you for breakfast," he said to Ashik, who had now introduced himself, before walking out through front of the tent, ducking underneath the flap, to join Satilde and two other doctors from the hospital in the large emergency tent.

"Good morning, Satilde. Were there any dramas overnight?"

"Good morning, Christian. No real dramas although I think we are going to be very busy today during debridement and dressings. Would you like a quick catch-up on each of the patients?"

"Yes, let's start with the ones that you've already seen and then we can do the rest together. Do we have a clearer idea of what happened at the airport?"

"We do. Bosco the Butcher with his boy soldiers tried to ambush Kariba's gang at the airport. They then started shooting and one of the bullets ignited the diesel tank. In the confusion some of the boys then tried to run and were shot; the others were obviously burned by the explosion. Bosco's gang was the worst affected and he retreated. From what we can understand, some of his boy soldiers were captured by Kariba and tortured. Those that survive he will send to his mines to work."

"Welcome to Africa," said one of the doctors from the hospital who had joined them and overheard the conversation.

The first four boys they reviewed had first and second degree burns. They were well hydrated, and with some ketamine all they would require would be antiseptic to their burns and light dressings. Looking at their faces, Christian could tell their pain was well controlled, but there was still a frightened and bewildered look. He asked Satilde to ask them how they were feeling. When she spoke to them, he noticed they cast their eyes down and did not reply. He looked at Satilde and she said,

"They won't say anything because they think that we going to sell them back to Kariba or Bosco and they might be beaten again or sent to the mines."

Feeling powerless that he could not remove these boys from their nightmare, Christian moved on to the next boy patient. Aged about twelve years, like the others he kept his eyes cast down, as they stood at his feet looking at his chart.

"This is Michelangelo," Satilde said. "He was the boy who was captured and was being beaten by Kariba's gang, but managed to escape when the first ambulance arrived. He has a broken left arm that we need to reduce and set in plaster. He has multiple lacerations on his back where he was whipped, which will need to be treated and dressed."

Christian lifted up the sheet and saw the slightly angulated left forearm. It had not broken the skin and therefore reducing it would be straightforward. As he indicated to the young boy to turn on his side so that he could inspect the deep lacerations on his back, instinct took over. In English, he whispered in his ear.

"Don't be afraid, we won't let you go back, I promise. Cindy will help."

Michelangelo did not turn over. He looked Christian directly in the eye and with tears welling up, said,

"Thank you, Doctor."

"You know him?" Satilde said obviously shocked, as Christian rearranged the sheet around Michelangelo.

"I don't know him, but I know of him. He is one of the boys who need to come back with us to Garanyi. I will explain on the way. Now let's take one of those permanent stretchers from the back of the ambulance. We can use that as the operating table and disinfect it between cases."

No one moved once Christian had stopped talking. They stood staring at him, he could sense their confusion. Would rescuing one boy from the situation make any difference, their eyes were saying. By the end of the day, they had completed thirty dressing changes and set six fractures. Christian had also taught Jean Miguel to suture simple wounds. As nightfall approached, Christian could not help but wonder when the relief would arrive from Medicines Sans Frontier. He was starting to feel unwell himself, nauseated with hot flushes every ten to fifteen minutes. Explosive diarrhoea he could feel was not very far away. He quickly excused himself from the large tent, and walking out into the cool night air before vomiting uncontrollably, next to a small tree on the lawn. Momentarily, he felt slightly better but then the waves of nausea returned. He searched frantically for the toilet that Satilde had mentioned. In the dark, he could just see the blue plastic constructed around four sticks two metres high. The side that faced the hospital was uncovered; the plastic doors rolled up and permanently open, for emergencies such as his. As he reached and quickly sat on the wooden seat, both ends exploded with an African velocity. He knew he was not going to be able to do any more operating that night. After what seemed like an eternity, the nausea settled and he made his way slowly back to the mattress in the small tent.

The night was devoid of any sleep, Christian's increasing fever causing him to constantly toss and turn. As waves of nausea built up into an uncontrollable surge, he crawled outside the tent to vomit. On his second or third excursion outside, Satilde lit the gas lantern. As he crawled back inside, he noticed her sitting next to his mattress with an intravenous line and bag of saline. He nodded his agreement, for he could feel that he was rapidly becoming dehydrated. Satilde inserted a needle into a vein on his hand before hooking up the bag of saline. John Miguel, who was also now awake, applied pressure to the bag to rehydrate him more quickly. He did not remember falling asleep, just a desperate act of pulling a perspiration-soaked sheet over his head to thwart the inevitable mosquito squadrons. When he did wake, small rays of sunshine were filtering into the tent and initially as he opened his eyes, he wondered whether he was delirious. Three people were sitting around his mattress with concerned looks on all of their faces. He tried to focus, squinting initially, and wiping his eyes with the back of his hand. It looked like Isabella; he must be delirious, he thought. Then she leaned forward, dabbed his face with a wet cloth, and whispered in his ear,

"Hello, we need to get you out of here urgently and treat your malaria and gastroenteritis. Old lovers don't die on my watch." She winked at him. "We are taking you back in the ambulance, Doctor Sudani's orders."

Christian smiled; despite it being ten years since he had seen Isabella, he still knew her voice. Her hair was not how he remembered, for she now had it cut very short. The black-rimmed glasses gave her an authoritative air.

"Isabella, it's so nice to see you again," he whispered. "However we can't leave yet as Medicines sans Frontier hasn't arrived and all those boys need to have the dressings changed and skin grafts done. Otherwise they're going to become infected."

"Don't worry. MSF will be here this evening and the Dutch or German surgeon who sometimes helps out at Garanyi has arrived. Satilde has briefed him and I went to speak to him to tell him that we are urgently evacuating you to Garanyi. I wondered whether his accent was Dutch. Some of the words he used had a South African inflection. "

"Don't forget to bring Michelangelo with us. I promised him."

"If you can make it in the cab, we will put Michelangelo plus three other boys in the back."

"I'll go in the cab."

Chapter 18

Isabella decided to treat Christian at the Sudani's. The only concern was whether Christian had drug-resistant malaria. She had learnt in London that most sub-Saharan malaria infections were drug-resistant. Fortunately, she had brought some malarone to use for herself as a preventative measure; she would give that to Christian. Keeping an eye on his fluid intake would then be the only other real concern. Within two days, he should be recovering.

After twenty hours of Isabella's care, Christian could feel his strength returning. He did not feel as delirious and although he was sleeping most of the day, he could feel the beginning of hunger and knew that was a good sign. After forty-eight hours, he stood up, clearheaded for the first time, and felt well enough to want to try Chantal's coffee. Chantal and Isabella both turned at the same time to look at him as he walked into the kitchen, a little unsteady on his feet. He knew, after three days of no food and little fluid, that physically he looked gaunt and unwell.

"I am feeling better even though I may still look terrible," he said trying to manage a smile.

"That you are standing is a significant advance and suggests that the malarone is dealing with the malaria."

"I'm not sure. Would you like to check my spleen, Isabella?"

"A sense of humour that returning is also a good clinical sign," Isabella said, raising an eyebrow in Chantal's direction and smiling.

"Are you up to a cup of coffee yet? We have had our first one but there is still some left."

"I would love to try."

"Sit down and I'll get you one then," Chantal said. "Then I'm going to the market and you two can catch up, which I'm sure there's a lot to do."

The coffee did not taste quite the same, with possibly the malarone affecting his taste. However, even though the coffee had an aluminium edge, it was great to taste something other than water, and not have the feeling that it was not going to reappear immediately in front of him. He looked at Isabella, enjoying having her close again. Her velvet coal dark hair still had the rich blackness, which he had often remembered. When they had had first met in Cape Town nine years ago, she had worn it shoulder length. He had really liked the longer length as she would wear it in so many different styles, all of which seemed to suit her. Now she wore it short and cropped into her neck, which emphasised her cheekbones. The large black rim glasses gave her an academic look and a mature sexiness. One thing had not changed, which he had long wondered about: the intense passionate desire for her was still present in abundance. The way that she looked at him suggested to him that it was for also there for her as well.

"You don't like the short hair, do you?"

"I really do. It's just not the memory that I have of you, although I can see and feel you are the same Isabella. I do like the new version."

"You look very much the same to me although your hair is a little bit longer, and after the last few days you are much thinner than I remember. However, when I saw you lying there on the plastic floor, burning up with a fever and delirious, I still had the same kind of feeling of desire that I had experienced when I first saw you in Cape Town."

Christian was initially taken aback by the boldness of the statement. There was a confidence about her now, which had replaced the teenage innocence he remembered. It was that confidence which he had noted when she had calmly taken over his care. That was to be expected; medicine had also given him a similar confidence. Isabella, like him, was trained to care for people. He held her gaze, realizing that she was scrutinizing him to see whether he felt the same. He smiled back his agreement. His mind wandered back to their meeting in Johannesburg, when they had discovered they were not brother and sister. Without the horrible thought that they had previously committed incest, they had discovered a sexual chemistry, which had threatened to overwhelm them both. In the months which had followed, Christian had moved back to Australia and the relationship intensity had waned. Until he had met Petrea on the plane, he had not felt that intensity of feelings for another woman. He had thought that the chemistry that they had had experienced was unique only to Isabella. The intensity that they had previously brought to their relationship came sharply back into focus; he wanted to feel strong enough to enjoy discovering the chemistry that they had previously had, again. Christian decided to try and match her boldness.

"Any particular therapy you would recommend which would speed my recovery?"

"There is good research that suggests direct skin contact stimulates endorphin release which is therapeutic in the healing process," Isabella replied looking directly at him and smiling mischievously.

"That was in a peer reviewed journal, I'm sure."

Isabella took off her glasses and moved her stool closer to his. Stroking his hair, she kissed him on the cheek and said.

"I need to take that intravenous needle out now that we no longer need to give you intravenous fluids. You will need to take off your shirt."

Christian was about to take his shirt off when he heard Chantal open the front door. He did up his top button as Isabella moved the stool back a little.

"Hello you two. Up to mischief, I hope," Chantal said, gently knocking on the doorway, as she peered into the bedroom.

Isabella laughed as Chantal handed the *Rwandan Times* newspaper to Christian. The front page covered the shooting in the Congo under the headlines 'Militias vie for control of resources'. He read the first few lines as Isabella read over his shoulder. The newspaper condemned the militia groups and argued that it was time that the area was controlled by a legitimate government force. Christian allowed Isabella to continue reading.

"Do you understand this fully?" Isabella said as she read on.

"I'm starting to understand it a little bit more each day. The world thinks it's an ethnic conflict but it's all about money and corruption and who controls one of the richest resource regions in the world."

"Would you two like some lunch?" Chantal called from the kitchen.

Christian and Isabella walked through into the kitchen, where Chantal was unpacking the fruit and vegetables that she had bought at the local market.

"Actually Mohammed has invited me to lunch via text message this morning. I feel strong enough to go, especially if I can take my doctor with me."

"Yes, I heard that Mohammed had been very helpful. You realize, of course, that some in the hospital might see that as Mohammed looking to gain influence with you and the community in general."

Christian nodded. He knew going to have lunch with Mohammed may well contribute to that feeling, which principally came from Emmanuel. With that in mind, he had asked Mohammed to meet at one of the small cafés in the main street. That, at least, he thought would be neutral territory.

"Chantal, I'm aware of what people might think of that. I have arranged to meet at one of the cafés in the main street, so that it can't be misunderstood. I am going to check on the boys in the hospital first though."

"Isabella, do you think he is strong enough?"

"Well he is certainly getting his cheekiness back, so I suspect he will manage a quick ward round. I will go with him to make sure he doesn't do too much and then after lunch, I have an outpatient clinic and he can walk back here."

The walk back up to the hospital was both tiring and rejuvenating. Christian's legs felt rubbery by the time they made it to the top of the hill, but after two days cast in bed, just walking was gratifying. Isabella told him as they walked that the four boys had been placed in the paediatric ward. The two older boys could possibly have been in the adult surgical ward, she said, however they all had burns, and it was easier to have them together in one ward for dressings and possibly skin grafting.

The paediatric ward was similar to the other wards, red plastic mattresses with a single sheet covering them, creamy yellow mosquito nets furled and tied to the ceiling above the beds. The major difference was mothers with two or three children occupied the beds. When Christian had first arrived, it had been difficult sometimes to determine which child was the patient.

201

Michelangelo was in the second bed and as Christian and Isabella entered, he looked up. There was no smile of recognition and he quickly cast his eyes down. The boy in the first bed appeared to be about the same age as Michelangelo. Christian stopped at the foot of the first bed and looked at the chart. The pulse and temperature were significantly elevated, suggestive of a developing infection. Christian looked at Isabella and the ward sister, Margarita, who had now joined them. Anticipating his question, the ward sister said that Doctor Nikita had started antibiotics the previous day. They would take twenty-four hours to start being effective in bringing down his temperature. Christian approached the bed to exam the boy's burns, feeling Michelangelo's eyes watching him. As he pulled back the sheet, he turned and glanced at Michelangelo who again quickly looked down.

"I think we will need to debride those burns in theatre tomorrow," Christian said as he pulled the sheet back up.

"Yes, Doctor Chris. I will organize that with theatre," Margarita said, writing instructions in her notebook

"Do we know whether any of these boys have family yet?"

"None that we know of."

"Good morning, Michelangelo," Christian said as he moved to the foot of next bed.

Michelangelo did not look up. Christian examined his chart and noted that there was only a slight temperature. Nothing to be alarmed about; however, what did concern him was that Michelangelo now gave the impression that he did not recognize him.

"None of the boys have said a word since we admitted them," Isabella said. "They will not even tell us their names or whether they have families. It's almost as though they are too frightened or shocked to talk."

Christian knew post-traumatic stress could cause such an effect. Just because violence was so endemic in the Congo did not mean that those subjected to it so frequently should be immune. Nevertheless, something still did not quite fit with Michelangelo, for he had responded initially. Christian's intuition told him there was something else happening that they did not quite understand.

"Margarita, could we get this patient down to theatre now? His wounds need to be dressed as soon as possible."

Isabella was about to protest when she sensed that Christian wanted Michelangelo away from the ward and the other boys. By the time they finished the rest of the ward, Josef, one of the orderlies, had already taken Michelangelo down to theatre.

"Care to tell me about this intuition with Michelangelo? Clearly you're not going to operate on him," said Isabella as they walked down the concrete pathway to theatre.

"Just a strange hunch at the moment."

Michelangelo was just inside the theatre door, and Josef had put his bag of intravenous saline hooked over a window catch. He again did not look up as Christian and Isabella entered. Christian picked up the wooden chair from behind the reception desk and pulled it up next to Michelangelo. He motioned to Isabella to stand beside him as he took Michelangelo's hand.

"Michelangelo, I know Cindy from the orphanage. She is a good friend of mine, and we're going to look after you and make sure you never go back to fighting or the mines. Cindy is coming tomorrow to see you. I know that you speak English. Is there anything that's frightening you that we can help with?" Christian squeezed his hand in reassurance as Isabella moved to the head of the bed and gently stroked his head. There was no response from Michelangelo. Christian looked up at Isabella who motioned to him to leave the reception area. He quizzed her with his eyes and Isabella responded by waving him in the direction of the door. He stood up, offered the chair to Isabella, and walked out the door, closing it quietly. He sat down on the concrete walkway next to the theatre door.

It seemed like half an hour before Isabella opened the door and said,

"We will need to get the dressings changed so that the other boys don't suspect anything."

Christian walked back in through the half-open theatre door and headed to where he knew Teresa kept the dressings. He quickly dressed the wounds, while Isabella went to organize Michelangelo's return to the ward. As he applied to the last piece of micropore tape, he looked up to see Michelangelo watching him. His eyes were filled with tears. Christian resolved instantly that this was one boy he would never let go back to the militias, even if it meant his own life. Josef and Isabella arrived back as he looked at Michelangelo and said,

"Just remember the promise that I made you."

"Come on. We need to make lunch with Mohammed," Isabella said closing the theatre door behind Josef and Michelangelo.

"You need to tell me what you found out first."

"Walk with me while I talk to you and explain."

They headed out hand-in-hand through the main entrance of the hospital towards the dirt road that led up to the town. Within five minutes, they had reached the main street of the town. Each side of the street was lined by two-story buildings with wooden frontages The rest of the buildings were made from traditional mud bricks, creating the impression of a western movie set that you would expect to see in Hollywood - not Africa. The shop openings all had wooden planks as a footpath separating them from the dusty main road. Balconies above the shop frontages appeared to be tailor-made for damsels in distress to wave from, although he could see they also had practical value as a place to dry washing. Hitching posts in front of some of the shops, added to the strange western movie set impression, while also suggesting that horses had only recently been substituted for by motorcycles. Further, up the main street several pedal-operated Singer sewing machines were busy, each with two or three people standing around them while clothing was repaired.

"So what did you find out? It's not all just post dramatic stress, is it?"

"No, it's not. The boy in the first bed is one of the sons of Kariba Offengowe. All the boys are terrified to say anything in case he comes back to get his son and kills them for running away."

"I knew there was something not right," Christian said, stopping as they got to the first building in the main street. "And we can't get them to a safe place until we've got them well."

"Exactly, Christian, but we need to let Emmanuel know. Perhaps we can transfer them to Kigali by ambulance which might be safer for them."

"Okay, that's worth thinking about. Let's have lunch with Mohammed and then I will go and talk to Emmanuel."

Mohammed was sitting at little wooden table half way up the main street. He spotted Christian and Isabella and waved.

"Good morning," Christian said as Mohammed stood up to greet them. "This is a friend of mine, Isabella, who is also a doctor."

"You forget that this is a small community. We have heard about your lady doctor friend, and that she has nursed you back to health, for which we are all very grateful. And I suppose he hasn't told you, Isabella, that he saved my son's life?"

"He did mention that to me."

"May I buy you both a coffee?"

"I didn't know that you were allowed to drink coffee as a Muslim. We are happy to drink water if you cannot join us," Christian replied.

"Muslims introduced coffee to the world. There has been debate about it being an intoxicant but mostly it is acceptable as long as it does not have pig's milk in it. Did you know it was discovered in the year 1400 in Yemen, and Muslims used it to stay awake to pray in the night? Then when it was exported to Europe, it was seen as an evil drink because of its association with Muslims."

"Well, I didn't know that. What an interesting bit of information," Isabella said, looking at Christian who smiled and turned to Mohammed.

"Mohammed, I wanted to thank you for sending all those medical supplies. They may well have saved many of the boys' lives including those that we brought back."

"Helping others and contributing to peace and harmony is what the Quran and the prophet Mohammed commands us to do."

"So that's not just other Muslims that you are commanded to help but everyone. I thought that there was a Hadith that indicated that this command applied only to Muslim brothers?"

"You are well informed, Christian, and with a name like that I suppose you should be when it comes to religious matters. Since ultimately we are working for Allah, to whom all people belong, we help everyone where there is a need."

"That's not too dissimilar to Christianity then. Perhaps there is more common ground than we think. However, I am sure extremists on both sides would never allow any kind of cooperation despite the good that might come from that."

"Unfortunately, Christian, I think you're right. Although I don't think that means that those of us who believe that it can be achieved should stop working for that goal. Within any religion, there will always be an old guard that sticks to the old ways. Many of us prefer the benign persuasion to gain popular support, but there are still those who believe in *al-sama'wa'l-ta'a*, and unfortunately they are the ones who capture the headlines."

"From what I could see, Mohammed, the way that you assisted with those children across the border, was so far from forceful coercion that it has to have impacted on some of those at the hospital who might have been resistant to the idea of any cooperation."

"Can we ask you what you know about the shooting?" Isabella asked.

"The truth is very disturbing on many levels. Young boys are kidnapped from their families and forced into being child soldiers. Other boys too young to be useful soldiers are forced into labour camps deep in the Congolese Bush. The most notorious of these, run by Kariba Offengowhe, is called Mount Golgotha. Hundreds of boys are sent down mine tunnels each day, each expected to fill 50 kg bags of rock containing Tin Tungsten and Tantalum. In temperatures of up to forty degrees, many die from exhaustion, and any who rebel are tortured or killed. Offengowe controls the flow of resources and money via the city of Goma, which Bosco the Butcher and his backers are attempting to take control over."

"Did not the United States pass a law making it illegal to deal with militias in the Congo?" Isabella said.

"That was intended to stop abuse and illegal trade, whereas in effect, it just increased the price of resources and contributed to greater corruption and violence."

Christian reflected for a few minutes on Mohammed's explanation before telling him that they had one of Kariba's sons on the hospital ward and that he was very sick.

"You may be in great danger. Kariba is an atavistic monster and when he finds out where his son is, none of those boys will be safe and you may not be."

"He has a serious infection, and if he takes him now, then he may well die."

"Then you will be blamed and he will kill you both."

Christian was about to tell Mohammed about Michelangelo when a text message registered on his phone. It was from Cindy telling him that Kim Yao had found out that Michelangelo was in hospital and would be arriving that evening to return him to the orphanage. Christian finished reading the text message and quickly explained to Mohammed that Cindy had concerns that the orphanage was being used to supply boys to the militia. She thought Michelangelo might have information about that which is why Kim Yao desperately wanted him back.

"You can bring him to us. We have brothers who will protect him."

"We could dress his wounds in the morning, and then switch him to oral antibiotics. Is there some way that we could get him to you, Mohammed, unnoticed?"

"One of our brothers supplies the pharmacy with soap. The pharmacy is next to the paediatric ward. If you were to transport him from the ward to the theatre to do his dressings, we could bring him back to us in the van. Now I must excuse myself for afternoon prayers."

Christian and Isabella sat in silence for quite some time after Mohammed left. Isabella looked at Christian and said,

"We are going to need to tell Emmanuel and try and get his cooperation."

"I agree. However I'm concerned, though, that he will see it as creating even greater influence for Mohammed within the hospital and may not agree. I had thought about taking Michelangelo back so that we can look after him at the Sudani's, but then that's the first place someone would look. Let's walk back and see whether he's in his office and I'll text Cindy to find out what time Kim Yao is arriving."

"I'll phone the hospital to find out where Emmanuel is. Can I borrow your phone, Isabella, as I've left mine at the Sudani's?"

"What's yours is nearly mine!" she said winking at him.

They found Emmanuel sitting in his office reading an article in *Newsweek* magazine on the Somali jihadists and Boko Haram.

"You might want to read this given what I hear about your developing friendships. Africa does not need these extremists and despite a moderate approach from those locally, they cannot control the extremists. Christianity may have its fundamentalists but they do not kill innocent people," Emmanuel said sliding the magazine across the desk towards Christian.

Christian took the magazine, thinking that the Crusades had not exactly been blameless when it came to killing innocent people. However, now was not the time to have that discussion with Emmanuel, especially with what he was about to ask.

Chapter 19

The last text from Cindy had indicated that Kim Yao would be at the hospital at 10 AM. Mohammed had organised to deliver the soap at 9 AM to the pharmacy. Emmanuel, after much discussion, had reluctantly agreed to the plan. Christian decided to review patients in Accident and Emergency early, while Isabella went to talk to Michelangelo, so that he understood what was going to happen. It was 8 AM by the time Christian finished. There were two machete injuries, which would require suturing in theatre, a possible appendicitis and two obstructed pregnancies.

Opening the door from onto the covered concrete walkway, he saw Isabella in the distance. She was running towards him frantically waving to him to stop.

"Kim Yao is already on the ward," she said breathlessly. "She's making arrangements to take Michelangelo back with her."

"Get John the orderly and I'll slow her down," Christian said running in the direction of the paediatric ward.

He slowed down as he entered the ward, composing himself and getting his growing anger under control. As he entered, Kim Yao was standing at the foot of Michelangelo's bed. The only sound that could be heard in the ward was her strident voice, instructing the two men on either side of her. Christian understood the French instructions were to carry Michelangelo to the waiting car. The nurses stood back as the two men placed a stretcher next to Michelangelo's bed. Each of the men carried a large machete in a pouch attached to their belt. Michelangelo, on seeing Kim Yao, had turned on his side with his knees pulled up under his chin and his hands over his head. Christian could see him shaking with tears trickling out of the corner of his eyes.

"If you take him, he will die."

Kim Yao didn't turn around or respond, continuing to instruct the two men to place Michelangelo on the stretcher.

"At least let us change his dressings before you take him."

Kim Yao turned to face Christian with a deliberately slow and unrushed movement designed to convey to him that it was she who was in charge. Despite being a head shorter than Christian, her demeanour insinuated control. Short black hair was cut to emphasise almond oriental eyes which concentrated the gaze of anyone looking at her, reinforcing the feeling that great power resided within. There seemed, as he looked at her, to be no soul connection, so devoid were they of any feeling. Facing him, she stood with both legs apart, the balance position, which allowed movement forwards or backwards quickly. Finishing her appraisal of Christian, she said in perfect English,

"You have fifteen minutes to do the dressings before we take him with us where our doctors will attend to him."

"His wounds need surgical debridement," Christian said wondering what happened to John the orderly.

Kim stood and looked at him. Christian could sense that she was deciding whether it was worthwhile continuing the discussion.

"Let me repeat, in case you did not understand, we have access to doctors who can treat him. You have fifteen minutes to get him ready."

At that moment, John trundled through the open door of the ward with the theatre trolley, a wobbly wheel making it difficult to negotiate the beds. Christian realized that he would also have to distract Kim in case she decided to follow Michelangelo to theatre.

"You will need to come with me to the superintendent's office to sign the release papers that frees the hospital from responsibility for his care. I would then like to inspect the vehicle that you're taking him back in. Could you please ask your two assistants to bring the vehicle around to the superintendent's office?"

Kim did not move and did not blink. Christian could feel the repulsion implicit in complying with an order; commands, he sensed, she was used to giving - not being forced to act upon. She shifted on her feet, changing balance so that Christian wondered if she was going to strike him. Then she turned to the two men holding the stretcher and issued commands in French to bring their vehicle to the superintendent's office. She picked up Michelangelo's observation chart, faced Christian again and stared unblinkingly for some time conveying the harm which may come to him if she wasn't happy with the outcome. As she walked past him and headed in the direction of the superintendent's office, John manoeuvred the theatre trolley next to Michelangelo's bed before helping him onto it.

Christian opened the door leading from the ward that ran down to theatre. John pushed the theatre trolley with Michelangelo onto the concrete walkway. Christian could see part way down the walkway that the pharmacy door was open. He quickly glanced back down the corridor door to make certain that Kim and her two assistants were not returning, before turning to John.

"John, you know what to do. Michelangelo is being taken to the safe place we told you about. Leave the trolley in theatre as I know they will come looking for it."

Christian watched through the door as John slowed the trolley in front of the pharmacy. Two dark arms in a white flowing robe quickly lifted Michelangelo into the pharmacy. As he heard the sound of the van being driven away, he relaxed slightly, knowing that Michelangelo, at least for the time being, was safe. The next challenge would be to deal with Kim Yao's anger. Christian closed the door offering a silent thank you to Mohammed. He walked slowly to Emmanuel's office; the black Range Rover with Kim Yao's two assistants was parked outside. Both doors were open and as Christian approached, he was invited to inspect the vehicle. A perfunctory glance was all that he needed. He closed the door and nodded to one of the assistants as Kim Yao strode out, waved the papers at Christian, and sat in the passenger seat. He watched as they drove off in the direction of theatre. He wondered how long they would wait outside before entering and finding the empty trolley.

Christian walked into Emmanuel's office, who was sitting at his battered wooden desk shuffling the newly signed papers. Emmanuel did not look up or smile when Christian entered. He continued shuffling the papers; after a few minutes he put them in the top drawer of the desk. Then he looked at Christian and said:

"You might have bitten off more than you can chew. Kim Yao gives the impression of getting what she wants and if she is involved with the militia, as you think she is, she is going to want her material witness back whatever it takes. I hope Mohammed knows what he's getting himself into, and that your solution to this problem doesn't involve anyone getting hurt."

In the previous day's discussion, Emmanuel had been reluctant to agree to hide Michelangelo with Mohammed and his family. It was only when they explained that he was a potential witness, not only to child slavery but also Chinese government involvement and that his life was at risk if he was returned to the orphanage, that Emmanuel relented.

"If Cindy is right and there is a Chinese government involvement, they are not going to want to create publicity."

"I hope you are right," Emmanuel said locking the papers in his drawer.

Christian walked out through the front door and headed back towards the operating theatre. Part way down the concrete walkway, he saw Kim and her two assistants coming out from the theatre. He stopped and watched as she calmly closed the theatre door behind her before almost running to where Christian was standing. Stopping less than a meter away, she fixed him with a rabid glare.

"I will find him. And when I do, I will find you again."

She then strode off collecting her two machete-carrying assistants before departing in the Range Rover, barely missing five new patients as it turned out through the front gate. Christian turned and headed back towards the surgical ward. He had been concerned about Kariba's son's increasing pulse and temperature, which he felt was going to be his next problem. As he entered the ward, he was still thinking about Kim's threat and did not immediately notice the three older boys sitting in the corner of the ward with their intravenous lines disconnected. Then he saw Sister Margarita standing in the middle of the ward fearfully unmoving. Standing in front of her, with an AK-47 slung over one shoulder and a large machete hanging from one hip, was a young man. A red bandanna tied around his head partly covered his severed left ear, testimony undoubtedly to some previous violent encounter. He wore a dirty green T-shirt with *Kariba's Army Rules OK* written across it. Christian walked in, and the young man turned away from the boys, taking up a stance between them and Christian. Looking to his left, Christian could see the two nurses were loading Kariba's son in the first bed onto a stretcher. They were being supervised by an older male who sat with his boots up on the ward desk, his AK-47 pointed in the direction of the two nurses. Kariba's henchmen had arrived to repatriate not only his son but also the other three injured boys. He looked at the older male who had now trained the AK-47 on him. A thin black moustache outlined voluminous lips. Yellowed sclera suggested he suffered from liver disease, as did the perspiration running from his brow.

"If you take him, he will die," Christian said, nodding in the direction of Kariba's son.

The mail with yellow eyes lowered the gun so that it centred on Christian's chest before speaking to one of the nurses in Kinyarwandan. When he had finished speaking to her, she walked to where Christian was standing at the foot of the bed. Her hand was shaking as she gestured to Christian to bend down so that she could whisper in his ear.

"He says that you need to go with them to make the boy well."

"Tell him that he needs surgery and the medicines that we only have here in the hospital."

Christian watched as she walked back and resumed a discussion in Kinyarwandan. As the nurse finished conveying Christian's instructions, sclerotic eyes focused unblinkingly on Christian.

"You come," he said

"He will die," Christian said as he heard Isabella walk into the ward behind him. Christian turned his head slightly, enough to see the look of horror on Isabella's face. The perspiring face behind the AK-47 moved the gun and pointed it in Isabella's direction as he indicated to one of the nurses to come closer. Once he finished talking to her, she approached Christian and again whispered in his ear.

"He is going to take Doctor Isabella and then if Kariba's son dies, she dies," she said.

He turned to explain what had been said to Isabella, when yellow eyes issued a command to the younger male in the red bandanna. The three boys in the corner then immediately stood up and walked out through the front door. Taking his boots off the desk, yellow eyes stood up and prodded Isabella in the same direction with his AK-47.

"Wait," Christian said, positioning himself between the barrel of the gun and Isabella. With one hand placed over the barrel of the gun, he stared at the jaundiced eyes. The black pupils were like coloured stones in sea of poisonous sulphur. As they stared at each other, he could feel Isabella push in behind him and take her phone out of the pocket of his white coat. Thankfully, she had remembered. At least they would have communication.

As Isabella was marched out of the ward, he could see the prescient fear in her eyes. The overwhelming feeling of wanting to protect her briefly threatened his rational thought. He turned away, knowing the best way to keep her safe was to keep Kariba's son alive. One of the nurses had put the young boy back in his bed and reattached his intravenous line. Christian checked that it was running correctly, and that he been given the correct dosage of antibiotics that morning.

Emmanuel put his head in his hands as Christian related the incident to him. Slowly he looked up to where Christian was sitting and shook his head.

"This is not good. I will need to inform the Minister of Police and the Minister of Health."

He then reached for the phone on his desk, and as he did so, it rang. Christian listened as Emmanuel spoke in a combination of French and Kinyarwandan. They were short words, and it was mostly Emmanuel who was listening and replying. After a minute, he put the phone down and looked at Christian.

"That was Kariba. He wanted to make it plain that if his son, Prince Kariba he called him, died then so did Isabella. And if there was any attempted rescue or publicity, he would kill her anyhow."

"I am going to go and see his son; I have been concerned about his temperature," Christian said, not quite certain what else to say or do.

He walked out onto the dirt roadway and headed towards the surgical ward. He noticed a small group walking up the hill towards him. They were three or four mothers and their children. Two of the children were strapped on their mothers' backs African style, swaying gently with each step; next to one of the mothers was a young boy in white flowing Muslim robes. When they drew level with Christian, he felt the young boy's hand momentarily touch his. A small piece of paper was pressed into his palm. Christian stopped and was about to say something to the boy when he noticed one of Kim Yao's assistants standing next to Accident and Emergency watching him. He squeezed the paper deeper into the palm of his hand and headed to the operating theatre where he knew he could read it unobserved.

Closing the theatre door behind him, he looked into theatre and the changing room to make sure he was alone before unfolding the paper. Mohammed had written that Michelangelo was well and they were doing his dressings twice a day as instructed. If Christian would like to come to five o'clock prayers at the mosque the next day, he could see and check up on Michelangelo's progress. Christian quietly sighed. At least that was one thing less to worry about. He would go and see Kariba's son, and see whether his temperature had come down as hoped.

Chapter 20

Christian found Emmanuel waiting outside the surgical ward. They walked down the hill together, both pleased to be out of the hospital and away from the day's trauma. Cicadas stretched their lymbals from a clicking sound to a raspy irreverent evening chorus. In another world, the night smells and sounds would have soothed his soul.

"Kariba's son. He is going to survive?"

"I don't think it's the burns that are going to be the major issue. We will clean those in theatre in the morning. They don't seem to be infected, but he is spiking a temperature and his pulse rate is above normal."

"Most of the children here have malaria; you should consider that. Perhaps treat him as though he has, since there is so much riding on his getting better."

"I was going to start him tomorrow on malarone that Isabella had brought me. I will switch to another antibiotic and hope I do not relapse. There is one piece of good news: Michelangelo is safe and doing well," Christian said as they turned into the Sudani's driveway.

"That's good to hear. You will also need to let Isabella's mother know what has happened."

"I was going to get my phone once we were inside and call my mother in Australia who has Nadine's number in Cape Town. I want to send Isabella a text as well so that she knows that we are thinking about her. Fortunately, she remembered to take her phone from my pocket when she was taken away."

Their feet crunching on the rock chips as they walked up the driveway alerted Chantal to their presence. As they approached the back door, she smiled and waved. Emmanuel, in the gathering darkness, fumbled for the key long enough to allow Chantal to unlock the door from the inside.

"Good evening, darling," she said to Emmanuel as she opened the door, the smell of her vegetable curry drifting past her to Christian.

He was instantly reminded that he had not eaten all day and was ravenous. However, he knew he could not relax until he had phoned his mother and sent a text message to Isabella. As Emmanuel turned into the kitchen, Christian continued down the hallway to his room. On the floor next to his bed, he noticed his rucksack. That was a little strange, he thought, as he had left it under his bed that morning. The other strange thing was that all the contents had been emptied and placed neatly alongside the rucksack. For a moment, he wondered whether Chantal had been tidying up. However, he was certain she would not have gone through his rucksack, nor could he imagine she would place everything in it in a neat tidy pile next to it if she had. He quickly reached inside his rucksack searching for his phone and the small bag, which held his passport and documents. He could not feel them. He searched the three zip pockets and in one of them, found his phone. He moved back from the bed to where there was light coming through the door from the kitchen. A small star in the top right hand corner indicated there was a message. He touched the screen to open the message on his note page. *We will find him* was all that it said. Kim Yao had clearly been through his belongings; he hoped she had not been able to access his address book, which contained Mohammed's number.

He walked back down the hallway to the kitchen and quickly glanced into Isabella's room. Her rucksack he could see tucked under the bed, undisturbed. In the kitchen, Emmanuel and Chantal were in one of their familiar, loving embraces.

"What is it , Chris?" Chantal said seeing the concern on his face as he walked in.

"My passport is missing; someone seems to have been through my things."

"Are you sure? The back door was locked when I came home and Anna our maid hasn't yet arrived."

"Yes, I double checked. My passport and health documents have all disappeared."

"I can't imagine who would be able to silently break in like that," Emmanuel said.

"I think it's pretty clear who it is," said Christian, holding up the phone with the message on it.

Christian could not enjoy the meal; he felt nauseated. He kept thinking about Kim's threat and how he needed to inform both Isabella's mother and his mother. He excused himself from the table and went through into the front room. He sat and thought about how difficult life had suddenly become before sending a text message to Isabella. *Stay strong, Kariba's son okay, we will see you soon.* He waited for a few minutes hoping that there might be a reply. There was not.

"You can use our phone to call your mother in Australia if you would like," Chantal said from the lounge room doorway, interrupting his thoughts.

Christian smiled and nodded his thanks. He dialled the Australian number and listened while the phone rang, trying to imagine the golden retriever sitting in her favourite position. He wondered whether she knew, in that instinctive way that dogs have of knowing things, that it was Christian phoning. He closed his eyes and imagined her soft ears, which she loved having scratched. He suddenly missed her intensely.

"Hello." His mother's voice interrupted his thoughts.

"Hi, mum. It's Christian."

"Yes, sweetheart, I should know your voice after all these years! And it is lovely to hear it again. How are you?"

"Mum, there is a bit of an issue which I need your help with."

Christian then explained about the events of the day. As he spoke, he could sense his mother processing the information; all of her intelligence, which normally analysed pathology, concentrated on what he was telling her. In addition, as he had come to expect when he finished, she took over. Telling him first that Isabella's mother, Nadine, would be contacted and not to worry about that. She would also send her an email with all the details in the morning. Moreover, Kariba's son may have drug-resistant TB. He should also consider that HIV might be a cause and start him on retroviral medication. She had a copy of all his documents, as well as passport and health certificates. The Department of Foreign Affairs she would contact in the morning to get special travel documents issued through the embassy in Kenya. When Christian told her about the lack of medications available in Garanyi, she said that Sibokwe was now the Minister of Health in South Africa and she would ask him to send antibiotics by courier the following day for Kariba's son. Christian put the phone down grateful for his mother's considerable resources, but still wondering whether he would sleep.

A mosquito's incessant buzzing on the mosquito net woke him. Partly opening his eyes, he could see the fingers of the early morning light reaching beneath the curtains into his room. A mosquito silhouetted, as a tiny black spot above his head. He watched, not moving, as it searched determinedly for a way through the net. Then without a second thought, he swatted it viciously. All that remained was a tiny smear of blood marking the spot on the torn net, an odious exclamatory epitaph. The satisfaction that the small smear of blood produced initially shocked him, as well as his angry reaction in killing the mosquito. For a minute or two, there had been intense satisfaction but then the feeling of frustration had returned. It was suppressed anger and frustration at not being able to protect Isabella.

There were no other sounds in the house - it was too early for Emmanuel and Chantal. He got up quietly and dressed, hoping that Kariba's son had improved overnight. Checking his phone as he pulled on his shirt, he was disappointed. There were no messages from Isabella. There was one from Cindy saying to call him when he could, and another from his mother saying to stay calm; everything is under control. He took the remaining malarone tablets and put them in his pocket for Prince Kariba, before letting himself out through the back door and snipping the lock. At 6:30 AM in the morning, there were only a few people out. Most were carrying some produce for the town market. A few who now knew him greeted him as he walked, but he was too busy processing the possible scenarios for Kariba's son to be able to respond cheerfully.

Walking in through the ward door, he knew the first thing that he would see was the temperature chart at the foot of the bed. As he walked towards it, he could see there had been a steady increase overnight. Kariba's son, he noted, was restless and a new nurse, whom Christian did not recognize, was trying to calm him down. She called Prince Kariba Matthew, and was dabbing at his perspiration with a small towel. From the foot of the bed he could see perspiration gathering in small pools on the plastic mattress. Christian said good morning to the nurse and felt for Matthew's pulse. He counted 120 beats per minute; Matthew had a tachycardia and was septic. Sepsis, if it not treated correctly, would result in death. He asked for a pair of scissors and quickly removed the bandages covering the burns. There was no sign of gross sepsis, meaning something else was causing his high temperature. Christian examined his abdomen and chest, and both looked fine but then as he took out his stethoscope, Matthew coughed. Dark green phlegm flecked with blood narrowly missed him and landed on the floor next to the bed. Putting his stethoscope on Matthew's chest, he heard the coarse crackles and bronchial breathing that is advanced lung disease associated with TB. To be sure of curing him, they would need the specific medicines from South Africa. If they did not get them within forty-eight hours, Matthew and Isabella may die.

He doubled the dose of the antibiotics, knowing that it would be of little benefit against the tuberculosis bacillus. Nevertheless, it felt like he was doing something, however irrational, to keep Isabella safe and alive. He checked the intravenous line to make sure that it was running correctly and then headed to the pharmacy and the computer. Once inside with the door locked, he scanned the shelves in case there was any isoniazid that he could give to Matthew—there wasn't.

The computer only took a few seconds and then the emails flashed up. True to Renata's word, her email was one of the first telling him that everything was under control. He saw that she had copied it to Nadine, Isabella's mother. Nadine's email, when he opened it, reminded him that she had the same efficient gene as his mother. She was concerned for Isabella but it was more about what needed to be done to get her back. Nadine quickly explained that she had been in contact with Sibokwe and that the drugs would be delivered within forty-eight hours. She had also contacted Mike and Galela, who were on their way to Garanyi, and they would bring the medication.

It was nine years since he had seen Galela, who with Mike had rescued both he and Isabella from the renegade white supremacist group in South Africa. Both, he knew, now belonged to the new National Government Intelligence Agency in South Africa. He knew that Mike had given up full-time anaesthetics and become head of the South African government's equivalent to the CIA. Galela, he had heard, remained the head of covert operations. Having them both would be great moral support.

As he closed off the computer, he remembered the text message from Cindy. He quickly sent a message asking if she was free to talk. The message quickly returned. *Be careful I am being watched, have new information about Kim and Michelangelo. Phone you later.* Thank goodness, Mike and Galela were coming he thought, things were starting to get out completely of his league. He closed down the computer and thought he would pay Matthew one final visit before he headed to the overnight carnage, which would be waiting in Accident and Emergency. Thankfully, Doctor Nikita was back which meant he would have the afternoon off from surgery. Peering through the open door into the ward, he could see that Matthew was more restless. In the middle of a coughing fit, the new nurse, Saone, had bought in the bottom half of an old Coca-Cola bottle as a spittoon. Christian could see that was already one third full of green phlegm and blood. However, next to his head, a woman was now seated. Christian assumed that Matthew's mother had arrived. If anything happened to Matthew, there would be no delaying the news to Kariba.

The morning's surgery he did on autopilot. Fractures reduced; lacerations sutured, two babies delivered by caesarean section. Teresa, who had been assisting him, had been her normal efficient self. She had sensed his stress, and quietly handed him the instruments and the sutures. Satilde had managed to keep the patients mostly restrained and without too much movement. After suturing the last patient, he tore off his surgical gloves, walked out through the small theatre reception room, and stood outside breathing in the fresh air. Part of him immediately wanted to check on Matthew in the hope that he was improving; the doctor in him knew that there would be no change without the new drugs. One of the reasons that he had opted for surgery is that it mostly eliminated uncertainty. If there was a problem, you could diagnose it, operate on it, and fix it. He had never been good at sitting and waiting. While thinking about how frustrated he felt, his phone vibrated in his pocket. He took it out and looked at it. There was a message was from an unknown number, although he recognized the prefix +27 as being from Cape Town. Touching the screen revealed the message: *Arriving early hours of the morning, with drugs, staying at the Lakeside hotel. Join us for breakfast. Mike.* Christian heaved a small sigh of relief. Mike and Galela would not only arrive early, but they had the drugs to help

Matthew survive and ensure Isabella's safe return. He decided to go and have lunch down by the lake to dissipate some of the stress. He would also treat himself to a cold beer before heading back up to the mosque to check on Michelangelo.

The Norfolk pines by the edge of the lake were over one hundred feet tall. The first Belgian colonials had planted them in the 1800s, as a reminder of Europe. Now mature and fully grown they stood as magnificent guardians of the lakeshore; acres of shade scattered underneath, a refuge from the hot African sun. Christian could have eaten his hamburger sandwich at the hotel, but the hotel's luxury and its magnificent swimming pool were so strangely at odds with the poverty around him; eating there would have seemed somewhat surreal. Sitting in the shade under a huge tree did not produce, he had found, the same discordant feeling. As he sat in the shade he could see groups of three or four people around him, some sleeping, others with children playing happily in the water, a reminder that poverty did not always preclude happiness.

As he ate his sandwich, one of three children playing in the water smiled and waved at him. Christian waved back, touching the cold primus beer bottle, enjoying the condensation on the glass and how refreshing it would be to drink. He took his first drink and closed his eyes to enhance the enjoyment of the scene, and temporarily close out the world. He then slowly opened his eyes to take in the vista that was the lake when he saw standing in front of him one of the young children who had been playing in the lake. Five or six years of age, the young boy was looking intently at Christian. Large eyes were framed by angelic face, curious perhaps to see someone so white in an area, which was normally African.

"Bonjour," said Christian.

There was no response other than a huge smile. It was then that Christian noted the red tinge to the boy's hair and his potbelly, all signs of malnutrition. The boy's gaze quickly shifted to Christian's hamburger. In the distance, he could sense the boy's parents watching. He wondered briefly whether they too had not eaten and for how long. He motioned to the boy to sit down next to him. Then he waved his arms at the other two children at the water's edge, indicating they should come and join their brother. When they were all sitting next to him, he divided the hamburger in three parts, giving one to each. They ate slowly, never taking their eyes off Christian, as if uncertain as to whether this was really happening to them. When they finished, they turned and looked at their parents, who smiled at Christian and waved their thank you. Then the three children got up and stood looking at Christian, hunger temporarily satiated, a gratitude lingered briefly in their eyes before they gave loud squeals and raced back to their parents. For several minutes, they all sat looking at each other smiling.

The beer tasted even better, as he watched the children splash about at the water's edge. He had not thought about the dramas at the hospital for at least twenty minutes, a small act of kindness reminding him of one of the reasons that he was in Africa. That contrasted with much of what he had learnt in the last few weeks. The Congo was one of the most beautiful and populous regions of the world, exploited mercilessly, by those interested only in power and money. The richness of resources, buried amongst poverty, with a great potential to alleviate, was obstructed by some strange Faustian agreement, by those whose souls' satanically worshiped money. Foreign governments, driven by a desire to drive their economies irrespective of the human cost, ignored the abuses of women and children, abuses which should have demanded their intervention not exploitation. The local militias were viciously protecting their interests while arguing flagitiously that without them, many would die of starvation. It was a devil's cauldron continuously fed by greed and the need for power, uncontrolled, unsanctioned, viewed by a world apathetic to its barbarism. He looked at his watch and saw that it was 3:30 PM, time to head back up to the town and the mosque. He stood up waved at the family who smiled and then headed back up the hill.

To get to the mosque he had to walk past the hospital. Despite it being his afternoon off, he needed to know about Matthew. Walking into the ward again, he knew that he should not have called in. Matthew had a large oxygen cylinder next to the head of his bed. He clearly was struggling to breathe, eyes wide open with anxiety that oxygen deprivation brings. His mother was sat holding his hand, dabbing repeatedly at his increasing perspiration. Matthew and, therefore, Isabella were going to need a miracle. Leaving the ward, he realised that he had hardly had a chance to think about Michelangelo. He walked out through the front gate and headed up the dirt road to the town. Despite the stream of people in both directions, making it difficult to isolate one person, he had the feeling he was being watched. He glanced around as casually as he could, but could see no one that he recognised. As he reached the main street, the wind blew and the curtains drifted back on the upstairs balcony of the shop selling spices. A small flash of yellow was momentarily exposed. He recognised it as the distinctive bright yellow jacket that Kim Yao had worn. From where she was watching, she would be able to see him enter the mosque. He stopped, uncertain as to whether to continue or to turn back. As he stood trying to make up his mind, he saw the young boy who had passed him the note approaching. As he passed Christian, he stumbled, bumping into him, grasping Christian's arm to rebalance. As he helped the young boy up, he pressed another sheet of paper into his hand. Not looking down at what he had been given, Christian searched for small side street that would be away from the prying eyes of those who watched him. Ten metres ahead he found a small alleyway, and without looking around, he casually turned into it and quickly looked at the piece of paper. *Go to the market, not the mosque.*

The market was at the far end of town. It took him ten minutes further walking to get there. The entrance was protected by two large oval gates. Walking through, he stopped and looked around. Dozens of stalls with clothing and handbags were intermingled with those selling live chickens, fruit, and vegetables. It was the fourth stall down on the right that caught his eye. The little boy who had passed the note to him in the street stood half hidden behind the handbags, beckoning him with his hand. By the time he got to the stall, the boy had gone but he could see at the far end sackcloth through which he must have disappeared. Christian parted the sackcloth and on the other side he could see the boy with two other men, dressed in Muslim robes. They both motioned to Christian to keep quiet. One of the men then walked back past him, opened the sackcloth, and peered out into the market. Satisfied that Christian had not been followed, he then handed him a flowing Black Muslim burqa to put on with full-face covering. Black gloves eliminated any trace of his white skin. The man who had handed him the clothes explained that Christian needed to follow them at a distance of several meters. He must not look at anyone just concentrate on the heels in front of him.

They left the market through the main gate. Christian concentrating on the heels in front of him, taking small steps so as his shoes did not show out under the front of the robe. They all reached the mosque as the call was going out on the loudspeakers summoning everyone to prayer. Inside the mosque, he removed his shoes as he saw everyone else doing. Then he noticed that the women were being directed to a separate room upstairs. Mohammed then appeared from a side door and stopped in front of him.

"Go into that small room over there," he said and walked on.

The wooden door had 'Praise Allah' written across it in large gold letters. Underneath was a picture of the prophet Mohammed. Christian opened the door into the room, which had a single chair in one corner with white flowing robes folded neatly on top of the chair. A small white prayer cap and turban rested neatly on top of the robes. Christian quickly exchanged the black robes and the burqa. He put on the prayer cap and wrapped the turban around the cap and his face so that only his eyes were visible. The long flowing robes would cover his hands as long as he kept them clasped. The turban securely tucked in, he heard a knock at the door. He opened it to see Mohammed again standing there. He looked Christian up and down, then smiled approvingly before saying,

"Go back into the mosque. There is a prayer mat in the fifth row from the front. Michelangelo will be next to you."

Christian walked back through the main entrance into the mosque. Walking up the side of the mosque, he could see there were at least 200 men, bent low, praying on mats that faced obliquely across the large hall. In the right hand corner was a small pulpit. As he slowly walked up the hall, he saw the vacant mat the fifth row from the front. Christian knelt on the vacant mat, before bending forward in the motion of prayer in the way that he saw the other men doing. Then he glanced under his right arm and saw Michelangelo's wide eyes looking back at him. There was uncertainty and a little fear until Christian winked. Then he heard Mohammed say,

"Glory be to my Lord, the most high."

That verse he had remembered hearing in a Christian church. As they stood up to pray, he could feel Michelangelo looking at him. As they finished the standing prayer and began the second prostration, he squeezed Michelangelo's hand. He could see that had caused a large smile. With the finish of prayer time, one of the men who had brought them to the mosque directed him to the front and took them behind the pulpit. A door led through to a small prayer room where Mohammed was now sitting on a chair.

"Please feel free to take off your turban and cap," he said as Christian walked in.

Unravelling the turban, Christian folded it and placed it neatly on the desk as he heard Michelangelo sit down and ask for a glass of water. Christian sat on one of the spare chairs next to Mohammed and held out his arms to Michelangelo. He rushed into Christian's arms grasping his flowing robes as though he intended never to let go.

"I promised you we wouldn't let you go back," Christian said holding him at arm's-length before taking his turban to wipe the tears from Michelangelo's eyes. Mohammed gave them a few minutes before saying:

"Kim Yao has been staying in that boarding house down the street since yesterday. She has five men with her. One of the brothers told us that she's been making inquiries about any boys fitting Michelangelo's description and the five men are checking on any families around town."

"A mosque seems to be a very safe place to be then."

"It usually is one of the safest places to be," Mohammed said smiling. "Michelangelo has joined our family and none of the brothers will say anything to anyone so he is quite safe. He has also started talking to us. It appears one of the boys at the orphanage who was trusted to serve at the meetings they held stole an iPad and showed it to Michelangelo. Then they beat the boy until he confessed. And to ensure that no details of that meeting should emerge all the boys, including Michelangelo, were delivered to Brutal Bosco, trusting they would be killed in the fighting with Kariba."

"Does he remember what was on the iPad?"

"Yes, there were details of the meeting. Those details were apparently transferred by an application that went to an iPhone, belonging to a friend of yours called Cindy. Michelangelo just wanted to clear diagrams so they could play minesweeper and pushed an application called Bump to clear the screen. Kim Yao would have only found out much later that that information had been transferred. She knows, therefore, that Michelangelo has seen that information and that it has been transferred to Cindy's phone."

"Do you remember anything that was on the iPad?" Christian said, looking at Michelangelo.

"Yes, the diagrams," Michelangelo quietly whispered.

"Keep him safe. I have two friends arriving tonight from the National Government Intelligence Agency in South Africa, and they might have suggestions on what we can do. I will call Cindy tonight. She may not realise that information is on her phone and the danger that she is in."

"Okay, we going to take you back to the market. We will dress you in the black robes and then take you back to our stall. You have my number; we will take good care of Michelangelo. Text me when you have met with your friends and have developed a plan."

Walking back through the town, Christian knew he was being observed. Now at least he knew how desperate Kim Yao was to get at Michelangelo. Hopefully Mike and Galela would have a plan to deal with her. He walked past the hospital but did not go and check on Matthew. He had enough to deal with, and he knew that Doctor Rashid would be doing his utmost with what they had, to ensure that Matthew survived. He turned left into Sudani's driveway, hoping the day had no more challenges left. Then remembering he had to contact Cindy, he hurriedly sent her a text message and waited a few minutes, but there was no response. He put the key in the lock to the back door and as it opened, he could smell the fresh coffee. Looking through into the kitchen, he was surprised to see Cindy sitting on one of the chairs. He locked the back door, by which time Cindy was in front of him hugging him as though he was a long lost friend.

"What a wonderful surprise!" he said as she extricated herself from his hug and let him by the hand into the kitchen.

"I just needed to see you and talk to you about what was going on. I have been so scared in the last few days after I found all the details of that meeting on my iPhone and of course I was worried about Michelangelo."

"Did you bring the iPhone?"

"Oh my God, you know about that?"

"I saw and talked to Michelangelo this afternoon."

"They demanded my phone but I refused. I realised after I read the information that was transferred, how important it was. I also knew that it was only a matter of time before they just came and took it with force so I caught the bus to you."

"I'm sure that they know you are here. I spotted Kim and some of her assistants in the town this morning hoping obviously that I would lead them to Michelangelo."

"Kim also knows that Michelangelo has a photographic memory; therefore they need both my iPhone and Michelangelo to ensure the Chinese government is not severely embarrassed."

"I assume Chantal knows that you are here and let you in?"

"Yes she was wonderful. Put on the coffee and said that I could use the bedroom where Isabella was staying."

"Do you have your iPhone?"

"It's in my bag. I'll go and get it!"

Cindy show Christian Notes on her phone where the Bump application had transferred the documents. The first document had a heading in English. It was titled Acquisition and Control of Resources/ Congo. What followed was a list of large Chinese corporate companies linked to a holding company in Beijing called Dragons Lair and located at the National Defence Ministry. Another diagram showed that Dragons Lair was in turn was an extension of Central Military Commission of the People's Republic of China. It was clearly official Chinese government business, the publication of which would be devastating.

The second document he opened outlined a strategy to provide direct access for Chinese companies to the resources of the Congo. A detailed plan included utilizing Rwandan support, both political and business. A list of prominent Rwandan executives and politicians was included in the first subsection. Humanitarian Aid was to be utilised as a front to boost China's international image and facilitate the takeover of Northern Congo. An orphanage within half an hour of the Congolese border was to be acquired with the help of the Rwandans, and to be fully supported by the Chinese National Defence Ministry. It would also coordinate the distribution of arms to supportive militia. A subsection in the second document was titled: Military support for the killing of Kariba Offengowe. The killing was proposed at a meeting outside of Goma. Comptoirs Assad and Segal, who controlled the resources out of Congo, were to be present and were to be blamed for the killing. The power vacuum that would ensue would allow China and Rwanda, through Brutal Bosco, full access to all the Congo's minerals.

A further document outlined the financial commitment of Chinese companies to the building in Rwanda of warehouses, factories to produce computers and mobile phones as well as repackaging centres for truckloads of ore. All resources would then be rebranded and sent to smelters, nominated by the Chinese National Defence Ministry. This document said it would avoid international approbation for extraction of mineral resources from the Congo utilising child and slave labor.

Christian looked up at Cindy once he had finished reading.

"Have you emailed this to someone you trust?"

"Yes, my brother in Wisconsin who is a judge."

"Good, as long as someone has it, that may well be then a guarantee against anything happening to you or Michelangelo."

"Can I see Michelangelo? I would love to give him a hug and just reassure him."

"I'm sure we can arrange that tomorrow. We might need to get you some long flowing robes," Christian said as Cindy gave him a puzzled look in return.

Chapter 21

"Christian."

Christian partly opened his eyes, and could see the small black silk surgical suture with which he had repaired the mosquito net. Beyond, he could see Emmanuel's concerned face staring at him.

"Christian, are you awake?" Christian now also felt a gentle shake of his shoulder through the mosquito net.

Half asleep, Emmanuel's question still struck him as one of those strange questions to ask someone, whether they were awake when you could clearly see that they were asleep.

"What is it?"

Christian opened his eyes fully, his brain starting to function. It must be something serious, as Emmanuel never came in to wake him up, only Chantal. That he was not smiling suggested something very significant.

"Is it Isabella?"

"No, get up and come through to the kitchen and I'll tell you what has happened at the hospital overnight."

"The friends of mine who arrived from South Africa, which I told you about last night, have medication for Matthew that we can start this morning," Christian said as he pulled on his clothes. However, Emmanuel had already walked back into the kitchen.

Christian walked into the kitchen tightening his belt; at one end of the bench was a cup of coffee, steam gently drifting upwards. Emmanuel was sitting at the other end, an empty bread and butter plate with a few scattered crumbs from recent toast, next to his cup. Christian sat down on the spare stool, looked at the steam rising from his coffee, and decided it was too hot to drink. He looked across at Emmanuel. He had not moved from the time that Christian had come into the room, and his eyes remained fixed on his coffee. The way in which both hands encircled the cup suggested to Christian that the news was even worse than what he anticipated. Emmanuel felt Christian's gaze and looked up.

"There is no easy way to say this; Matthew died last night."

Christian felt the sickening feeling rise in his throat, and briefly wondered whether he would throw up. Matthew was dead; what hope was there now for Isabella?

"The only hope for Isabella is to try to get her back from Kariba. I think I should come and meet those friends of yours who arrived from South Africa last night. There is a small window of opportunity as Matthew's mother left to go and look after one of her other sick children last night. She will not get the news of Matthew's death until later this morning."

"I was going to meet them for breakfast at 7 AM; I'll just let Cindy know what we are doing."

Emmanuel and Christian walked the 1 km to the Lakeside Hotel in silence. Christian had given Cindy Mohammed's phone number and suggested that she text him after the morning prayers. He would, Christian knew, work out a way to get Cindy to see Michelangelo. The Lakeside Hotel car park was lined with old Victorian style lights, another reminder of the homesick Belgian colonials. The antique lights contrasted vividly with many sparkling new four-wheel drive vehicles parked side-by-side, the United Nations logo loudly emblazoned on their doors.

The young girl behind the reception desk smiled broadly as they walked in and welcomed Emmanuel as a friend. After a few minutes of chatting, Emmanuel turned and said to Christian,

"Your friends are waiting for us out on the deck next to the pool. Follow me."

A sliding door led out onto a large wooden deck on which were half a dozen round tables. Each had shelter provided by a large green canvas umbrella. An enormous kidney-shaped swimming pool stretched beyond the deck towards the lake. At the third table to the left, as they walked out through the sliding door, he could see Mike McMahon and Galela. When he had visited Cape Town immediately before doing medicine, Mike and his wife Sian had looked after him. They had also helped in the search for information on his father, Jannie de Villiers. Mike, in addition, had also been the anaesthetist and coordinator of his father's liver transplant program. Mike and Sian had then introduced him to Sibokwe, his father's first successful child liver transplant recipient. Sibokwe was now Minister of Health in South Africa. Galela at the time was the only black operative in the white apartheid Bureau of State Security [B.O.S.S.]. He had never established whether Galela had another name. He had always just known him as Galela. Mike and Galela had rescued both he and Isabella from the mine where a white supremacist group had held them hostage. Both had become firm friends with his mother and he knew they remained in regular email contact.

As he looked across to where they both sat, the familiar tousled hair and profile of Mike was reassuring to see. He looked as fit and as athletic as when he had last seen him in Cape Town. Mike was casually dressed in a light blue polo neck shirt, short sleeves displaying the muscular forearms related to his long-term interest in the martial arts. Galela with his back to him was still instantly recognizable. Broad shoulders, a thick muscular neck, and a height of 193 cm still suggested great physical power and dominance—a power which had been instrumental in saving Christian's life.

Mike immediately stood up on seeing them walk out through the sliding door and called out.

"Christian, great to see you!" before closing the space between them with two big strides, grinning broadly and then taking Christian in a firm embrace.

"Great to see you too, Mike. It doesn't seem like nine years; you look as fit and healthy as when I last saw you in Cape Town," Christian said, before turning to introduce Emmanuel.

Galela pushed his chair back from the table and waited for Christian to disentangle himself from Mike before grasping Christian's hand and with a knowing smile, saying:

"Good to see you, young man. You have turned out to be the spitting image of your dad. Come and sit down; we have got lots to talk about and not much time, I think."

The large green umbrella shaded the table from the early morning sun, but not the dazzling glare from the crystal-clear swimming pool. Christian positioned himself with his back to the swimming pool to reduce the glare, while Mike and Galela reached for their sunglasses. It was, Christian felt, a little surreal, almost like a scene from some spy movie, two genuine spooks in sunglasses, he with information for the next mission.

"Would you like coffee or breakfast?" Mike said as he pulled out a long sealed cardboard tube from a brown leather bag next to his chair.

"I will have bacon and eggs and sausages," Emmanuel quickly replied, scanning the menu, while Mike extracted what appeared to be a map from the cardboard tube.

"Nothing for me," Christian said to the waiter who was now taking Emmanuel's order.

Christian watched Mike straighten out the rolled up paper. He placed the pepper grinder on one corner, then the saltshaker on the other, and finally the sugar bowl at the bottom edge to prevent the paper curling up. Christian moved a little closer to see what had been unfurled. It was, from the markings, a satellite map on which a line had been drawn indicating the Congolese and Rwandan borders. On the Congolese side was marked North and South Kivu, and in the northern part of the map, there were three distinct triangles; one was circled. All were approximately fifteen to twenty kilometres inside the Congo, he estimated according to the scale on the side of the map. Christian wanted to ask how they had satellite maps when South Africa had no satellites. Mike, reading his mind, pointed at the bottom of the map where it was stamped *International Intelligence Community.*

"Those are the three locations where we think Isabella might be held," Galela said. "We have asked our friends in IIC to monitor that region and they have narrowed it down to that site there which has been circled, which also is the closest to one of the largest mining operations at Mount Golgotha and has a fully functional airport next to it for the export of ore to Goma. This is the magnified version of that circled area."

Christian and Emmanuel looked at the high-powered high-resolution photograph that Galela overlaid on the map. The detail was remarkable, almost as though someone had flown above it in a helicopter and photographed it from approximately eight hundred metres. It was a compound with one large multiform Weston style villa, surrounded on all sides by fences with one road leading to the main gate. All buildings were clearly visible, with fifteen or twenty small huts scattered throughout for security and some workers. There were sentry towers placed on each corner of the compound overseeing the airport. To Christian, it looked a formidable fortress.

"Isabella has her mobile phone with her," Mike said more as a statement then a question.

"Yes, she does, but I don't know whether it has been confiscated or switched off or disabled, as she hasn't replied to any of my text messages."

"That doesn't matter; we have checked. Kariba has created his own telecommunications tower which means we were able to access her phone. We have confirmed that the circle is currently the place where she's kept. The other places with silver triangles are where we have received other GPS coordinates. He obviously keeps moving her around."

"How did you manage that if the phone was either switched off or flat?" Emmanuel asked.

"We remotely uploaded a program Plan B to her phone. Nadine, Isabella's mother, found the details of her phone that she had purchased before going to London. We weren't certain from your email whether she had her phone with her, but when we uploaded Plan B, it automatically switched on her GPS locator in the phone. We texted 'locate' to the phone and the GPS coordinates confirmed that was the main house."

"You may only have a small window of opportunity to get her back," Emmanuel interrupted. "Matthew's mother will be returning to the hospital today and will find out that Matthew has died which will mean, given Kariba's reputation, he will kill Isabella."

"We need to move quickly then," Mike said looking at Emmanuel. "Do you have a vehicle that we could use to get close to the compound where she is being held in North Kivu?"

"The old ambulance that we used to get the boys back from the Congo, could we use that?" Christian said.

"You can certainly use that. I will walk up to the hospital and send it to meet you as I would assume that you're not going to go and try and rescue her empty-handed."

"We have come prepared, thanks to our friends in the airline who know how to get weaponry through customs."

"I want to come with you."

"Christian, knowing your father and your mother as I do, I thought you might say that. But this is potentially dangerous and I do not want to risk your mother's wrath again!"

"I know it's dangerous, but I have done dangerous with you before, remember, and the priority is to get Isabella out. In addition, if we can get photographic evidence of the abuse, it might help shock the world out of its lethargy when it comes to child slavery. I have not told you about Michelangelo and the Chinese development yet, but I suspect that is all involved. Besides which, Isabella brought me a 500 mm telephoto lens as a birthday present from my mother, which means I could record images safely from four hundred metres while you did your thing."

"Stubborn, just like your father was - and obviously with his gene to try and rectify wrongs in the world. All right, you can come with us but you are the driver. The deal is that you stay well back once we go to rescue Isabella. Agreed?"

"Agreed."

"We are also fully aware of the Chinese involvement and the desire for exclusive access to the minerals."

Within fifteen minutes John had arrived with the M.A.S.H. ambulance.

"Good luck," he said as he handed the keys to Christian. "Emmanuel has put your camera and telephoto lens under the front seat."

Mike and Galela quickly transferred two wooden boxes to the back of the ambulance from their four-wheel-drive, and then lashed them in place. Once secure, the combinations on the boxes were opened, and Christian could see that the first box contained first aid equipment: bandages, IV lines, and air splints. In the second were an assortment of weapons, some with telescopic sights, others short nosed machine pistols, and handguns.

"Let's go," Mike said, squeezing himself into the front seat alongside Galela, and closing the door. Both had on green and brown camouflage clothing with black leather gloves, the fingers of which had been cut out.

Christian headed out through the car park, turned right and up the hill past the hospital. The thought suddenly occurred to him that they would have to go through the main street and Kim might be watching. She might assume that they were going to rescue Michelangelo. He was clearly visible in the old truck, and pulling down the sunshade he knew would not fully obscure him from her view. The number of people streaming down the road meant he could not drive faster than first gear. If she was where she was the other day, she would certainly spot him. As they drew level with the balcony and window that she had been watching from the previous day, he quickly glanced up. Fortunately, there was no one in the window, no tell-tale splash of yellow from Kim's jacket. He quickly glanced down the alleyway next to the building. No black Range Rover to be seen. Twenty minutes beyond the town, the stream of people started to decrease and Christian could speed up a little bit. With concentration easier, Christian told Mike and Galela about Michelangelo. Mike, who had been watching the GPS tracker said without looking up, "Let us deal with Isabella first, if and then, we can sort out Michelangelo, who appears to be safe with Mohammed."

"Five minutes and then we take the left turn," Galela said as he glanced at Mike's GPS tracker.

The left-hand turned out to be not much more than a goat track. The old ambulance shook and bounced along the ruts. Every deep rut, it creaked or banged and sounded like many parts were about to break loose.

"Stop for a second," Mike said.

Christian stopped, Mike opened the door and climbed up on the tray of the ambulance. A few seconds after, he heard the wooden box closing and Mike was quickly back in the cab. He handed a small submachine gun to Galela. Christian watched as he checked the safety catch before putting the gun on the floor of the cab under his feet. Mike had a rifle with a telescopic sight and a silencer. He rested his on his knee.

"Okay, Christian, let's keep going. Ten minutes and then we need to proceed on foot."

"How far away are we?"

"Far enough away for you not to get hurt, but close enough that your mother might never ever talk to me again. Does that answer your question, my young friend?"

Christian nodded, and he sensed from the intensity on their faces that both Mike and Galela had switched into professional mode. They were both now watching the GPS tracker intently.

"Okay, stop here. Christian, stay here with the ambulance; turn it round to face back to where we need to go, in case we need to get out of here in a hurry."

Christian did not say anything, but he could not imagine the ambulance going anywhere in a hurry on the road that they had just come up. He realised also that plans had changed; he had hoped to at least be close enough to use his telephoto lens.

"How long do I wait for you and what happens if you don't come back?"

"We always come back," Galela winked at him. "We may also have had a little bit of luck; the GPS coordinates on Isabella suggest she has been taken out to the mine at Mount Golgotha, fifteen minutes from the main compound. That will be less heavily defended and easier to get her back. It also means we do not have to go past the main compound."

Christian glanced at the screen that Mike held as Galela pointed at the track through the bush to the mine. It would avoid the major road from the mine, which ran past the main compound. Mike and Galela assembled their hardware on the side of the track while Christian tried to turn the ambulance around. Finally, with it pointed back in the direction which they had come, in his rear vision mirror he could see Mike and Galela disappearing over the first rise in the goat track. He reached under the seat grabbed the camera case and lens, stashed keys under the rear tire, then headed quickly up the road after Mike and Galela.

Christian stopped at the first rise and found that he was able to clearly see them both 800 m ahead. He watched as they diverged left off the track into the bush. He gave them five minutes and then followed, making a note of the small rock where they had turned off. The bush was dense green foliage and it wrapped itself around his legs, but having been crushed by Mike and Galela, also provided a path for him to follow. Ten minutes later however, the beaten bush path stopped. Christian looked around, there was just dense jungle on all sides, and in front of him was a large rock. A miniature Uluru, he thought, in the middle of the Congo. He found a foothold and climbed up the face. On the far side, he could see the Mike and Galela's tracks starting again. Working his way carefully down the fifteen feet to the bottom, he turned around to look at the path when he noticed Mike crouching looking at him.

"I thought I told you to stay with the ambulance. This is not a mission for sightseers or photographers," he said looking at Christian's photography bag.

"Come on, Mike. You knew that I couldn't stay there waiting for you. I am my father's son as you said."

"Stay behind us then; do not say anything unless we speak to you."

Galela emerged from the bush ahead and they preceded single file in silence, stopping every fifteen minutes to check their position. An hour later without turning around, Galela indicated an immediate stop. Christian watched and followed as Mike and Galela lowered themselves to the ground before crawling to the top of the small rise in front of them. Mike pulled out pulled out the satellite-tracking screen, and Galela pinged Isabella's mobile phone. A small dot appeared, blinking on the screen.

"Over the next ridge, due north 800 metres away."

Christian wriggled his way through the undergrowth and stinging nettles, to position himself between Mike and Galela. Beyond the ridge was a scene that seemed to belong to another planet. Hundreds, if not thousands of boys, were traversing and excavating the side of a mountain. Denuded of all forest and undergrowth, all that remained was the brown earth pockmarked with excavations. It resembled the far away pockmarked surface of the moon, other than the fact that unlike the moon, it was a reechy faecal brown colour from all the ore tailings. He watched as boys were forced to extract large bags of ore from the various excavations. Many of the boys, only eight or nine years of age, struggled to pull huge hessian sacks over the lips of the craters. Christian knew the bags must weigh at least 50 kg. Then the boys, who all looked scrawny and malnourished, also had to carry heavy primitive digging tools on their backs. He could see how they struggled to manage so much weight. When some of the bags threatened to fall back into the excavation sites, one of the armed guards would rush to and with whips, try to beat them into a greater effort. Cries of anguish constantly reverberated around the hillside. The 50 kg bags of ore out of the small mines were met by an older male who rolled the bags down the hill to a conveyor belt and waiting trucks.

Christian, as he looked through his telephoto lens, could see some of the excavations were very small, only able to only fit two very young boys. For these excavations, seven or eight-year-old boys with torches strapped to their heads were sent down the mine to dig. Christian estimated the heat in the mine shafts could be close to 45 degrees. That would possibly explain the lifeless bodies he saw being pulled up out of some of the holes. Young boys unconscious from heat stroke, ropes tied around their hands like a dead animal, were slung over men's shoulders and taken down the mountain to a hut with a grass-thatched roof. Christian wondered whether that was a makeshift morgue.

"Can you see Isabella?" Mike whispered to Galela who had the binoculars.

"The GPS locates her down there at the bottom of the hill in that small hut with the grass-thatched roof where those lifeless young boys are being taken, but I can't see her in there."

"We need to make sure that she is in there and it is not just her phone that someone has taken."

Christian took the powerful binoculars and focused on the hut. There were eight boys lying on the floor. Christian could make out intravenous fluids hanging from the wooden poles. It was not a morgue, but a treatment hut, where they were being rehydrated so that they could be returned to the mountain excavations. As he scanned the boys with the binoculars, a movement inside the hut caught his eye. He could see someone connecting intravenous lines to the new arrivals. He refocused and suddenly saw that it was Isabella. He tugged at Mike's sleeve, and showed him what he had seen.

"We will need a diversion," Mike said. "Ingcuka, you will probably be able to get closer to where Isabella is, if I cause a diversion."

"Because I'm black and I will blend in better?" Galela winked at Mike.

Christian remembered their banter and camaraderie when he was rescued in South Africa. They were completely professional, working together as a lethal team, not diverted by any change in circumstances, however still able to lighten a situation with banter.

"If you can get close enough to that hut, then I will fire a phosphorous grenade to the section of the hill close to everyone. That will start a small fire and the ensuing chaos will give you five or ten minutes to get Isabella out."

"You stay here, Christian. This time I mean it. You can photograph anything that you like but once you see that Ingcuka has Isabella, head back to the truck as fast as you can."

Christian nodded, thinking that was one of the few times he had heard Galela's African name. No wonder everyone just called him Galela. He would ask Mike what it meant when they got out.

Christian screwed on the 500 mm telephoto lens as Galela backtracked to head down the mountain.

"Wait," he said a little too loudly. "There is a vehicle approaching the main gate."

Mike took the binoculars back as Christian focused on the approaching vehicle with his camera.

"Mike, it's the Chinese woman, Kim Yao, whom I was telling you about."

"Interesting that she is paying a visit to Kariba; she has obviously heard the rumour that Brutal Bosco has terminal cancer and might surrender to the ICC in order to get treatment in Europe. She's now, I suspect, hedging Chinas bets."

"If that's the case, then they wouldn't need to kill Kariba."

"And the Chinese and Rwandans end up with exclusive access to some of the world's most precious and scare resources. She may have brought a peace offering, so make sure you photograph this, Christian. We have the documents on Cindy's phone; however, a picture is still worth a thousand words."

"Mike, before you go, what you think those blue drums are stacked up at the airport, beneath the sentry tower?"

"I'm not sure. They could be stored fuel. See if you can see any markings with the digital binoculars."

"The writing is Arabic on the drums so I guess we are going to be none the wiser."

"Take a photo of one of them with that long lens of yours, Bluetooth that to my satellite pad, and we'll see what the smart boys in Johannesberg can tell us."

Christian took quite a few photos of the blue drums, uploaded them to Mike's satellite pad, and then watched as the distinctive black Range Rover pulled up at the gate. The armed guard temporarily left the thatched hut and spoke to Kim through the passenger window. The guard pointed to a parking space and the Range Rover moved forward parking next to the treatment hut. Kim Yao in her distinctive bright yellow jacket climbed out of the driver's seat, walked around, and with one of her assistants opened the doors and the boot. Six boys scrambled out, one of whom had on a T-shirt *Save the Children Orphanage*. Christian kept taking pictures as several older males escorted the boys up the hill to various excavation sites.

"The boys are obviously part of a peace offering to Kariba."

"Undoubtedly. I wonder what else the Chinese are now offering. That Range Rover looks like a better prospect to escape in than the ambulance we came in."

"We would have to get rid of the driver."

"I cannot see that that will be a great problem to Ingcuka. We just need to get him out of the way."

"She's heading up the hill in the direction of those boys."

"Okay." Mike whispered into his radio to Galela, "Let's do it. If the Range Rover is available, grab it, or if that's too well defended, shoot out the tyres. We don't want them following us."

Christian lay quietly next to Mike, photographing Kim Yao as she inspected some of the excavations. Then out of the corner of his eye, he saw a message flashing on Mike's pad. 'In position' was all that it said. Mike reached into his bag, pulled out a pistol, and turned towards Christian.

"In case anything happens, this is a Glock 20 pistol. It is on semiautomatic and you have fifteen rounds in the magazine. The tab on the pistol grip shows the safety is on. Turn this and the safety is off and the pistol is ready to use. Use it only if you are threatened, and whatever you do, do not tell your mother that I taught you to use this!"

"Thanks Mike. Hopefully I won't need it, but good protection nonetheless. I definitely won't tell her."

Mike quickly took another gun from the sack and fired a grenade. It whistled through the air and then exploded on the hillside with a bright yellow flame and clouds of white smoke. As the fire took hold amongst the scrub on the hillside, pandemonium broke out. Boys rapidly climbed out of excavations, supervisors with whips scrambled further up the hill. Galela emerged from the bush and ran crouched over towards the hut. The armed guard had moved to the corner of the hut to observe the growing fire. Galela knocked him out with the butt of his rifle. Moments later he emerged with Isabella, and crouched over, they ran towards the Range Rover. Christian watched as they frantically tried to open the doors which were locked. Then shouts erupted from the hill. Kim had spotted them and some of the guards were firing. Galela, still holding on to Isabella, ran and disappeared into the nearby bush.

"Christian, you head back to the truck. Ingcuka has enough on his plate getting Isabella out. I'm going to make sure the tires on that Range Rover are flat."

Christian put the Glock pistol in the camera case and headed back down into the undergrowth of the surrounding bush. The track was easy to follow and twenty minutes later, he emerged onto the track when he had left the ambulance. Before emerging from the bush, he checked to see that there was no one visible in either direction. Then emerging from the undergrowth, he hurried to where he had left the keys under the rear tire. Walking around the tray to the cab, he was about to open the door and when he sensed something moving in the bush, a little way from where he had exited. Mike could not have moved that quickly, he thought. Possibly an animal he thought, and opened the door. He was loading the camera case into the cab and was about to place it under it under the seat when he felt something prod him in the back.

"Ne déplacez pas."

Christian could feel the barrel hard up against his spine and knew not to move.

"Déplacer à l'arrière du camion."

He moved around to the back of the truck as instructed. The person with the gun standing behind him was not allowing Christian a view of who he was. At the rear of the truck, he was instructed in French again, to climb up and remain face down on the tray. Clambering up onto the tray, he wished he had kept his camera case with him. As he turned to see who it was pointing the gun at him, he heard a small cry and heard the gun fall to the ground. He looked around; his assailant had collapsed beside the goat track, blood streaming from a head wound. Christian looked up and saw Mike emerging from the track giving a thumbs-up sign. Beyond Mike a little bit further up the road, Galela and Isabella were hurrying towards the ambulance. He jumped down off the tray and climbed back in the cab. He had the engine started before they arrived. Isabella put her head through the drive's door, gave him a kiss on the cheek, and mouthed thank you before clambering up on the back of the truck with Mike. Galela got in the right-hand passenger door, his automatic weapon laid on the floor under his feet, a canvas bag similar to what he had seen Mike carrying placed on the seat next to him.

"If there was one, there are liable to be more. Don't stop driving. Just let me and Mike deal with it," Galela said as he used the rifle butt to smash the half-broken windscreen in front of him.

Christian drove as fast as he thought the ambulance would allow. Despite being designed as an off-road ambulance, the huge wheels were more suited for mud than the dry rutted African dirt and volcanic rocks. He glanced down at the speedometer; 20 mph was all he could manage. If they were pursued in anything more modern, they would be caught. Then he heard Mike start firing from the back of the ambulance. Glancing in the rear vision mirror, he could see the black Range Rover. He could see men were hanging from the windows firing indiscriminately in their direction. Christian instinctively crouched lower over the wheel, as he heard some of the bullets lodge in the cab. Galela was now out the passenger window looking to assist Mike. He heard the distinctive clatter from Mike's weapon. As they rounded a corner, he knew they were fifteen minutes from the town. Suddenly as he rounded the corner there was another large black four-wheel-drive across the road in front of him. Two men stood in front of it with automatic weapons aimed at them. He shouted at Galela as he applied the brakes.

"Don't stop. Go round them!" Galela said as he expertly shot the two men through the missing windscreen before jumping out of the passenger door rolling into the bush. Glancing back, he could see Mike had done the same, taking Isabella with him. Christian swerved to get around the rear of the black Mercedes four-wheel-drive, when he felt the wheels of the ambulance slide down the hill. It refused to go any further despite him trying to reverse back.

"Get out," he heard Mike shout from the bush.

Scrambling out of the cab, he grabbed the camera bag and crawled through the bush close to where he had seen Galela roll. In the distance, he could see the top of the black Range Rover parked across the road. An eerie quiet had descended upon the road. Christian knew the occupants of the Range Rover would be making their way through the bush towards them. Christian reached into the camera bag. He had a feeling he might need the Glock pistol. He also removed the SD card from the camera and slipped it into his rear pocket.

"They will try and get in front of us," Galela whispered in his ear having crawled up next to him. "We need that black Mercedes; can you crawl around the back while I cover you? Keep your head down and when you are ready to start, signal me with a fist in the air, and Mike and I will cover you."

Christian nodded and smiled at Galela and began crawling through the undergrowth to get to far side of the vehicle. At the rear of the black Mercedes, and still protected by the bush, he could see one of the men whom Galela had shot still holding the keys to the car. To be able to get them he would be in full view of whoever was up the road. However, if he did not get them, they all might die on the side of the road. He broke cover from the bush and ran as hard as he could, crouched over. As he drew level with the rear wheel, he heard the passenger window shatter above his head, sprinkling him with glass. Instinctively he dived to the ground, sliding to be within reach of the keys. He pulled the keys out of the hand of the dead driver, and rolled into the bush at the front of the Mercedes. Then he heard another bullet strike the front tire and the tire behind him. Kim and Kariba's gang were trying to isolate the Mercedes. Christian crawled up the bank to see whether the Mercedes was sitting on flat tires and whether they could still use it. As he peered through the grass at the top of the bank, he heard another shot and suddenly felt a burning in his right flank. As he looked down, blood was oozing through his shirt.

He called out to Galela, "I've been shot."

"Have you got the keys?"

"Yes," he shouted back.

"Stay where you are. I'll come and get you."

Christian ripped his shirt and then could see a bullet hole beneath his right rib cage. It had exited through his back; the real issue was what important organ it had hit and missed inside his abdomen. He knew that he was going to need surgery. If the bullet had sliced his liver, he doubted whether there would be anyone with the skill to repair it. At least there was the small comfort that if he did die, it was in the same continent that his father had died on. He could hear Galela crawling through the bush and wondered how much time he had as the blood had now soaked half of his shirt. Looking up, he saw Galela crawling across the road and crouching behind the rear wheel of the Mercedes. More shots struck the far side of the vehicle.

"Hang on, Christian. We going to get you out," Galela shouted to him under the car.

"I'm going to throw the keys to you underneath the car."

Christian threw the keys underneath the car and watched Galela pick them up. More gunfire erupted from close to the black Range Rover. There was no way that they would get into the car; as soon as they did, they would be sitting ducks and all would be killed. The firing then momentarily stopped. In the relative quiet, Christian could detect another car coming up the road from the direction of the town. If they were Kariba's men, they were going to be sandwiched. Galela heard the approaching vehicle and turned his gun to face the oncoming threat. A red Civic Honda then appeared around the corner and slid to a halt in a cloud of dust fifty metres from where they were. Four men leapt out carrying automatic weapons.

"Don't shoot!" they shouted as they ran crouched before diving into the bush next to them.

"Mohamed's friendly jihadists. We heard you were in trouble," one of the young man called out from his hiding place in the bush. Christian watched a series of hand signals. The long grass started to move as the one of the young man from the red Honda Civic crawled and then stood behind the front wheel of the Mercedes. Signalling silently to three of his friends, they positioned themselves behind with the Mercedes between them and the black Range Rover. Then as one stood and opened fire on the bush on either side of the Range Rover.

"Christian, the next time they do that, crawl towards their car," Galela shouted.

Christian watched as they reloaded magazines into their weapons, wondering how much blood he would lose crawling to the car, when he felt Mike and Isabella alongside him.

"Mike, I've been shot. I think it's serious and the bullet has gone through my liver. I'm going to need a laparotomy to stop the bleeding. I can feel my pulse is already 84 bpm so I'm losing a significant volume of blood."

Mike looked up and saw Galela pointing repeatedly at the red car. Mike turned and explained to the nearest gunman what they intended to do. He nodded showing Mike five fingers. As the fifth finger went up, the four young men stood up and started firing again as Mike and Isabella dragged Christian to the red Honda Civic. Once in the back seat, Isabella quickly removed Christian's shirt, tearing it using parts to plug the entrance and exit wounds.

"Doctor Sudani," Mike said into his mobile phone as they headed towards Garanyi. "Christian has been shot and is going to need a laparotomy. I can do the anaesthetic but we are going to need a surgeon a bit more experienced than a generalist. Is there anyone who is close that you could get urgently? We will be at the hospital in fifteen minutes."

"Hang on, Christian," Mike said as he switched his phone off. "We are in luck. The visiting surgeon from Syria, Josef Strauss, is at the hospital. He's going to wait for us in theatre, and he's previously done all kinds of complex surgery according to Emmanuel."

Arriving at the hospital, Mike and Galela lifted Christian out of the red Civic and carried him in through the theatre door. Emmanuel met them and quickly inserted an intravenous line into Christian's arm.

"Joseph is in theatre scrubbed up as is Teresa. All you need to do, Mike, is familiarise yourself with the ventilator and the drugs. Satilde is also here to help you do that. The changing room is there to your right."

Christian heard Mike changing and then walking through into the theatre.

"This will make you feel better," He said as he opened his medical supply bag and took out some propofol.

Emmanuel had changed into surgical scrubs as had John, who had appeared when he heard that it was Christian who was going to be operated on. They both lifted Christian onto the operating table and, looking up, Christian could only see the deep blue eyes of Josef Strauss.

"I think it has gone through my liver."

"Don't you worry; I have operated on many livers and even replaced some of them. You will be fine, besides which you also have an excellent anaesthetist."

Mike had his intravenous line running and started to trickle in the propofol. For a moment, he stopped and looked up, uncertain as to what disturbed him about Josef Straus. It was the last comment he had made, but surgeons often said things like that. Flattering the anaesthetist was a ritual that surgeons regularly indulged in partly because they did not really understand what the anaesthetists did. The top of the table was considered a bit of a black magic zone. Banter aside, there was something familiar about the way that Josef stood; also his accent wasn't clearly German or Dutch. Mike hoped he wasn't one of those rogue surgeons who had been kicked out of his home country and now operated unsupervised in Africa.

Christian looked up, starting to relax as the propofol took effect. He was finding it difficult to focus, but he could see the concern in Mike's eyes. As he drifted off to sleep, he hoped that Josef Strauss knew what he was doing.

Chapter 22

The voices all sounded some way off as he struggled to wake up from the anaesthetic. The sedative effects of the morphine made it difficult to focus. Blinking a few times, he was aware of many blurred faces standing around the foot of his bed. A yellowish light filtering through a small window above his bed created a surreal effect. As his mind started to clear, he understood where he was: the recovery area outside of theatre. Squinting to focus, he could just make out Cindy; she was closest to him and holding his hand. He looked up at and smiled. When he tried to turn to look at her he winced, the pain in his abdomen reminding him of his surgery. Picking up the sheet, he looked underneath; there was an incision just below his right rib margin. However, it was not a midline incision; it was a Kocher's incision, very specific for liver injuries. Whoever the surgeon was, he had had great surgical experience, and in addition, he had neatly repaired his skin.

"Christian." He heard another voice next to his ear.

He turned his head away from Cindy and tried to focus again. He recognised Isabella's voice; as he turned slowly to his right, he could see her sitting in a chair next to his bed, stethoscope and blood pressure cuff in hand.

"I need to check your blood pressure again," she said as she unfurled the sphygmomanometer. "How are you feeling and how's your pain level?"

"Pain about 4/10; otherwise I feel okay. Who was the surgeon who operated on me?"

Christian did not really understand the silence that followed his question. He looked towards the foot of the bed where Mike and Galela were standing next to each other. Mike gave the thumbs up sign while Galela just winked and smiled at him. Dr. Sudani was standing next to Galela, but the person next to him he did not recognise. He had on a white coat so Christian knew he was probably a doctor. However, he was wearing a surgical mask that covered most of his face, and beneath the mask there was, protesting its containment, a full bristly beard. It disguised his features, keeping all well hidden, other than piercing blue eyes. Christian remembered Isabella's description from when they were triaging the boys in the Congo; the description fitted the surgeon Josef Strauss.

"You must be Josef Strauss. Thank you for saving my life. And doing such a neat job of stitching me closed."

"Great to see you awake, Christian."

"You obviously had some experience dealing with livers from where you put the incision."

"Quite a bit of experience in actual fact, which I'm happy to tell you about when you are feeling a little better."

As Josef finished his last sentence, Christian was aware of Mike and Galela smiling as if part of some intrigue. They were looking at Josef Strauss as though expecting him to make some kind of grand pronouncement. Christian looked back to Josef. He noticed he quickly averted his eyes, but not before Christian had seen the tears gathering in the corners. He then turned and quickly walked out the door with Mike following closely behind.

"What's going on?" Christian said, looking both at Cindy and at Isabella for an answer. "Doesn't Josef think that I will recover?"

He felt Cindy squeeze his hand tighter while Isabella put the stethoscope down and looked at him.

"You're going to be fine; Josef did a wonderful job of repairing your liver and the inferior vena cava, which the bullet had torn. Without his experience you might have died. Your haemoglobin is now five but we think that you are going to be fine without a transfusion. You will just be tired for a few weeks as you would know, but the plan is for Mike and Galela to take you back to Cape Town on a special plane which Sibokwe has organised in a week's time."

"So why did Josef walk out with tears in his eyes?"

"It was a very emotional experience, and with you bleeding, we didn't know whether we would lose you on the table."

"So you were assisting Josef."

"Yes I was."

"And do I look as good on the inside as I do on the outside?"

"Very cute, I mean you look very cute on the inside as well, everything where it should be, and nice to hear the sense of humour returning - that's always a good clinical indicator."

"But that doesn't really explain Josef's reaction just now. Surgeons are trained not to be emotional and with the experience that he must have, judging by that perfect incision, that does not really fit either. What is it that you're not telling me?"

"We just want you to get well first."

"Get well first before what. Come on, Isabella, we are all adults here. My haemoglobin maybe five but my pulse rate is down. I'm not bleeding, therefore I'm going to recover, my sense of humour has returned. I'm capable of dealing with whatever you need to tell me."

"Okay, let me go and talk to your surgeon," said Isabella disconnecting the blood pressure cuff.

Isabella stood up and placed the sphygmomanometer on the seat. She looked at Cindy, raising her eyebrows in a way which indicated the inevitability of supplying an answer to Christian's question. Christian noticed the look and stared at Cindy to see whether he could determine a clue to what was going on from her facial expression. She looked at him, smiled and squeezed his hand. That did not tell him much, but she did not look away so he interpreted that as a positive sign.

"Tell me what happened then to Kariba's gang. I know that I can manage to hear about that." Christian winked at Cindy.

"The men that Mohammed sent to find you shot two of Kariba's men. They think three others got away and that Kariba was one of them."

"That's a pity that he escaped. In a way if he hadn't, that would have been raw jungle justice."

"Yes, it would have been, but dying by the sword would have been too easy for someone who has inflicted so much pain and suffering on so many. However, there is some good news. Bosco the Brutal surrendered to European authorities and is to be tried for war crimes committed in the Congo. Mike told us that he has lung cancer and the only treatment for his particular type of lung cancer is in the Netherlands."

"Mike hinted at that when we were at the mine. The only issue with that is that Kariba will see the whole of the Congo as his unrivalled kingdom; there will be nothing to restrain him, especially with unrestricted Chinese support. By the way, have you seen Michelangelo?"

"Yes I did. He is doing really well and wants to come and see you after late afternoon prayers with Mohammed and say thank you for everything that you did for him."

"Now that's really good news. I'll look forward to that. I take that to mean, now that Mike and Galela are here, that Kim Yao is no longer a threat."

"Before you went into theatre, Mike checked all your pockets and found the disc with the photos that you had taken with your telephoto lens of Kim dumping boys at Mount Golgotha. He uploaded them to his laptop as well as the data from the meeting at the orphanage, which was on my phone. He then e-mailed them to the Chinese embassy in Cape Town threatening to release them to the media. Kim and her entourage, we heard, left the orphanage in a great rush in the middle of the night and they haven't been seen since."

"So who's running the orphanage now?"

"Gabriella and I," Cindy said smiling contentedly.

"Well Cindy, sounds like you're going to have your hands full. You may not be able to leave, you realise."

"I was thinking exactly that and how wonderful that might be."

Christian heard the theatre door open again. Mike and Galela walked in, followed by Josef Strauss and Isabella. Josef had removed his surgical mask, and without looking directly at Christian, sat on the chair next to his bed. Christian looked more closely at Josef; strangely, it was like looking at a bearded, older version of himself. Josef turned and looked Christian directly in the eyes; a shout of primal recognition reverberated deep within Christian followed by a strange sense of peace. It was a feeling that Christian had never experienced before.

"Christian, do you remember what struck you most when you first went to Dr Sudani's house?"

Christian thought it was a very strange question with which to begin a conversation, especially with someone you had just operated on. In addition, he could not imagine that Dr Sudani's house would explain all the looks that had been exchanged between everyone in the room previously.

"I thought it was very reminiscent of some of the houses that I had seen in Cape Town."

"You are absolutely correct. I designed it when I thought that I was going to live here. Then unfortunately I couldn't."

"Well, I've heard that the houses in Cape Town are very similar to those in Holland or Germany. I guess, though, the interesting bit is why you couldn't live there?"

"I know you're not prepared for this, although a few minutes ago I sensed a brief recognition in your soul. What I am going to tell you next there is no preparation for. For more than twenty years, you have had no father and for more than twenty years, I have had no son. However, there is not a day that has gone by that I have not thought about you or your mother. I am your father Jannie, who you thought had been killed in Cape Town. A man named Van der Walt tried to kill me to prevent me disclosing information, which would severely embarrass the South African apartheid government. It was only because Galela fought with him that I wasn't executed in the back garden of our home in Wynberg. I knew the threat of documents being released would keep you and your mother alive, but if Van der Walt knew I was alive, he would not rest until he found me and tortured me for the location of the documents. When I arrived at the mortuary in Cape Town, a doctor friend of mine pronounced me dead although it was he who resuscitated me. I thought I could live and do surgery in Rwanda as Josef Strauss but someone recognised me from the time I had been here doing research. Therefore, despite my newly acquired beard, my German name and accent, I had to disappear before Van der Walt came looking for me again."

Christian could have touched the silence in the room. All eyes he knew were on him as he struggled to take in the enormity of Josef's revelation.

"Are you really my father? I saw you shot by Van der Walt next to the pool at our house in Wynberg Cape Town and mum and I weren't unable to resuscitate you."

"When Van der Walt shot your father, he was about to put a bullet through his head and then kill me so that I would get the blame for the killing. We fought and the noise of the fighting attracted the lady next door. That combination saved your father a fatal headshot," said Galela.

"I saw all of that," Christian said. "I'd climbed back up on the tree stump and saw what was happening."

251

"I seem to remember telling you to stay hidden no matter what you heard," Josef said smiling at Christian. "Must be those rebellious genes which you inherited from your mother."

"But she was certain that you were dead, and she is a good doctor!"

"Your mother could not feel a pulse because I had lost a significant amount of blood. The paramedic also thought I was dead and took me directly to the Salt River mortuary. A friend of mine, Dr Sandy van de Merwe, was a pathologist working there and was about to put a tag on my toe which would identify my corpse, when he noticed some eye movement. He started CPR again. Sandy sutured my neck wound with some of the suture material he used on the corpses, and put up an intravenous line. He said that within fifteen minutes, I was sitting up and talking."

"Seeing you dead next to our swimming pool gave me nightmares for many years. Almost ten years ago, I went back to Cape Town and our home in Wynberg, to try to put the memory to rest."

"Mike and Galela have told me that part of the story and that you went back just after you finished high school and found the folder that I had buried in the back garden."

"It was Isabella who worked out the cryptic clue from the *Wind in the Willows.*"

Isabella interrupted. "The Mole was bewitched, entranced, fascinated. By the side of the pool, he trotted as one trots, when very small, by the side of a man who holds one spellbound by exciting stories. And when tired at last, he sat beneath the willow, while the pool still chattered on to him, a babbling procession of the best stories in the world, sent from the heart of the earth to be told at last to the insatiable sea."

"Perfect memory, Isabella, and it was there by the side of the pool that I had changed the original quote that you both worked out which led you to the folder."

"That's right," Christian said. "But surely you could have in some way let us know that you were alive."

Josef looked at Mike and Galela before replying.

"Van der Walt, as I said, would have hunted you down and killed you and your mother. If he knew that I was alive, there was always a threat, not only to himself for crimes against humanity, but also to governments which had been covertly involved with the South African apartheid. Before he tried to kill me, I was about to reveal the South African apartheid government's involvement in a secret germ warfare programme. I also knew about South Africa's nuclear weapons development in which France, Israel, and the United States were covertly involved. I wasn't certain that the security forces in those countries wouldn't have cooperated with Van der Walt's threat to find and kill me if he thought I was alive."

"He's dead. Galela shot him."

"Yes, I know. Mike and Galela told me."

"Does my mother know yet that you're alive?"

"No. What we are planning on doing is a medical evacuation of you to Cape Town."

"So that would mean that Nadine, Isabella's mother, knows that you're alive. Don't you think Renata should know, especially since you had an affair with Nadine?"

"I know that you know about that, and for that you may judge me harshly and quite rightly. Isabella and I have talked about it and she knows it's one of those mistakes we both made which we regret, but more importantly in the years that I have been in Rwanda, I have realised how much I loved your mother."

"What's your favourite song?"

Christian scrutinised Jannie's face as he thought about the response. Jannie held his stare, and Christian knew that he knew and therefore what he would say.

"'Tom Jones, She's a Lady'. Did I pass?"

"Not so fast." Christian smiled. "Sing or hum the first four lines."

Christian watched as Jannie took a deep breath and then in a deep baritone quietly sang.

"Well, she's all you'd ever want

She's the kind I like to flaunt and take to dinner

But she always knows her place

She's got style, she's got grace--she's a winner'

Everyone applauded as Jannie finished and Isabella bent over and kissed him on the cheek.

"Okay, well, I think you have a chance," Christian said with a wry smile.

"That means we can keep it a surprise from your mother?"

"I won't tell her. Does she know that I'm okay?"

"I have spoken to Renata and Nadine," Mike said. "I told Renata what had happened and that you are okay. She's obviously anxious to get to Cape Town and makes certain for herself that her number one son is intact."

"We need to discuss a bit of business," interrupted Galela. "With Kariba still being alive and having all kinds of informants in this area, we need to take precautions. He has been known to travel to Angola just to kill someone who crossed him. He still may want to even things up with you because of his son's death. We're going to keep you here in this area because it's secure and easier to control than a general ward. We will each take turns to do a shift keeping an eye on you. If you are okay after three days, we will move you to Dr Sudani's."

"Christian, now I need to tell you this as your anaesthetist. Your dad is going to tell you about the operation when we leave you two alone to chat in a few minutes. If for any reason you start bleeding again, we would need to operate fast. So do not be concerned. In that table next to your bed I have left 100 mg of propofol drawn up in a syringe. That is so we know where everything is just in case we need it. So if you open that drawer, don't get concerned that I have just left drugs lying around; it's to make everything easier if there was an emergency, which we don't think there will be. If you have a plan B, then you don't usually need to use it if you follow the logic."

"I understand that. Mike, is there anything else? What about analgesics?"

"Those are locked in theatre. We will take those out as we need to or as you require. Isabella is going to do the first shift until 6 PM and then your dad will take over until midnight. Dr Sudani is going to put a bed in here, so you'll be able to find out whether your dad snores."

"Thanks, everyone."

"All right. We will leave you and your dad to get reacquainted, and let him tell you the neat piece of surgery that he did inside you."

Chapter 23

"Your blood pressure and pulse are good. Do you need any analgesic?" Isabella asked, folding up the blood pressure cuff and placing it on the chair at the foot of the bed.

"No thanks, Issy. That last injection of morphine seems to have taken away the pain completely."

"That's good; I like my patients to be comfortable and happy with my care."

"Well, no complaints from this patient. Although, it is a very strange way to be reacquainted, do you not think?"

"I agree; certainly not the way that I visualised seeing you again in bed - as my patient. Well, part of that I could rephrase."

"Yes. I imagined picking you up from the bus and wondering whether those original feelings and chemistry would surge back as I saw you."

"Lying on that piece of plastic burning up from malaria, I imagine that would have been furthest thing from your mind and you would have had only feelings for survival?"

"That's true. I cannot remember whether there were any feelings really other than the primal one of being glad to see someone who knew what I desperately needed to survive. Seeing you walk in there was part of me that just was relieved knowing you were someone who knew what they were doing. I thought if I did die, least it wouldn't be because someone hadn't done everything possible."

"It was awful seeing you lying there, weak with a fever and dehydrated. Certainly not the memory of that strong and vibrant person you were in Cape Town. My feelings for you at that moment were as a doctor and what I needed to do to get you better."

"I did wonder what you would remember when you saw me."

"I think it was only once I got you back to Dr Sudani's and that I could think about you and what you meant to me then and how I felt now. You are still very attractive to me, if that is what you are really asking. Which, being the boy that you are, it probably is." Isabella looked at Christian and raised a quizzical eyebrow.

Christian smiled. "I see you have lost none of that insight which was so attractive."

"Nine years ago, Christian, neither of us had discovered what sex was about. We met, we were enormously attracted to each other, and thought this was a love forever; it seemed to us at the time like winning the relationship lottery. In addition, we turned our virginal hormones loose on each other. There was no rational thought after that for quite some time. Indeed, for almost eighteen months, I thought that there was no one else in the whole world that I could be compatible with. This may disappoint you, but I tried a number of times to create that intensity with others before I realised the intensity of something which you do for the first time is really difficult, if not impossible to recreate."

"It was really intense, wasn't it? You were my first lover and in many ways, I knew nothing but felt I knew everything. Since then, I have also struggled to replicate the intensity of those feelings and wondered whether it was just because it wasn't you that I was with, or that it was just the first time where, as you say, that it's impossible then to recreate that intensity."

"I think part of the issue is you can only climb Everest once, and there are not many who would get the same kind of feeling even if it was possible to climb it again. Which means it can then be hugely confusing if you have had that kind of experience for a first relationship. Chemistry and its intensity become defined by what you first experienced and you think that should be present in every relationship. When they are not, you accept that what we experienced was a one-off event in terms of intensity and adjust to a lesser chemistry. However, like you, I have a curiosity, partly through not being able to achieve the level of intensity in other relationships, and wonder whether that meant that I could only achieve that with you because of our unique interaction."

"Yes, it has been the same for me."

"It didn't come back when you saw me again." Isabella flicked her hair back and smiled in the slightly flirtatious way he remembered.

Christian laughed, hesitated for a few seconds, and then said,

"It's difficult to answer that given the state that I was in, wondering whether I was going to die in Africa."

"That's not like a surgeon to squib on an answer; although I suppose it was an emotional question and we know how surgeons don't deal with those." Isabella laughed again.

"I hesitated a little, Issy, only because I didn't really know how to answer your question properly, given the circumstances that we met under again. I have had girlfriends since you and we've had good physical relationships, but I kept thinking back, wondering whether ours was better, or whether it was just because it was the first time for us. Did we have something special that I couldn't find in another relationship?"

"When did you lose that feeling that ours was the only chemistry that would work?"

"That's what I'm trying to say. I don't think I ever lost that feeling that our chemistry was unique. It might be that what we had was so different to anyone else, that it wasn't just the first encounter, that it really was something special to us, and us alone."

"Or it could be that it was just the intensity of the first time, just to keep your feet on the ground, and so that you are not disappointed when you are feeling better."

"Realistically, I know you could be right. Did you lose the feeling that our chemistry was unique?"

"Like you, after I got over our relationship, I tried quite a few others. I hope that doesn't shock you, but most girls have on average five relationships before they make a choice."

"I don't think I ever want to hear the details about other lovers, but if surgery has taught me anything, it's that you have to deal with the realities of life, or withdraw and be incarcerated with your hopes and fears."

"Okay, well I wouldn't go into detail anyhow. However, I think it is important to give you just some background so that you understand a bit better, how I have evolved. I realise there is a risk in this that you may not want to try again but I think it's important that you have insight into me beyond what you remember as a seventeen-year-old. The first boy I met was called Manfred, not really like the first part of this name unfortunately. He was very sweet, dressed beautifully, and was considerate but too effeminate. I was left thinking what a contrast to the raw physicality what we had. Manfred lasted six months and then Benjamin swept me off my feet. He was a coloured South African like me. Very good-looking, charismatic, and I hope this is not too hurtful, but he was wonderful in bed."

"Sounds like you found a perfect replacement for me then," Christian said with a rueful smile.

Isabella laughed. "I see surgery has dissected out humility."

"I was mostly just teasing, but I guess I wished in some strange way, that you had said that there had been no-one else who was as good, and therefore that what we had was not replicable with anyone else."

"Now where is that surgeon who is grounded in reality?"

"Well, there is part of me that still retains romantic delusions. Surgery hasn't completely excised the dreamer."

"Alright, no more details about Benjamin. Suffice it to say that I thought I had someone with the same kind of chemistry as you and I had, then the relationship broke down after several months, partly because he was more in love with himself, which I doubt you would ever be. The postscript therefore is the chemistry that you and I had was still superior."

"I had one of those relationships that you described with Benjamin. April was a design arts student, who looked like she had just stepped out of *Teen Vogue* magazine. It took her an hour to prepare if we were just going to go out for a drink or barbecue. She was obsessed with her beauty and while she was gorgeous to look at, it was almost as though when you went to bed, the primary point was to admire her body. There was little of what we had, in addition to which she was incredibly insecure and jealous. I would get multiple text messages through the day asking where I was and who I was talking to."

"It was a little bit the same with Benjamin. After we broke up, I then swapped sides, thinking that another female at least be on a similar wave-length when it came to understanding needs."

"You have really tried to answer the chemistry question. A female lover, how did that work?"

"Are you sure that you are able to deal with this. Should I check your blood pressure and pulse again to make sure that we're not stressing you too much?"

"No, this is very therapeutic; it's keeping my mind off the wound. Keep going, Issy."

"Her name was Simone; she was a black American third-year medical student. Her father was a diplomat in Cape Town. I first saw her in the university bar, surrounded by three or four rugby players. That was not surprising given her stunning looks, long black hair, and a figure to die for. What was surprising was that when the rugby players left, she came over to me and we got chatting. Within five minutes, we were like old excited friends and then she told me that I really turned her on. I was so taken aback that I do not think I replied for two minutes. I had never really considered sex with another woman before, and then I thought why not? It would be something new, fun, and definitely unknown chemistry."

"So you are gay? And if the answer to that is yes, I guess there goes any future chance of revisiting our chemistry."

"That's a very cute pout. And don't interrupt; although I suppose that I should be grateful that you weren't like most boys and didn't say something such as was it as good as being with me?"

"Well, was it?"

"Christian!"

"Okay, I was teasing. I promise to behave; please keep going."

"I'm not sure yet whether I'm gay. There was an enormous warmth and fun with Simone. I loved exploring her body and its softness and having her explore mine. In many ways, because you know your own body so well, you instinctively know what can give pleasure. Many males can't spell clitoris. You of course are one of the exceptions, I should add quickly, let alone finding it and causing pleasure. In my small research group, most seem to think it was down there somewhere, and a hard penis was all that was required."

"That doesn't sound like you want to cross back too soon."

"Don't go pretending that you are all hurt and rejected. What we had was very special, and you were very sensitive and stimulating as a lover, which is why I'm not completely won over to the other side."

"So there's a chance still."

"Maybe. You had better hurry up and get better if you want to find out," She said, standing at the foot of his bed smiling mischievously.

"Quick, place your healing hands on me then."

259

Christian looked at Isabella sitting at the foot of his bed. She hadn't taken her eyes off him, in a way that girls do when they're intent on conveying pleasure and availability. He tried to think about being well again and whether they could recapture what they had, when he heard a light knock at the door. Isabella looked at her watch and said to Christian,

"It's probably Mike, although he's half an hour early according to my reckoning. He will most probably want to make certain that you have not been using the propofol!"

Isabella unlatched the door slightly and then stood back quickly as it was pushed open from the outside. Michelangelo appeared, a shocked look on his face, and then tripped on the step, falling facedown at the foot of Christian's bed. Isabella helped him up and as she did so, Christian noticed him looking anxiously towards the door. Through the open doorway, Christian could make out the shapes of three men in the darkness beyond. None looked like Mohammed in his flowing robes. Michelangelo ran and hid behind Isabella when one of the men walked into the room. He was a tall muscular black man, hair carefully plaited with long golden earrings. A camouflage shirt was completely unbuttoned and rolled to his shoulders. A black T-shirt, worn underneath, had *welcome to Kariba's hell* emblazoned in red letters. Evil emanated from under the bony ridges which shaped his eyes. He looked at Christian and then at Isabella.

"Stay where you are and I won't kill you!" He half spat at Isabella.

Turning away from Isabella, he looked at Christian. He said,

"Your turn to die, Muzungu. You killed my son. Now it's your turn to die."

"I didn't kill your son; his disease killed him."

"You didn't save my son so that means you killed him, and in Kariba's world, it's a life for a life. You should be grateful that you are going to die; I could just rip your eyes out and eat them. My brother is a devil worshipper and that is what he wants me to do. Eating a Muzungu's eyes will let me see things in the dark. The king should be able to see in the dark; however, I want you to see the hell that you are going to and feel your breath disappearing as my son did." He then laughed in a way, Christian thought, that suggested he was high on some drug.

"Muzungu bitch, who escaped from me. Come and inject this morphine," he said, pulling out two dirty 50 ml syringes from his pocket while pointing the pistol with his other hand at Isabella's head."

Isabella remained at the foot of the bed and shook her head.

"If you don't do it, both of you will die, but I will kill Michelangelo in front of you first and then rape you."

Christian looked across to where Michelangelo was and saw that he was now sitting in the corner curled up, his arms over his head, his tears already staining the floor.

"And in case you were thinking that Mohammed was going to ride your rescue again, he is presently talking to Allah." Kariba laughed maniacally.

"Stupid white Muzungu bitch, you have ten seconds to get over here. Otherwise I kill Michelangelo," he said aiming his pistol at the crouching shape in the corner.

"If I inject myself, will you let the other two go?" Christian quickly said.

"Too late, you stupid son-killing Muzungu. I've changed my mind. Michelangelo can inject you. He's about the same age as my son. And then he gets the pleasure of coming to work for me."

"That will ruin his life," Isabella said.

"Shut up, stupid Muzungu bitch. Kariba gave you a chance, now in a short while, if you're lucky, he's going give you HIV."

"Just let me do it. I will inject myself, but let Isabella and Michelangelo go free," Christian pleaded.

Kariba spat in his direction and strode to the corner of the room. He yanked Michelangelo up by one arm, silencing the whimper by holding the pistol to his head, before dragging him back to Christian's bed and the intravenous line running into Christian's vein. Michelangelo hung limply by one arm, eyes closed as Kariba tried to connect the first syringe filled with morphine to Christian's intravenous line. However because he had not remove the cover from the needle, Kariba could not connect it to Christian's intravenous line. Then recognising his mistake, he dropped Michelangelo onto the floor so that he could use two hands. Michelangelo quickly crawled under Christian's bed. Kariba cursed and let go of the syringe, attempting to stamp on Michelangelo's leg as he disappeared under the bed. Missing Michelangelo with his army boot, he bent down to look under the bed.

"Come to daddy," he called mockingly, pointing his pistol in the direction that Michelangelo had crawled.

Christian quickly looked at Isabella who nodded. He pulled the sheath off the syringe, leaned over the bed, and plunged it into the side of Kariba's exposed neck. His hope, before he pushed the plunger, was that it was in the internal jugular vein. It needed to strike the large vein to have an instant effect. There was primitive guttural cry of shock from Kariba under the bed, who knocked his head as he reached for the syringe. Christian pushed harder, 30 mils were injected. If it was in the right place, that would be enough to knock out but not enough to kill him. Kariba fired his gun, the bullet shattering the front of the desk as he pulled the syringe from his neck. Isabella slammed the door closed and locked it. The loud beating on the door from Kariba's henchmen almost drowned out Kariba's cursing. As he pulled himself out from under Christian's bed, the rage in his eyes was incandescent. He fired another shot that went up through Christian's mattress, missing his left leg by centimetres.

Kariba then pulled himself out from underneath the bed and sat on the floor facing Christian. Slowly he brought his pistol up and aimed at Christian's head. The pounding on the door matched the pounding in Christian's head. He wondered whether the pounding was the last sound that he would ever hear. He was about to close his eyes and accept his fate when then the pistol wavered a little, tracking down to his abdomen, the morphine was starting to take effect. Kariba's black eyes, he could see, were now struggling to focus, and desperation brought his second hand up to steady the gun. However, even with two hands he could not hold the gun steady and again it drifted away to the left. Momentarily trained on the wall, Isabella in one motion picked up the chair and smashed it across Kariba's head. The gun discharged as he fell, shattering the small window above Christian's head.

"Thanks, Issy. That doorway will not hold the others for long."

"I have Mike on speed dial," Isabella said as she pushed the number seven on her phone.

"It will take him fifteen minutes to get here; they will be in by then. Give me Kariba's gun and you and Michelangelo come over here behind me."

Isabella took the pistol out of Kariba's hand and handed it to Christian as suddenly the pounding on the door stopped. Perhaps others were coming after hearing the shots and those outside had left them, thought Christian. Then thirty seconds later, the pounding restarted, this time with what sounded like an iron bar against the wooden door. Although the wooden door was constructed in two layers, Christian knew it would not last long against an iron bar. He motioned to Isabella to crouch down behind his bed.

He took aim at the door as the iron bars shattered the top part of the frame. In the darkness, he could just make out a black hand reaching in, searching for the latch. Christian thought about shooting at the hand, but knew that he had to wait to be certain of killing them. He watched as the black hand lifted the latch and slowly withdrew. Christian glanced down to make sure the safety catch had not flicked on with the pistol falling on the floor. It was off and ready to use.

The door slowly swung, creaking on its hinges, pushed by a hand that he now could not see. He squinted into the darkness beyond the door, wondering if whoever was out there would know that he had Kariba's gun. Just as he was wondering about firing a warning shot, Mike's voice drifted through the door.

"Don't shoot. We have neutralised both of Kariba's men."

Christian lowered the pistol as Isabella stood up and kissed him on the forehead.

"My goodness, you get yourself into situations," Mike said, as he walked through the door with a smiling Galela behind him.

"You got my phone call then," said Isabella, clutching onto a shaking Michelangelo.

"I was already on the way deciding to come early when I got your call. Galela had come with me, wanting to get out for some fresh air."

"Have you killed him?" Galela said looking in Kariba's direction.

"I don't think so. I can see him just breathing, and I only managed to inject 30 mls of morphine, not the 50 mls that was in the syringe."

"That will indeed keep him quiet. But we'd better tie him up in case he is a fast metaboliser."

"Or we could give him the other 20 mls and that would completely deal with the problem if he stops breathing completely," said Galela

"Considering how many people he has killed, I don't think anyone would complain," Mike replied

"What you think, Christian? You gave him the first 30 mls, and given the chance, he was probably going to kill all three of you. Shall we give him the extra 20 mils and stop his breathing?"

"I have a better idea. Killing him would be too easy for him when you think of the number of people he has tortured and raped. There is an international warrant out for his arrest, and I happen to know and have the phone number of one of the international prosecutors. They would love to have him and prosecute him for his crimes against humanity. That way he gets to spend life in jail."

"Okay, it'll need to happen quickly. Even though we've taken care of his two henchmen outside, others might come looking for him. We will tie him up and lock him in the mortuary. Is your phone at Dr Sudani's?"

Christian nodded.

"I'll go and get it," Isabella said. "I know where it is. And I can get Cindy to look after Michelangelo."

"Are you sure you're okay to go by yourself?"

"I will be fine. You have all these terrorists tied up. And I need to get Michelangelo out of here and into Cindy's safe arms. Do you know what's happened to Mohammed?"

"No, but I have sent Heinrich and Suleiman, two of our best agents from NIA, to check on him. They arrived last night, and when I got your message just now, they came with us in case we needed a hand but I have sent them to check on Mohammed."

"I'll drop Michelangelo with Cindy and bring Jannie back. He'll want to know what has been happening, although given what he knows about his adventurous son, I'm sure he won't be totally surprised."

"All right, but phone me if there are any issues."

"I will," Isabella said, scooping up Michelangelo and telling him that it was all over and that he was going to be safe with Cindy.

"So young man, who is this prosecutor you know at The Hague."

"I met her on a plane on the way to London. She had warned me about child trafficking, and human rights abuses in the Congo, and to be careful. Then after I had been here for a few weeks, she sent me a text message saying there was now a warrant for Kariba's arrest and a reward of five million dollars."

"When Isabella brings my phone back, I can text her. If we could get him across the border to Goma, I'm sure they send a plane to pick up Kariba."

"Yes, we can always stick him in the ambulance and get him to Goma airport."

"What are you going to do with five million dollars? That's far too much money for a young man to have." Mike smiled.

"I'm sure Cindy could use it at the orphanage and it would rebuild part of the hospital that is falling down."

"Do you know who has the key to the mortuary? " Galela asked.

"Dr Sudani has one," Christian replied

"Let me text Isabella to bring the key back."

Before Mike could finish texting, they heard the sound of feet running down the concrete pathway from the hospital. Mike quickly switched off the light and Galela crouched low in the doorway. Christian watched as he brought up his Glock pistol and pointed it in the direction of the footsteps.

"It's okay," said Mike. "Heinrich and Suleiman are back."

Galela went outside while Mike again switched the light on. Christian could hear the animated discussion through the door, some in English and some in Afrikaans.

"Kariba killed Mohammed," Galela said as he walked back in through the door. "Heinrich and Suleiman found his family tied up in the mosque and have freed them. We will need to notify the local police chief."

"I will do that," Mike said. "I talked to him after the Kariba incident so I have his phone number."

"Mike, why don't we get Heinrich and Suleiman to put Kariba and his two henchmen in the mortuary. I am just a little concerned about Isabella. Raoul Assad could be out there somewhere if Kariba is," Galela said.

"All right, Heinrich and Suleiman can wait here for Dr. Sudani and the key to the mortuary. Let's follow up on that gut instinct of yours; it's always been right in the past."

As Isabella rounded the corner to the Sudani's house, she could feel Michelangelo shivering. It could have been the cool night air, but it more likely was the shock of what he had been through. She stopped at the driveway entrance and took off her jacket, wrapping it around Michelangelo's shoulders. He looked up at her, smiled at her, and said thank you. Further up the driveway, she could see the light on in the kitchen. She took hold of Michelangelo's hand before realising he had no shoes. She picked him up and walked along the edge of the granite chips, noting that the washing was still on the line, which was somewhat unusual. Chantal always took it in to avoid it disappearing during the night. Just before she turned the corner, she looked up and saw Jannie, Cindy, Emmanuel, and Chantal sitting at the kitchen bench. None of them were talking; all were looking in the direction of the doorway. She motioned to Michelangelo to keep quiet and crept forward.

Standing a little closer to the window, she could just make out the bulging outline of Raoul Assad. Isabella could not make out or hear what he was saying, but the terrified look in Cindy's eyes spoke volumes. Isabella withdrew into the darkness and taking Michelangelo by the hand, she headed quietly back down the pathway. Once she was obscured by the hedge, she texted Mike. Within minutes, a message returned. *Stay put will be there in 10 min.*

Within two minutes, Mike and Galela appeared out of the darkness slowing to a jog as they approached Isabella.

"That was quick. I have only just finished texting you."

"Ingcuka just had this gut feeling about the Syrian so we decided to check up on you just in case he appeared somewhere."

Isabella quickly told them what she had seen.

"Mike, that Syrian is ex-military. He will want to shoot his way out."

"Yes, I know. I have read his rap sheet and his predilection for young girls. We need to be able to try and lure him out or distract him."

"You can't see him through the window. He is standing in the darkness of the hallway so I doubt whether you could get a good shot through the kitchen window."

Mike looked up. "They have both fires burning."

"Yes, that usually heats the front room and the kitchen on cold nights," Isabella confirmed.

"If we could plug the chimneys, we might be able to smoke them out."

"He would hear you get on the roof," Galela said.

"Not if someone was light and small," Mike said looking at Michelangelo.

"You can't ask him to do that after the trauma that he has been through," Isabella said horrified.

"I want to do it. That's one of the men that killed Mohammed," Michelangelo said, pulling away from Isabella.

"Let's take the washing off the line. We can use that to stuff down the chimneys. If you stand on Galela's shoulders, Michelangelo, you will be able to pull yourself up onto the roof. Be very careful. There may be loose tiles. We will wrap all the washing in Isabella's jacket and hand it up to you. Block each of those pipes and then we will help you down."

Isabella gathered up the washing with great reluctance, four of Emmanuel's shirts and two of Chantal's skirts. She wrapped them all in the jacket and tied the sleeves together. Mike positioned Michelangelo on Galela's shoulders as they stood next to the wall. He pulled himself up onto the roof and then Mike threw up the jacket full of washing. They retreated down the driveway so that they could see Michelangelo, his white top clear in the darkness. A few minutes later, the smoke from this first chimney stopped. Moments after that, smoke from the second chimney stopped and Michelangelo was back at the edge of the house. Mike quickly ran forward and caught Michelangelo as he jumped from the edge of the house.

"Isabella, take Michelangelo up the road a little in case there is any shooting. We will position ourselves at the back and front doors."

Isabella only made it to the front gate when she heard the smashing of glass. She turned around and in the darkness could see Galela positioned next to the front door. Mike was standing at the corner of the house, which allowed him to view the back door. There was more glass smashing followed by loud coughing, the smoke inside the house taking effect. Then the front door was suddenly thrown open, smoke billowed out followed quickly by a coughing Raoul Assad. He stumbled onto the veranda, coughing repeatedly, clutching a wet tea cloth to his mouth, a gun in his other hand. Galela struck quickly with the back of his pistol, and Assad collapsed lifeless on the veranda. A whistle to Mike signalled the all clear and Isabella could see him disappear around the back corner of the house. In a few minutes Jannie, Emmanuel, Cindy, and Chantal were all standing on the front lawn, coughing, and tears streaming from their eyes.

"Is Christian all right?" Jannie stammered as he wiped his eyes.

"Yes, he is fine," Isabella said. "Once everything is settled here, I'll explain and take you back up to him."

"Unfortunately, I don't think there is an international arrest warrant for Raoul," Mike said looking at Galela.

"The lake is not very far away," Galela said shrugging his shoulders; the statement was more a question seeking Mike's approval.

"Let's see if he can swim, although the Tilapia may not find him to their taste. For him to contribute to the ecosystem of the planet, ironically, might be one of his only positive contributions; it would also make for less paperwork."

Chapter 24

Christian could hear Isabella and Mike's footsteps as they walked up the pathway towards theatre. Heinrich and Suleiman, upon hearing their voices, peered out the door into the darkness.

"I can see everyone coming; they are about fifty metres away," Suleiman said turning back inside the door to face Christian.

A few minutes later, Mike appeared in the doorway smiling. Christian could see Jannie and Isabella standing behind him.

"Everyone is okay," Mike said, as he walked in and stood at the foot of Christian's bed. "No problems here, I hope."

"No sir. The only problem has been the mosquitoes," Suleiman said smiling.

"I hope you are taking your antimalarial tablets." Isabella quickly offered her advice.

"So what happened at the Sudani's?" Christian asked.

"Well the short version, and your father can give you the longer version, is that Kariba in his drug confused state of mind, had blackmailed Assad into holding your father, Cindy, and the Sudanis in case he ran into any problems dealing with us."

"Michelangelo smoked us out," Jannie said, interrupting Mike and smiling in Michelangelo's direction.

"I can't imagine how he did that but obviously it all had a good conclusion and what happened to Mr Assad?"

"Let's just say that he wasn't a very good swimmer," Galela said looking in the direction of Heinrich and Suleiman, who both smiled knowingly.

Christian tried to imagine what had happened and realised that he obviously needed the full picture to understand. Hopefully, his father would fill in the details later.

"Well, I'm glad it all worked out. Now we only need to deal with Kariba."

"After all the drama and once the smoke cleared, I did get your phone," Isabella said handing it to Christian.

"Thanks. Perhaps now we can find out what the ICC would like us to do with Kariba."

"We will leave you to deal with that. Galela and I are going to go and check the mortuary and Kariba, Heinrich, and Suleiman will stay here for the rest of the night in case any of Kariba's gang are brave enough to return. Emmanuel has suggested that if the ICC can evacuate Kariba from Goma, we could sedate him and transport across in an ambulance. See if your contact at the ICC can organise a plane to pick him up from Goma airport."

"Christian, Cindy and I are going to go and help the Sudanis clean up their house. Jannie, if you want to talk to Christian, could you check his blood pressure and pulse? They were fine when I left him. You could tell him about what happened and then come and join us."

"We will also give you a bit of space with Christian," Heinrich said. "We will just be outside, so just shout if you need anything."

"Sounds like a plan, as they say in South Africa. So you people go on. I will talk to my son here a little bit more and we will see what the woman from the ICC has to say.

Christian looked in his address book briefly wondering about the time. It was now 10 PM in Garanyi, an hour earlier in Brussels. He found Petrea's number and sent a text explaining that they had Kariba in custody.

"How do you think your mother will react when she hears about your latest adventure?"

"She's very phlegmatic as you may remember. She will be concerned, however delighted that everything is okay, and I can just imagine she's going to want to be in Cape Town when we arrive."

"I think it's amazing that she hasn't remarried. She is such an attractive woman still judging by those photos on your phone."

"I often wondered that same thing. Nothing ever seemed to get started with her from a relationship point of view. I remember that there was one anaesthetist who turned up when I was about fourteen years of age. He seemed to be interested in her but it never progressed beyond friendship. It was the same with a number of other men and I wondered whether she had lost interest in men when you disappeared from her life. That Tom Jones record I asked you about, she plays that about every six months or so. At least she did up until about a year ago. I think she had a candle burning for you, and I assumed it was really a love that you two had shared that she couldn't replace."

"That was very much the same for me. Over the years there have been visiting doctors. One very attractive German woman specialising in tropical diseases came and worked at the clinic. I was attracted to her but not in the sense that I was with your mother. I knew then that your mother was the love of my life and perhaps there was no other."

"Well, it's going to be interesting to say the least to see you two in the same room again."

"Yes, I can't wait, but I'm uncertain about the whole surprise element. That might just be too much for her after this long."

"Come on, dad, if you're into that kind of Tom Jones music, you've got to be a romantic."

"Yes I know, but we have been apart long time and even though I feel this way, there might be a lot of other feelings that your mother has to deal with, such as anger, before there can be any kind of reconciliation."

"It will be fine; Mike and Sian will be there along with Isabella's mother, Nadine, for support."

"I know we haven't talked about the affair that I had with Nadine, and I will need to obviously with your mother, but it's encouraging that she has obviously dealt with it in her way and still has feelings for me."

"Strangely Renata and Nadine have become really good friends. It took a bit of adjusting initially, but when it was established that Isabella was not your daughter, they were able to talk and become friends. Nadine apologised to mum and said it was only a few times that things happened and that she knew you really loved mum."

"Yes, it wasn't even really an affair. There were three nights when I had been operating late. Things went too far and then we realised that it wasn't something we wished to continue."

"Dad, I don't really need to know any more than that."

"Yes, I'm sorry that you had to find out about that and then deal with it. From what I've seen of Isabella, she is a wonderful young woman and Doctor."

"When I met her in Cape Town, I thought she was the love of my life. I think I must have inherited some of your genes because I haven't been able to experience that same feeling with any of the other girls that I have been out with so far."

"Does Isabella feel the same way?"

"We were talking about that just before Kariba burst in. I wasn't completely convinced that she felt how I felt about things, but I think she was curious for us to see whether we could recreate any magic once we got Cape Town."

"Well, it could be an interesting little gathering for a number of reasons then," Jannie said smiling.

Christian felt the phone vibrate in his hand. He looked down and saw a message from Petrea. *Outstanding news about Kariba. Plane in Goma tomorrow at 2 PM. Do not forget the $5 million reward. Currently in Cape Town, I have missed you.*

"What did it say?" Jannie asked. "The ICC will cooperate?"

Christian did not reply for a few seconds. It was the last three words of the text, which he had not expected, and which had taken him a little by surprise. 'I have missed you' brought back all the memories of the discussions on the plane with Petrea, and how, when he saw her leave in London, he realised he had similar feelings to when he met Isabella for the first time.

"Christian, are you okay? You look deep in thought; not good news from your contact at the ICC."

"They can pick Kariba up in Goma tomorrow and will have a plane there at 2 PM." Christian looked at Jannie, wondering if he was noticing the feelings that he was experiencing.

"Judging by your reaction, I would say the representative from the ICC, without knowing her, has at some stage touched part of your soul. Would that be a good guess by a father who hasn't seen you for twenty years?"

Christian smiled. "Very intuitive. I did wonder where I got those genes from. It is not something that I can say that I have seen in mum. Petrea is the ICC prosecutor whom I met on a plane going to London. She has coordinated the pickup of Kariba, but she is currently in Cape Town and we might also meet up."

"My paternal intuition further tells me it is going to be a very interesting meeting in Cape Town." Jannie laughed.

"I'll text her back, and let her know that that's okay for 2 PM tomorrow. And then I had better let Mike and Galela know so that they can start getting transport organised," said Christian.

"Here is a bit of fatherly advice based on that intuition. Why don't you text Petrea to call you? Then you can absolutely confirm all the details for tomorrow and any other details for Cape Town. I'll go and wait outside with Heinrich and Suleiman."

"That's a very good suggestion. Thank you. I'll do that."

After Jannie had walked out through the partly broken door, Christian could hear him speaking to Suleiman in Afrikaans. It reminded him of the past that he had not yet talked to his father about. He looked at the text message again. Despite what she had texted, and a flirtatious conversation on the plane, he had convinced himself that someone in her position would have many others who would be of more interest. Besides which, he had not yet established whether Isabella was the only one he could have great chemistry with. He knew Isabella wanted to try again to answer the same question. The only thing to do, he resolved, was to tell Petrea about Isabella, and keep the meeting in Cape Town with her at a professional level.

Chapter 25

"I hear if we get Kariba to Goma airport, the ICC will pick him up?" Mike said walking back in through the door.

"Yes, that's all arranged. They will have a plane there at 2 PM with security people and all the papers to be served on him. They just asked whether they would need a medical person to accompany him and I said no."

"Okay, that's great. And we discovered some other very good news."

"Well given what's happened recently," Jannie said, "good news is always going to be welcome. What did you manage to find out, Mike?"

"Heinrich and Suleiman were talking to the locals and they told them that Raoul always flies in to Goma on a Lear jet. Dr. Sudani allowed them to take the ambulance, and they drove across and the Lear jet is parked on the runway, refuelled and waiting for his return. They also found out the two pilots are staying at the Ihusi Hotel. They have persuaded them to fly us all to Cape Town tomorrow!"

"Is that legal?" Jannie asked.

"Well, we did suggest that the Lear jet could be impounded by the Congolese authorities when we reveal what Raoul was involved with; the pilots suddenly offered to fly us to Cape Town, then be allowed to directly return to Damascus," Mike said with a smile and a wink at Christian.

"Well, that sounds very legal, co-opting a plane for a real medical evacuation! I believe Lear jets have a full-length bed, which will also make it easier for Christian. I have to smile; Mike, some things over the years clearly haven't changed with you."

Mike laughed. "Well, you know what they say, keep the best parts and improve the worst. And it's great to have you back, Jannie."

"Okay, now that you two have finished eulogising the past, have you let Sian know and Renata or Nadine?"

"I spoke to Sian on the phone, and she contacted Renata and found out she has managed to get a flight from Australia tomorrow and will get in at 9 PM. Renata said to say hi to you and that she was looking forward to seeing you and had a surprise to show you."

"Well, she doesn't realise obviously the surprise that we are bringing might well upstage hers," Christian said, smiling and looking in the direction of his dad.

"No indeed. I can't wait to see the look on her face when she sees you, Jannie."

"Mike, will you have enough room for us all to stay at your place?" Christian asked.

"What we thought we would do, since we will arrive first, is take you and Jannie to our place. Nadine is going to be at the airport to pick up Isabella. Given your history with Nadine Jannie, it might well be prudent to keep you hidden so that Renata is the first to see you the next day."

"Yes, I agree with that. I've had a brief chat with Christian. He agrees that would be much more sensitive and then I can hopefully, with Renata's help if she forgives me, deal with the Nadine saga later on."

"So where is mum going to stay?"

"At the Mount Nelson, a beautiful old Victorian hotel, fifteen minutes from where we live. Renata arrives at about midnight, so Sian has arranged a car to pick her up and take her to the hotel. We thought it would be less disruptive that way even though your mum is keen to see you. And then we thought that if your mum and dad get on as we expect they will, they might need a little bit of romantic downtime together!"

"Way too much information for a son." Christian smiled

"Sian thought that Renata would also be a little bit jetlagged and that we should arrange for her to come to our place for lunch. Jannie, would that make you the entree or the main course?"

"Very funny, Mike. As I said, some things don't change!"

"And of course Christian, with the great progress that you are making, we expect you to be walking by the weekend. With your bowels now working, we can move you up to eating something more solid."

"That sounds good, dad. I am starting to get a bit hungry which I guess is another good clinical sign and I don't have any pain."

"Okay you two. Enough of a clinical discussion. Here are the details. Heinrich and Suleiman are staying at the Ihusi Hotel to make sure we have pilots in the morning. Heinrich is an amateur pilot so he will check and make sure everything is ready. Dr. Sudani is going to come with us in the ambulance. We all have white coats to make it look more official and Galela will ride with Michael in the front."

"With the damage to the door here, we are going to move you down to Dr. Sudani's tonight, Christian, in the ambulance. Then we'll all leave from there in the morning."

"Dad, you might want to talk to Isabella tonight a little bit about what happened with you and her mother."

"We have already done that, so don't worry. She was as understanding as you. I just hope your mother is when I meet her."

"I'm sure she will be, dad, especially with some positive input from your son."

"Cut!" Mike interjected. "You'll both have me in tears soon."

"As though that would happen," Jannie said laughing aloud.

Half an hour later the ambulance arrived. With Isabella's help, Christian walked to the ambulance and up the back steps for the short journey to Dr. Sudani's. The few bumps along the way reminded him of his abdominal wound. He put his hand under his T-shirt and felt the very fine wound. He thought he must thank his dad again for doing such a good job.

Chantal was at the front door as they arrived and waved the ambulance up the driveway. The door was opened from the outside, and Christian was confronted by Emmanuel's smiling face, as he made to walk down the rear steps of the ambulance.

"Let me come in and give you a hand."

"He's walking by himself," Isabella said proudly from inside the ambulance.

Christian, holding onto his intravenous line, walked carefully down the steps, with Emmanuel holding his elbow for extra support as he stepped onto the ground.

"So nice to see you back and in one piece," Chantal said as he walked up the back stairs.

"Nice to be back and in one piece," Christian said smiling at her.

"We have rearranged the bedrooms. I have put a spare bed in your room, and Isabella is going to sleep in there, in case anything happens such as a temperature or you wanting to vomit. We are going to put your father in the front room."

"That's great. Thank you," said Christian.

"I will make sure he behaves," Isabella said with a mock reassurance, causing Chantal to laugh.

"The big thing is going to be everyone getting a good sleep after all the drama. There is a five hour flight to Cape Town tomorrow. Now that Christian can eat a little, how about an early supper and then we all have an early night."

"Eating Chantal's food again sounds great," said Christian.

Chantal made ratatouille as she thought Christian may not be up to spicy food. The mix of tomatoes, garlic, onions, and courgette with a little bit of basil, was just what Christian needed to satiate his hunger. He was also desperate to try a slice of Chantal's home-made bread, but Jannie intervened and suggested they just wait and see how he got on with the ratatouille. Bread, he reminded Christian, in the early stage of bowel functioning can clog things up. At the end of the meal, the conversation turned to the departure in the morning and all the events of the last few weeks.

"We will be sorry to see you all go," said Emmanuel.

"I think I would like to come back at some stage," Isabella said, "if you would have me. It seems like here I could use my training in tropical medicine to the best advantage."

"We would be delighted to have you back, Isabella, as well as Christian with Jannie."

"I think I can say from everyone that we are extremely grateful to you and Chantal for looking after us. I think we all need to sort out a few things in Cape Town and then stay in touch and see where things lead us. And then contact you about returning," said Christian.

"I couldn't agree more," said Emanuel.

"And of course, the Sudanis could always visit us in Australia, dad. Couldn't they?"

277

"Maybe, but perhaps it's going to depend a little on your mother!"

"Well, on that note, I think we should all go to bed. It will be quite involved and busy day tomorrow," said Mike.

Christian got into bed, having decided with Isabella's help that he no longer needed intravenous drip. He released the mosquito net as Isabella searched through her backpack. Uncertain as to whether he should watch, he politely turned his back. The sound of her getting undressed was strangely exciting.

"And what might you be thinking? I can feel you thinking something," said Isabella from behind his back.

"The thought of you naked in the same room as me brings back some of those great memories."

"Don't get too excited. I'm still in my underwear which, this being Africa, is not as pretty or as exotic as you may remember."

Christian felt the mosquito net lift up and as he glanced up and saw Isabella's face next to his. She kissed him on the cheek.

"That's all the foreplay you are allowed before Cape Town. Doctors' orders and if you misbehave, I'll have the surgeon talk to you."

Christian laughed. "Good night, Isabella. Sleep well. See you in the morning. Can't wait for Cape Town"

The smell from Chantal's coffee drifted into the bedroom. Christian stirred, looked across at Isabella, who was still sound asleep under her mosquito net, and wondered what it would be like making love to her again. Would there be that same wonderful feeling?

"Are you two awake yet?" Chantal called from outside the door. "Coffee is made; Mike and Galela are just checking the ambulance again outside and then coming in for coffee."

Christian quickly got dressed. He lifted up the mosquito net covering Isabella and kissed her gently on the cheek.

"Mike and Galela are here. Time to go."

Christian waited for Isabella to dress and then they quickly walked through into the kitchen. Sitting on the stools around the kitchen bench, each with a steaming cup of coffee, were Mike and Galela.

"Did you sleep well, my young friend? I hope your snoring didn't disturb Isabella," Mike said smiling at Chantal.

"No, it didn't," Isabella said over Christian's shoulder. "And there was no sleepwalking either, if that's what you were thinking, Mike."

"Can't imagine I would be thinking that about you two at all," Mike laughed.

"We have Kariba sedated in a coffin in the ambulance. We will need to go in about fifteen minutes. The Goma border is ten minutes down the road. He will remain sedated for about twenty minutes," Galela said.

"And if there are any delays and he wakes up?" Jannie asked.

"We have a small bore intravenous line tracking out through the bottom of the coffin. Isabella and I will be in the back of the ambulance with you and if he makes any noise, we will give him a 20 mg bolus of propofol."

Chantal wished them luck, hugging both Christian and Isabella before they climbed into the back of the ambulance. Mike said goodbye to Chantal, and climbed in through the back door and sat next to Isabella. Christian lay under a sheet on the bed opposite the coffin. Jannie and Mike then quickly hooked a dummy intravenous line before taping it realistically to Christian's arm. Mike then peered through one of the tiny peepholes in the coffin at Kariba. After a few seconds, he stood up and smiled at them all and said,

"Perfect – breathing but not stirring."

The connecting window to the cab slid back and Emanuel's face appeared.

"All ready to go," he said

Mike nodded as Emanuel held up the paperwork and signalled to Galela sitting next to him to start driving towards the border. Fortunately, being early in the morning, the roads were not yet crowded with people walking to and from the border. Galela, however, couldn't avoid all the potholes, each of which caused a disconcerting dull thump as Kariba's body knocked against the side of the coffin. Christian hoped it wasn't too much of a stimulus that could wake him up. It took about six or seven minutes from the Sudani's to get to the border crossing. Christian felt the ambulance slowing and knew that they must be close.

"Border crossing coming up in one-minute," Emanuel called through the sliding window, which he then closed.

Christian felt the ambulance stop. The front door then opened and he could hear Emmanuel explaining to the security guards that they had patients for transfer to Goma hospital. His French wasn't good enough to understand much more but he heard the conversation moving along the side of the ambulance to the rear door. He looked at Isabella and Mike.

"Isabella, do you understand what they're saying?"

"They want to look inside the coffin to make sure nothing else was being transported across the border."

"Shit!" Mike said. "We need to give him 10 mg of propofol to make sure he doesn't move when I open the coffin."

Christian watched as Mike quickly took a syringe already loaded with the propofol. Jannie lifted the top end of the coffin so that Mike could find the IV line connected through the coffin to Kariba.

"There is a chance that this could overdose and kill him. But better to take that chance than to be charged with human trafficking," Mike said as he injected the propofol and then tucked the intravenous line underneath the coffin again. He had just sat back on the bed next Isabella when the back door opened. Emmanuel rolled his eyes in a look of fatalistic expectation. Behind him were two guards in military uniforms, each with an automatic weapon. One of the guards handed his weapon to the other and climbed into the back of the ambulance.

He stood between Jannie and Christian looking at the coffin. He then tapped it several times with his gun before looking at Isabella and Mike.

"You can open," he said to Mike.

Mike nodded. The coffin was hinged on one side and secured on the other with four adjustable wing nuts. As the guard stood to one side, Mike unscrewed them. Then looking at the guard, who indicated he should open the coffin, Mike lifted up one side so that was open facing towards Christian. Jannie reached across and held it open. Kariba was lying on his side, his face away from the guard and therefore not recognisable. Christian looked into the coffin and could not detect any breathing; perhaps Mike had overdosed him. The guard stood and looked for a few seconds, and then nodded his head and indicated to Jannie to close the coffin. Without any further checks, he turned and climbed back out of the ambulance. Galela closed the back doors of the ambulance, giving them all a thumbs up as he did, while Emmanuel climbed into the cab again and started the engine.

"I think you need to check on Kariba," Christian said. "I couldn't see any breathing when the coffin was open."

Mike and Isabella sat on Christian's bed as Jannie lifted up the coffin edge again. They all looked in and there was no movement and no breathing; Mike looked concernedly at Jannie when suddenly Kariba heaved and coughed. Jannie slammed the lid down and Mike quickly started screwing up the wing nuts, smiling.

"Seems like he got just the right dose."

At Goma airport, there was less intense security. Emmanuel talked to the security guard explaining who they were, and the barrier was raised allowing them to pass. The guard had pointed beyond the main entrance to a large hangar next to which they should find the Lear jet. They drove slowly so as not to attract too much attention in the ambulance, and as they drove past the large hangar, they saw the Lear jet; its front door was open and Suleiman was standing at the top of the stairs waving at them. Galela stopped at the bottom of the stairs.

"Isabella and Jannie, you help Christian get on board. We will deliver Kariba, who should be waking up any minute, to your friends from the ICC on the other side of the tarmac and then join you."

Christian disconnected the intravenous line as Isabella and Jannie gathered up both of their bags. As he climbed out of the ambulance, Jannie took his elbow until he was firmly on the tarmac. Christian looked up, and half a kilometre away was an Airbus 737 with a large European Union insignia on its tail, engines running. The ambulance stopped next to it and Christian watched as half a dozen men in uniform took the coffin up the stairs. He knew they would release him once they had taken off. Kariba was getting more comfort for his extradition to The Hague, more than he deserved.

"Are you okay going up the stairs?" Jannie said to Christian.

"Feeling stronger by the minute, dad, thanks to that excellent surgeon."

"Don't get overconfident, kiddo. I don't need to be doing any more surgery mid-flight!"

"Welcome aboard," said Suleiman as they reached the top of the stairs. "You will see halfway along, we have made provision for a bed for you if you need it."

"Yes, you might need some sleep before you get to Cape Town," said Isabella said winking at Christian.

"I'm actually feeling quite good. So I think I'll start out sitting up and at least we can all chat on the way, which I think given what's gone on, would also be therapeutic."

It was almost an hour later before Mike, Galela, and Emanuel returned.

"Everything okay?" Isabella asked as Mike poked his head in through the front door.

"Took Kariba a while to wake up from that dose of propofol we had to give him en route. But everything is now fine. Christian's friend from the ICC had a full security detail plus lawyers and an intensive care doctor to monitor him. Once we had him awake, they served the extradition papers on him and read his rights."

"I would like to have seen his face when that happened."

"To be honest, Christian, I don't think he really realised where he was or what was happening, but was awake enough to be served and for us to witness that he understood he was being extradited."

"Well, I'm going to leave you now that everything is done," Emanuel said. "I hope you have a smooth flight back and thank you all for helping us to get rid of this monster."

"I'm not sure that it's going to contribute much to the long-term problem of child labour and the abuse of women. There will eventually be someone else who takes Kariba's place," Galela said.

"Is there anything else that you think that we could do?"

"I think if in some way you could let the world know what goes on and those people like Raoul Saad who support the Karibas of the world could be exposed, that might be something positive."

"We'll see what we can do. Goodbye, Emmanuel, and thank you for everything. I hope we meet again soon."

"Au revoir, my friends." With a final wave, Emanuel disappeared down the stairs.

Mike and Galela walked down the aisle and sat on the couch opposite Christian and Isabella.

"Heinrich and Suleiman just need to load a few things and then we will leave," Mike said.

Christian looked out the window and saw that they were loading weapons from beneath the front seat of the ambulance into the rear hold. Just as well the ambulance had not been more thoroughly searched at the border crossing!

Suleiman returned and closed and locked the front door. Heinrich had positioned himself next to the second officer. As they banked, right over Lake Kivu, Christian wondered whether he would ever be back. He hoped so, for there was so much one could contribute, much more than he had previously appreciated or experienced in medicine.

"When do you think you will come back?" He said turning to Isabella.

"As soon as we have you sorted out in Cape Town."

"Okay you two, I know where this is going," Jannie said as both Mike and Galela smiled knowingly.

"Now listen dad, if there is anyone who should be talking about romance and the impact that you're about to make, then there's no comparison yours is going to be unsurpassed in terms of romantic drama."

"Let's hope your mother sees it that way."

"What a pity we don't have that Tom Jones recording that you both like so much. I can just imagine that in the background as she walks in and sees you."

"I can see 'like father like son' when it comes to romance," Mike laughed. "I'll make sure Sian has lots of tissues."

"Mike, you said there wouldn't be an issue with me not having a passport."

"No, Jannie. We have organised that. Galela made a phone call last night - one of the advantages of being employees of the National Intelligence Agency. Temporary papers will be delivered as we land. Heinrich already has your photo and you will have a passport within two days. In case you want to go on honeymoon to somewhere like Mauritius."

They all laughed and Christian tried to imagine the look on his mother's face after all these years. He hoped that she would understand that his father had been trying to protect them, while not understanding that the major threat to all their lives, Van der Walt, was dead. He closed his eyes and tried to imagine what it would be like having a mother and father again. Weird was the only thought that he could come up with. It would clearly take them all a while to adjust.

Chapter 26

Christian woke up as Heinrich announced that they were descending into Cape Town, having fallen asleep on the couch. Looking out through the small side window, he could make out the dark forbidding shadow of Table Mountain, the lights of Cape Town sprinkled like glow-worms at its feet.

"How is the wound feeling?" Jannie said to Christian from the opposite seat.

"It's feeling really good, dad. No pain when I move, no ooze from the wound, I might even be able to jog on the beach at the Strand in a couple of days."

"Just remember you're a patient, and think like a doctor - at least another week before that kind of vigorous activity!"

"Hear hear," Isabella added, winking at Christian. "Looks you are going to need a doctor to keep an eye on you."

Christian smiled inwardly, the conversation was the kind of banter that he had missed having with his father. Despite the initial awkwardness, it already felt good having him around. However, he knew it would be a bigger adjustment for his mother. While he wondered again what her surprise was, Galela walked back to them from where he had been chatting to Heinrich.

"Heinrich says it's time to fasten seatbelts."

"Now is everyone certain that my appearance should be as a surprise to Renata?" Jannie said to everyone but no one in particular.

"Did you lose all that surgical confidence in Rwanda?" Mike turned in his seat and asked Jannie.

"It will be fine, dad. Trust me. Especially if Sian can find that Tom Jones music!"

Jannie reached over and playfully ruffled Christian's hair.

"We will be met by my colleagues from NIA. They will bring a car out to the plane. Sian and Nadine will be waiting inside the terminal so we will take everyone through except Jannie. Once Nadine and Isabella have departed, we will come back and pick you up, Jannie. That should only take fifteen or twenty minutes. Everyone happy with those arrangements?"

Christian could remember ten years previously, approaching Cape Town for the first time, the pilot did a fly past of Table Mountain; its white cloud tablecloth tumbled down sheer sides. At the mountain's southernmost point, the Atlantic and Indian oceans embracing each other with their obtesting currents, the conflict produced fierce whitecaps. There had been a sense of anticipation of embarking on a potential journey of discovery to find out more about his father. He had left with many answers. Isabella was not his half-sister, and his father had gone to extreme lengths to protect Christian and his mother. There had not been the slightest suggestion or thought that his father might be alive. Not only was he alive, now he was going to land at the city of his birth with his father. Excitement about what might transgress with his father meeting with his mother was eclipsed only by what he might finally discover with Isabella.

As the pilots switched the engines off, Suleiman and Heinrich opened the front door in response to a tap from the outside. Two colleagues greeted them at the top of the steps, before handing them a leather pouch with NIA stamped across it in big letters. Heinrich thanked them in Afrikaans, opened the bag, and then handed the official papers to Jannie.

"Welcome back, Dr. de Villiers," Mike said. "You and Heinrich hang on here; we will be back in fifteen minutes after we have dropped off Christian and Isabella."

Waiting for them at the bottom of the steps was a black BMW X5. Christian and Isabella sat in the back with Suleiman. Mike and Galela sat up front with the driver. Christian for the first time felt the excitement of Isabella's body next to him. Perhaps after all on this trip, he was going to have the answer to another question, which had persisted since he had met Isabella: that they had a special chemistry unique to them and which he had not been able to replicate with anyone else. He glanced sideways at Isabella, and saw her smile.

The BMW pulled up outside an entrance which, Christian could see in the headlights, was marked private. Christian held the door for Isabella as Mike punched in a number on the keypad next to the door. As the door clicked and opened, Mike turned to Christian and Isabella.

"You two go first. Walk down the corridor until you see the VIP lounge on the right, go in there and you will find Nadine and Sian will be waiting."

Fifty metres down the corridor they saw the VIP sign. Christian looked at Isabella.

"After you, Issy."

Isabella opened the door and Christian recognised both Nadine and Sian in the background chatting animatedly. Nadine turned as she heard the door open and saw Isabella before shouting her name.

"Isabella!"

Christian watched as Nadine advanced rapidly, her arms wide open. Isabella smiled broadly at her mother's greeting, pushing the door fully open which allowed Christian to see a tall dark beautiful African woman, staring intently at them both. Nadine embraced Isabella with tears streaming down her cheeks and as they embraced, there was so much kissing that Christian did not notice that Sian had come up beside him and tapped him on the shoulder.

"So where's my greeting, handsome?" she said.

"Sian, it's fantastic to see you again."

"Is your wound okay? Mike told me you had an excellent surgeon." Sian winked at him.

"Yes, a fantastic surgeon. I was so lucky to have him there. I cannot wait for you to meet him," Christian whispered in Sian's ear.

Nadine finally disentangled herself from Isabella and held out her arms to Christian.

"Christian, so nice to see you again, and all in one piece."

Christian put his arms around Nadine while she kissed him on the cheek. Over her shoulder, he could see the unknown African woman smiling at Isabella, who stood looking at her surprised, overwhelmed, and with her hand over her mouth. Within minutes, as Christian watched, Isabella began passionately kissing Simone, oblivious to everyone else in the room. Christian looked across at Sian and raised his eyebrows as if to say what was going on? Sian's shrug of her shoulders and the way she pulled the corner of her mouth down indicated she was just as puzzled as to what was going on. Nadine fully disentangled from Christian's embrace looked up and saw the puzzlement on his face. She grasped his hand and said,

"Come on. Let's introduce you and break these two up."

Nadine, as she walked up behind, pulled on Isabella's jeans' pocket to get her attention. Isabella slowly turned around, not looking directly at Christian, but staring adoringly at the African girl whose hand she now held tightly.

"Isabella, how rude! You haven't introduced Simone to Christian."

Isabella took her eyes slowly off Simone and looked at Christian apologetically.

"I'm sorry. I was genuinely looking forward to seeing whether we could find our old chemistry, but as soon as I saw Simone, this wonderful feeling came back, a feeling I know that you were hoping to find with me again."

"That's okay, Issy. I know feelings can be surprisingly irrational; however, if you have found that with Simone, it might be possible for me to find something similar as well."

"Alright everyone," Mike said, walking into the room completely oblivious to the discussion. "Time to get moving, darling. You've got the BMW at the back entrance, haven't you?"

"Yes, I'll just see Nadine off with Simone and Isabella."

Nadine and Sian, with Simone and Isabella hand-in-hand, walked out through the door. Isabella stopped and put one hand on the door frame before turning and looking at Christian. She smiled and blew him a kiss off her hand before leaving.

"What was that all about? Did I miss something?" Said Mike

"I think Isabella has decided that she's gay."

"Well, not quite certain how to answer that, because I know that you were hoping that things might work out between the two of you. But these things happen in life and I believe when one door closes, another opens. So watch out for an open door that has lots of excitement on the other side is my advice."

"Thanks, Mike, good advice but still a bit of a shock."

"Well, maybe it's good preparation for your father meeting your mother tomorrow morning!"

Christian smiled. "Let's hope it is not that dramatic."

"Well, he must be dying to get off that plane, so let's get into the car and home. Of course he's going to be interrogated on the way home by Sian."

Suleiman came down the steps from the Lear jet to meet them as they drove up. Mike wound down the window.

"All clear?" Suleiman asked.

"All clear. Tell Jannie to come and join us."

Solomon gave the thumbs up sign to Heinrich standing at the top of the stairs and within a few minutes, Jannie was in the front seat next to Mike.

"Did it all go well inside?"

"Not quite according to plan, dad."

Jannie turned around to look at his son.

"That wasn't quite the overjoyed expression I was expecting to see. Is your wound okay?"

"The wound is fine, dad. It's a bit complicated but I'll tell you when we get back to Mike and Sian's. Prepare yourself though; Mike says Sian is so excited to see you again that none of us may get a word in until we get to their house!"

"Well, I do remember that she'd love to chat and we did get on really well as a couple, didn't we, Mike?"

"Yes, we did and Sian has lost none of the ability to find all the pieces of the jigsaw and put them together. So be warned, my friend."

"In a strange way I am looking forward to it. It's like putting all parts together of my life that had been hidden. Seeing Renata again is going to be wonderful. I just hope it's not too much of a shock to her."

"It's going to be, dad, but I think she's had a small candle burning for you. I'm sure it may take a while but that claim might burn brightly again when she gets over the shock of knowing that you're alive."

"Okay you two, enough of the philosophising. There's Sian waving. Let the interrogation begin."

They pulled up next to Sian and Jannie opened the front door and stepped out. Sian rushed at him, threw her arms around him, and started crying. Christian watched as they embraced, rocking each other backwards and forwards.

"Well then, not quite the interrogation I was expecting, but then they were such great friends," said Mike turning to Christian. "And I think, young man, you going to have to get in the front seat with me so that we can put those two in the back seat and Sian can ask her 1000 questions on the way home."

Christian remembered the drive, the shantytowns lining either side of the roadway not clearly visible in the dark but nonetheless still there. He could hear Sian in the back seat, hardly allowing his father to reply before asking another question. That sequence was interrupted when Jannie tapped Mike on the shoulder.

"Do you still have any association with the Groote Schuur hospital?"

"Yes and I'm planning on taking you and Renata there, but there are not many of the old faces left. You probably won't recognise it; there have been so many changes."

The large, electronically-operated gates were remotely opened by Mike. They drove up the driveway that Christian knew so well and stopped at the foot of the steps. Mike tooted the horn, the front door opened, and Ruby stood there waiting for them.

"She's so excited to see you again," said Sian to Christian. "We didn't tell her about you, Jannie, just to prepare an extra room, so be prepared for lots of tears and hugs when she sees you."

"Master Christian, Master Christian, it is so wonderful to see you and have you back," said Ruby as Christian reached her at the top of the stairs.

"Thank you, Ruby. It's great to be back, and I brought a surprise for you."

"You didn't need to do that, Master Christian."

"Brace yourself for the surprise, Ruby," said Mike as he walked past her into the house.

Ruby peered into the darkness towards the car. Jannie was partly obscured by the open boot and Ruby turned back to Christian and Sian.

"The surprise, is it in the boot?" She smiled

"In a way it is." said Sian laughing as Jannie started to walk up the stairs towards them.

Three steps from the top, Ruby screamed.

"Oh my God, it's Master Jannie, its Master Jannie, oh my God, I can't believe it, he's meant to be dead!"

"As you can see, Ruby, he's very much alive which we are all thrilled about."

Christian looked at Ruby, the tears rolling down her cheeks as his father made it to the top step. For a second they both stopped and looked at each other, smiled, and then embraced. Christian thought the hug may go on all night.

"Come on, you two old friends. Let's get everyone inside where it's warm and I'm sure these two need to get some sleep as there is a big day planned tomorrow."

"Still the wonderful Rwandan coffee to look forward to," said Christian to Ruby as they walked through the kitchen.

"Yes, Master Christian, and I remember how you like yours, black with no sugar or milk."

"Very good memory," said Christian.

"I'll show you to your rooms and we can have breakfast at whatever time you wake up. It's too late to call Renata, but she's going to be here tomorrow morning at 10:30 AM. So if you want to sleep in, don't worry."

"It's whether I will get to sleep is the real issue, I think." said Jannie.

Chapter 27

Christian knew he would struggle to get to sleep. Every time he closed his eyes, he could see Isabella and Simone embracing. It did not trouble him that she had chosen Simone over him; the more interesting question to him was how she had decided. Their discussions in Rwanda had left him believing that she had not found the type of chemistry with Simone that they had had. He woke up thinking about Isabella. He wondered whether he would get to talk to her now that Simone was her partner.

Rubbing his eyes, he looked across at the digital clock and saw that it was 9 AM. Downstairs he could hear his father's voice and Sian laughing. The smell of Ruby's coffee, just as he remembered, filled the room with a rich Arabica aroma. He rolled over and looked down at his phone on the floor next to his bed. There were three messages. The first message, which surprised him, was from Isabella: *We won't come to your reunion today, but Simone and I would love to talk to you.* His mother's message was next: *So looking forward to seeing you, love mum.* The third message was from Petrea: *Kariba successfully picked up, we need to talk about the $5 million reward, would love to see you, staying at the Waterfront hotel.* He replied to his mother, then to Petrea suggesting they meet at the Mount Nelson hotel for lunch, and left Isabella's reply for later until he had thought about it a little more.

"Good morning, Master Christian," Ruby said, as Christian walked into the kitchen. "I hope you had a good night's sleep."

"Wonderful sleep, that bed is as comfortable as I remember it, and it's so nice to be back, Ruby."

"Everyone is out on the stoep. I'm sure you remember how to get out there." She smiled, as Christian walked out through the open doorway.

"Good morning, dad. Isn't that just a magnificent view of Table Mountain?"

"It is. I was just commenting to Mike, you forget how much you miss things, until you see them again. A bit like you. It's a wonderful feeling after all this time to have you as close as you are."

"I seem to recall mum saying you were much more clinical in your observations."

Jannie smiled as Mike and Sian both laughed.

"I can see it hasn't taken you two long to establish a relationship with a cheeky edge."

"Yes, it's funny isn't it, after all these years; perhaps it's that genetic link that just breaks through all the barriers that would normally require months of dismantling to get to the point where we are now."

"I'm sure that's the way that it will work with mum when she arrives."

"Here's hoping. I'm still a little nervous about that, despite all the confidence around me."

"You have indeed changed, Jannie. Nothing ever seemed to make you nervous in the past," said Sian

"Well, there is a lot to be forgiven and adjusted to, despite Christian's encouragement. I'm sure that she has changed and may not feel the same as I do. I'm trying to be realistic, especially with the disappointment of Isabella and Christian fresh in our minds still."

"I'm sure there will be some adjustment necessary on both sides but you're both mature, have the ability to talk through issues, and love, when it's there, can repair even the most damaged relationships."

"So how do you think we should surprise her when she arrives?" Jannie asked.

"We will need to let her get over meeting Christian first, which will take a good twenty minutes. I will leave the big French doors open out onto the stoep. You stay out here and then after about twenty minutes or so, plug-in the iPod and let the Tom Jones song float in through the doors. I'm sure that will make her curious enough to come out, and then find you. The rest, as they say, will be up to you."

"Okay, Mike, let's go with that plan. Do you have a spare pair of jeans and a clean shirt that I could change into?"

"I have. Just as well you haven't put on any weight over the years!"

Christian watched as Mike and Jannie walked up the stairs, arm in arm, like two old mates at a rugby reunion. The wall clock then chimed ten o'clock. His mother, who was always on time, would be arriving in thirty minutes. Strangely, he now felt a little nervous, possibly he thought because of the disappointing Isabella outcome. Successful conclusions were never guaranteed in life just because you hoped for them. The meeting of his mother and father, while he was seriously hoping that it would have a good conclusion, did have a number of potential hurdles.

"It will be okay," Sian said as if reading his mind. "They are both intelligent and wonderful people. It may take a bit of adjusting in the beginning, but I'm sure it will all work out."

Christian smiled at Sian, hoping the disquiet that he felt in his spirit was related only to the Isabella episode the previous day. He got up from the couch, taking his coffee cup, and walked through to the kitchen. As he stood in the kitchen refilling his coffee cup, he tried to imagine what it was going to be like not only having a father, but potentially now a family. He had not told his father about the golden retriever, whom he knew at least would have no problems adjusting to more affection and potential walks. He sat on the kitchen bench for the next twenty minutes slowly drinking his coffee, until he heard the front gates open.

"Dad," he shouted up the stairs. "You'll need to hurry; mum's here."

Jannie appeared at the top of stairs in Mike's new shirt and jeans.

"How do I look, kiddo?" he said smiling.

"Handsome, dad, but get your skates on. I can hear the car doors opening."

Jannie ruffled his hair on the way down the stairs, and then disappeared out through the French doors onto the stoep. Christian sat for a second, offered a prayer to whoever was listening, and then walked to the front door. Sian and Ruby were already at the top of the stairs, and all he could hear were indecipherable excited greetings. He momentarily thought about waiting in the family room, so that by the time everyone reached him, they would be much more settled. There was also a strange feeling of needing to show solidarity with his dad.

"Christian!" Renata said excitedly as she walked in through the front door smiling." I don't think I'm ever letting you go to Africa again."

Christian laughed before he said, "Good to see you, mum; I think that's what you said last time as well."

As she walked up to him, he put his arms around her and felt her squeeze him tightly. For a minute, she just stood holding him her head nestled under his chin, not saying a word.

"Mum, my shirt is getting wet."

"That's what you have to put up with if you go getting yourself shot," she said, standing back and looking at him, still smiling.

"In fact you look very good for someone who's been shot; Mike told me that you were lucky enough to have an experienced liver surgeon who operated on you. That was very fortunate in the middle of the Congo. I would like to meet him at some stage and personally thank him. Someone upstairs was obviously looking out for you."

"Yes, mum, someone obviously was."

"You're going to have to tell me all about it; you know what mothers are like. They need to have all the details. But firstly there's someone I want you to meet, the surprise that I talked about."

Christian looked beyond his mother to the doorway. Mike was standing in the doorway, making strange hand signals and pointing out towards the stoep, where Jannie was sitting. Christian could not work out what Mike was trying to tell him and then Renata turned round and saw Mike gesticulating.

"What is that Mike up to, Christian? He always had a trick or two up his sleeve."

"I don't know, mum. Perhaps related to your surprise."

"I thought Isabella and Nadine might be here, or are they coming later?"

"Just us for coffee. As you will see, it's a bit of a long story. We thought we might all be able to do lunch later."

"Well, if Mike and Sian are not going to bring my surprise in here to meet you, let's go and join them in the kitchen."

Christian followed his mother through into the kitchen, his inner disquiet returning. Ruby was her busy self, and did not look up as he walked in. In the far corner, Mike and Sian were talking to someone he vaguely recognised as having visited their house in

Adelaide a few times. As he looked closer, he recognised Tim Mickelson, an anaesthetist who had been to their house a few times for coffee with his mother.

"Christian, you will remember Tim who's been to the house a few times. We decided to get engaged last week, but we didn't want to tell anyone until we could tell you. So now it's official and you're the first one to know, which is how I wanted it."

Christian looked at Mike and Sian. They both just looked back at him wide-eyed and shocked. He realised he needed to quickly get to his father and prepare him for the shock that was coming.

"Christian, nice to see you again and great to hear that you're okay. I hope this is not too much of a shock for you," Tim said turning and shaking Christian's hand.

"Tim, I am extremely happy for you both, and please don't think me rude but there is something I have got to do urgently, which you will understand later," Christian said, turning to head out towards the stoep and his father. He had only taken one step when he heard the Tom Jones song begin and the words drift in through the open door.

"Where's that music coming from?" Renata asked.

"I must have left the iPod on. I will go and turn it off," Christian said over his shoulder as he headed for the doorway.

"That's strange. I didn't hear it before, and that's one of my favourite songs."

"Yes, mum, I know it is. Wait here and I'll go and switch it off."

Christian walked out of the kitchen into the family room and stopped. His mother was right behind him.

"Mum, best if you stay in the kitchen with Tim."

"You have forgotten that mothers have instincts like no other human beings, especially when it comes to sons. You are hiding something from me."

"Mum, it's better if you let me handle this," Christian said, turning to face her, putting his hands on her waist, to stop her coming any further into the family room. Then he heard his father's voice from behind him.

"Renata."

He could see Mike and Sian watching from the doorway, a concerned look on both their faces. He took his hands off his mother's waist and stepped aside to allow her to fully see his father.

"Oh my God! Is that you, Jannie? It can't be you! I buried you!"

"It is me, Renata. I was the surgeon who operated on Christian. I have explained to him that I had survived the shooting that took place at our house in Wynberg, thanks to a Dr. Sandy van Andover at the Salt River Mortuary where I was taken. I have been in hiding in Rwanda hoping that if Van der Walt believed that I was dead, that you and Christian would be safe. Mike and Christian have told me how he was killed down the mine in Johannesburg, and is no longer a threat to any of us. It is so wonderful to see you again. You are just as I remembered and I'm sorry that I haven't been here for you."

Christian watched as his mother looked away from Jannie and slowly sat down on the sofa. Mike and Sian sat next to her and put an arm around her as she started to cry. Tim was standing in the doorway looking very perplexed. Christian looked at his father, who had not heard the conversation in the kitchen - that his mother had become engaged to Tim. Jannie was looking at Christian as if to say 'what do I do now?'

"Dad, I'm sorry. There is no easy way of doing this. This is Tim Mickelson who in the last few minutes officially became engaged to mum."

Christian watched as Jannie stared at Tim for sixty seconds, feeling his hopes dissipating. Then to Christian's surprise he walked across to where Tim was standing, reached out with his hand and said,

"Congratulations, Tim, you have made an excellent choice."

"I, along with everyone else, thought you were dead Jannie - if you will excuse the bluntness. I'm sorry you had to confront this after all you have obviously been through."

"That's okay, Tim. Surprises sometimes don't work out the way that you hope, and you, along with everyone else, would never have expected me to return like this. It was always going to be a long shot to integrate back into Christian and Renata's life, let alone seamlessly. It was, in many ways, an unrealistic expectation."

"Jannie, I think it's fantastic that you have survived. The reality now is that you two need some time alone. There will be much that you have to discuss and provide each other answers about, as well as catching up on Christian's adventures. Ren, I'm going to go back to the hotel. Either give me a call when you're finished or I'm sure Mike will bring you down as an alternative."

"Thanks, Tim, for being so understanding," Renata said tearfully from where she was sitting on the sofa. "Jannie and I obviously need to have a discussion which will take some time. I'll call you when we're finished."

Christian heard the front door close and turned to look at his mother. Mike had gone through to the kitchen, and his father was now sitting on the sofa next to his mother. He looked at them both and thought they looked like they belonged together, then wondered whether that was wishful dreaming. Sian then got up and went to join Mike in the kitchen, who was making fresh coffee. Christian started to feel uncomfortable as both his parents just looked at each other, not saying anything. He stood up to go and join Mike and Sian when Mike walked back in with the coffee and placed it on the small table in front of Renata. As he walked back out with Mike, he heard his father say:

"Renata, I just need to say how sorry I am. I know how extremely difficult it must have been for you and while it doesn't help with much of the hurt, there wasn't a day that went past that I didn't think about you. I have missed out on over twenty years of sharing a life with you and Christian, which I would love to hear about, but I'm also realistic and I'm not expecting to walk back into your life. I would love to share certain aspects and at worst, be your friend and father to Christian."

Christian stopped just beyond the doorway. He needed to know how his mother was going to respond to his father.

"Why didn't you just let us know that you were alive somewhere?"

"Van der Walt had threatened to kill you and Christian unless I gave him all my research and the documents that I had taken. I knew that if I did that, he might kill us all. As long as he thought I was dead and had the documents, then there was no reason to come after you and Christian."

"But why didn't you at least try and contact us, or Mike and Sian?"

"Van der Walt had the ability to monitor everything coming into and going out of South Africa, and had friends in Mossad and the CIA. If he or they had suspected that I was alive, with the documents I had about germ warfare and nuclear research, they might have thought that I had contacted you which would put you in danger again. Believe me, there wasn't a day when I wished that I could."

"I have a whole new life now, Jannie. For so long I missed you and couldn't form a relationship with anyone else because I had loved you so much. For the first time, I have now met someone and I had felt the love that we had."

"I understand that, Renata. Christian has filled me in on small parts of the twenty years in Australia. As I said, I don't expect to walk back into your life. I just hope over a period of time you will forgive me for what happened and that would be my greatest expectation fulfilled. I would like to come to Australia and be a father to Christian. He has grown up into a magnificent young man; you have done a wonderful job."

"Thank you. I wouldn't be concerned about you coming to Australia. I do understand that you did what you did to protect us, and part of me is very grateful for that. It is so nice to see you alive even though it will take me some time to adjust to you being around. I'm sure Christian was as shocked as I am, but I can see that he has already formed a bond with you. I'm sure in some way we can function again as a family."

"Thanks, Renata. That is as much as I can realistically expect and to be a father to Christian again as well as perhaps a good friend of yours and Tim. If that works out, it would be wonderful bonus."

Christian looked back in through the doorway. His mother looked up, wiped the tears from her eyes with the back of her hand, then reached out and took his father's hand. She held it for a few minutes before saying,

"Jannie, you never left my heart and I suspect you never will. Coming back to Australia would be wonderful for Christian. I am prepared to help you get back there and settled and perhaps we could be, as you say, good friends. I have so many questions that I want to ask you but I feel in a state of shock, and perhaps we just need a little space first. I will also need to go and need reassure Tim. Perhaps we can talk about this tomorrow, once everything has settled a little," Renata said looking at Sian.

"I suppose it depends on how Tim feels; we could all have lunch today at the Mount Nelson and invite Nadine and Isabella if you want."

"Tim, I'm sure will be fine, and that sounds like a really great idea to have everyone sitting around, talking in a less strained atmosphere, getting to know each other."

"We might need to extend that invitation to Isabella and Simone," Christian said looking at Mike.

"The more that we have, the easier it might be. Who is Simone?"

"It's a short story, Mike. I'll explain a little bit later."

Renata stood up as Sian offered her a box of tissues which Renata waved away.

"I'll take you back to the Mount Nelson."

"Is it all right if I tag along as far as the hotel?" Christian asked. "I have someone to meet there."

"Is that the lady from the ICC?"

"Yes. She wants me to sign some papers and indicate how the reward should be used."

"Well, perhaps the five of us should just have a glass of wine together. It might make it easier tomorrow for Tim. What do you think, Christian?" Mike asked.

Christian looked at his father, who just smiled and nodded.

"Well, we will give you three a twenty minute head start and then I will bring Jannie in the car. That will also give Jannie and me a chance to debrief."

The fifteen-minute trip to the Mount Nelson Hotel seemed much longer. Christian had no idea as to what he should say to his mother as they drove, other than he was sorry that he had not let her know ahead of time. He also had little idea of what he would talk to Tim about; however he knew that it was important from his mother's point of view that Tim felt involved.

Sian, in her inimitable way, kept up a monologue that included comments on everything from corruption in local politics, to the beautiful springtime weather. The brightness of her commentary, Christian thought, was a useful distraction, which moderated both the awkwardness and the shock they were all feeling. It also allowed him time to text Petrea as they drove. *'Meet you in the foyer, looking forward to seeing you'* was the reply he received within a few seconds.

Chapter 28

Sian turned left off Wilkinson Street, beneath the giant Roman columns guarding the entrance to the Mount Nelson Hotel. On either side of the red brick driveway were giant palm trees, each with huge poorly coiffured fronds, irritated incessantly by the southerly Cape Town breeze, sweeping visitors to the grand entrance of the hotel. At the top of the driveway, Sian parked the BMW between the steps and a large pond bordered by bright pink and white petunias. The hotel, Christian thought, was from the early nineteen hundreds, but had been lovingly restored and painted in a non-period pinkish hue. Modern polished white sandstone blocks that had been added extended out in front of the hotel to create an outdoor food and drinks area. Dotted with white corrugated iron tables, each covered by a pink and white umbrella, the presence of numerous couples and families created the atmosphere of twenty-first-century conviviality. Circumscribing the hotel were manicured gardens with a variety of native plants that he had not previously seen in Africa.

Christian got out and opened the front door for his mother. Renata gave him a big hug and said,

"Don't worry, honey; I'm sure it's all going to work out."

Christian hugged her back then held her at arm's length, smiled, and hugged her again. Renata hooked her arm through his, as Sian gave her keys to the valet, and Christian headed toward the steps.

`"Wait for me," said Sian as she hurried to join them.

Sian, on catching up with them, took Christian's free arm and they all ascended the steps in unison. As they arrived at the top of the steps, Christian looked up and saw Tim waiting for them. Renata let go of his arm to embraced Tim.

"Tim, I'm so sorry. I had no idea that was going to happen."

"Renata, that's fine. I don't blame you at all. It would have been a surprise with amazing potential, if we had not met. However, I think there will be many issues that you two should work out, just so that you can be certain about us. I have booked a flight back on Monday and suggest that you, Christian, and Jannie sort out what needs to be sorted out and then come back to Australia and we can go from there."

"Tim, don't you think that is something that we should have discussed first?"

"I know how I feel about you, Renata, and I know that you would have tried to persuade me not to, but I think this is seriously the right decision so that we can all then clearly see the way ahead."

"Tim, after all this time, I'm certain you are the one that I want to be with. I can understand what a shock this has been. However, I think you're right that there are issues to be worked through so that there is no confusion, particularly for us going forward."

"Tim, I'm so sorry I had no idea that you and mum were seeing each other, let alone thinking about becoming engaged. It was my idea to arrange it as a surprise. I feel badly now that it has worked out the way it has. I'm sorry that I also spoilt your surprise for me."

"Christian, you have been through an enormous amount, so don't worry. Your intentions were all good. We are all mature adults and will all work through this to find a solution for everyone. So why don't we all sit down and have lunch here in the beautiful sunshine. Maybe a good bottle of Stellenbosch wine or two will ease some of the tensions."

"That's a good idea, Tim. I think Christian needed to sign some papers with the woman from the ICC. Maybe, honey, you would like to invite her to lunch as well."

"If you are sure that you don't want to be alone, that would be great. I had texted her so assume that she's waiting inside at reception. I will go and find her and bring her back."

"Great. We'll be at the table over there, number twelve," Tim said pointing to his left.

Christian walked into the reception area. Standing at the far end, he spotted the unforgettable shape of Petrea. She was dressed in the pinstriped trouser suit he had so admired at Adelaide airport, and a crisp white professional shirt, which also emphasised her femininity. Almost at the same time as he saw her, Petrea spotted him and waved, holding the briefcase in one hand and pointing to it.

Christian smiled and looked at her, and the attraction he had felt when he first met her instantly returned. Swinging the briefcase, she strode towards him with an authority that he had not previously noted. It added to her attraction. As she walked, she kept her eyes on him, he tried unsuccessfully to remember her advice about interpreting body language. Within a few seconds she was standing in front of him, holding out her hand.

"Great to see you again, Christian; fantastic that Kariba is now all locked up in The Hague and Brutal Bosco has surrendered to the Ugandans. We have applied to extradite Bosco and they will both then be tried for war crimes and crimes against humanity."

"I have to admit I had a lot of help," Christian said, shaking her hand.

"Modesty is quite sexy when done genuinely well, and is that all the girl gets after a few months' absence?" she looked at his hand shaking hers.

Christian laughed, bent forward, and kissed her on the cheek.
"Better?"

"Acceptable for the moment," she said smiling. "Shall we go and find an espresso coffee and you can tell me all about what happened, then I will get you to sign the necessary papers."

They walked through to the small dining room but stopped when the lift door opened, and a young African couple walked out. Christian and Petrea paused as they surveyed the reception area, when from the back of the lift, laughing, Simone and Isabella walked out hand-in-hand. In their preoccupation with each other, they almost bumped into Christian and Petrea. There was an awkward silence as they all stood and faced each other.

"Christian, I'm so sorry. I didn't know that you were going to be here," Isabella said.

"Isabella, don't worry. It's great to see you happy, seriously."

"Would you like to come and join us for lunch?"

"No thanks, Isabella. Mum, Tim, and Sian are at a table outside. Mike and Jannie are joining us in half an hour and we have been invited to join them. Isabella, this is Petrea. She is the lawyer from the ICC who extradited Kariba. She has some papers that I need to sign with regards to Kariba and the reward."

"Nice to meet you, Isabella. I have heard lots about you."

"Petrea, this is my partner Simone whom you have possibly heard a little about from Christian."

Petrea reached her hand out towards Simone who ignored it and instead kissed her on the cheek.

"Delighted to meet you, Petrea. And nice to see you again, Christian. I'm sorry that it was all so rushed at the airport and Isabella and I didn't have a chance to talk to you."

"That's okay. Perhaps in the next few days we can all meet up for coffee," Christian said.

"We will let you get on with signing the papers then. If you have time, come and have a chat. Otherwise I will phone you to organise a time to talk," Isabella said as she walked off with Simone hand-in-hand.

"Now that's something I didn't see coming," Petrea said.

"I had no idea that was going to happen either, although Isabella had told me about Simone. I thought it was just a past experiment. Simone was waiting for Isabella at the airport and my guess is that they haven't been apart since."

"So are you devastated that you never got to find out whether it was just a first love thing with Isabella, or whether it was her chemistry which was unique to you both and never to be replicated?"

"I was a little bit stunned at the airport. However, there has been so much happening with my mum and dad that I have not really thought about it too much. Other than thinking it was a chapter now definitely closed that I was hoping to reopen and find some answers."

"Maybe you need a new book to read," Petrea said, with a mischievous smile.

"Any suggestions? Do-it-yourself chemistry?"

"That is quite funny, Christian, but self-pleasure I have found lacks the intensity that I enjoy. Therefore, it would not be my first choice for you either. I have just realised that I have left one of the documents that I need you to sign in my room. I don't want to leave that lying up there on the table as it is highly confidential. Why don't you come with me? I'll get it and then we can come down to lunch."

Christian looked at Petrea; he could not imagine her leaving a confidential document on the table in her room. She seemed far too organised for that; however, putting a little distance between him and Isabella for a few minutes was attractive.

The lift took them to the second floor in silence. Petrea stood close enough to him that he could feel her hand against his leg. There was nothing more than the faintest contact but the effect was such that it completely distracted him from his thoughts about the Isabella encounter. He was not certain whether it was his imagination, or whether Petrea was exerting gentle pressure against his leg. Notoriously bad at interpreting any kind of body language, he reassured himself that it was his imagination. Then as her perfume drifted up, he had an overwhelming desire to feel the softness of her skin next to his. He closed his eyes and tried to picture his golden retriever until he felt the lift stop. He opened his eyes to see Petrea standing in front of him smiling, almost as though she knew what he had been thinking.

"Follow me," she said, walking out of the lift.

The corridor was lined with paintings of African wildflowers. Underneath each one was a small brass plaque detailing the history of the artist. They stopped in front of Petrea's room, and Christian could see next to her door bright red pistol Aloes set against the backdrop of Table Mountain. It captured the beauty of the Cape and was, he thought, very Freudian given his thoughts in the lift. As Petrea swiped her door card, Christian saw the artist was a Margaret van Zyl and started to read some of her details on the brass plaque, when Petrea unlocked the door. Holding it open, she said,

"Coming in? Or are you going to stand out there reading history?"

Christian walked towards her and as he did so, her perfume reached up again and embraced his desire. As he turned sideways to pass her in the doorway, he glanced down at her beautiful cleavage, delicately framed by her white shirt. He heard Petrea lock the door behind him. Turning around to face her, he watched as she put the hard briefcase down on the floor in front of him. She then took off her jacket and threw it on the nearest chair, before standing on the briefcase in front of him smiling. Slowly Petrea stretched and stood on her toes before reaching up and taking his face in her hands and then gently kissing him. Christian leaned back against the wall, feeling the softness of her breasts, as she pushed her body in against his. He wrapped his arms around her, pulling her gently towards him, while her tongue danced along the edge of his lips. He held her tightly against his body, feeling her tongue hesitate before exploring the edges of his mouth. Then she gently forced open his lips, touching the tip of his tongue with hers in small sensual circles.

Christian opened his eyes and looked at Petrea. Her eyes were closed but her sensuality was undiminished. He closed his eyes again, and kissed her with a passion that only the deep desire to make love could generate.

"Wait," she whispered, opening her eyes and looking up at him before putting one finger on his lips to prevent a question.

"I want this to be the most remarkable first encounter."

As she proceeded to place delicate soft kisses all over his neck, he did heard her whisper,

"I want you so much, deep inside of me, where you can touch a part of me that tells you how much I want you."

Taking her head in his hands, he kissed her with a raw passion, before she broke free laughing, kissing the tip of his nose, before pushing him gently back against the wall. Then, unbuttoning his shirt, she began teasing each of his nipples with the tip of her tongue, lightly caressing each nipple until they each became erect with desire. Her passionate need climbed over his body invading every pore, threatening his control. Every fibre within him became more demanding of release; the hardness of his desire begged for an orgasmic tumult. She rubbed her body against his, enjoying his desire and then said,

"Come with me." She took his hand and led him into the bedroom.

Christian followed, enjoying feeling the all-consuming passion that he had not experienced since Isabella; at the foot of the bed, he could no longer control his desire and pulled her to him, kissing her with an uncontrolled intensity. They both stumbled back landing on the bed laughing, struggling in their passion to remove each other's clothes. Petrea undid the remaining buttons on his shirt as he lay back on the bed before finally pulling his shirt off and throwing it on the floor. Teasing his nipples with her tongue again, she stroked his abdomen, stopping teasingly at the top of his jeans. Slowly she touched his hardness, stroking it lightly, she gasped and said,

"That feels so hard and beautiful I just want to kiss all of it and then feel you deep inside of me."

He stood up and slipped off his jeans, watching as she removed her bra - displaying beautiful breasts. He hung his jeans over the chair next to the bed, as Petrea lay back naked on the bed watching him, teasingly stroking the firmness of her nipples. Christian could not believe that everything about her was so beautiful, from her breasts to her dark beautifully trimmed, dark enchanting forest.

Stepping out of his boxers, he lay down next to her feeling the sensual softness of her skin. Bending forward he kissed her nipples softly, taking each between his lips, sucking and caressing them with his tongue. As he traced his tongue across the tips, Petrea whispered,

"Christian, that is beautiful."

Christian looked up to see Petrea smiling at him. Reaching down, he stroked her inner thighs with the back of his fingers. He then traced the outlines of her soft dark hair. He heard her sigh and call his name again.

"Make love to me," she whispered in his ear as she lay on his chest. Christian reached down and held her hips with both hands.

"Christian, that's beautiful," she said as the intimacy of Christian's love-making overwhelmed her.

Christian looked up. Petrea's eyes were closed, but her smile revealed the intensity of her pleasure.

"Christian."

Petrea called more loudly as Christian's passionate fire infused her whole body. As their ecstasy climaxed he called her name, holding her tightly. After several small contractions, Petrea stopped moving, lying silently on his chest. He held her tightly, overwhelmed by the intensity of their passion, not wanting the moment or the feeling to end.

"So do you like the new book?" she said lifting her head off his chest to look at him, smiling mischievously.

"Very cute. I am, as you know, an avid reader. How many chapters do think there might be in this new book?"

"How many chapters would you like there to be?"

"From that experience, many more. However, I suspect we may not get beyond page one with you living in The Hague and with me in Australia."

"Well, if you enjoyed that first chapter as much as me, we may get to create a few more chapters shortly. I'm taking up a position with a law firm in Sydney."

"Could be the best read I have ever had then," Christian said laughing. "Shall we get dressed and go and have lunch with my mother, and you can fill me in on some of the details."

"That sounds great, but I do need you to sign the papers."

Christian dressed slowly as Petrea showered, reflecting on how his journey had begun and evolved into an adventure he could never have imagined. He left Adelaide for an overseas surgical experience, and hopefully to see whether Isabella was the unique alchemist when it came to his passion; the trauma of the shooting, finding his father, and then wondering whether the question with Isabella would remain forever unanswered. Then, in another twist, Petrea emphatically answered part of the Isabella question. Chemistry was an equation with many different evolutionary elements; the unique order which those elements interacted caused the combustible reaction, which promotes passion and desire to Himalayan heights.

"Sign here, gorgeous man," Petrea said, walking up to the table where Christian was sitting. He looked at her silk dressing gown distractingly covering of parts of her wet body. Christian suddenly wanted her passion again. He ignored the paper that she had put on the table, pulling her to him and undoing her gown.

"Hold on, Tiger! I want more of you too. However, your mother will be wondering what has happened to you, and we don't want security knocking on the door as we're shouting each other's names!"

Christian laughed.

"No, that wouldn't do. I'll stop if you promise me we can start again later."

"I'm here for another two days. You can stay with me if you have the stamina! Now sign this while I get dressed."

Riding down in the lift, Christian put his arm around Petrea's waist, closing his eyes and reliving the wonderful lovemaking. As the door of the lift opened, Christian turned to Petrea and said,

"Mothers know."

"I'm sure she will if you keep smiling like that as will ex-girlfriends if she is still around!"

They walked through the foyer out onto the covered front deck. Christian looked to his left. Seated at table twelve, he could see his mother, father, Tim, Mike, and Sian. It was indeed a day of continuing surprises. His father, upon seeing him, waved. Christian walked over to the table turning and introducing Petrea, briefly explaining who she was and her involvement with the ICC. He tried not to look at his mother whom he could feel staring at him when Mike said very mischievously,

"You are missing several of the buttons on your shirt."

"I think you need a good lawyer if you attempt to reply to that," Petrea said, smiling at Christian as she sat down on a chair that Jannie had pulled up next to him.

Christian took the chair next to his mother, who gave him a knowing look that only mothers, with their deep instincts for their children, can manage. Then, with what Christian had come to understand was an approving smile, she handed Christian and Petrea a menu.

"We ordered about half an hour ago but they are incredibly slow here. I think that was about the time that you went to sign your papers! Did you manage to get those all signed?" Renata said looking at Christian.

"My lawyer was happy," Christian said looking in Petrea's direction.

"If you decide what you would like for lunch, I'll go inside and see whether I have any influence with the chef," Mike suggested.

"That would be great, Mike."

Christian quickly glanced at the menu.

"I'll go with the salmon salad."

"Make that two," said Petrea.

"Mike, there was one thing that I've been meaning to ask since we rescued Isabella that day in the bush. The blue drums that were stacked up at the bottom of the mountain. Did you ever find out what they were?"

"I sent your photographs of them to our office in Johannesburg and they identified them as drums of Tabin nerve gas. They were supplied by the Syrian. We are now helping the Congolese destroy those drums safely."

"So the twelve hundred South African troops that are now helping the Congolese army, to secure that North Kivu region and all its resources, are under no pressure to secure supplies for the major mining companies in South Africa?" Petrea asked.

Mike collected up the menus, before looking at Petrea.

"I would like to plead the Fifth Amendment on that."

Renata turned and looked at Christian.

"Just to update you, Tim and I are going to put our engagement on hold, while your father and I spend the next few days catching up and sorting out a few decades. Then we are going to fly back to Australia with you."

"Mum, I'm obviously happy with what you decide. I know it's a really difficult situation. That does sound like a good suggestion though. It will give also you a chance to catch up with Nadine and Isabella."

"Isabella is sitting over there in the far corner with Simone, so I have already organised that for lunch tomorrow. Sian provided a full breakdown on what happened at the airport. It's good to see that it has not had a significant impact on your medical recovery."

"We literally ran into them, Mum, as they came out of the lift."

"Well, now that you and Petrea are better acquainted, I'm sure it would ease the tension a little if you and Petrea had coffee with them later. That is, if we ever get any food."

"I think there are still a couple of documents that Petrea still needs to have signed later, perhaps after that,"

Christian said looking across at Petrea.

"I'm sure there must be some unsigned documents up there somewhere," Petrea replied, looking directly at Christian, as everyone laughed.

THE END